P9-DFR-892

THE BONE COLLECTOR

By the author of

A Maiden's Grave
Praying for Sleep
The Lesson of Her Death
Mistress of Justice
Hard News
Death of a Blue Movie Star
Manhattan Is My Beat

and

Writing as William Jefferies

Shallow Graves
Bloody River Blues

THE
BONE COLLECTOR
JEFFERY DEAVER

Viking

VIKING
Published by the Penguin Group
Penguin Books USA Inc., 375 Hudson Street,
New York, New York 10014, U.S.A.
Penguin Books Ltd, 27 Wrights Lane,
London W8 5TZ, England
Penguin Books Australia Ltd, Ringwood,
Victoria, Australia
Penguin Books Canada Ltd, 10 Alcorn Avenue,
Toronto, Ontario, Canada M4V 3B2
Penguin Books (N.Z.) Ltd, 182–190 Wairau Road,
Auckland 10, New Zealand

Penguin Books Ltd, Registered Offices:
Harmondsworth, Middlesex, England

First published in 1997 by Viking Penguin,
a division of Penguin Books USA Inc.

3   5   7   9   10   8   6   4   2

Copyright © Jeffery Deaver, 1997
All rights reserved

PUBLISHER'S NOTE
This is a work of fiction. Names, characters, places, and incidents either are the
product of the author's imagination or are used fictitiously, and any resemblance
to actual persons, living or dead, events, or locales is entirely coincidental.

LIBRARY OF CONGRESS CATALOGING-IN-PUBLICATION DATA
Deaver, Jeffery.
The bone collector / Jeffery Deaver.
p.   cm.
ISBN 0-670-86871-X
I. Title.
PS3554.E1755B66   1997
813'.54—dc20   96-35457

This book is printed on acid-free paper.
∞

Printed in the United States of America
Set in Janson
Designed by Jaye Zimet

Without limiting the rights under copyright reserved above, no part of this
publication may be reproduced, stored in or introduced into a retrieval system,
or transmitted, in any form or by any means (electronic, mechanical, photo-
copying, recording or otherwise), without the prior written permission of both
the copyright owner and the above publisher of this book.

For my family,
Dee, Danny, Julie, Ethel
and Nelson . . .
Apples don't fall far.
And for Diana too.

CONTENTS

I
KING FOR A DAY

The present in New York is so powerful
that the past is lost.

—JOHN JAY CHAPMAN

ONE

S he wanted only to sleep.

The plane had touched down two hours late and there'd been a marathon wait for the luggage. And *then* the car service had messed up; the limo'd left an hour ago. So now they were waiting for a cab.

She stood in the line of passengers, her lean body listing against the weight of her laptop computer. John rattled on about interest rates and new ways of restructuring the deal but all she could think was: Friday night, 10:30. I wanna pull on my sweats and hit the hay.

Gazing at the endless stream of Yellow Cabs. Something about the color and the similarity of the cars reminded her of insects. And she shivered with the creepy-crawly feeling she remembered from her childhood in the mountains when she and her brother'd find a gut-killed badger or kick over a red-ant nest and gaze at the wet mass of squirming bodies and legs.

T.J. Colfax shuffled forward as the cab pulled up and squealed to a stop.

The cabbie popped the trunk but stayed in the car. They had to load their own luggage, which ticked John off. He was used to people doing things for him. Tammie Jean didn't care; she was still occasionally surprised to find that she had a secretary to type and file for her. She tossed her suitcase in, closed the trunk and climbed inside.

John got in after her, slammed the door and mopped his pudgy face and balding scalp as if the effort of pitching his suit-bag in the trunk had exhausted him.

"First stop East Seventy-second," John muttered through the divider.

"Then the Upper West Side," T.J. added. The Plexiglas between the front and back seats was badly scuffed and she could hardly see the driver.

The cab shot away from the curb and was soon cruising down the expressway toward Manhattan.

"Look," John said, "that's why all the crowds."

He was pointing at a billboard welcoming delegates to the UN peace conference, which was starting on Monday. There were going to be ten thousand visitors in town. T.J. gazed up at the billboard—blacks and whites and Asians, waving and smiling. There was something wrong about the artwork, though. The proportions and the colors were off. And the faces all seemed pasty.

T.J. muttered, "Body snatchers."

They sped along the broad expressway, which glared an uneasy yellow under the highway lights. Past the old Navy Yard, past the Brooklyn piers.

John finally stopped talking and pulled out his Texas Instruments, started crunching some numbers. T.J. sat back in the seat, looking at the steamy sidewalks and sullen faces of people sitting on the brownstone stoops overlooking the highway. They seemed half-comatose in the heat.

It was hot in the cab too and T.J. reached for the button to lower the window. She wasn't surprised to find that it didn't work. She reached across John. His was broken too. It was then that she noticed that the door locks were missing.

The door handles too.

Her hand slid over the door, feeling for the nub of the handle. Nothing—it was as if someone had cut it off with a hacksaw.

"What?" John asked.

"Well, the doors . . . How do we open them?"

John was looking from one to the other when the sign for the Midtown Tunnel came and went.

"Hey!" John rapped on the divider. "You missed the turn. Where're you going?"

"Maybe he's going to take the Queensboro," T.J. suggested. The bridge meant a longer route but avoided the tunnel's toll. She sat forward and tapped on the Plexiglas, using her ring.

"Are you taking the bridge?"

He ignored them.

"Hey!"

And a moment later they sped past the Queensboro turnoff.

"Shit," John cried. "Where're you taking us? Harlem. I'll bet he's taking us to Harlem."

T.J. looked out the window. A car was moving parallel to them, passing slowly. She banged on the window hard.

"Help!" she shouted. "Please . . ."

The car's driver glanced at her once, then again, frowning. He slowed and pulled behind them but with a hard jolt the cab skidded down an exit ramp into Queens, turned into an alley and sped through a deserted warehouse district. They must've been going sixty miles an hour.

"What're you *doing?*"

T.J. banged on the divider. "Slow down. Where are?—"

"Oh, God, no," John muttered. "Look."

The driver had pulled on a ski mask.

"What do you want?" T.J. shouted.

"Money? We'll give you money."

Still, silence from the front of the cab.

T.J. ripped open her Targus bag and pulled out her black laptop. She reared back and slammed the corner of the computer into the window. The glass held though the sound of the bang seemed to scare the hell out of the driver. The cab swerved and nearly hit the brick wall of the building they were speeding past.

"Money! How much? I can give you a lot of money!" John sputtered, tears dripping down his fat cheeks.

T.J. rammed the window again with the laptop. The screen flew off under the force of the blow but the window remained intact.

She tried once more and the body of the computer split open and fell from her hands.

"Oh, shit . . ."

They both pitched forward violently as the cab skidded to a stop in a dingy, unlit cul-de-sac.

The driver climbed out of the cab, a small pistol in his hand.

"Please, no," she pleaded.

He walked to the back of the cab and leaned down, peering into the greasy glass. He stood there for a long time, as she and John scooted backwards, against the opposite door, their sweating bodies pressed together.

The driver cupped his hands against the glare from the streetlights and looked at them closely.

A sudden crack resonated through the air, and T.J. flinched. John gave a short scream.

In the distance, behind the driver, the sky filled with red and blue fiery streaks. More pops and whistles. He turned and gazed up as a huge, orange spider spread over the city.

Fireworks, T.J. recalled reading in the *Times*. A present from the mayor and the UN secretary-general for the conference delegates, welcoming them to the greatest city on earth.

The driver turned back to the cab. With a loud snap he pulled up on the latch and slowly opened the door.

———

The call was anonymous. As usual.

So there was no way of checking back to see *which* vacant lot the RP meant. Central had radioed, *"He said Thirty-seven near Eleven. That's all."*

Reporting parties weren't known for Triple A directions to crime scenes.

Already sweating though it was just nine in the morning, Amelia Sachs pushed through a stand of tall grass. She was walking the strip search—what the Crime Scene people called it—an

S-shaped pattern. Nothing. She bent her head to the speaker/mike pinned to her navy-blue uniform blouse.

"Portable 5885. Can't find anything, Central. You have a further-to?"

Through crisp static the dispatcher replied, "Nothing more on location, 5885. But one thing . . . the RP said he hoped the vic was dead. K."

"Say again, Central."

"The RP said he hoped the victim was dead. For his sake. K."

"K."

Hoped the vic was dead?

Sachs struggled over a wilted chain-link and searched another empty lot. Nothing.

She wanted to quit. Call in a 10-90, unfounded report, and go back to the Deuce, which was her regular beat. Her knees hurt and she was hot as stew in this lousy August weather. She wanted to slip into the Port Authority, hang with the kids and have a tall can of Arizona iced tea. Then, at 11:30—just a couple of hours away—she'd clean out her locker at Midtown South and head downtown for the training session.

But she didn't—couldn't—blow off the call. She kept going: along the hot sidewalk, through the gap between two abandoned tenements, through another vegetation-filled field.

Her long index finger pushed into her flattop uniform cap, through the layers of long red hair piled high on her head. She scratched compulsively then reached up underneath the cap and scratched some more. Sweat ran down her forehead and tickled and she dug into her eyebrow too.

Thinking: My last two hours on the street. I can live with it.

As Sachs stepped farther into the brush she felt the first uneasiness of the morning.

Somebody's watching me.

The hot wind rustled the dry brush and cars and trucks sped noisily to and from the Lincoln Tunnel. She thought what Patrol officers often did: This city is so damn loud somebody could come up right behind me, knife-range away, and I'd never know it.

Or line up iron sights on my back . . .

She spun around quickly.

Nothing but leaves and rusting machinery and trash.

Climbing a pile of stones, wincing. Amelia Sachs, thirty-one—
a *mere* thirty-one, her mother would say—was plagued by arthritis. Inherited from her grandfather as clearly as she'd received
her mother's willowy build and her father's good looks and career (the red hair was anybody's guess). Another jolt of pain as
she eased through a tall curtain of dying bushes. She was fortunate to stop herself one pace from a sheer thirty-foot drop.

Below her was a gloomy canyon—cut deep into the bedrock of
the West Side. Through it ran the Amtrak roadbed for trains
bound north.

She squinted, looking at the floor of the canyon, not far from
the railroad bed.

What *is* that?

A circle of overturned earth, a small tree branch sticking out of
the top? It looked like—

Oh, my good Lord . . .

She shivered at the sight. Felt the nausea rise, prickling her
skin like a wave of flame. She managed to step on that tiny part
inside her that wanted to turn away and pretend she hadn't seen
this.

He hoped the victim was dead. For his sake.

She ran toward an iron ladder that led down from the sidewalk
to the roadbed. She reached for the railing but stopped just in
time. Shit. The perp might've escaped this way. If she touched it
she might screw up any prints he'd left. Okay, we do it the hard
way. Breathing deeply to dull the pain in her joints, she began
climbing down the rock face itself, slipping her issue shoes—
polished like silver for the first day of her new assignment—into
crevices cut in the stone. She jumped the last four feet to the
roadbed and ran to the grave.

"Oh, man . . ."

It wasn't a branch sticking out of the ground; it was a hand.
The body'd been buried vertical and the dirt piled on until just

the forearm, wrist and hand protruded. She stared at the ring finger; all the flesh had been whittled away and a woman's diamond cocktail ring had been replaced on the bloody, stripped bone.

Sachs dropped to her knees and began to dig.

Dirt flying under her dog-paddling hands, she noticed that the uncut fingers were splayed, stretched beyond where they could normally bend. Which told her that the vic had been alive when the last shovelful of dirt was spooned onto the face.

And maybe still was.

Sachs dug furiously into the loosely packed earth, cutting her hand on a bottle shard, her dark blood mixing into the darker earth. And then she came to the hair and a forehead below it, a cyanotic bluish-gray from the lack of oxygen. Digging further until she could see the dull eyes and the mouth, which had twisted into a horrible grin as the vic had tried in the last few seconds to stay above the rising tide of black earth.

It wasn't a woman. Despite the ring. He was a heavyset man in his fifties. As dead as the soil he floated in.

Backing away, she couldn't take her eyes off his and nearly stumbled over a railroad track. She could think of absolutely nothing for a full minute. Except what it must've been like to die that way.

Then: Come *on*, honey. You got yourself a homicide crime scene and you're first officer.

You know what to do.

ADAPT

A is for Arrest a known perp.

D is for Detain material witnesses and suspects.

A is for Assess the crime scene.

P is for . . .

What was *P* again?

She lowered her head to the mike. "Portable 5885 to Central. Further-to. I've got a 10-29 by the train tracks at Three-eight and Eleven. Homicide, K. Need detectives, CS, bus and tour doctor. K."

"Roger, 5885. Perp in custody, K?"

"No perp."

"Five-eight-eight-five, K."

Sachs stared at the finger, the one whittled down to the bone. The incongruous ring. The eyes. And the grin . . . oh, that fucking grin. A shudder ripped through her body. Amelia Sachs had swum among snakes in summer-camp rivers and had boasted truthfully she'd have no problem bungee-jumping from a hundred-foot bridge. But let her think of confinement . . . think of being trapped, immobile, and the panic attack'd grab her like an electric shock. Which was why Sachs walked fast when she walked and why she drove cars like light itself.

When you move they can't getcha . . .

She heard a sound and cocked her head.

A rumble, deep, getting louder.

Scraps of paper blowing along the roadbed of the tracks. Dust dervishes swirling about her like angry ghosts.

Then a low wail . . .

Five-foot-nine Patrol Officer Amelia Sachs found herself facing down a thirty-ton Amtrak locomotive, the red, white and blue slab of steel approaching at a determined ten miles an hour.

"Hold up, there!" she shouted.

The engineer ignored her.

Sachs jogged onto the roadbed and planted herself right in the middle of the track, spread her stance and waved her arms, signaling him to stop. The locomotive squealed to a halt. The engineer stuck his head out the window.

"You can't go through here," she told him.

He asked her what she meant. She thought he looked woefully young to be driving such a big train.

"It's a crime scene. Please shut off the engine."

"Lady, I don't see any crimes."

But Sachs wasn't listening. She was looking up at a gap in the chain-link on the west side of the train viaduct, at the top, near Eleventh Avenue.

That would have been one way to get the body here without being seen—parking on Eleventh and dragging the body through the narrow alley to the cliff. On Thirty-seventh, the cross street, he could be spotted from two dozen apartment windows.

"That train, sir. Just leave it right there."

"I can't leave it here."

"Please shut off the engine."

"We don't shut off the engines of trains like this. They run all the time."

"And call the dispatcher. Or somebody. Have them stop the southbound trains too."

"We can't do that."

"Now, sir. I've got the number of that vehicle of yours."

"Vehicle?"

"I'd suggest you do it immediately," Sachs barked.

"What're you going to do, lady? Gimme a ticket?"

But Amelia Sachs was once again climbing back up the stone walls, her poor joints creaking, her lips tasting limestone dust, clay and her own sweat. She jogged to the alley she'd noticed from the roadbed and then turned around, studying Eleventh Avenue and the Javits Center across it. The hall was bustling with crowds—spectators and press. A huge banner proclaimed, *Welcome UN Delegates!* But earlier this morning, when the street was deserted, the perp could easily have found a parking space along here and carried the body to the tracks undetected. Sachs strode to Eleventh, surveyed the six-lane avenue, which was jammed with traffic.

Let's do it.

She waded into the sea of cars and trucks and stopped the north-bound lanes cold. Several drivers tried end runs and she had to issue two citations and finally drag trash cans out into the middle of the street as a barricade to make sure the good residents did their civic duty.

Sachs had finally remembered the next of the first officer's ADAPT rules.

P is for Protect the crime scene.

The sound of angry horns began to fill the hazy morning sky, soon supplemented by the drivers' angrier shouts. A short time later she heard the sirens join the cacophony as the first of the emergency vehicles arrived.

Forty minutes later, the scene was swarming with uniforms and investigators, dozens of them—a lot more than a hit in Hell's Kitchen, however gruesome the cause of death, seemed to warrant. But, Sachs learned from another cop, this was a hot case, a media groper—the vic was one of two passengers who'd arrived at JFK last night, gotten into a cab and headed for the city. They'd never arrived at their homes.

"CNN's watching," the uniform whispered.

So Amelia Sachs wasn't surprised to see blond Vince Peretti, chief of the Central Investigation and Resource Division, which oversaw the crime scene unit, climb over the top of the embankment and pause as he brushed dust from his thousand-dollar suit.

She was, however, surprised to see him notice her and gesture her over, a faint smile on his clean-cut face. It occurred to her she was about to receive a nod of gratitude for her *Cliffhanger* routine. Saved the fingerprints on *that* ladder, boys. Maybe even a commendation. In the last hour of the last day of Patrol. Going out in a blaze of glory.

He looked her up and down. "Patrolwoman, you're no rookie, are you? I'm safe in making that assumption."

"I'm sorry, sir?"

"You're not a rookie, I assume."

She wasn't, not technically, though she had only three years' service under her belt, unlike most of the other Patrol officers her age; they had nine or ten years in. Sachs had foundered for a few years before attending the academy. "I'm not sure what you're asking."

He looked exasperated and the smile vanished. "You were first officer?"

"Yessir."

"Why'd you close down Eleventh Avenue? What were you *thinking* of?"

She looked along the broad street, which was still blocked by her trash-can barricade. She'd gotten used to the honking but realized now it was really quite loud; the line of cars extended for miles.

"Sir, the first officer's job is to arrest a perp, detain any witnesses, protect—"

"I know the ADAPT rule, officer. You closed the street to protect the crime scene?"

"Yessir. I didn't think the perp would park on the cross street. He could be seen too easily from those apartments. See, there? Eleventh seemed like a better choice."

"Well, it was a wrong choice. There were no footprints on *that* side of the tracks, and two sets going to the ladder that leads up to Thirty-seven."

"I closed Thirty-seven too."

"That's my point. That's all that needed to be closed. And the train?" he asked. "Why'd you stop that?"

"Well, sir. I thought that a train going through the scene might disturb evidence. Or something."

"Or *something*, officer?"

"I didn't express myself very well, sir. I meant—"

"What about Newark Airport?"

"Yessir." She looked around for help. There were officers nearby but they were busily ignoring the dressing-down. "What exactly about Newark?"

"Why didn't you shut that down too?"

Oh, wonderful. A schoolmarm. Her Julia Roberts lips grew taut but she said reasonably, "Sir, in my judgment, it seemed likely that—"

"The New York Thruway would've been a good choice too. And the Jersey Pike and Long Island Expressway. I-70, all the way to St. Louis. Those are likely means of escape."

She lowered her head slightly and stared back at Peretti. The two of them were exactly the same height, though his heels were higher.

"I've gotten calls from the commissioner," he continued, "the head of the Port Authority, the UN secretary-general's office, the head of that expo—" He nodded toward the Javits Center.

"We've fucked up the conference schedule, a U.S. senator's speech and traffic on the entire West Side. The train tracks were fifty feet from the vic and the street you closed was a good two hundred feet away and thirty above. I mean, even Hurricane Eva didn't fuck up Amtrak's Northeast Corridor like this."

"I just thought—"

Peretti smiled. Because Sachs was a beautiful woman—her "foundering" before attending the academy had involved steady assignments for the Chantelle Modeling Agency on Madison Avenue—the cop chose to forgive her.

"Patrolwoman Sachs"—he glanced at the name tag on her chest, flattened chastely by the American Body Armor vest—"an object lesson. Crime scene work is a balance. It'd be nice if we could cordon off the whole city after every homicide and detain about three million people. But we can't do that. I say this constructively. For your edification."

"Actually, sir," she said brusquely, "I'm transferring out of Patrol. Effective as of noon today."

He nodded, smiled cheerfully. "Then, enough said. But for the record, it *was* your decision to stop the train and close the street."

"Yessir, it was," she said smartly. "No mistake about that."

He jotted this into a black watchbook with slashing strokes of his sweaty pen.

Oh, please . . .

"Now, remove those garbage cans. You direct traffic until the street's clear again. You hear me?"

Without a yessir or nosir or any other acknowledgment she wandered to Eleventh Avenue and slowly began removing the garbage cans. Every single driver who passed her scowled or muttered something. Sachs glanced at her watch.

An hour to go.

I can live with it.

T W O

With a terse flutter of wings the peregrine dropped onto the window ledge. The light outside, midmorning, was brilliant and the air looked fiercely hot.

"There you are," the man whispered. Then cocked his head at the sound of the buzzer of the door downstairs.

"Is that him?" he shouted toward the stairs. "Is it?"

Lincoln Rhyme heard nothing in response and turned back to the window. The bird's head swiveled, a fast, jerky movement that the falcon nevertheless made elegant. Rhyme observed that its talons were bloody. A piece of yellow flesh dangled from the black nutshell beak. It extended a short neck and eased to the nest in movements reminiscent not of a bird's but a snake's. The falcon dropped the meat into the upturned mouth of the fuzzy blue hatchling. I'm looking, Rhyme thought, at the only living creature in New York City with no predator. Except maybe God Himself.

He heard the footsteps come up the stairs slowly.

"Was that him?" he asked Thom.

The young man answered, "No."

"Who was it? The doorbell rang, didn't it?"

Thom's eyes went to the window. "The bird's back. Look, bloodstains on your windowsill. Can you see them?"

The female falcon inched into view. Blue-gray like a fish, iridescent. Her head scanned the sky.

"They're always together. Do they mate for life?" Thom wondered aloud. "Like geese?"

Rhyme's eyes returned to Thom, who was bent forward at his trim, youthful waist, gazing at the nest through the spattered window.

"Who was it?" Rhyme repeated. The young man was stalling now and it irritated Rhyme.

"A visitor."

"A visitor? Ha." Rhyme snorted. He tried to recall when his last *visitor* had been here. It must have been three months ago. Who'd it been? That reporter maybe or some distant cousin. Well, Peter Taylor, one of Rhyme's spinal cord specialists. And Blaine had been here several times. But she of course was not a *vis-i-tor*.

"It's freezing," Thom complained. His reaction was to open the window. Immediate gratification. Youth.

"Don't open the window," Rhyme ordered. "And tell me who the hell's here."

"It's freezing."

"You'll disturb the bird. You can turn the air conditioner down. *I'll* turn it down."

"We were here first," Thom said, further lifting the huge pane of window. "The birds moved in with full knowledge of you." The falcons glanced toward the noise, glaring. But then they always glared. They remained on the ledge, lording over their domain of anemic ginkgo trees and alternate-side-of-the-street parkers.

Rhyme repeated. "Who *is* it?"

"Lon Sellitto."

"Lon?"

What was he doing here?

Thom examined the room. "The place is a mess."

Rhyme didn't like the fuss of cleaning. He didn't like the bustle, the noise of the vacuum—which he found particularly irritating. He was content here, as it was. This room, which he called his office, was on the second floor of his gothic townhouse on the Upper West Side of the city, overlooking Central Park. The room was large, twenty-by-twenty, and virtually every one of those feet was occupied. Sometimes he closed his eyes, playing a game, and tried to detect the smell of the different objects in the room here. The thousands of books and magazines, the Tower of Pisa stacks of photocopies, the hot transistors of the TV, the dust-frosted lightbulbs, the cork bulletin boards. Vinyl, peroxide, latex, upholstery.

Three different kinds of single-malt Scotch.

Falcon shit.

"I don't want to see him. Tell him I'm busy."

"And a young cop. Ernie Banks. No, he was a baseball player, right? You really should let me clean. You never notice how filthy someplace is till people come to call."

"Come to call? My, that sounds quaint. Victorian. How does *this* sound? Tell 'em to get the hell out. How's that for fin-de-siècle etiquette?"

A mess . . .

Thom was speaking of the room but Rhyme supposed he meant his boss too.

Rhyme's hair was black and thick as a twenty-year-old's—though he was twice that age—but the strands were wild and bushy, desperately in need of a wash and cut. His face sprouted a dirty-looking three days' growth of black beard and he'd wakened with an incessant tickle in his ear, which meant that those hairs needed trimming as well. Rhyme's nails were long, finger and toe, and he'd been wearing the same clothes for a week—polka-dotted pajamas, god-awful ugly. His eyes were narrow, deep brown, and set in a face that Blaine had told him on a number of occasions, passionate and otherwise, was handsome.

"They want to talk to you," Thom continued. "They say it's very important."

"Well, bully for them."

"You haven't seen Lon for nearly a year."

"Why does that mean I want to see him now? Have you scared off the bird? I'll be pissed if you have."

"It's important, Lincoln."

"*Very* important, I recall you saying. Where's that doctor? He might've called. I was dozing earlier. And you were out."

"You've been awake since six a.m."

"No." He paused. "I woke up, yes. But then I dozed off. I was sound asleep. Did you check messages?"

Thom said, "Yes. Nothing from him."

"He said he'd be here midmorning."

"And it's just past eleven. Maybe we'll hold off notifying air-sea rescue. What do you say?"

"Have you been on the phone?" Rhyme asked abruptly. "Maybe he tried to call while you were on."

"I was talking to—"

"Did I say anything?" Rhyme asked. "Now you're angry. I didn't say you shouldn't be making phone calls. You can do that. You've always been able to do that. My point is just that he might've called while you were on the line."

"No, your point this morning is to be a shit."

"There you go. You know, they have this thing—call waiting. You can get two calls at once. I wish we had that. What does my old friend Lon want? And *his* friend the baseball player?"

"Ask them."

"I'm asking *you*."

"They want to see you. That's all I know."

"About something vay-ree im-por-tant."

"Lincoln." Thom sighed. The good-looking young man ran his hand through his blond hair. He wore tan slacks and a white shirt, with a blue floral tie, immaculately knotted. When he'd hired Thom a year ago Rhyme had said he could wear jeans and T-shirts if he wanted. But he'd been dressed impeccably every day since. Rhyme didn't know why it contributed to the decision to keep the young man on, but it had. None of Thom's predecessors had lasted more than six weeks. The number of those who quit was exactly equal to the firees.

"All right, what did you tell them?"

"I told them to give me a few minutes to make sure you were decent then they could come up. Briefly."

"You did that. Without asking me. Thank you very much."

Thom retreated a few steps and called down the narrow stairway to the first floor, "Come on, gentlemen."

"They told you something, didn't they?" Rhyme said. "You're holding out on me."

Thom didn't answer and Rhyme watched the two men approach. As they entered the room Rhyme spoke first. He said to Thom, "Close the curtain. You've already upset the birds way too much."

Which really meant only that he'd had enough of the sputtering sunlight.

———

Mute.

With the foul, sticky tape on her mouth she couldn't speak a word and that made her feel more helpless than the metal handcuffs tight on her wrists. Than the grip of his short, strong fingers on her biceps.

The taxi driver, still in his ski mask, led her down the grimy, wet corridor, past rows of ducts and piping. They were in the basement of an office building. She had no idea where.

If I could talk to him . . .

T.J. Colfax was a player, the bitch of Morgan Stanley's third floor. A negotiator.

Money? You want money? I'll get you money, lots of it, boy. Bushels. She thought this a dozen times, trying to catch his eye, as if she could actually force the words into his thoughts.

Pleeeeeeeease, she begged silently, and began thinking about the mechanics of cashing in her 401(k) and giving him her retirement fund. *Oh, please . . .*

She remembered last night: The man turning back from the fireworks, dragging them from the cab, handcuffing them. He'd thrown them into the trunk and they'd begun driving again. First over rough cobblestones and broken asphalt then smooth roads then rough again. She heard the whir of wheels on a bridge. More turns, more rough roads. Finally, the cab stopped and the driver got out and seemed to open a gate or some doors. He drove into a garage, she thought. All the sounds of the city were cut off and the car's bubbling exhaust rose in volume, reverberating off close walls.

Then the cab trunk opened and the man pulled her out. He yanked the diamond ring off her finger and pocketed it. Then he led her past walls of spooky faces, faded paintings of blank eyes staring at her, a butcher, a devil, three sorrowful children— painted on the crumbling plaster. Dragged her down into a moldy basement and dumped her on the floor. He clopped up- stairs, leaving her in the dark, surrounded by a sickening smell— rotting flesh, garbage. There she'd lain for hours, sleeping a little, crying a lot. She'd wakened abruptly at a loud sound. A sharp explosion. Nearby. Then more troubled sleep.

A half hour ago he'd come for her again. Led her to the trunk and they'd driven for another twenty minutes. Here. Wherever *here* was.

They now walked into a dim basement room. In the center was a thick black pipe; he handcuffed her to it then gripped her feet and pulled them out straight in front of her, propping her in a sitting position. He crouched and tied her legs together with thin rope—it took several minutes; he was wearing leather gloves. Then he rose and gazed at her for a long moment, bent down and tore her blouse open. He walked around behind her and she gasped, feeling his hands on her shoulders, probing, squeezing her shoulder blades.

Crying, pleading through the tape.

Knowing what was coming.

The hands moved down, along her arms, and then under them and around the front of her body. But he didn't touch her breasts. No, as the hands spidered across her skin they seemed to be searching for her ribs. He prodded them and stroked. T.J. shivered and tried to pull away. He gripped her tight and ca- ressed some more, pressing hard, feeling the give of the bone.

He stood. She heard receding footsteps. For a long moment there was silence except for the groans of air conditioners and elevators. Then she barked a frightened grunt at a sound right behind her. A repetitive noise. *Wsssh. Wsssh.* Very familiar but something she couldn't place. She tried to turn to see what he was doing but couldn't. What was it? Listening to the rhythmic sound, over and over and over. It took her right back to her mother's house.

Wsssh. Wsssh.

Saturday morning in the small bungalow in Bedford, Tennessee. It was the only day her mother didn't work and she devoted most of it to housecleaning. T.J. would wake up to a hot sun and stumble downstairs to help her. *Wsssh.* As she cried at this memory she listened to the sound and wondered why on earth he was sweeping the floor and with such careful, precise strokes of the broom.

He saw surprise and discomfort on their faces.

Something you don't find very often with New York City homicide cops.

Lon Sellitto and young Banks (Jerry, not Ernie) sat where Rhyme gestured with his bush-crowned head: twin dusty, uncomfortable rattan chairs.

Rhyme had changed considerably since Sellitto had last been here and the detective didn't hide his shock very well. Banks had no benchmark against which to judge what he was seeing but he was shocked nonetheless. The sloppy room, the vagrant gazing at them suspiciously. The smell too certainly—the visceral aroma surrounding the creature Lincoln Rhyme now was.

He immensely regretted letting them up.

"Why didn't you call first, Lon?"

"You would've told us not to come."

True.

Thom crested the stairs and Rhyme preempted him. "No, Thom, we won't be needing you." He'd remembered that the young man always asked guests if they wanted something to drink or eat.

Such a goddamn Martha Stewart.

Silence for a moment. Large, rumpled Sellitto—a twenty-year vet—glanced down into a box beside the bed and started to speak. Whatever he'd been about to say was cut off by the sight of disposable adult diapers.

Jerry Banks said, "I read your book, sir." The young cop had a bad hand when it came to shaving, lots of nicks. And what a charming cowlick in his hair! My good Lord, he can't be more than twelve. The more worn the world gets, Rhyme reflected, the younger its inhabitants seem to be.

"Which one?"

"Well, your crime scene manual, of course. But I meant the picture book. The one a couple years ago."

"There were words too. It was *mostly* words, in fact. Did you read them?"

"Oh, well, sure," Banks said quickly.

A huge stack of remaindered volumes of *The Scenes of the Crime* sat against one wall of his room.

"I didn't know you and Lon were friends," Banks added.

"Ah, Lon didn't trot out the yearbook? Show you the pictures? Strip his sleeve and show his scars and say these wounds I had with Lincoln Rhyme?"

Sellitto wasn't smiling. Well, I can give him even less to smile about if he likes. The senior detective was digging through his attaché case. And what does he have in *there?*

"How long were you partnered?" Banks asked, making conversation.

"There's a verb for you," Rhyme said. And looked at the clock.

"We weren't partners," Sellitto said. "I was Homicide, he was head of IRD."

"Oh," Banks said, even more impressed. Running the Central Investigation and Resource Division was one of the most prestigious jobs in the department.

"Yeah," Rhyme said, looking out the window, as if his doctor might be arriving via falcon. "The two musketeers."

In a patient voice, which infuriated Rhyme, Sellitto said, "Seven years, off and on, we worked together."

"And good years they were," Rhyme intoned.

Thom scowled but Sellitto missed the irony. Or more likely ignored it. He said, "We have a problem, Lincoln. We need some help."

Snap. The stack of papers landed on the bedside table.

"Some help?" The laugh exploded from the narrow nose Blaine had always suspected was the product of a surgeon's vision though it was not. She also thought his lips were too perfect (Add a scar, she'd once joked and during one of their fights she nearly had). And why, he wondered, does her voluptuous apparition keep rising today? He'd wakened thinking about his ex and had felt compelled to write her a letter, which was on the computer screen at that moment. He now saved the document on the disk. Silence filled the room as he entered the commands with a single finger.

"Lincoln?" Sellitto asked.

"Yessir. Some help. From me. I heard."

Banks kept an inappropriate smile on his face while he shuffled his butt uneasily in the chair.

"I've got an appointment in, well, any minute now," Rhyme said.

"An appointment."

"A doctor."

"Really?" Banks asked, probably to murder the silence that loomed again.

Sellitto, not sure where the conversation was going, asked, "And how've you been?"

Banks and Sellitto hadn't asked about his health when they'd arrived. It was a question people tended to avoid when they saw Lincoln Rhyme. The answer risked being a very complicated, and almost certainly an unpleasant, one.

He said simply, "I've been fine, thanks. And you? Betty?"

"We're divorced," Sellitto said quickly.

"Really?"

"She got the house and I got half a kid." The chunky cop said this with forced cheer, as if he'd used the line before, and Rhyme supposed there was a painful story behind the breakup. One he had no desire to hear. Still, he wasn't surprised that the marriage had tanked. Sellitto was a workhorse. He was one of the hundred or so first-grade detectives on the force and had been for years— he got the grade when they were handed out for merit not just time served. He'd worked close to eighty hours a week. Rhyme hadn't even known he was married for the first few months they'd worked together.

"Where you living now?" Rhyme asked, hoping a nice social conversation would tucker them out and send them on their way.

"Brooklyn. The Heights. I walk to work sometimes. You know those diets I was always on? The trick's not dieting. It's exercise."

He didn't look any fatter or thinner than the Lon Sellitto of three and a half years ago. Or the Sellitto of fifteen years ago for that matter.

"So," collegiate Banks said, "a doctor, you were saying. For a . . ."

"A new form of treatment?" Rhyme finished the dwindling question. "Exactly."

"Good luck."

"Thank you *so* much."

It was 11:36 a.m. Well past midmorning. Tardiness is inexcusable in a man of medicine.

He watched Banks's eyes twice scan his legs. He caught the pimply boy a second time and wasn't surprised to see the detective blush.

"So," Rhyme said. "I'm afraid I don't really have time to help you."

"But he's not here yet, right, the doctor?" asked Lon Sellitto in the same bulletproof tone he'd used to puncture homicide suspects' cover stories.

Thom appeared at the doorway with a coffeepot.

Prick, Rhyme mouthed.

"Lincoln forgot to offer you gentlemen something."

"Thom treats me like a child."

"If the bootie fits," the aide retorted.

"All right," Rhyme snapped. "Have some coffee. I'll have some mother's milk."

"Too early," Thom said. "The bar isn't open." And weathered Rhyme's glowering face quite well.

Again Banks's eyes browsed Rhyme's body. Maybe he'd been expecting just skin and bones. But the atrophying had stopped not long after the accident and his first physical therapists had exhausted him with exercise. Thom too, who may have been a prick at times and an old mother hen at others, was a damn good PT. He put Rhyme through passive ROM exercises every day. Taking meticulous notes on the goniometry—measurements of the range of motion that he applied to each joint in Rhyme's body. Carefully checking the spasticity as he kept the arms and legs in a constant cycle of abduction and adduction. ROM work wasn't a miracle but it built up some tone, cut down on debilitating contractures and kept the blood flowing. For someone whose muscular activities had been limited to his shoulders, head and left ring finger for three and a half years, Lincoln Rhyme wasn't in such bad shape.

The young detective looked away from the complicated black ECU control sitting by Rhyme's finger, hardwired to another controller, sprouting conduit and cables, which ran to the computer and a wall panel.

A quad's life is wires, a therapist had told Rhyme a long time ago. The rich ones, at least. The lucky ones.

Sellitto said, "There was a murder early this morning on the West Side."

"We've had reports of some homeless men and women disappearing over the past month," Banks said. "At first we thought it might be one of them. But it wasn't," he added dramatically. "The vic was one of those people last night."

Rhyme trained a blank expression on the young man with the dotted face. "Those *people?*"

"He doesn't watch the news," Thom said. "If you're talking about the kidnapping he hasn't heard."

"You don't watch the news?" Sellitto laughed. "You're the SOB read four papers a day and recorded the local news to watch when he got home. Blaine told me you called her Katie Couric one night when you were making love."

"I only read literature now," Rhyme said pompously, and falsely.

Thom added, " 'Literature is news that stays news.' "

Rhyme ignored him.

Sellitto said, "Man and woman coming back from business on the Coast. Got into a Yellow Cab at JFK. Never made it home."

"There was a report about eleven-thirty. This cab was driving down the BQE in Queens. White male and female passenger in the back seat. Looked like they were trying to break a window out. Pounding on the glass. Nobody got tags or medallion."

"This witness—who saw the cab. Any look at the driver?"

"No."

"The woman passenger?"

"No sign of her."

Eleven forty-one. Rhyme was furious with Dr. William Berger. "Nasty business," he muttered absently.

Sellitto exhaled long and loud.

"Go on, go on," Rhyme said.

"He was wearing her ring," Banks said.

"*Who* was wearing *what?*"

"The vic. They found this morning. He was wearing the woman's ring. The other passenger's."

"You're sure it was hers?"

"Had her initials inside."

"So you've got an unsub," Rhyme continued, "who wants you to know he's got the woman and she's still alive."

"What's an unsub?" Thom asked.

When Rhyme ignored him Sellitto said, "Unknown subject."

"But you know how he got it to fit?" Banks asked, a little wide-eyed for Rhyme's taste. "Her ring?"

"I give up."

"Cut the skin off the guy's finger. All of it. Down to the bone."

Rhyme gave a faint smile. "Ah, he's a smart one, isn't he?"

"Why's that smart?"

"To make sure nobody came by and took the ring. It was bloody, right?"

"A mess."

"Hard to see the ring in the first place. Then AIDS, hepatitis. Even if somebody noticed, a lot of folks'd take a pass on that trophy. What's her name, Lon?"

The older detective nodded to his partner, who flipped open his watchbook.

"Tammie Jean Colfax. She goes by T.J. Twenty-eight. Works for Morgan Stanley."

Rhyme observed that Banks too wore a ring. A school ring of some sort. The boy was too polished to be just a high-school and academy grad. No whiff of army about him. Wouldn't be surprised if the jewelry bore the name Yale. A homicide detective? What was the world coming to?

The young cop cupped his coffee in hands that shook sporadically. With a minuscule gesture of his own ring finger on the Everest & Jennings ECU panel, to which his left hand was strapped, Rhyme clicked through several settings, turning the AC down. He tended not to waste controls on things like heating and air-conditioning; he reserved it for necessities like lights, the computer and his page-turning frame. But when the room got too cold his nose ran. And *that's* fucking torture for a quad.

"No ransom note?" Rhyme asked.

"Nothing."

"You're the case officer?" Rhyme asked Sellitto.

"Under Jim Polling. Yeah. And we want you to review the CS report."

Another laugh. "Me? I haven't looked at a crime scene report in three years. What could I possibly tell you?"

"You could tell us tons, Linc."

"Who's head of IRD now?"

"Vince Peretti."

"The congressman's boy," Rhyme recalled. "Have him review it."

A moment's hesitation. "We'd rather have you."

"Who's we?"

"The chief. Yours truly."

"And how," Rhyme asked, smiling like a schoolgirl, "does Captain Peretti feel about this vote of no confidence?"

Sellitto stood and paced through the room, glancing down at the stacks of magazines. *Forensic Science Review.* Harding & Boyle Scientific Equipment Company catalog. *The New Scotland Yard Forensic Investigation Annual. American College of Forensic Examiners Journal. Report of the American Society of Crime Lab Directors.* CRC Press *Forensics. Journal of the International Institute of Forensic Science.*

"Look at them," Rhyme said. "The subscriptions lapsed ages ago. And they're all dusty."

"*Everything* in here's fucking dusty, Linc. Why don't you get off your lazy ass and clean this pigsty up?"

Banks looked horrified. Rhyme squelched the burst of laughter that felt alien inside him. His guard had slipped and irritation had dissolved into amusement. He momentarily regretted that he and Sellitto had drifted apart. Then he shot the feeling dead. He grumbled, "I can't help you. Sorry."

"We've got the peace conference starting on Monday. We—"

"What conference?"

"At the UN. Ambassadors, heads of state. There'll be ten thousand dignitaries in town. You heard about that thing in London two days ago?"

"*Thing?*" Rhyme repeated caustically.

"Somebody tried to bomb the hotel where UNESCO was meeting. The mayor's scared shitless somebody's going to move on the conference here. He doesn't want ugly *Post* headlines."

"There's also the little problem," Rhyme said astringently, "that Miss Tammie Jean might not be enjoying her trip home either."

"Jerry, tell him some details. Whet his appetite."

Banks turned his attention from Rhyme's legs to his bed, which was—Rhyme readily admitted—by far the more interesting of the two. Especially the control panel. It looked like something off the space shuttle and cost just about as much. "Ten hours after they're snatched we find the male passenger—John Ulbrecht—shot and buried alive in the Amtrak roadbed near Thirty-seventh and Eleventh. Well, we find him dead. He'd *been* buried alive. Bullet was a .32." Banks looked up and added, "The Honda Accord of slugs."

Meaning there'd be no wily deductions about the unsub from exotic weaponry. This Banks seems smart, Rhyme thought, and all he suffers from is youth, which he might or might not outgrow. Lincoln Rhyme believed he himself had never been young.

"Rifling on the slug?" Rhyme asked.

"Six lands and grooves, left twist."

"So he's got himself a Colt," Rhyme said and glanced over the crime scene diagram again.

"You said 'he,' " the young detective continued. "Actually it's 'they.' "

"What?"

"Unsubs. There're two of them. There were two sets of footprints between the grave and the base of an iron ladder leading up to the street," Banks said, pointing to the CS diagram.

"Any prints on the ladder?"

"None. It was wiped. Did a good job of it. The footprints go to the grave and back to the ladder. Anyway, there *had* to be two of 'em to schlepp the vic. He weighed over two hundred pounds. One man couldn't've done it."

"Keep going."

"They got him to the grave, dropped him in, shot him and buried him, went back to the ladder, climbed it and vanished."

"Shot him in the grave?" Rhyme inquired.

"Yep. There was no blood trail anywhere around the ladder or the path to the grave."

Rhyme found himself mildly interested. But he said, "What do you need me for?"

Sellitto grinned ragged yellow teeth. "We got ourselves a mystery, Linc. A buncha PE that doesn't make any fucking sense at all."

"So?" It was a rare crime scene when every bit of physical evidence made sense.

"Naw, this is real weird. Read the report. Please. I'll put it here. How's this thing work?" Sellitto looked at Thom, who fitted the report in the page-turning frame.

"I don't have time, Lon," Rhyme protested.

"That's quite a contraption," Banks offered, looking at the frame. Rhyme didn't respond. He glanced at the first page then read it carefully. Moved his ring finger a precise millimeter to the left. A rubber wand turned the page.

Reading. Thinking: Well, this *is* odd.

"Who was in charge of the scene?"

"Peretti himself. When he heard the vic was one of the taxi people he came down and took over."

Rhyme continued to read. For a minute the unimaginative words of cop writing held his interest. Then the doorbell rang and his heart galloped with a great shudder. His eyes slipped to Thom. They were cold and made clear that the time for banter was over. Thom nodded and went downstairs immediately.

All thoughts of cabdrivers and PE and kidnapped bankers vanished from the sweeping mind of Lincoln Rhyme.

"It's Dr. Berger," Thom announced over the intercom.

At last. At long last.

"Well, I'm sorry, Lon. I'll have to ask you to leave. It was good seeing you again." A smile. "Interesting case, this one is."

Sellitto hesitated then rose. "But will you read through the report, Lincoln? Tell us what you think?"

Rhyme said, "You bet," then leaned his head back against the pillow. Quads like Rhyme, who had full head-and-neck movement, could activate a dozen controls just by three-dimensional movements of the head. But Rhyme shunned headrests. There were so few sensuous pleasures left to him that he was unwilling to abdicate the comfort of nestling his head against his two-hundred-dollar down pillow. The visitors had tired him out. Not even noon, and all he wanted to do was sleep. His neck muscles throbbed in agony.

When Sellitto and Banks were at the door Rhyme said, "Lon, wait."

The detective turned.

"One thing you should know. You've only found half the crime scene. The important one is the other one—the primary scene. His house. That's where he'll be. And it'll be hard as hell to find."

"Why do you think there's another scene?"

"Because he didn't shoot the vic at the grave. He shot him there—at the primary scene. And that's probably where he's got the woman. It'll be underground or in a very deserted part of the city. Or both . . . Because, Banks"—Rhyme preempted the young detective's question—"he wouldn't risk shooting someone and holding a captive there unless it was quiet and private."

"Maybe he used a silencer."

"No traces of rubber or cotton baffling on the slug," Rhyme snapped.

"But how could the man've been shot there?" Banks countered. "I mean, there wasn't any blood spatter at the scene."

"I assume the victim was shot in the face," Rhyme announced.

"Well, yes," Banks answered, putting a stupid smile on his own. "How'd you know?"

"Very painful, very incapacitating, very little blood with a .32. Rarely lethal if you miss the brain. With the vic in that shape the unsub could lead him around wherever he wanted. I say unsub singular because there's only one of them."

A pause. "But . . . there were two sets of prints," Banks nearly whispered, as if he were defusing a land mine.

Rhyme sighed. "The soles're identical. They were left by the same man making the trip twice. To fool us. And the prints going north are the same depth as the prints going south. So he wasn't carrying a two-hundred-pound load one way and not the other. Was the vic barefoot?"

Banks flipped through his notes. "Socks."

"Okay, then the perp was wearing the vic's shoes for his clever little stroll to the ladder and back."

"If he didn't come down the ladder how *did* he get to the grave?"

"He led the man along the train tracks themselves. Probably from the north."

"There're no other ladders to the roadbed for blocks in either direction."

"But there *are* tunnels running parallel to the tracks," Rhyme continued. "They hook up with the basements of some of the old warehouses along Eleventh Avenue. A gangster during Prohibition—Owney Madden—had them dug so he could slip shipments of bootleg whisky onto New York Central trains going up to Albany and Bridgeport."

"But why not just bury the vic near the tunnel? Why risk being seen schlepping the guy all the way to the overpass?"

Impatient now. "You *do* get what he's telling us, don't you?"

Banks started to speak then shook his head.

"He *had* to put the body where it'd be seen," Rhyme said. "He needed someone to find it. That's why he left the hand in the air. He's *waving* at us. To get our attention. Sorry, you may have only one unsub but he's plenty smart enough for two. There's an access door to a tunnel somewhere nearby. Get down there and dust it for prints. There won't be any. But you'll have to do it just the same. The press, you know. When the story starts coming out . . . Well, good luck, gentlemen. Now, you'll have to excuse me. Lon?"

"Yes?"

"Don't forget about the primary crime scene. Whatever happens, you'll have to find it. And fast."

"Thanks, Linc. Just read the report."

Rhyme said of course he would and observed that they believed the lie. Completely.

THREE

He had the best bedside manner Rhyme had ever encountered. And if anyone had had experience with bedside manners it was Lincoln Rhyme. He'd once calculated he'd seen seventy-eight degreed, card-carrying doctors in the past three and a half years.

"Nice view," Berger said, gazing out the window.

"Isn't it? Beautiful."

Though because of the height of the bed Rhyme could see nothing except a hazy sky sizzling over Central Park. That—and the birds—had been the essence of his view since he'd moved here from his last rehab hospital two and half years ago. He kept the shades drawn most of the time.

Thom was busy rolling his boss—the maneuver helped keep his lungs clear—and then catheterizing Rhyme's bladder, which had to be done every five or six hours. After spinal cord trauma, sphincters can be stuck open or they can be stuck closed. Rhyme was fortunate that his got jammed closed—fortunate, that is, provided someone was around to open up the uncooperative little tube with a catheter and K-Y jelly four times a day.

Dr. Berger observed this procedure clinically and Rhyme paid no heed to the lack of privacy. One of the first things crips get over is modesty. While there's sometimes a halfhearted effort at draping—shrouding the body when cleaning, evacuating and examining—serious crips, real crips, *macho* crips don't care. At Rhyme's first rehab center, after a patient had gone to a party or been on a date the night before, all the wardmates would wheel over to his bed to check the patient's urine output, which was the barometer of how successful the outing had been. One time Rhyme earned his fellow crips' undying admiration by registering a staggering 1430 cc's.

He said to Berger, "Check out the ledge, doctor. I have my own guardian angels."

"Well. Hawks?"

"Peregrine falcons. Usually they nest higher. I don't know why they picked me to live with."

Berger glanced at the birds then turned away from the window, let the curtain fall back. The aviary didn't interest him. He wasn't a large man but he looked fit, a runner, Rhyme guessed. He seemed to be in his late forties but the black hair didn't have a trace of gray in it and he was as good-looking as any news anchor. "That's quite a bed."

"You like it?"

The bed was a Clinitron, a huge rectangular slab. It was an air-fluidized support bed and contained nearly a ton of silicone-coated glass beads. Pressurized air flowed through the beads, which supported Rhyme's body. If he had been able to feel, it would have felt as if he was floating.

Berger was sipping the coffee that Rhyme had ordered Thom to fetch and that the young man had brought, rolling his eyes, whispering, "Aren't we suddenly social?" before retreating.

The doctor asked Rhyme, "You were a policeman, you were telling me."

"Yes. I was head of forensics for the NYPD."

"Were you shot?"

"Nope. Searching a crime scene. Some workmen'd found a body at a subway-stop construction site. It was a young patrolman who'd disappeared six months before—we had a serial killer shooting cops. I got a request to work the case personally and when I was searching it a beam collapsed. I was buried for about four hours."

"Someone was actually going around murdering policemen?"

"Killed three and wounded another one. The perp was a cop himself. Dan Shepherd. A sergeant working Patrol."

Berger glanced at the pink scar on Rhyme's neck. The telltale insignia of quadriplegia—the entrance wound for the ventilator tube that remains embedded in the throat for months after the accident. Sometimes for years, sometimes forever. But Rhyme had—thanks to his own mulish nature and his therapists' herculean efforts—weaned himself off the ventilator. He now had a pair of lungs on him that he bet could keep him underwater for five minutes.

"So, a cervical trauma."

"C4."

"Ah, yes."

C4 is the demilitarized zone of spinal cord injuries. An SCI above the fourth cervical vertebra might very well have killed him. Below C4 he would have regained some use of his arms and hands, if not his legs. But trauma to the infamous fourth kept him alive though virtually a total quadriplegic. He'd lost the use of his legs and arms. His abdominal and intercostal muscles were mostly gone and he was breathing primarily from his diaphragm. He could move his head and neck, his shoulders slightly. The only fluke was that the crushing oak beam had spared a single, minuscule strand of motor neuron. Which allowed him to move his left ring finger.

Rhyme spared the doctor the soap opera of the year following the accident. The month of skull traction: tongs gripping holes drilled into his head and pulling his spine straight. Twelve weeks of the halo device—the plastic bib and steel scaffolding around his head to keep the neck immobile. To keep his lungs pumping, a large ventilator for a year then a phrenic nerve stimulator. The catheters. The surgery. The paralytic ileus, the stress ulcers, hypotension and bradycardia, bedsores turning into decubitus ulcers, contractures as the muscle tissue began to shrink and threatened to steal away the precious mobility of his finger, the infuriating phantom pain—burns and aches in extremities that could feel no sensation.

He did, however, tell Berger about the latest wrinkle. "Autonomic dysreflexia."

The problem had been occurring more often recently. Pounding heartbeat, off-the-charts blood pressure, raging headaches. It could be brought on by something as simple as constipation. He explained that nothing could be done to prevent it except avoiding stress and physical constriction.

Rhyme's SCI specialist, Dr. Peter Taylor, had become concerned with the frequency of the attacks. The last one—a month ago—was so severe that Taylor'd given Thom instructions in how to treat the condition without waiting for medical help and insisted that the aide program the doctor's number into the phone's speed dialer. Taylor had warned that a severe enough bout could lead to a heart attack or stroke.

Berger took in the facts with some sympathy then said, "Before I got into my present line I specialized in geriatric orthopedics. Mostly hip and joint replacements. I don't know much neurology. What about chances for recovery?"

"None, the condition's permanent," Rhyme said, perhaps a little too quickly. He added, "You understand my problem, don't you, doctor?"

"I think so. But I'd like to hear it in your words."

Shaking his head to clear a renegade strand of hair, Rhyme said, "Everyone has the right to kill himself."

Berger said, "I think I'd disagree with that. In most societies you may have the power but *not* the right. There's a difference."

Rhyme exhaled a bitter laugh. "I'm not much of a philosopher. But I don't even have the power. That's why I need you."

Lincoln Rhyme had asked four doctors to kill him. They'd all refused. He'd said, okay, he'd do it himself and simply stopped eating. But the process of wasting himself to death became pure torture. It left him violently stomach-sick and racked with unbearable headaches. He couldn't sleep. So he'd given up on that and, during the course of a hugely awkward conversation, asked Thom to kill him. The young man had grown tearful—the only time he'd shown that much emotion—and said he wished he could. He'd sit by and watch Rhyme die, he'd refuse to revive him. But he wouldn't actually kill him.

Then, a miracle. If you could call it that.

After *The Scenes of the Crime* had come out, reporters had appeared to interview him. One article—in *The New York Times*—contained this stark quotation from author Rhyme:

"No, I'm not planning any more books. The fact is, my next big project is killing myself. It's quite a challenge. I've been looking for someone to help me for the past six months."

That screeching-stop line got the attention of the NYPD counseling service and several people from Rhyme's past, most notably Blaine (who told him he was nuts to consider it, he had to quit thinking only about himself—just like when they'd been together—and, now that she was here, she thought she should mention that she was remarrying).

The quotation also caught the attention of William Berger, who'd called unexpectedly one night from Seattle. After a few moments of pleasant conversation Berger explained that he'd read the article about Rhyme. Then a hollow pause and he'd asked, "Ever hear of the Lethe Society?"

Rhyme had. It was a pro-euthanasia group he'd been trying to track down for months. It was far more aggressive than Safe Passage or the Hemlock Society. "Our volunteers are wanted for questioning in dozens of assisted suicides throughout the country," Berger explained. "We have to keep a low profile."

He said he wanted to follow up on Rhyme's request. Berger refused to act quickly and they'd had several conversations over the past seven or eight months. Today was their first meeting.

"There's no way you can pass, by yourself?"

Pass . . .

"Short of Gene Harrod's approach, no. And even that's a little iffy."

Harrod was young man in Boston, a quad, who decided he

wanted to kill himself. Unable to find anyone to help him he finally committed suicide the only way he was able to. With the little control he had he set a fire in his apartment and when it was blazing drove his wheelchair into it, setting himself aflame. He died of third-degree burns.

The case was often raised by right-to-deathers as an example of the tragedy that anti-euthanasia laws can cause.

Berger was familiar with the case and shook his head sympathetically. "No, that's no way for anyone to die." He assayed Rhyme's body, the wires, the control panels. "What are your mechanical skills?"

Rhyme explained about the ECUs—the E&J controller that his ring finger operated, the sip-and-puff control for his mouth, the chin joysticks, and the computer dictation unit that could type out words on the screen as he spoke them.

"But everything has to be set up by someone else?" Berger asked. "For instance, someone would have to go to the store, buy a gun, mount it, rig the trigger and hook it up to your controller?"

"Yes."

Making that person guilty of a conspiracy to commit murder, as well as manslaughter.

"What about your equipment?" Rhyme asked. "It's effective?"

"Equipment?"

"What you use? To, uhm, do the deed?"

"It's very effective. I've never had a patient complain."

Rhyme blinked and Berger laughed. Rhyme joined him. If you can't laugh about death what can you laugh about?

"Take a look."

"You have it with you?" Hope blossomed in Rhyme's heart. It was the first time he'd felt that warm sensation in years.

The doctor opened his attaché case and—rather ceremonially, Rhyme thought—set out a bottle of brandy. A small bottle of pills. A plastic bag and a rubber band.

"What's the drug?"

"Seconal. Nobody prescribes it anymore. In the old days suicide was a lot easier. These babies'd do the trick, no question. Now, it's almost impossible to kill yourself with modern tranquilizers. Halcion, Librium, Dalmane, Xanax . . . You may sleep for a long time but you're going to wake up eventually."

"And the bag?"

"Ah, the bag." Berger picked it up. "That's the emblem of the Lethe Society. Unofficially, of course—it's not like we have a logo. If the pills and the brandy aren't enough then we use the bag. Over the head, with a rubber band around the neck. We add a little ice inside because it gets pretty hot after a few minutes."

Rhyme couldn't take his eyes off the trio of implements. The bag, thick plastic, like a painter's drop cloth. The brandy was cheap, he observed, and the drugs generic.

"This's a nice house," Berger said, looking around. "Central Park West . . . Do you live on disability?"

"Some. I've also done consulting for the police and the FBI. After the accident . . . the construction company that was doing the excavating settled for three million. They swore there was no liability but there's apparently a rule of law that a quadriplegic automatically wins any lawsuits against construction companies, no matter who was at fault. At least if the plaintiff comes to court and drools."

"And you wrote that book, right?"

"I get some money from that. Not a lot. It was a 'better-seller.' Not a best-seller."

Berger picked up a copy of *The Scenes of the Crime*, flipped through it. "Famous crime scenes. Look at all this." He laughed. "There are, what, forty, fifty scenes?"

"Fifty-one."

Rhyme had revisited—in his mind and imagination, since he'd written it after the accident—as many old crime scenes in New York City as he could recall. Some solved, some not. He'd written about the Old Brewery, the notorious tenement in Five Points, where thirteen unrelated murders were recorded on a single night in 1839. About Charles Aubridge Deacon, who murdered his mother on July 13, 1863, during the Civil War draft riots, claiming former slaves had killed her and fueling the rampage against blacks. About architect Stanford White's love-triangle murder atop the original Madison Square Garden and about Judge Crater's disappearance. About George Metesky, the mad bomber of the '50s, and Murph the Surf, who boosted the Star of India diamond.

"Nineteenth-century building supplies, underground streams, butler's schools," Berger recited, flipping through the book, "gay baths, Chinatown whorehouses, Russian Orthodox churches . . . How d'you learn all this about the city?"

Rhyme shrugged. In his years as head of IRD he'd studied as much about the city as he had about forensics. Its history, politics, geology, sociology, infrastructure. He said, "Criminalistics doesn't exist in a vacuum. The more you know about your environment, the better you can apply—"

Just as he heard the enthusiasm creep into his voice he stopped abruptly.

Furious with himself that he'd been foxed so easily.

"Nice try, Dr. Berger," Rhyme said stiffly.

"Ah, come on. Call me Bill. Please."

Rhyme wasn't going to be derailed. "I've heard it before. Take a big, clean, smooth piece of paper and write down all the reasons why I should kill myself. And then take another big, clean smooth piece of paper and write all the reasons why I shouldn't. Words like *productive, useful, interesting, challenging* come to mind. Big words. Ten-dollar words. They don't mean shit to me. Besides, I couldn't pick up a fucking pencil to save my soul."

"Lincoln," Berger continued kindly, "I have to make sure you're the appropriate candidate for the program."

" 'Candidate'? 'Program'? Ah, the tyranny of euphemism," Rhyme said bitterly. "Doctor, I've made up my mind. I'd like to do it today. Now, as a matter of fact."

"Why today?"

Rhyme's eyes had returned to the bottles and the bag. He whispered, "Why not? What's today? August twenty-third? That's as good a day to die as any."

The doctor tapped his narrow lips. "I *have* to spend some time talking to you, Lincoln. If I'm convinced that you really want to go ahead—"

"I do," Rhyme said, noting as he often did how weak our words sound without the body gestures to accompany them. He wanted desperately to lay his hand on Berger's arm or lift his palms beseechingly.

Without asking if he could, Berger pulled out a packet of Marlboros and lit a cigarette. He took a folding metal ashtray from his pocket and opened it up. Crossed his thin legs. He looked like a foppish frat boy at an Ivy League smoker. "Lincoln, you understand the problem here, don't you?"

Sure, he understood. It was the very reason why Berger was here and why one of Rhyme's own doctors hadn't "done the deed." Hastening an inevitable death was one thing; nearly one-third of practicing doctors who treated terminal patients had prescribed or administered fatal doses of drugs. Most prosecutors turned a blind eye toward them unless a doctor flaunted it—like Kevorkian.

But a quad? A hemi? A para? A crip? Oh, that was different. Lincoln Rhyme was forty years old. He'd been weaned off the ventilator. Barring some insidious gene in the Rhyme stock, there was no medical reason why he couldn't live to eighty.

Berger added, "Let me be blunt, Lincoln. I also have to be sure this isn't a setup."

"Setup?"

"Prosecutors. I've been entrapped before."

Rhyme laughed. "The New York attorney general's a busy man. He's not going to wire a crip to bag himself a euthanasist."

Glancing absently at the crime scene report.

> . . . *ten feet southwest of victim, found in a cluster on a small pile of white sand: a ball of fiber, approximately six centimeters in diameter, off-white in color. The fiber was sampled in the energy-dispersive X-ray unit and found to consist of $A_2 B_5 (Si, Al)_8 O_{22} (OH)_2$. No source was indicated and the fibers could not be individuated. Sample sent to FBI PERT office for analysis.*

"I just have to be careful," Berger continued. "This is my whole professional life now. I gave up orthopedics completely. Anyway, it's more than a job. I've decided to devote my life to helping others end theirs."

> *Adjacent to this fiber, approximately three inches away were found two scraps of paper. One was common newsprint, with the words "three p.m." printed in Times Roman type, in ink consistent with that used in commercial newspapers. The other scrap appeared to be the corner of a page from a book with the page number "823" printed on it. The typeface was Garamond and the paper was calendared. ALS and subsequent ninhydrin analysis reveal no latent friction-ridge prints on either. . . . Individuation was not possible.*

Several things nagged Rhyme. The fiber, for one. Why hadn't Peretti caught on as to what it was? It was so obvious. And why was this PE—the newspaper scraps and the fiber—all clustered together? Something was wrong here.

"Lincoln?"

"Sorry."

"I was saying . . . You're not a burn victim in unbearable pain. You're not homeless. You've got money, you've got talent. Your police consulting . . . that helps a lot of people. If you want one, you could have a, yes, *productive* life ahead of you. A long life."

"Long, yes. That's the problem. A long life." He was tired of being on good behavior. He snapped, "But I don't *want* a long life. It's as simple as that."

Berger said slowly, "If there's the slightest chance you might've regretted your decision, well, see, *I'm* the one who'd have to live with it. Not you."

"Who's ever certain about something like this?"

Eyes slipping back to the report.

> *An iron bolt was found on top of the scraps of paper. It was a hex bolt, head-stamped with the letters "CE." Two inches long, clockwise twist, $^{15}/_{16}$" in diameter.*

"I've got a busy schedule for the next few days," Berger said, looking at his watch. It was a Rolex; well, death has always been lucrative. "Let's take an hour or so now. Talk for a while, then have a cooling-off day and I'll come back."

Something was nagging at Rhyme. An infuriating itch—the curse of all quads—though in this case it was an intellectual itch. The kind that had plagued Rhyme all his life.

"Say, doctor, I wonder if you could do me a favor. That report there. Could you flip through it? See if you could find a picture of a bolt."

Berger hesitated. "A picture?"

"A Polaroid. It'll be glued in somewhere toward the back. The turning frame takes too long."

Berger lifted the report out of the frame and turned the pages for Rhyme.

"There. Stop."

As he gazed at the photo a twinge of urgency pricked at him. Oh, not here, not now. *Please, no.*

"I'm sorry, could you flip back to the page where we were?"

Berger did.

Rhyme said nothing and read carefully.

The paper scraps . . .

Three p.m. . . . page 823.

Rhyme's heart was pounding, sweat popped out on his head. He heard a frantic buzzing in his ears.

Here's a headline for the tabloids. MAN DIES DURING TALK WITH DEATH DOC. . . .

Berger blinked. "Lincoln? Are you all right?" The man's canny eyes examined Rhyme carefully.

As casually as he could, Rhyme said, "You know, doctor, I'm sorry. But there's something I've got to take care of."

Berger nodded slowly, uncertainly. "Affairs aren't in order after all?"

Smiling. Nonchalant. "I'm just wondering if I could ask you to come back in a few hours."

Careful here. If he senses *purpose* he'll mark you down nonsuicidal, take his bottles and his plastic bag and fly back to Starbucks land.

Opening a date book, Berger said, "The rest of the day isn't good. Then tomorrow . . . No. I'm afraid Monday's the earliest. Day after tomorrow."

Rhyme hesitated. Lord . . . His soul's desire was finally within his grasp, what he'd dreamed of every day for the past year. Yes or no?

Decide.

Finally, Rhyme heard himself say, "All right. Monday." Plastering a hopeless smile on his face.

"What exactly's the problem?"

"A man I used to work with. He asked for some advice. I wasn't paying as much attention to it as I should have. I have to call him."

No, it wasn't dysreflexia at all—or an anxiety attack.

Lincoln Rhyme was feeling something he hadn't felt in years. He was in one big fucking hurry.

"Could I ask you to send Thom up here? I think he's downstairs in the kitchen."

"Yes, of course. I'd be happy to."

Rhyme could see something odd in Berger's eyes. What was it? Caution? Maybe. It almost seemed like disappointment. But there was no time to think about it now. As the doctor's footsteps receded down the stairs Rhyme shouted in a booming baritone, "Thom? Thom!"

"What?" the young man's voice called.

"Call Lon. Get him back here. Now!"

Rhyme glanced at the clock. It was after noon. They had less than three hours.

FOUR

The crime scene was staged," Lincoln Rhyme said.

Lon Sellitto had tossed his jacket off, revealing a savagely wrinkled shirt. He now leaned back, arms crossed, against a table strewn with papers and books.

Jerry Banks was back too and his pale-blue eyes were on Rhyme's; the bed and its control panel no longer interested him.

Sellitto frowned. "But what story's the unsub tryin' to sell us?"

At crime scenes, especially homicides, perps often monkeyed with PE to lead investigators astray. Some were clever about it but most weren't. Like the husband who beat his wife to death then tried to make it look like a robbery—though he only thought to steal *her* jewelry, leaving his gold bracelets and diamond pinkie ring on his dresser.

"That's what's so interesting," Rhyme continued. "It's not about what happened, Lon. It's what's *going to* happen."

Sellitto the skeptic asked, "What makes you think so?"

"The scraps of paper. They mean three o'clock today."

"Today?"

"Look!" Nodding toward the report, an impatient jerk of his head.

"That one scrap says three p.m.," Banks pointed out. "But the other's a page number. Why do you think it means today?"

"It's *not* a page number." Rhyme lifted an eyebrow. They still didn't get it. "Logic! The only reason to leave clues was to tell us something. If that's the case then 823 has to be something more than just a page number because there's no clue as to what book it's from. Well, if it's not a page number what is it?"

Silence.

Exasperated, Rhyme snapped, "It's a *date!* Eight twenty-three. August twenty-third. Something's going to happen at three p.m. today. Now, the ball of fiber? It's asbestos."

"Asbestos?" Sellitto asked.

"In the report? The formula? It's hornblende. Silicon dioxide. That *is* asbestos. Why Peretti sent it to the FBI is beyond me. So. We have asbestos on a railbed where there shouldn't be any. And we've got an iron bolt with decaying oxidation on the head but none on the threads. That means it's been bolted someplace for a long time and just recently removed."

"Maybe it was overturned in the dirt," Banks offered. "When he was digging the grave?"

Rhyme said, "No. In Midtown the bedrock's close to the surface, which means so are the aquifers. All the soil from Thirty-fourth Street up to Harlem contains enough moisture to oxidize iron within a few days. It'd be completely rusted, not just the head, if it'd been buried. No, it was unbolted from someplace, carried to the scene and left there. And that sand . . . Come on, what's white sand doing on a train roadbed in Midtown Manhattan? The soil composition there is loam, silt, granite, hardpan and soft clay."

Banks started to speak but Rhyme cut him off abruptly. "And what were these things doing all clustered together? Oh, he's telling us something, our unsub. You bet he is. Banks, what about the access door?"

"You were right," the young man said. "They found one about a hundred feet north of the grave. Broken open from the inside. You were also right about the prints. Zip. And no tire tracks or trace evidence either."

A lock of dirty asbestos, a bolt, a torn newspaper . . .

"The scene?" Rhyme asked. "Intact?"

"Released."

Lincoln Rhyme, the crip with the killer lungs, exhaled a loud hiss of air, disgusted. "Who made *that* mistake?"

"I don't know," Sellitto said lamely. "Watch commander probably."

It was Peretti, Rhyme understood. "Then you're stuck with what you've got."

Whatever clues as to who the kidnapper was and what he had in mind were either in the report or gone forever, trampled under the feet of cops and spectators and railroad workers. Spade-work—canvassing the neighborhood around the scene, inter-viewing witnesses, cultivating leads, traditional *detective* work—was done leisurely. But crime scenes themselves had to be worked "like mad lightning," Rhyme would command his officers in IRD. And he'd fired more than a few CSU techs who hadn't moved fast enough for his taste.

"Peretti ran the scene himself?" he asked.

"Peretti and a full complement."

"Full complement?" Rhyme asked wryly. "What's a *full complement?*"

Sellitto looked at Banks, who said, "Four techs from Photo, four from Latents. Eight searchers. ME tour doctor."

"*Eight* crime scene searchers?"

There's a bell curve in processing a crime scene. Two officers are considered the most efficient for a single homicide. By your-self you can miss things; three and up you tend to miss more things. Lincoln Rhyme had always searched scenes alone. He let the Latents people do the print work and Photo do the snap-shooting and videoing. But he always walked the grid by himself.

Peretti. Rhyme had hired the young man, son of a wealthy politico, six, seven years ago and he'd proved a good, by-the-book CS detective. Crime Scene is considered a plum and there's always a long waiting list to get into the unit. Rhyme took per-verse pleasure in thinning the ranks of applicants by offering them a look at the family album—a collection of particularly gruesome crime-scene photos. Some officers would blanch, some would snicker. Some handed the book back, eyebrows raised, as if asking, So what? And those were the ones that Lincoln Rhyme would hire. Peretti'd been one of them.

Sellitto had asked a question. Rhyme found the detective looking at him. He repeated, "You'll work with us on this, won't you, Lincoln?"

"Work with you?" He coughed a laugh. "I can't, Lon. No. I'm just spitting out a few ideas for you. You've got it. Run with it. Thom, get me Berger." He was now regretting the decision to postpone his tête-à-tête with the death doctor. Maybe it wasn't too late. He couldn't bear the thought of waiting another day or two for his *passing*. And Monday . . . He didn't want to die on Monday. It seemed common.

"Say please."

"Thom!"

"All right," the young aide said, hands raised in surrender.

Rhyme glanced at the spot on his bedside table where the bottle, the pills and the plastic bag had sat—so very close, but like everything else in this life wholly out of Lincoln Rhyme's reach.

Sellitto made a phone call, cocked his head as the call was answered. He identified himself. The clock on the wall clicked to twelve-thirty.

"Yessir." The detective's voice sank into a respectful whisper. The mayor, Rhyme guessed. "About the kidnapping at Kennedy. I've been talking to Lincoln Rhyme. . . . Yessir, he has some thoughts on it." The detective wandered to the window, staring blankly at the falcon and trying to explain the inexplicable to the man running the most mysterious city on earth. He hung up and turned to Rhyme.

"He and the chief both want you, Linc. They asked specifically. Wilson himself."

Rhyme laughed. "Lon, look around the room. Look at *me!* Does it seem like I could run a case?"

"Not a normal case, no. But this isn't a very normal one now, is it?"

"I'm sorry. I just don't have time. That doctor. The treatment. Thom, did you call him?"

"Haven't yet. Will in just a minute."

"Now! Do it now!"

Thom looked at Sellitto. Walked to the door, stepped outside. Rhyme knew he wasn't going to call. Bugger the world.

Banks touched a dot of razor scar and blurted, "Just give us some thoughts. Please. This unsub, you said he—"

Sellitto waved him silent. He kept his eyes on Rhyme.

Oh, you prick, Rhyme thought. The old silence. How we hate it and hurry to fill it. How many witnesses and suspects had caved under hot, thick silences just like this. Well, he and Sellitto *had* been a good team. Rhyme knew evidence and Lon Sellitto knew people.

The two musketeers. And if there was a third it was the purity of unsmiling science.

The detective's eyes dipped to the crime scene report. "Lincoln. What do you think's going to happen today at three?"

"I don't have any idea," Rhyme pronounced.

"Don'tcha?"

Cheap, Lon. I'll get you for that.

Finally, Rhyme said. "He's going to kill her—the woman in the taxi. And in some real bad way, I guarantee you. Something that'll rival getting buried alive."

"Jesus," Thom whispered from the doorway.

Why couldn't they just leave him alone? Would it do any good to tell them about the agony he felt in his neck and shoulders? Or about the phantom pain—far weaker and far eerier—roaming through his alien body? About the exhaustion he felt from the daily struggle to do, well, everything? About the most overwhelming fatigue of all—from having to rely on someone else?

Maybe he could tell them about the mosquito that'd gotten into the room last night and strafed his head for an hour; Rhyme grew dizzy with fatigue nodding it away until the insect finally landed on his ear, where Rhyme let it stab him—since that was a place he could rub against the pillow for relief from the itch.

Sellitto lifted an eyebrow.

"Today," Rhyme sighed. "One day. That's it."

"Thanks, Linc. We owe you." Sellitto pulled up a chair next to the bed. Nodded Banks to do the same. "Now. Gimme your thoughts. What's this asshole's game?"

Rhyme said, "Not so fast. I don't work alone."

"Fair enough. Who d'you want on board?"

"A tech from IRD. Whoever's the best in the lab. I want him here with the basic equipment. And we better get some tactical boys. Emergency Services. Oh, and I want some phones," Rhyme instructed, glancing at the Scotch on his dresser. He remembered the brandy Berger had in his kit. No way was he going out on cheap crap like that. His *Final Exit* number would be courtesy of either sixteen-year-old Lagavulin or opulent Macallan aged for decades. Or—why not?—both.

Banks pulled out his own cellular phone. "What kind of lines? Just—"

"Landlines."

"In here?"

"Of course not," Rhyme barked.

Sellitto said, "He means he wants people to make calls. From the Big Building."

"Oh."

"Call downtown," Sellitto ordered. "Have 'em give us three or four dispatchers."

"Lon," Rhyme asked, "who's doing the spadework on the death this morning?"

Banks stifled a laugh. "The Hardy Boys."

A glare from Rhyme took the smile off his face. "Detectives Bedding and Saul, sir," the boy added quickly.

But then Sellitto grinned too. "The Hardy Boys. Everybody calls 'em that. You don't know 'em, Linc. They're from the Homicide Task Force downtown."

"They look kind of alike is the thing," Banks explained. "And, well, their delivery is a little funny."

"I don't want comedians."

"No, they're good," Sellitto said. "The best canvassers we got. You know that beast 'napped that eight-year-old girl in Queens last year? Bedding and Saul did the canvass. Interviewed the entire 'hood—took twenty-two *hundred* statements. It was 'causa them we saved her. When we heard the vic this morning was the passenger from JFK, Chief Wilson himself put 'em on board."

"What're they doing now?"

"Witnesses mostly. Around the train tracks. And sniffing around about the driver and the cab."

Rhyme yelled to Thom in the hallway, "Did you call Berger? No, of course you didn't. The word 'insubordination' mean anything to you? At least make yourself useful. Bring that crime scene report closer and start turning the pages." He nodded toward the turning frame. "That damn thing's an Edsel."

"Aren't we in a sunny mood today?" the aide spat back.

"Hold it up *higher*. I'm getting glare."

He read for a minute. Then looked up.

Sellitto was on the phone but Rhyme interrupted him. "Whatever happens at three today, if we can find where he's talking about, it's going to be a crime scene. I'll need someone to work it."

"Good," Sellitto said. "I'll call Peretti. Toss him a bone. I know his nose'll be out of joint 'cause we're tiptoeing around him."

Rhyme grunted. "Did I ask for Peretti?"

"But he's the IRD golden boy," Banks said.

"I don't want him," Rhyme muttered. "There's somebody else I want."

Sellitto and Banks exchanged glances. The older detective smiled, brushing pointlessly at his wrinkled shirt. "Whoever you want, Linc, you got him. Remember, you're king for a day."

Staring at the dim eye.

T.J. Colfax, dark-haired refugee from the hills of Eastern Tennessee, NYU Business School grad, quick-as-a-whip currency trader, had just swum out of a deep dream. Her tangled hair stuck to her cheeks, sweat crawling in veins down her face and neck and chest.

She found herself looking into the black eye—a hole in a rusty pipe, about six inches across, from which a small access plate had been removed.

She sucked mildewy air through her nose—her mouth was still taped shut. Tasting plastic, the hot adhesive. Bitter.

And John? she wondered. Where was he? Refusing to think about the loud crack she'd heard last night in the basement. She'd grown up in Eastern Tennessee and knew what gunshots sounded like.

Please, she prayed for her boss. Let him be all right.

Stay calm, she raged to herself. You fucking start to cry again, you remember what happened. In the basement, after the gunshot, she'd lost it completely, breaking down, sobbing in panic, and had nearly suffocated.

Right. Calm.

Look at the black eye in the pipe. Pretend it's winking at you. The eye of your guardian angel.

T.J. sat on the floor, surrounded by a hundred pipes and ducts and snakes of conduit and wires. Hotter than her brother's diner, hotter than the back seat of Jule Whelan's Nova ten years ago. Water dripped, stalactites drooped from the ancient girders above her head. A half-dozen tiny yellow bulbs were the only illumination. Above her head—directly above—was a sign. She couldn't read it clearly, though she caught the red border. At the end of whatever the message might have been was a fat exclamation point.

She struggled once more but the cuffs held her tight, pinching against the bone. From her throat rose a desperate cry, an animal's cry. But the thick tape on her mouth and the insistent churning of machinery swallowed up the sound; no one could've heard her.

The black eye continued to stare. You'll save me, won't you? she thought.

Suddenly the silence was broken by a clanging slam, an iron

bell, far away. Like a ship's door slamming shut. The noise came from the hole in the pipe. From her friendly eye.

She jerked the cuffs against the pipe and tried to stand. But she couldn't move more than a few inches.

Okay, don't panic. Just relax. You'll be all right.

It was then that she happened to see the sign above her head. In her jockeying for slack she'd straightened up slightly and moved her head to the side. This gave her an oblique view of the words.

Oh, no. Oh, Jesus in my heart . . .

The tears began again.

She imagined her mother, her hair pulled back from her round face, wearing her cornflower-blue housedress, whispering, "Be all raht, honey love. Doan' you worry."

But she didn't believe the words.

She believed what the sign said.

> *Extreme Danger! Superheated steam under High Pressure. Do not remove plate from pipe. Call Consolidated Edison for access. Extreme danger!*

The black eye gaped at her, the eye that opened into the heart of the steam pipe. It stared directly at the pink flesh of her chest. From somewhere deep inside the pipe came another clink of metal on metal, workers hammering, tightening old joints.

As Tammie Jean Colfax cried and cried she heard another clink. Then a distant groan, very faint. And it seemed to her, through her tears, that the black eye finally winked.

FIVE

H ere's the situation," Lincoln Rhyme announced. "We've got a kidnap victim and a three p.m. deadline."

"No ransom demands"—Sellitto supplemented Rhyme's synopsis, then turned aside to answer his chirping phone.

"Jerry," Rhyme said to Banks, "brief them about the scene this morning."

There were more people hovering in Lincoln Rhyme's dark room than in recent memory. Oh, after the accident friends had sometimes stopped by unannounced (the odds were pretty good that Rhyme'd be home of course) but he'd discouraged that. And he'd stopped returning phone calls too, growing more and more reclusive, drifting into solitude. He'd spend his hours writing his book and, when he was uninspired to write another one, reading. And when that grew tedious there were rental movies and pay-per-view and music. And then he'd given up TV and the stereo and spent hours staring at the art prints the aide had dutifully taped up on the wall opposite the bed. Finally they too had come down.

Solitude.

It was all he craved, and oh how he missed it now.

Pacing, looking tense, was compact Jim Polling. Lon Sellitto was the case officer but an incident like this needed a captain on board and Polling had volunteered for the job. The case was a time bomb and could nuke careers in a heartbeat so the chief and the dep coms were happy to have him intercept the flak. They'd be practicing the fine art of distancing and when the Betacams rolled their press conferences would be peppered with words like *delegated* and *assigned* and *taking the advice of* and they'd be fast to glance at Polling when it came time to field the hardball questions. Rhyme couldn't imagine why any cop in the world would volunteer to head up a case like this one.

Polling was an odd one. The little man had pummeled his way through Midtown North Precinct as one of the city's most successful, and notorious, homicide detectives. Known for his bad temper, he'd gotten into serious trouble when he'd killed an unarmed suspect. But he'd managed, amazingly, to pull his career together by getting a conviction in the Shepherd case—the cop-serial-killer case, the one in which Rhyme'd been injured. Promoted to captain after that very public collar, Polling went through one of those embarrassing midlife changes—giving up blue jeans and Sears suits for Brooks Brothers (today he wore navy-blue Calvin Klein casual)—and began his dogged climb toward a plush corner office high in One Police Plaza.

Another officer leaned against a nearby table. Crew-cut, rangy Bo Haumann was a captain and head of the Emergency Services Unit. NYPD's SWAT team.

Banks finished his synopsis just as Sellitto pushed disconnect and folded his phone. "The Hardy Boys."

"Anything more on the cab?" Polling asked.

"Nothing. They're still beating bushes."

"Any sign she was fucking somebody she shouldn't've been?" Polling asked. "Maybe a psycho boyfriend?"

"Naw, no boyfriends. Just dated a few guys casually. No stalkers, it looks like."

"And still no ransom calls?" Rhyme asked.

"No."

The doorbell rang. Thom went to answer it.

Rhyme looked toward the approaching voices.

A moment later the aide escorted a uniformed police officer up the stairs. She appeared very young from a distance but as she drew closer he could see she was probably thirty or so. She was tall and had that sullen, equine beauty of women gazing out from the pages of fashion magazines.

We see others as we see ourselves and since the accident Lincoln Rhyme rarely thought of people in terms of their bodies. He observed her height, trim hips, fiery red hair. Somebody else'd weigh those features and say, What a knockout. But for Rhyme that thought didn't occur to him. What did register was the look in her eyes.

Not the surprise—obviously, nobody'd warned he was a crip—but something else. An expression he'd never seen before. It was as if his condition was putting her at ease. The exact opposite of how most people reacted. As she walked into the room she was relaxing.

"Officer Sachs?" Rhyme asked.

"Yessir," she said, catching herself just as she was about to extend a hand. "Detective Rhyme."

Sellitto introduced her to Polling and Haumann. She'd know about the latter two, by reputation if nothing else, and now her eyes grew cautious once more.

She took in the room, the dust, the gloominess. Glanced at one of the art posters. It was partially unrolled, lying under a table. *Nighthawks*, by Edward Hopper. The lonely people in a diner late at night. That one had been the last to come down.

Rhyme briefly explained about the 3:00 p.m. deadline. Sachs nodded calmly but Rhyme could see the flicker of what?—fear? disgust?—in her eyes.

Jerry Banks, fingers encumbered by a class ring but not a wedding band, was attracted immediately by the lamp of her beauty and offered her a particular smile. But Sachs's single glance in response made clear that no matches were being made here. And probably never would be.

Polling said, "Maybe it's a trap. We find the place he's leading us to, walk in and there's a bomb."

"I doubt it," Sellitto said, shrugging, "why go to all this trouble? If you want to kill cops all you gotta do is find one and fucking shoot him."

Awkward silence for a moment as Polling looked quickly from Sellitto to Rhyme. The collective thought registered that it was on the Shepherd case that Rhyme had been injured.

But faux pas meant nothing to Lincoln Rhyme. He continued, "I agree with Lon. But I'd tell any Search and Surveillance or HRT teams to keep an eye out for ambush. Our boy seems to be writing his own rules."

Sachs looked again at the poster of the Hopper painting. Rhyme followed her gaze. Maybe the people in the diner really weren't lonely, he reflected. Come to think of it, they all looked pretty damn content.

"We've got two types of physical evidence here," Rhyme continued. "Standard PE. What the unsub didn't mean to leave behind. Hair, fibers, fingerprints, maybe blood, shoeprints. If we can find enough of it—and if we're lucky—that'll lead us to the primary crime scene. That's where he lives."

"Or his hidey-hole," Sellitto offered. "Something temporary."

"A safe house?" Rhyme mused, nodding. "Bet you're right, Lon. He needs someplace to operate out of." He continued, "Then there's the planted evidence. Apart from the scraps of paper—which tell us the time and date—we've got the bolt, the wad of asbestos and the sand."

"A fucking scavenger hunt," Haumann growled and ran a hand through his slick buzz cut. He looked just like the drill sergeant Rhyme recalled he'd been.

"So I can tell the brass there's a chance of getting the vic in time?" Polling asked.

"I think so, yes."

The captain made a call and wandered to the corner of the room as he talked. When he hung up he grunted, "The mayor. The chief's with 'im. There's gonna be a press conference in an hour and I gotta be there to make sure their dicks're in their pants and their flies're zipped. Anything more I can tell the big boys?"

Sellitto glanced at Rhyme, who shook his head.

"Not yet," the detective said.

Polling gave Sellitto his cellular phone number and left, literally jogging out the door.

A moment later a skinny, balding man in his thirties ambled up the stairs. Mel Cooper was as goofy-looking as ever, the nerdy neighbor in a sitcom. He was followed by two younger cops carrying a steamer trunk and two suitcases that seemed to weigh a thousand pounds each. The officers deposited their heavy loads and left.

"Mel."

"Detective." Cooper walked up to Rhyme and gripped his useless right hand. The only physical contact today with any of his guests, Rhyme noted. He and Cooper had worked together for years. With degrees in organic chemistry, math and physics, Cooper was an expert both in identification—friction-ridge prints, DNA and forensic reconstruction—and in PE analysis.

"How's the world's foremost criminalist?" Cooper asked him.

Rhyme scoffed good-naturedly. The title had been bestowed on him by the press some years ago, after the surprising news that the FBI had selected him—a city cop—as adviser in putting together PERT, their Physical Evidence Response Team. Not satisfied with "forensic scientist" or "forensic specialist," reporters dubbed Rhyme a "criminalist."

The word had actually been around for years, first applied in the United States to the legendary Paul Leland Kirk, who ran the UC Berkeley School of Criminology. The school, the first in the country, had been founded by the even more legendary Chief August Vollmer. The handle had recently become chic, and when techs around the country sidled up to blondes at cocktail parties now they described themselves as criminalists, not forensic scientists.

"Everybody's nightmare," Cooper said, "you get into a cab and turns out there's a psycho behind the wheel. And the whole world's watching the Big Apple 'causa that conference. Wondered if they might not bring you out of retirement for this one."

"How's your mother?" Rhyme asked.

"Still complaining about every ache and pain. Still healthier than me."

Cooper lived with the elderly woman in the Queens bungalow where he'd been born. His passion was ballroom dancing—the tango his specialty. Cop gossip being what it is, there'd been speculation around IRD as to the man's sexual preference. Rhyme had had no interest in his employees' personal lives but had been as surprised as everyone else to finally meet Greta, Cooper's steady girlfriend, a stunning Scandinavian who taught advanced mathematics at Columbia.

Cooper opened the large trunk, which was padded with velvet. He lifted out parts for three large microscopes and began assembling them.

"Oh, house current." He glanced at the outlets, disappointed. He pushed his metal-rimmed glasses up on his nose.

"That's because it's a house, Mel."

"I assumed you lived in a lab. Wouldn't have been surprised."

Rhyme stared at the instruments, gray and black, battered. Similar to the ones he'd lived with for over fifteen years. A standard compound microscope, a phase-contrast 'scope, and a polarized-light model. Cooper opened the suitcases, which contained a Mr. Wizard assortment of bottles and jars and scientific instruments. In a flash, words came back to Rhyme, words that had once been part of his daily vocabulary. EDTA vacuum blood-collection tubes, acetic acid, orthotolidine, luminol reagent, Magna-Brush, Ruhemann's purple phenomenon . . .

The skinny man looked around the room. "Looks just like your office used to, Lincoln. How do you *find* anything? Say, I need some room here."

"Thom." Rhyme moved his head toward the least cluttered table. They moved aside magazines and papers and books, revealing a tabletop Rhyme had not seen in a year.

Sellitto gazed at the crime scene report. "Whatta we call the unsub? We don't have a case number yet."

Rhyme glanced at Banks. "Pick a number. Any number."

Banks suggested, "The page number. Well, the date, I mean."

"Unsub 823. Good as any."

Sellitto jotted this on the report.

"Uhm, excuse me? Detective Rhyme?"

It was the patrolwoman who'd spoken. Rhyme turned to her.

"I was supposed to be at the Big Building at noon." Coptalk for One Police Plaza.

"Officer Sachs . . ." He'd forgotten about her momentarily. "You were first officer this morning? At that homicide by the railroad tracks."

"That's right, I took the call." When she spoke, she spoke to Thom.

"I'm *here*, officer," Rhyme reminded sternly, barely controlling his temper. "Over here." It infuriated him when people talked to him through others, through *healthy* people.

Her head swiveled quickly and he saw the lesson had been learned. "Yessir," she said, a soft tone in her voice but ice in her eyes.

"I'm decommissioned. Just call me Lincoln."

"Would you just get it over with, please?"

"How's that?" he asked.

"The reason why you brought me here. I'm sorry. I wasn't thinking. If you want a written apology I'll do it. Only, I'm late for my new assignment and I haven't had a chance to call my commander."

"Apology?" Rhyme asked.

"The thing is, I didn't have any real crime scene experience. I was sort of flying by the seat of my pants."

"What are you talking about?"

"Stopping the trains and closing Eleventh Avenue. It was *my* fault the senator missed his speech in New Jersey and that some of the senior UN people didn't make it in from Newark Airport in time for their meetings."

Rhyme was chuckling. "Do you know who I am?"

"Well, I've heard of you of course. I thought you . . ."

"Were dead?" Rhyme asked.

"No. I didn't mean that." Though she had. She continued quickly, "We all used your book in the academy. But we don't hear about you. Personally, I mean . . ." She looked up at the wall and said stiffly, "In my judgment, as first officer, I thought it was best to stop the train and close the street to protect the scene. And that's what I did. Sir."

"Call me Lincoln. And you're . . ."

"I—"

"Your first name?"

"Amelia."

"Amelia. After the aviatrix?"

"Nosir. A family name."

"Amelia, I don't want an apology. You were right and Vince Peretti was wrong."

Sellitto stirred at this indiscretion but Lincoln Rhyme didn't care. He was, after all, one of the few people in the world who could stay flat on his ass when the president of the United States himself walked into the room. He continued, "Peretti worked the scene like the mayor was looking over his shoulder and that's the A-number-one way to screw it up. He had too many people, he was dead wrong to let the trains and traffic move and he should never have released the scene as early as he did. If we'd kept the tracks secure, who knows, we might've just found a credit card receipt with a name on it. Or a big beautiful thumbprint."

"That may be," Sellitto said delicately. "But let's just keep it to ourselves." Giving silent orders, his eyes swiveling toward Sachs and Cooper and young Jerry Banks.

Rhyme snorted an irreverent laugh. Then turned back to Sachs, whom he caught, like Banks that morning, staring at his legs and body under the apricot-colored blanket. He said to her, "I asked you here to work the next crime scene for us."

"What?" No speaking through interpreters this time.

"Work for us," he said shortly. "The next crime scene."

"But"—she laughed—"I'm not IRD. I'm Patrol. I've never done CS work."

"This is an unusual case. As Detective Sellitto himself'll tell you. It's real *weird*. Right, Lon? True, if it was a classic scene, I wouldn't want you. But we need a fresh pair of eyes on this one."

She glanced at Sellitto, who said nothing. "I just . . . I'd be no good at it. I'm sure."

"All right," Rhyme said patiently. "The truth?"

She nodded.

"I need somebody who's got the balls to stop a train in its tracks to protect a scene and to put up with the heat afterwards."

"Thank you for the opportunity, sir. Lincoln. But—"

Rhyme said shortly, "Lon."

"Officer," the detective grunted to Sachs, "you're not being given any options here. You've been assigned to this case to assist at the crime scene."

"Sir, I have to protest. I'm transferring out of Patrol. Today. I've got a medical transfer. Effective an hour ago."

"Medical?" Rhyme inquired.

She hesitated, glancing unwilling at his legs again. "I have arthritis."

"Do you?" Rhyme asked.

"Chronic arthritis."

"I'm sorry to hear that."

She continued quickly, "I only took that call this morning because someone was home sick. I didn't plan on it."

"Yes, well, I had other plans too," Lincoln Rhyme said. "Now, let's look at some evidence."

SIX

"T he bolt."

Remembering the classic crime scene rule: Analyze the most unusual evidence first.

Thom turned the plastic bag over and over in his hands as Rhyme studied the metal rod, half rusted, half not. Dull. Worn.

"You're sure about the prints? You tried small-particle reagent? That's the best for PE exposed to the elements."

"Yup," Mel Cooper confirmed.

"Thom," Rhyme ordered, "get this hair out of my eyes! Comb it back. I told you to comb it back this morning."

The aide sighed and brushed at the tangled black strands. "Watch it," he whispered ominously to his boss and Rhyme jerked his head dismissively, mussing his hair further. Amelia Sachs sat sullenly in the corner. Her legs rested under the chair in a sprinter's starting position and, sure enough, she looked like she was just waiting for the gun.

Rhyme turned back to the bolt.

When he headed IRD, Rhyme had started assembling databases. Like the federal auto-paint-chip index or the BATF's tobacco files. He'd set up a bullet-standards file, fibers, cloth, tires, shoes, tools, motor oil, transmission fluid. He'd spent hundreds of hours compiling lists, indexed and cross-referenced.

Even during Rhyme's obsessive tenure, though, IRD had never gotten around to cataloging hardware. He wondered why not and he was angry at himself for not taking the time to do it and angrier still at Vince Peretti for not thinking of it either.

"We need to call every bolt manufacturer and jobber in the Northeast. No, in the *country*. Ask if they make a model like this and who they sell to. Fax a description and picture of the bolt to our dispatchers at Communications."

"Hell, there could be a million of them," Banks said. "Every Ace Hardware and Sears in the country."

"I don't think so," Rhyme responded. "It's got to be a viable clue. He wouldn't have left it if it was useless. There's a limited source of these bolts. I bet you."

Sellitto made a call and looked up a few minutes later. "I've got you dispatchers, Lincoln. Four of them. Where do we get a list of manufacturers?"

"Get a patrolman down to Forty-second Street," Rhyme replied. "Public Library. They have corporate directories there. Until we get one, have the dispatchers start working through the Business-to-Business Yellow Pages."

Sellitto repeated this into the phone.

Rhyme glanced at the clock. It was one-thirty.

"Now, the asbestos."

For an instant, the word glowed in his mind. He felt a jolt—in places where no jolts could be felt. What was familiar about asbestos? Something he'd read or heard about—recently, it seemed, though Lincoln Rhyme no longer trusted his sense of time. When you lie on your back frozen in place month after month after month, time slows to near-death. He might be thinking of something he'd read two years ago.

"What do we know about asbestos?" he mused. No one answered but that didn't matter; he answered himself. As he preferred to do anyway. Asbestos was a complex molecule, silicate polymer. It doesn't burn because, like glass, it's already oxidized.

When he'd run crime scenes of old murders—working with forensic anthropologists and odontologists—Rhyme often found himself in asbestos-insulated buildings. He remembered the peculiar taste of the face masks they'd had to wear during the excavation. In fact, he now recalled, it'd been during an asbestos-removal cleanup at the City Hall subway stop three and a half years ago that crews found the body of one of the policemen murdered by Dan Shepherd dumped in a generator room. As Rhyme had bent down over it slowly to lift a fiber from the officer's light-blue blouse, he'd heard the crack and groan of the oak beam. The mask had probably saved him from choking to death on the dust and dirt that caved in around him.

"Maybe he's got her at a cleanup site," Sellitto said.

"Could be," Rhyme agreed.

Sellitto ordered his young assistant, "Call EPA and city Environmental. Find out if there're any sites where cleanup's going on right now."

The detective made the call.

"Bo," Rhyme asked Haumann, "you have teams to deploy?"

"Ready to roll," the ESU commander confirmed. "Though I gotta tell you, we've got over half the force tied up with this UN thing. They're on loan to the Secret Service and UN security."

"Got some EPA info here." Banks gestured to Haumann and they retired to a corner of the room. They moved aside several stacks of books. As Haumann unfurled one of ESU's tactical maps of New York something clattered to the floor.

Banks jumped. "Jesus."

From the angle where he lay, Rhyme couldn't see what had fallen. Haumann hesitated then bent down and retrieved the bleached piece of spinal column and replaced it on the table.

Rhyme felt several pairs of eyes on him but he said nothing about the bone. Haumann leaned over the map, as Banks, on the phone, fed him information about asbestos-cleanup sites. The commander marked them in grease pencil. There appeared to be a lot of them, scattered all over the five boroughs of the city. It was discouraging.

"We have to narrow it down more. Let's see, the sand," Rhyme said to Cooper. " 'Scope it. Tell me what you think."

Sellitto handed the evidence envelope to the tech, who poured the contents out onto an enamel examination tray. The glistening powder left a small cloud of dust. There was also a stone, worn smooth, which slid into the center of the pile.

Lincoln Rhyme's throat caught. Not at what he saw—he didn't yet know *what* he was looking at—but at the flawed nerve impulse that shot from his brain and died halfway to his useless right arm, urging it to grab a pencil and to probe. The first time in a year or so he'd felt that urge. It nearly brought tears into his eyes and his only solace was the memory of the tiny bottle of Seconal and the plastic bag that Dr. Berger carried with him— images that hovered like a saving angel over the room.

He cleared his throat. "Print it!"

"What?" Cooper asked.

"The stone."

Sellitto looked at him inquiringly.

"The rock doesn't belong there," Rhyme said. "Apples and oranges. I want to know why. Print it."

Using porcelain-tipped forceps, Cooper picked up the stone and examined it. He slipped on goggles and hit the rock with a beam from a PoliLight—a power pack the size of a car battery with a light wand attached.

"Nothing," Cooper said.

"VMD?"

Vacuum metal deposition is the Cadillac of techniques for raising latent prints on nonporous surfaces. It evaporates gold or zinc in a vacuum chamber containing the object to be tested; the metal coats the latent print, making the whorls and peaks very visible.

But Cooper didn't have a VMD with him.

"What *do* you have?" asked Rhyme, not pleased.

"Sudan black, stabilized physical developer, iodine, amido black, DFO and gentian violet, Magna-Brush."

He'd also brought ninhydrin for raising prints on porous surfaces and a Super Glue frame for smooth surfaces. Rhyme re-called the stunning news that had swept the forensic community some years ago: A technician working in a U.S. Army forensic lab in Japan had used Super Glue to fix a broken camera and found to his amazement that the fumes from the adhesive raised latent fingerprints better than most chemicals made for that purpose.

This was the method Cooper now used. With forceps he set the rock in a small glass box and put a dab of glue on the hot plate inside. A few minutes later he lifted the rock out.

"We've got something," he said. He dusted it with long-wavelength UV powder and hit it with the beam from the PoliLight wand. A print was clearly visible. Dead center. Cooper photographed it with Polaroid CU-5, a 1:1 camera. He showed the picture to Rhyme.

"Hold it closer." Rhyme squinted as he examined it. "Yes! He rolled it."

Rolling prints—rocking a finger onto a surface—produced an impression different from one made by picking up an object. It was a subtle difference—in the width of the friction ridges at various points on the pattern—but one that Rhyme now recognized clearly.

"And look, what's that?" he mused. "That line." There was a faint crescent mark above the print itself.

"It looks almost like—"

"Yep," Rhyme said, "her fingernail. You wouldn't normally get that. But I'll bet he tipped the stone just to make sure it got picked up. It left an oil impression. Like a friction ridge."

"Why would he do that?" Sachs asked.

Once more miffed that nobody seemed to be picking up these points as fast as he was, Rhyme explained tersely, "He's telling us two things. First, he's making sure we know the victim's a woman. In case we didn't make the connection between her and the body this morning."

"Why do that?" Banks asked.

"To up the ante," Rhyme said. "Make us sweat more. He's let us know there's a woman at risk. He's valuated the victims—just like we all do—even though we claim we don't." Rhyme happened to glance at Sachs's hands. He was surprised to see that, for such a beautiful woman, *her* fingers were a mess. Four ended in fleshy Band-Aids and several others were chewed to the quick. The cuticle of one was caked with brown blood. He noticed too the red inflammation of the skin beneath her eyebrows, from plucking them, he assumed. And a scratch mark beside her ear. All self-destructive habits. There're a million ways to do yourself in besides pills and Armagnac.

Rhyme announced, "The other thing he's telling us I already warned you about. He knows evidence. He's saying, Don't bother with regular forensic PE. I won't be leaving any. That's what *he* thinks of course. But we'll find something. You bet we will." Suddenly Rhyme frowned. "The map! We need the map. Thom!"

The aide blurted, "What map?"

"You *know* what map I mean."

Thom sighed. "Not a clue, Lincoln."

Glancing out the window and speaking half to himself, Rhyme mused, "The railroad underpass, the bootleg tunnels and access doors, the asbestos—those're all old. He likes *historical* New York. I want the Randel map."

"Which is where?"

"The research files for my book. Where else?"

Thom dug through folders and pulled out a photocopy of a long, horizontal map of Manhattan. "This?"

"That, yes!"

It was the Randel Survey, drawn in 1811 for the commissioners of the city to plan out the grid of streets in Manhattan. The map had been printed horizontally, with Battery Park, south, to the left and Harlem, north, to the right. Laid out this way, the island resembled the body of a dog leaping, its narrow head lifted for an attack.

"Pin it up there. Good."

As the aide did, Rhyme blurted, "Thom, we're going to deputize you. Give him a shiny badge or something, Lon."

"Lincoln," he muttered.

"We need you. Come on. Haven't you always wanted to be Sam Spade or Kojak?"

"Only Judy Garland," the aide replied.

"Jessica Fletcher then! You'll be writing the profile. Come on now, get out that Mont Blanc you're always letting stick vainly out of your shirt pocket."

The young man rolled his eyes as he lifted his Parker pen and took a dusty yellow pad from a stack under one of the tables.

"No, I've got a better idea," Rhyme announced. "Put up one of those posters. Those art posters. Tape it up backwards and write on the back in marker. Write big now. So I can see it."

Thom selected a Monet lily pads and mounted it to the wall.

"On the top," the criminalist ordered, "write 'Unsub 823.' Then four columns. 'Appearance. Residence. Vehicle. Other.' Beautiful. Now, let's start. What do we know about him?"

Sellitto said, "Vehicle . . . He's got a Yellow Cab."

"Right. And under 'Other' add that he knows CS—crime scene—procedures."

"Which," Sellitto added, "maybe means he's had his turn in the barrel."

"How's that?" Thom asked.

"He might have a record," the detective explained.

Banks said, "Should we add that he's armed with a .32 Colt?"

"Fuck yes," his boss confirmed.

Rhyme contributed, "And he knows FRs. . . ."

"What?" Thom asked.

"Friction ridges—fingerprints. That's what they are, you know, ridges on our hands and feet to give us traction. And put down that he's probably working out of a safe house. Good job, Thom. Look at him. He's a born law enforcer."

Thom glowered and stepped away from the wall, brushing at his shirt, which had picked up a stringy cobweb from the wall.

"There we go, folks," Sellitto said. "Our first look at Mr. 823."

Rhyme turned to Mel Cooper. "Now, the sand. What can we tell about it?"

Cooper lifted the goggles onto his pale forehead. He poured a sample onto a slide and slipped it under the polarized-light 'scope. He adjusted dials.

"Hmm. This is curious. No birefringence."

Polarizing microscopes show birefringence—the double refraction of crystals and fibers and some other materials. Seashore sand birefringes dramatically.

"So it isn't sand," Rhyme muttered. "It's something ground up. . . . Can you individuate it?"

Individuation . . . The goal of the criminalist. Most physical evidence can be *identified*. But even if you know what it is there are usually hundreds or thousands of sources it might have come from. *Individuated* evidence is something that could have come from only one source or a very limited number of sources. A fingerprint, a DNA profile, a paint chip that fits into a missing spot on the perp's car like a jigsaw-puzzle piece.

"Maybe," the tech responded, "if I can figure out *what* it is."

"Ground glass?" Rhyme suggested.

Glass is essentially melted sand but the glassmaking process alters the crystalline structure. You don't get birefringence with ground glass. Cooper examined the sample closely.

"No, I don't think it's glass. I don't know what it is. I wish I had an EDX here."

A popular crime lab tool was a scanning electron microscope married to an energy-dispersive X-ray unit; it determined what elements were in trace samples found at crime scenes.

"Get him one," Rhyme ordered Sellitto, then looked around the room. "We need more equipment. I want a vacuum metal fingerprint unit too. And a GC-MS." A gas chromatograph broke down substances into their component elements, and mass photospectrometry used light to identify each one of them. These instruments let criminalists test an unknown sample as small as one millionth of a gram and compare it against a database of a hundred thousand known substances, cataloged by identity *and* name brand.

Sellitto phoned the wish list in to the CSU lab.

"But we can't wait for the fancy toys, Mel. You'll have to do it the old-fashioned way. Tell me more about our phony sand."

"It's mixed with a little dirt. There's loam, flecks of quartz, feldspar and mica. But minimal leaf and decomposed-plant fragments. Flecks here of what could be bentonite."

"Bentonite." Rhyme was pleased. "That's a volcanic ash that builders use in slurry when they're digging foundations in watery areas of the city where the bedrock's deep. It prevents cave-ins. So we're looking for a developed area that's on or near the water, probably south of Thirty-fourth Street. North of that the bedrock's much closer to the surface and they don't need slurry."

Cooper moved the slide. "If I had to guess, I'd say this is mostly calcium. Wait, something fibrous here."

The knob turned and Rhyme would've paid anything to be looking through that eyepiece. Flashed back to all the evenings he'd spent with his face pressed against the gray sponge rubber, watching fibers or flecks of humus or blood cells or metal shavings swim into and out of focus.

"Here's something else. A larger granule. Three layers. One similar to horn, then two layers of calcium. Slightly different colors. The other one's translucent."

"Three layers?" Rhyme spat out angrily. "Hell, it's a seashell!" He felt furious with himself. He should have thought of that.

"Yep, that's it." Cooper was nodding. "Oyster, I think."

The oyster beds around the city were mostly off the coasts of Long Island and New Jersey. Rhyme had hoped that the unsub would limit the geographic area of the search to Manhattan—where the victim that morning was found. He muttered, "If he's opening up the whole metro area the search'll be hopeless."

Cooper said, "I'm looking at something else. I think it's lime. But very old. Granular."

"Concrete maybe?" Rhyme suggested.

"Possibly. Yes.

"I don't get the shells then," Cooper added reflectively. "Around New York the oyster beds're full of vegetation and mud. This is mixed with concrete and there's virtually no vegetable matter at all."

Rhyme barked suddenly. "Edges! What are the edges of the shell like, Mel?"

The tech gazed into the eyepiece. "Fractured, not worn. This's been pulverized by dry pressure. Not eroded by water."

Rhyme's eyes slipped over the Randel map, scanning right and left. Focusing on the leaping dog's rump.

"Got it!" he cried.

In 1913 F. W. Woolworth built the sixty-story structure that still bears his name, terra-cotta-clad, covered with gargoyles and Gothic sculpture. For sixteen years it was the world's tallest building. Because the bedrock in that part of Manhattan was more than a hundred feet below Broadway, workmen had to dig deep shafts to anchor the building. It wasn't long after the groundbreaking that workmen discovered the remains of Manhattan industrialist Talbott Soames, who'd been kidnapped in 1906. The man's body was found buried in a thick bed of what looked like white sand but was really ground oyster shells, a fact the tabloids had a hey-day with, noting the obese tycoon's obsession with rich food. The shells were so common along the lower eastern tip of Manhattan they'd been used for landfill. They were what had given Pearl Street its name.

"She's downtown somewhere," Rhyme announced. "Probably the east side. And maybe near Pearl. She'll be underground, about five to fifteen feet down. Maybe a construction site, maybe a basement. An old building or tunnel."

"Cross-check the EPA diagram, Jerry," Sellitto instructed. "Where they're doing asbestos cleanup."

"Along Pearl? Nothing." The young officer held up the map he and Haumann were working from. "There're three-dozen cleanup sites—in Midtown, Harlem and the Bronx. But nothing downtown."

"Asbestos . . . asbestos . . ." Rhyme mused again. *What* was so familiar about it?

It was 2:05 p.m.

"Bo, we've got to move. Get your people down there and start a search. All the buildings along Pearl Street. Water Street too."

"Man," the cop sighed, "that's beaucoup buildings." He started for the door.

Rhyme said to Sellitto, "Lon, you better go too. This's going to be a photo finish. They'll need all the searchers they can get. Amelia, I want you down there too."

"Look, I've been thinking—"

"Officer," Sellitto snapped, "you got your orders."

A faint glower crossed her beautiful face.

Rhyme said to Cooper, "Mel, you drive over here in a bus?"

"An RRV," he answered.

The city's big crime scene buses were large vans—filled with instruments and evidence-collection supplies, better equipped than the entire labs of many small towns. But when Rhyme was running IRD he'd ordered smaller crime scene vehicles— station wagons basically—containing the essential collection- and-analysis equipment. The Rapid Response Vehicles looked placid but Rhyme had bullied Transportation into getting them fitted with turbocharged Police Interceptor engines. They often beat Patrol's squad cars to the scene; on more than one occasion the first officer was a seasoned crime scene tech. Which is every prosecutor's dream.

"Give Amelia the keys."

Cooper handed them to Sachs, who stared briefly at Rhyme then wheeled and hurried down the stairs. Even her footsteps sounded angry.

"All right, Lon. What's on your mind?"

Sellitto glanced at the empty hallway and walked up close to Rhyme. "You really want P.D. for this?"

"P.D.?"

"I mean her. Sachs. P.D.'s a nickname."

"For what?"

"Don't say it around her. Ticks her off. Her dad was a beat cop for forty years. So they call her the Portable's Daughter."

"You don't think I should've picked her?"

"Naw, I don't. Why d'you want her?"

"Because she climbed down a thirty-foot embankment so she

wouldn't contaminate the scene. She closed a major avenue and an Amtrak line. That's initiative."

"Come on, Linc. I know a dozen CS cops'd do something like that."

"Well, she's the one I wanted." And Rhyme gave Sellitto a grave look, reminding him, subtly but without debate, what the terms of this bargain had been.

"All I'll say is," the detective muttered, "I just talked to Polling. Peretti's fucking outa joint about being flanked and if— no, I'll say *when*—the brass finds out somebody from Patrol's walking the grid at the scene, there'll be fucking trouble."

"Probably," Rhyme said softly, gazing at the profile poster, "but I have a feeling that's going to be the least of our trouble today."

And let his weary head ease back into the thick down pillow.

SEVEN

The station wagon raced toward the dark, sooty canyons of Wall Street, downtown New York.

Amelia Sachs's fingers danced lightly on the steering wheel as she tried to imagine where T.J. Colfax might be held captive. Finding her seemed hopeless. The approaching financial district had never looked so enormous, so full of alleys, so filled with manholes and doorways and buildings peppered with black windows.

So many places to hide a hostage.

In her mind she saw the hand sticking out of the grave beside the railroad tracks. The diamond ring sitting on the bloody bone of a finger. Sachs recognized the type of jewelry. She called them consolation rings—the sort lonely rich girls bought themselves. The sort she'd be wearing if she were rich.

Speeding south, dodging bicycle messengers and cabs.

Even on this glaring afternoon, under a choked sun, this was a spooky part of town. The buildings cast grim shadows and were coated with grime dark as dried blood.

Sachs took a turn at forty, skidding on the spongy asphalt, and punched the pedal to bring the station wagon back up to sixty.

Excellent engine, she thought. And decided to see how well the wagon handled at seventy.

UNSUB 823

Appearance	Residence	Vehicle	Other
	• Prob. has safe house	• Yellow Cab	• knows CS proc. • possibly has record • knows FR prints • gun = .32 Colt

Years before, while her old man slept—he worked the three-to-eleven watch usually—teenage Amie Sachs would palm the keys to his Camaro and tell her mother Rose she was going shopping, did she want anything from the Fort Hamilton pork store? And before her mother could say, "No, but you take the train, you're not driving," the girl would disappear out the door, fire up the car and race west.

Coming home three hours later, pork-less, Amie would sneak up the stairs to be confronted by a mother frantic and angry, who—to her daughter's amusement—would lecture her about the risks of getting pregnant and how that would ruin her chances to use her beautiful face to make a million dollars at modeling. And when finally the woman learned that her daughter wasn't sleeping around but was merely driving a hundred mph on Long Island highways, she grew frantic and angry and would lecture the girl about smashing up her beautiful face and ruining her chances to make a million dollars at modeling.

Things grew even worse when she got her driver's license.

Sachs now sliced between two double-parked trucks, hoping that neither a passenger nor a driver would open his door. In a Doppler whisper she was past them.

When you move they can't getcha. . . .

Lon Sellitto kneaded his rotund face with blunt fingertips and paid no attention to the Indy 500 driving. He talked with his partner about the case like an accountant discussing a balance sheet. As for Banks, though, he was no longer stealing infatuated glances at Sachs's eyes and lips and had taken to checking the speedometer every minute or so.

They skidded in a frantic turn past the Brooklyn Bridge. She thought again of the woman captive, picturing T.J.'s long, elegant nails, while she tapped her own picked fingers on the wheel. She saw again in her mind the image that refused to go away: the white birch branch of a hand, sticking up out of the moist grave. The single bloody bone.

"He's kind of loony," she blurted suddenly, to change the direction of her thoughts.

"Who?" Sellitto asked.

"Rhyme."

Banks added, "Ask me, he looks like Howard Hughes's kid brother."

"Yeah, well, that surprised me," the older detective admitted. "Wasn't looking too good. Used to be a handsome guy. But, well, you know. After what he's been through. How come if you drive like this, Sachs, you're a portable?"

"Where I got assigned. They didn't ask, they *told* me." Just like you did, she reflected. "Was he really as good as that?"

"Rhyme? Better. Most CSU guys in New York handle two hundred bodies a year. Tops. Rhyme did double that. Even when he was running IRD. Take Peretti, he's a good man but he gets out once every two weeks or so and only on media cases. You're not hearing this from me, officer."

"Nosir."

"But Rhyme'd run the scenes himself. And when he wasn't running scenes he'd be out walking around."

"Doing what?"

"Just walking around. Looking at stuff. He walked miles. All over the city. Buying things, picking up things, *collecting* things."

"What kinds of things?"

"Evidence standards. Dirt, food, magazines, hubcaps, shoes, medical books, drugs, plants . . . You name it, he'd find it and catalog it. You know—so when some PE came in he'd have a better idea where the perp might've been or what he'd been doing. You'd page him and he'd be in Harlem or the Lower East Side or Hell's Kitchen."

"Police in his blood?"

"Naw. Father was some kind of scientist at a national laboratory or something."

"Is that what Rhyme studied? Science?"

"Yeah. Went to school at Champaign-Urbana, got a coupla fancy degrees. Chemistry and history. Which I have no idea why. His folks're gone since I knew him, that'd be, hell, coming on fifteen years now. And he doesn't have any brothers or sisters. He grew up in Illinois. That's why the name, Lincoln."

She wanted to ask if he was, or had been, married but didn't. She settled for: "Is he really that much of a . . ."

"You can say it, officer."

"A shit?"

Banks laughed.

Sellitto said, "My ma had this expression. She said somebody was 'of a mind.' Well, that describes Rhyme. He's of a mind. One time this dumb-ass tech sprayed luminol—that's a blood reagent—on a fingerprint, instead of ninhydrin. Ruined the print. Rhyme fired him on the spot. Another time a cop took a leak at a scene and flushed the toilet. Man, Rhyme went ballistic, told him to get his ass down to the basement and bring back whatever was in the sewer trap." Sellitto laughed. "The cop, he had rank, he said, 'I'm not doing that, I'm a lieutenant.' And Rhyme said, 'Got news. You're a plumber now.' I could go on and on. Fuck, officer, you doing eighty?"

They streaked past the Big Building and she thought, achingly, That's where I oughta be right now. Meeting fellow information officers, sitting through the training session, soaking up the air-conditioning.

She steered expertly around a taxi that was oozing through a red light.

Jesus, this is hot. Dust hot, stink hot, gas hot. The ugly hours of the city. Tempers spurted like gray water shooting from hydrants up in Harlem. Two Christmases ago, she and her boyfriend had an abbreviated holiday celebration—from 11:00 p.m. to midnight, the only mutual free time their watches allowed—in the four-degree night. She and Nick, sitting at Rockefeller Center, outside, near the skating rink, drinking coffee and brandy. They'd agreed they'd rather have a week of cold than a single hot August day.

Finally, streaking down Pearl she spotted Haumann's command post. Leaving eight-foot skid marks, Sachs put the RRV into a slot between his car and an EMS bus.

"Damn, you drive good." Sellitto climbed out. For some reason Sachs was delighted to notice Jerry Banks's sweaty fingerprints remained prominently on the window when he pushed the rear door open.

EMS officers and Patrol uniforms were everywhere, fifty or sixty of them. And more were on their way. It seemed as if the entire attention of Police Plaza was focused on downtown New York. Sachs found herself thinking idly that if anybody wanted to try an assassination or to take over Gracie Mansion or a consulate, this'd be the time to do it.

Haumann trotted up to the station wagon. He said to Sellitto, "We're doing door-to-door, seeing about construction along Pearl. Nobody knows anything about asbestos work and nobody's heard any calls for help."

Sachs started to climb out but Haumann said, "No, officer. Your orders're to stay here with the CS vehicle."

She got out anyway.

"Yessir. Who exactly said that?"

"Detective Rhyme. I just talked to him. You're supposed to call in to Central when you're at the CP."

Haumann was walking away. Sellitto and Banks hurried toward the command post.

"Detective Sellitto," Sachs called.

He turned. She said, "Excuse me, detective. The thing is, who's my watch commander? Who'm I reporting to?"

He said shortly, "You're reporting to Rhyme."

She laughed. "But I can't be *reporting* to him."

Sellitto gazed at her blankly.

"I mean, aren't there liability issues or something? Jurisdiction? He's a *civilian*. I need somebody, a shield, to report to."

Sellitto said evenly, "Officer, listen up. We're *all* reporting to Lincoln Rhyme. I don't care whether he's a civilian or he's the chief or he's the fucking Caped Crusader. Got that?"

"But—"

"You wanna complain, do it in writing and do it tomorrow."

And he was gone. Sachs stared after him for a moment then returned to the front seat of the wagon and called in to Central that she was 10-84 at the scene. Awaiting instructions.

She laughed grimly as the woman reported, "Ten-four, Portable 5885. Be advised. Detective Rhyme will be in touch shortly, K."

Detective Rhyme.

"Ten-four, K," Sachs responded and looked in the back of the wagon, wondering idly what was in the black suitcases.

Two-forty p.m.

The phone rang in Rhyme's townhouse. Thom answered. "It's a dispatcher from headquarters."

"Put 'em through."

The speakerphone burst to life. "Detective Rhyme, you don't remember me but I worked at IRD when you were there. Civilian. Did phone detail then. Emma Rollins."

"Of course. How're the youngsters, Emma?" Rhyme had a memory of a large, cheerful black woman, supporting five children with two jobs. He recalled her blunt finger stabbing buttons so hard she once actually broke one of the government-issue phones.

"Jeremy's starting college in a couple weeks and Dora's still acting, or she thinks she is. The little ones're doing just fine."

"Lon Sellitto recruited you, did he?"

"Nosir. I heard you were working on the case and I booted some child back to 911. Emma's taking this job, I told her."

"What've you got for us?"

"We're working out of a directory of companies making bolts. And a book that lists places wholesaling them. Here's what we found. It was the letters did it. The ones stamped on the bolt. The *CE.* They're made special for Con Ed."

Hell. Of course.

"They're marked that way because they're a different size than most bolts this company sells—fifteen-sixteenths of an inch, and a lot more threads than most other bolts. That'd be Michigan Tool and Die in Detroit. They use 'em in old pipes only in New York. Ones made sixty, seventy years ago. The way the parts of the pipe fit together they have to be real close seals. Fit closer'n a bride and groom on their wedding night's what the man told me. Trying to make me blush."

"Emma, I love you. You stay on call, will you?"

"You bet I will."

"Thom!" Rhyme shouted. "This phone isn't going to work. I need to make calls myself. That voice-activation thing in the computer. Can I use it?"

"You never ordered it."

"I didn't?"

"No."

"Well, I need it."

"Well, we don't have it."

"Do *something*. I want to be able to make calls."

"I think there's a manual ECU somewhere." Thom dug through a box against the wall. He found a small electronic console and plugged one end into the phone and the other into a stalk control that mounted next to Rhyme's cheek.

"That's too awkward!"

"Well, it's all we've got. If we'd hooked up the infrared above your eyebrow like I suggested, you could've been making phone-sex calls for the past two years."

"Too many fucking wires," Rhyme spat out.

His neck spasmed suddenly and knocked the controller out of reach. "Fuck."

Suddenly this minute task—not to mention their mission—seemed impossible to Lincoln Rhyme. He was exhausted, his neck hurt, his head. His eyes particularly. They stung and—this was *more* painful to him—he felt a chip of urge to rub the backs of his fingers across his closed lids. A tiny gesture of relief, something the rest of the world did every day.

Thom replaced the joystick. Rhyme summoned patience from somewhere and asked his aide, "How does it work?"

"There's the screen. See it on the controller? Just move the stick till it's on a number, wait one second and it's programmed in. Then do the next number the same way. When you've got all seven, push the stick here to dial."

He snapped, "It's not working."

"Just practice."

"We don't have time!"

Thom snarled, "I've been answering the phone for you way too long."

"All right," Rhyme said, lowering his voice—his way of apology. "I'll practice later. Could you please get me Con Ed? And I need to speak to a supervisor."

The rope hurt and the cuffs hurt but it was the noise that scared her the most.

Tammie Jean Colfax felt all the sweat in her body run down her face and chest and arms as she struggled to saw the handcuff links back and forth on the rusty bolt. Her wrists were numb but it seemed to her that she was wearing through some of the chain.

She paused, exhausted, and twitched her arms this way and that to keep a cramp at bay. She listened again. It was, she thought, the sound of workmen tightening bolts and hammering parts into place. Final taps of hammers. She imagined they were just finishing up their job on the pipe and thinking of going home.

Don't go, she cried to herself. Don't leave me. As long as the men were there, working, she was safe.

A final bang, then ringing silence.

Git on outa thayr, girl. G'on.

Mamma . . .

T.J. cried for several minutes, thinking of her family back in Eastern Tennessee. Her nostrils clogged but as she began to choke she blew her nose violently, felt an explosion of tears and mucus. Then she was breathing again. It gave her confidence. Strength. She began to saw once more.

————————

"I appreciate the urgency, detective. But I don't know how I can help you. We use bolts all over the city. Oil lines, gas lines . . ."

"All right," Rhyme said tersely and asked the Con Ed supervisor at the company's headquarters on Fourteenth Street, "Do you insulate wiring with asbestos?"

A hesitation.

"We've cleaned up ninety percent of that," the woman said defensively. "Ninety-*five*."

People could be so irritating. "I understand that. I just need to know if there's still any asbestos used for insulation."

"No," she said adamantly. "Well, never for electricity. Just the steam and that's the smallest percentage of our service."

Steam!

It was the least-known and the scariest of the city's utilities. Con Ed heated water to 1,000 degrees then shot it through a hundred-mile network of pipes running under Manhattan. The blistering steam itself was superheated—about 380 degrees—and rocketed through the city at seventy-five miles an hour.

Rhyme now recalled an article in the paper. "Didn't you have a break in the line last week?"

"Yessir. But there was no asbestos leak. That site had been cleaned years ago."

"But there *is* asbestos around some of your pipes in the system downtown?"

She hesitated. "Well . . ."

"Where was the break?" Rhyme continued quickly.

"Broadway. A block north of Chambers."

"Wasn't there an article in the *Times* about it?"

"I don't know. Maybe. Yes."

"And did the article mention asbestos?"

"It did," she admitted, "but it just said that in the past asbestos contamination'd been a problem."

"The pipe that broke, was it . . . does it cross Pearl Street farther south?"

"Well, let me see. Yes, it does. At Hanover Street. On the north side."

He pictured T.J. Colfax, the woman with the thin fingers and long nails, about to die.

"And the steam's going back on at three?"

"That's right. Any minute now."

"It can't!" Rhyme shouted. "Somebody's tampered with the line. You can't turn that steam back on!"

Cooper looked up uneasily from his microscope.

The supervisor said, "Well, I don't know . . ."

Rhyme barked to Thom, "Call Lon, tell him she's in a basement at Hanover and Pearl. The north side." He told him about the steam. "Get the fire department there too. Heat-protective outfits."

Rhyme shouted into the speakerphone. "Call the work crews! Now! They can't turn that steam back on. They *can't!*" He repeated the words absently, detesting his exquisite imagination, which showed, in an endless loop, the woman's flesh growing pink then red then splitting apart under the fierce clouds of sputtering white steam.

———

In the station wagon the radio crackled. It was three minutes to three by Sachs's watch. She answered the call.

"Portable 5885, K—"

"Forget the officialese, Amelia," Rhyme said. "We don't have time."

"I—"

"We think we know where she is. Hanover and Pearl."

She glanced over her shoulder and saw dozens of ESU officers running flat-out toward an old building.

"Do you want me to—"

"They'll look for her. You have to get ready to work the scene."

"But I can help—"

"No. I want you to go to the back of the station wagon. There's a suitcase in it labeled zero two. Take it with you. And in a small black case there's a PoliLight. You saw one in my room. Mel was using it. Take that too. In the suitcase marked zero three you'll find a headset and stalk mike. Plug it into your Motorola and get over to the building where the officers are. Call me back when you're rigged. Channel thirty-seven. I'll be on a landline but you'll be patched through to me."

Channel thirty-seven. The special ops citywide frequency. The priority frequency.

"What?—" she asked. But the dead radio did not respond.

She had a long black halogen flashlight on her utility belt so she left the bulky twelve-volter in the back of the wagon and grabbed the PoliLight and the heavy suitcase. It must have weighed fifty pounds. Just what my damn joints need. She adjusted her grip and, teeth clamped together against the pain, hurried toward the intersection.

Sellitto, breathless, ran to the building. Banks joined them.

"You hear?" the older detective asked. Sachs nodded.

"This is it?" she asked.

Sellitto nodded toward the alley. "He had to take her in this way. The lobby's got a guard station." They now trotted down the shadowy, cobblestoned canyon, steaming hot, smelling of piss and garbage. Battered blue Dumpsters sat nearby.

"There," Sellitto shouted. "Those doors."

The cops fanned out, running. Three of the four doors were locked tight from the inside.

The fourth had been jimmied open and was now chained shut. The chain and lock were new.

"This's it!" Sellitto reached for the door, hesitated. Thinking probably about fingerprints. Then he grabbed the handle and yanked. It opened a few inches but the chain held tight. He sent three of the uniforms around to the front to get into the basement from the inside. One cop worked a cobblestone loose from the alley floor and began pounding on the door handle. A half-dozen blows, a dozen. He winced as his hand struck the door; blood gushed from a torn finger.

A fireman ran up with a Halligan tool—a combination pickax and crowbar. He rammed the end into the chain and ripped the padlock open. Sellitto looked at Sachs expectantly. She gazed back.

"Well, go, officer!" he barked.

"What?"

"Didn't he tell you?"

"Who?"

"Rhyme."

Hell, she'd forgotten to plug in the headset. She fumbled it, finally got it plugged in. Heard: "Amelia, where—"

"I'm here."

"Are you at the building?"

"Yes."

"Go inside. They shut the steam off but I don't know if it was in time. Take a medic and one ESU trooper. Go to the boiler room. You'll probably see her right away, the Colfax woman. Walk to her but not directly, not in a straight line from the door to her. I don't want you to disturb any footprints he might've left. Understand?"

"Yes." She nodded emphatically, not thinking that he couldn't see her. Gesturing the medic and an Emergency Services trooper after her, Sachs stepped forward into the murky corridor, shadows everywhere, the groan of machinery, dripping water.

"Amelia," Rhyme said.

"Yes."

"We were talking about ambush before. From what I know about him now I don't think that's the case. He's not there, Amelia. That would be illogical. But keep your shooting hand free."

Illogical.

"Okay."

"Now go! Fast."

EIGHT

A murky cavern. Hot, black, damp.

The three of them moved quickly down the filthy hallway toward the only doorway Sachs could see. A sign said BOILER ROOM. She was behind the ESU officer, who wore full body armor and helmet. The medic was in the rear.

Her right knuckles and shoulder throbbed from the weight of the suitcase. She shifted it to her left hand, nearly dropped it and readjusted her grip. They continued to the door.

There, the SWAT officer pushed inside and swung his machine gun around the dimly lit room. A flashlight was attached to the barrel and it cast a line of pale light in the shreds of steam. Sachs smelled moisture, mold. And another scent, loathsome.

Click. "Amelia?" The staticky burst of Rhyme's voice scared the absolute hell out of her. "Where are you, Amelia?"

With a shaking hand she turned down the volume.

"Inside," she gasped.

"Is she alive?"

Sachs rocked on her feet, staring at the sight. She squinted, not sure at first what she was seeing. Then she understood.

"Oh, no." Whispering. Feeling the nausea.

The sickening boiled-meat smell wafted around her. But that wasn't the worst of it. Neither was the sight of the woman's skin, bright red, almost orange, peeling off in huge scales. The face completely stripped of skin. No, what brought the dread home was the angle of T.J. Colfax's body, the impossible twisting of her limbs and torso as she'd tried to get away from the spray of ravaging heat.

He hoped the vic was dead. For his sake. . . .

"Is she alive?" Rhyme repeated.

"No," Sachs whispered. "I don't see how . . . No."

"Is the room secure?"

Sachs glanced at the officer, who'd heard the transmission and nodded.

"Scene secure."

Rhyme told her, "I want the ESU trooper out then you and the medic go check on her."

Sachs gagged once on the smell and forced herself to control the reflex. She and the medic walked in an oblique path to the pipe. He bent unemotionally forward and felt the woman's neck. He shook his head.

"Amelia?" Rhyme asked.

Her second body in the line of duty. Both in one day.

The medic said, "DCDS."

Sachs nodded, said formally into the mike, "We have a deceased, confirmed dead at the scene."

"Scalded to death?" Rhyme asked.

"Looks like it."

"Tied to the wall?"

"A pipe. Handcuffed, hands behind. Feet tied with clothesline. Duct-tape gag. He opened the steam pipe. She was only a couple of feet from it. God."

Rhyme continued, "Back the medic out the way you came. To the door. Watch where you put your feet."

She did this, staring at the body. How could the skin be so red? Like a boiled crab shell.

"All right, Amelia. You're going to work the scene. Open the suitcase."

She said nothing. Kept staring.

"Amelia, are you at the door? . . . Amelia?"

"*What?*" she shouted.

"Are you at the door?"

His voice was so fucking calm. So different from the snide, demanding voice of the man she remembered in the bedroom. Calm . . . and something else. She didn't know what.

"Yes, I'm at the door. You know, this is crazy."

"Utterly insane," Rhyme agreed, almost cheerfully. "Is the suitcase open?"

She flipped up the lid and glanced inside. Pliers and forceps, a flex mirror on a handle, cotton balls, eyedroppers, pinking sheers, pipettes, spatulas, scalpels . . .

What *is* all this?

. . . a Dustbuster, cheesecloth, envelopes, sifting screens, brushes, scissors, plastic and paper bags, metal cans, bottles—5 percent nitric acid, ninhydrin, silicone, iodide, friction-ridge-printing supplies.

Impossible. Into the mike she said, "I don't think you believed me, detective. I really *don't* know anything about CS work."

Eyes on the woman's ruined body. Water dripped off her peeled nose. A bit of white—bone—showed through the cheek. And her face was drawn into an anguished grin. Just like the vic that morning.

"I believed you, Amelia," he said dismissively. "Now, the case is open?" He was calm and he sounded . . . what? Yes, *that* was the tone. Seductive. He sounds like a lover.

I hate him, she thought. It's wrong to hate a cripple. But I fucking hate him.

"You're in the basement, right?"

"Yessir."

"Listen, you've got to call me Lincoln. We're going to know each other very well by the time this is over."

Which is gonna be about sixty minutes, tops.

"You'll find some rubber bands in the suitcase, if I'm not mistaken."

"I see some."

"Put them around your shoes. Where the ball of your foot is. If there's any confusion as to footprints you'll know which ones are yours."

"Okay, done."

"Take some evidence bags and envelopes. Put a dozen of each in your pocket. Can you use chopsticks?"

"What did you say?"

"You live in the city, right? You ever go to Mott Street? For General Tsao's chicken? Cold noodles with sesame paste?"

Her gorge rose at the talk of food. She refused to glance at the woman dangling in front of her.

"I can use chopsticks," she said icily.

"Look in the suitcase. I'm not sure you'll find them. They kept them there when I was running scenes."

"I don't see any."

"Well, you'll find some pencils. Put those in your pocket. Now you're going to walk a grid. Cover every inch. Are you ready?"

"Yes."

"First tell me what you see."

"One big room. Maybe twenty by thirty. Full of rusted pipes. Cracked concrete floor. Walls're brick. Mold."

"Any boxes? Anything on the floor?"

"No, it's empty. Except for the pipes, oil tanks, the boiler. There's the sand—the shells, a pile of it spilling out of a crack in the wall. And there's some gray stuff too—"

" 'Stuff'?" he jumped. "I don't recognize that word. What's *'stuff'?*"

A burst of anger tore through her. She calmed and said, "It's the asbestos but not wadded up like this morning. It's in crumbling sheets."

"Good. Now, the first sweep. You're looking for footprints and any staged clues that he's left for us."

"You think he left more?"

"Oh, I'll betcha," Rhyme said. "Put on the goggles and use the

PoliLight. Keep it low. Grid the room. Every inch. Get going. You know how to walk a grid?"

"Yes."

"How?"

She bristled. "I don't need to be tested."

"Ah, humor me. How?"

"Back and forth in one direction, then back and forth in the perpendicular direction."

"Each step, no more than one foot in length."

She hadn't known that. "I know," she said.

"Go ahead."

The PoliLight flashed on with an eerie, otherworldy glow. She knew it was something called an ALS—alternative light source— and that it made fingerprints and semen and blood and some shoeprints fluoresce. The brilliant bile-green light made shadows dance and jump and more than once she nearly drew down on a dark form that turned out to be a mere phantom of darkness.

"Amelia?" Rhyme's voice was sharp. She jumped again.

"Yes? What?"

"Do you see any footprints?"

She continued to stare at the floor. "I, uh, no. I see streaks in the dust. Or something." She cringed at the careless word. But Rhyme, unlike Peretti that morning, paid no attention. He said, "So. He swept up afterwards."

She was surprised. "Yeah, that's it! Broom marks. How'd you know?"

Rhyme laughed—a jarring sound to Sachs in this rank tomb— and he said, "He was smart enough to cover his tracks this morning; no reason to stop now. Oh, he's good, this boy is. But we're good too. Keep going."

Sachs bent over, her joints on fire, and began the search. She covered every square foot of the floor. "Nothing here. Nothing at all."

He picked up on the note of finality in her voice. "You've only just started, Amelia. Crime scenes are three-dimensional. Remember that. What you mean is there's nothing on the floor.

Now search the walls. Start with the spot farthest away from the steam and cover every inch."

She slowly circled the horrible marionette in the center of the room. She thought of a Maypole game she'd played at some Brooklyn street feast when she was six or seven, as her father proudly took home movies. Circling slowly. It was an empty room and yet there were a thousand different places to search.

Hopeless . . . Impossible.

But it wasn't. On a ledge, about six feet above the floor, she found the next set of clues. She barked a fast laugh. "Got something here."

"In a cluster?"

"Yes. A big splinter of dark wood."

"Chopsticks."

"What?" she asked.

"The pencils. Use them to pick it up. Is it wet?"

"Everything in here's wet."

"Sure, it would be. The steam. Put it in a paper evidence bag. Plastic keeps the moisture in and in this heat bacteria'll destroy the trace evidence. What else is there?" he asked eagerly.

"It's, I don't know, hairs, I think. Short, trimmed. A little pile of them."

"Loose or attached to skin?"

"Loose."

"There's a role of two-inch tape in the suitcase. 3M. Pick them up with that."

Sachs lifted most of the hairs, placed them in a paper envelope. She studied the ledge around the hairs. "I see some stains. Looks like rust or blood." She thought to hit the spot with the Poli-Light. "They're fluorescing."

"Can you do a presumptive blood test?"

"No."

"Let's just assume it's blood. Could it be the victim's?"

"Doesn't seem to be. It's too far away and there's no trail to her body."

"Does it lead anywhere?"

"Looks like it. To a brick in the wall. It's loose. No prints on it. I'm going to move it aside. I—oh, Jesus!" Sachs gasped and stumbled back a foot or two, nearly fell.

"What?" Rhyme asked.

She eased forward, staring in disbelief.

"Amelia. Talk to me."

"It's a bone. A bloody bone."

"Human?"

"I don't know," she answered. "How would I . . . ? I don't know."

"Recent kill?"

"Looks like it. About two inches long and two in diameter. There's blood and flesh on it. It's been sawn off. Jesus. Who the fuck'd do something—"

"Don't get rattled."

"What if he got it from another victim?"

"Then we better find 'im pretty damn soon, Amelia. Bag it. Plastic for the bone."

As she did this, he asked, "Any other staged clues?" He sounded concerned.

"No."

"That's all? Hairs, a bone and a splinter of wood. He's not making it very easy, is he?"

"Should I bring it back to your . . . office?"

Rhyme was laughing. "He'd like us to call it quits. But no. We're not through yet. Let's find out a little more about Unsub 823."

"But there's nothing here."

"Oh, yes there is, Amelia. There's his address and his phone number and his description and his hopes and aspirations. They're all around you."

She was furious at his professor's tone and remained silent.

"You have the flashlight?"

"I've got my issue halogen—"

"No," he grumbled. "Issue lights are too narrow. You need the twelve-volt broad beam."

"Well, I didn't bring it," she snapped. "Should I go back and get it?"

"No time. Check out the pipes."

She searched for ten minutes, climbing up to the ceiling, and with the powerful light she illuminated spots that perhaps hadn't been lit in fifty years. "No, I don't see a thing."

"Go back to the door. Hurry."

She hesitated and returned.

"Okay, I'm here."

"Now. Close your eyes. What do you smell?"

"Smell? Did you say smell?" Was he crazy?

"Always smell the air at a crime scene. It can tell you a hundred things."

She kept her eyes wide and breathed in. She said, "Well, I don't *know* what I smell."

"That's not an acceptable answer."

She exhaled in exasperation and hoped the hiss was coming through his telephone loud and clear. She jammed her lids closed, inhaled, fought the nausea again. "Mold, mustiness. The smell of hot water from the steam."

"You don't know where it's from. Just describe it."

"Hot water. The woman's perfume."

"Are you sure it's hers?"

"Well, no."

"Are you wearing any?"

"No."

"How 'bout aftershave? The medic? The ESU officer?"

"I don't think so. No."

"Describe it."

"Dry. Like gin."

"Take a guess, man's aftershave or woman's perfume."

What had Nick worn? Arrid Extra Dry.

"I don't know," she said. "Man's."

"Walk to the body."

She glanced once at the pipe then down to the floor.

"I—"

"Do it," Lincoln Rhyme said.

She did. The peeling skin was like black-and-red birch.

"Smell her neck."

"It's all . . . I mean, there isn't much skin left."

"I'm sorry, Amelia, but you have to do it. We have to see if it's her perfume."

She did, inhaled. Gagged, nearly vomited.

I'm going to puke, she thought. Just like Nick and me that night at Pancho's, done in by those damn frozen daiquiris. Two hard-ass cops, swigging down sissy drinks with blue plastic swordfish swimming in them.

"Do you smell the perfume?"

Here it comes . . . Gagging again.

No. No! She closed her eyes, concentrated on her aching joints. The most painful one—her knee. And, miraculously, the wave of nausea passed. "It's not her perfume."

"Good. So maybe our boy's vain enough to wear a lot of after-shave. That could be a social-class indicator. Or maybe he wants to cover up some other smell he might've left. Garlic, cigars, fish, whisky. We'll have to see. Now, Amelia, listen carefully."

"What?"

"I want you to be him."

Oh. Psychoshit. Just what I need.

"I really don't think we have time for this."

"There's never enough time in crime scene work," Rhyme continued soothingly. "But that doesn't stop us. Just get into his head. You've been thinking the way we think. I want you to think the way he does."

"Well, how do I do that?"

"Use your imagination. That's why God gave us one. Now, you're him. You've got her cuffed and gagged. You take her into the room there. You cuff her to the pipe. You scare her. You're enjoying this."

"How do you know he's enjoying it?"

"*You're* enjoying it. Not *him*. How do I know? Because nobody goes to this much trouble to do something they don't enjoy. Now, you know your way around. You've been here before."

"Why d'you think that?"

"You had to check it out earlier—to find a deserted place with a feeder pipe from the steam system. And to get the clues he left by the train tracks."

Sachs was mesmerized by his fluid, low voice. She forgot completely that his body was destroyed. "Oh. Right."

"You take the steam-pipe cover off. What are you thinking?"

"I don't know. That I want to get it over with. Get out."

But the words were hardly out of her mouth before she thought: Wrong. And she wasn't surprised when she heard Rhyme's tongue click in her headset. "Do you really?" he asked.

"No. I want to make it last."

"Yes! I think that's exactly what you want. You're thinking about what the steam will do to her. What else do you feel?"

"I . . ."

A thought formed in her mind, vague. She saw the woman struggling to free herself. Saw something else . . . some*one* else. Him, she thought. Unsub 823. But what about him? She was close to understanding. What . . . *what?* But suddenly the thought vanished. Gone.

"I don't know," she whispered.

"Do you feel any urgency? Or are you pretty cool about what you're doing?"

"I'm in a hurry. I have to leave. The cops could be here at any minute. But I still . . ."

"What?"

"Shhhh," she ordered, and scanned the room again, looking for whatever had put the seed of the vanished thought in her mind.

The room was swimming, a black, starry night. Swirls of darkness and distant, jaundiced lights. Lord, don't let me faint!

Maybe he—

There! That's it. Sachs's eyes were following the steam pipe. She was looking at another access plate in a shadowy alcove of

the room. It would have been a better hiding place for the girl—
you couldn't see it from the doorway if you were walking past—
and the second plate had only four bolts on it, not eight, like the
one he chose.

Why not that pipe?

Then she understood.

"He doesn't want . . . *I* don't want to leave just yet because I
want to keep an eye on her."

"Why do you think that?" he inquired, echoing her own words
just moments before.

"There's another pipe I could've chained her to but I picked
the one that was in the open."

"So you could see her?"

"I think so."

"Why?"

"Maybe to make sure she can't get away. Maybe to make sure
the gag's tight. . . . I don't know."

"Good, Amelia. But what does it *mean?* How can we *use* that
fact?"

Sachs looked around the room for the place where he'd have
the best view of the girl without being seen. It turned out to be a
shadowy spot between two large heating-oil tanks.

"Yes!" she said excitedly, looking at the floor. "He was here."
Forgetting the role-playing. "He swept up."

She scanned the area with the bile glow of the PoliLight wand.

"No footprints," she said, disappointed. But as she lifted the
light to shut it off, a smudge glowed on one of the tanks.

"I've got a print!" she announced.

"A print?"

"You get a better view of the girl if you lean forward and support yourself on a tank. That's what he did, I'm sure. Only, it's
weird, Lincoln. It's . . . deformed. His hand." She shivered looking at the monstrous palm.

"In the suitcase there's an aerosol bottle labeled DFO. It's a
fluorescent stain. Spray that on the print, hit the PoliLight and
shoot the image with the one-to-one Polaroid."

She told him when she'd finished this and he said, "Now Dust-bust the floor between the tanks. If we're lucky he scratched off a hair or chewed a fingernail."

My habits, Sachs thought. It was one of the things that had finally ruined her modeling career—the bloody nail, the worried eyebrow. She'd tried and tried and tried to stop. Finally gave up, discouraged, bewildered that a tiny habit could change the direction of your life so dramatically.

"Bag the vacuum filter."

"In paper?"

"Yes, paper. Now, the body, Amelia."

"What?"

"Well, you've *got* to process the body."

Her heart sank. Somebody else, please. Have somebody else do it. She said, "Not until the ME's finished. That's the rule."

"No rules today, Amelia. We're making up our own. The medical examiner'll get her after us."

Sachs approached the woman.

"You know the routine?"

"Yes." She stepped close to the destroyed body.

Then froze. Hands inches from the victim's skin.

I can't do it. She shuddered. Told herself to keep going. But she couldn't; the muscles weren't responding.

"Sachs? You there?"

She couldn't answer.

I can't do this. . . . It was as simple as that. Impossible. I *can't.*

"Sachs?"

And then she looked into herself and, somehow, saw her father, in uniform, stooping low on the hot, pitted sidewalk of West Forty-second Street, sliding his arm around a scabby drunk to help him home. Then was seeing her Nick as he laughed and drank beer in a Bronx tavern with a hijacker who'd kill him in a second if he knew the young cop was working undercover. The two men in her life, doing what they had to do.

"Amelia?"

These two images bobbed in her thoughts, and why they calmed her, or where that calm came from, she couldn't begin to guess. "I'm here," she said to Lincoln Rhyme and went about her business as she'd been taught. Taking the nail scrapings, combing the hair—pubic and head. Telling Rhyme what she did as she did it.

Ignoring the dull orbs of eyes . . .

Ignoring the crimson flesh.

Trying to ignore the smell.

"Get her clothing," Rhyme said. "Cut off everything. Put a sheet of newsprint under them first to pick up any trace that falls off."

"Should I check the pockets?"

"No, we'll do that here. Wrap them up in the paper."

Sachs cut the blouse and skirt off, the panties. She reached out for what she thought was the woman's bra, dangling from her chest. It felt curious, disintegrating in her fingers. Then, like a slap she realized what she held and she gave a short scream. It wasn't cloth, it was skin.

"Amelia? Are you all right?"

"Yes!" she gasped. "I'm fine."

"Describe the restraints."

"Duct tape for the gag, two inches wide. Standard-issue cuffs for hands, clothesline for the feet."

"PoliLight her body. He might've touched her with his bare hands. Look for prints."

She did. "Nothing."

"Okay. Now cut the clothesline—but not through the knot. Bag it. In plastic."

Sachs did. Then Rhyme said, "We need the cuffs."

"Okay. I've got a cuff key."

"No, Amelia. Don't open them."

"What?"

"The cuff lock mechanism is one of the best ways to pick up trace from the perp."

"Well, how'm I supposed to get them off without a key?" She laughed.

"There's a razor saw in the suitcase."

"You want me to cut off the cuffs?"

There was a pause. Rhyme said, "No, not the cuffs, Amelia."

"Well, what *do* you want me to . . . Oh, you can't be serious. Her *hands?*"

"You have to." He was irritated at her reluctance.

Okay, that's it. Sellitto and Polling've picked a nutcase for a partner. Maybe *their* careers're tanking but I'm not going down with them.

"Forget it."

"Amelia, it's just another way to collect evidence."

Why did he sound so reasonable? She thought desperately for excuses. "They'll get blood all over them if I cut—"

"Her heart's not beating. Besides," he added like a TV chef, "the blood'll be cooked into a solid."

The gorge rising again.

"Go on, Amelia. Go to the suitcase. Get the saw. In the lid." He added a frosty, "Please."

"Why'd you have me scrape under her nails? I could've just brought you back her hands!"

"Amelia, we need the cuffs. We have to open them here and we can't wait for the ME. It has to be done."

She walked back to the doorway. Unsnapped the thongs, lifted the wicked-looking saw from the case. She stared at the woman, frozen in her tortured pose in the center of the vile room.

"Amelia? *Amelia?*"

Outside, the sky was still clogged with stagnant, yellow air and the buildings nearby were covered with soot like charred bones. But Sachs had never been so glad to be out in the city air as now. The CU suitcase in one hand, the razor saw in the other, the headset dangling dead around her neck. Sachs ignored the huge crowd of cops and spectators staring at her and walked straight toward the station wagon.

As she passed Sellitto she handed him the saw without pausing, practically tossed it to him. "If he wants it done that badly tell him he can damn well walk down here and do it himself."

II
LOCARD'S PRINCIPLE

*In real life, you only get one shot at the
homicide crime scene.*

—VERNON J. GEBERTH,
LIEUTENANT COMMANDER (RET.)
NEW YORK POLICE DEPARTMENT

NINE

I've got myself into a situation here, sir."

The man across the desk looked like a TV show's idea of a big-city deputy police commissioner. Which happened to be his rank. White hair, a temperate jowl, gold-rimmed glasses, posture to die for.

"Now what's the problem, officer?"

Dep Com Randolph C. Eckert looked down his long nose with a gaze that Sachs recognized immediately; his nod to equali-ty was to be as stern with the female officers as with the male ones.

"I've got a complaint, sir," she said stiffly. "You heard about that taxi kidnapping case?"

He nodded. "Ah, has *that* got the city in double dutch."

She believed that was a schoolchild's game of jump rope but wouldn't presume to correct a deputy commissioner.

"That damn UN conference," he continued, "and the whole world's watching. It's unfair. People don't talk about crime in Washington. Or Detroit. Well, Detroit they do. Say, Chicago. Never. No, it's New York that people thump on. Richmond, Virginia, had more murders per capita than we did last year. I looked it up. And I'd rather parachute unarmed into Central Harlem than drive windows-up through South East D.C. any day."

"Yessir."

"Understand they found that girl dead. It was on all the news. Those reporters."

"Downtown. Just now."

"Now that's a pity."

"Yessir."

"They just killed her? Like that? No ransom demand or anything?"

"I didn't hear about any ransom."

"What's this complaint?"

"I was first officer in a related homicide this morning."

"You're Patrol?" Eckert asked.

"I *was* Patrol. I was supposed to be transferring to Public Affairs today at noon. For a training session." She lifted her hands, tipped with flesh-colored Band-Aids, and dropped them in her lap. "But they shanghaied me."

"Who?"

"Detective Lon Sellitto, sir. And Captain Haumann. And Lincoln Rhyme."

"Rhyme?"

"Yessir."

"Not the fellow was in charge of IRD a few years ago?"

"Yessir. That's him."

"I thought he was dead."

Egos like that will never die.

"Very much alive, sir."

The dep com was looking out his window. "He's not on the force anymore. What's he doing involved in this?"

"Consultant, I guess. It's Lon Sellitto's case. Captain Polling's overseeing it. I've been waiting for this reassignment for eight months. But they've got me working crime scene. I've never *done* crime scene. It doesn't make any sense and frankly I resent being assigned to a job I've had no training for."

"Crime scene?"

"Rhyme ordered me to run the whole scene. By myself."

Eckert didn't understand this. The words weren't registering. "Why is a civilian ordering uniformed officers to do *anything?*"

"My point, sir." She set the hook. "I mean, I'll help up to a point. But I'm just not prepared to dismember victims . . ."

"What?"

She blinked as if surprised he hadn't heard. She explained about the handcuffs.

"Lord in heaven, what the hell're they thinking of? Pardon my French. Don't they know the whole country's watching? It's been on CNN all day, this kidnapping. Cutting off her hands? Say, you're Herman Sachs's daughter."

"That's right."

"Good officer. *Excellent* officer. I gave him one of his commendations. The man was what a beat cop ought to be. Midtown South, right?"

"Hell's Kitchen. My beat."

My *former* beat.

"Herman Sachs probably prevented more crime than the entire detective division solves in a year. Just calming everything down, you know."

"That was Pop. Sure."

"Her hands?" Eckert snorted. "The girl's family'll sue us. As soon as they find out about it. They sue us for everything. There's a rapist suing us now 'cause he got shot in the leg coming at an officer with a knife. His lawyer's got this theory he's calling the 'least deadly alternative.' Instead of shooting, we're supposed to taze them or use Mace. Or ask them politely, I don't know. I better give the chief and the mayor a heads-up on this one. I'll make some calls, officer." He looked at a wall clock. It was a little after four. "Your watch over for the day?"

"I have to report back to Lincoln Rhyme's house. That's where we're working out of." She thought of the hacksaw. She said coolly, "His bedroom really. That's our CP."

"A civilian's bedroom is your command post?"

"I'd appreciate anything you can do, sir. I've waited a long time for that transfer."

"Cut her hands off. My good Lord."

She stood and walked to the door and out into one of the cor-

ridors that would soon be her new assignment. The feeling of relief took only a little longer to arrive than she'd expected.

————————

He stood at the bottle-glass window, watching a pack of wild
dogs prowl though the lot across the street.

He was on the first floor of this old building, a marble-clad Federal dating to the early 1800s. Surrounded by vacant lots and tenements—some abandoned, some occupied by paying tenants though
most by squatters—this old mansion had been empty for years.

The bone collector took the piece of emery paper in his hand
once more and continued to rub. He looked down at his handi-
work. Then out the window again.

His hands, in their circular motion, precise. The tiny scrap of
sandpaper whispering, *shhhhh*, *shhhhh* . . . Like a mother hushing
her child.

A decade ago, the days of promise in New York, some crazy
artist had moved in here. He'd filled the dank, two-story place
with broken and rusting antiques. Wrought-iron grilles, hunks
of crown molding and framed squares of spidered stained
glass, scabby columns. Some of the artist's work remained on the
walls. Frescoes on the old plaster: murals, never completed, of
workers, children, angst-ridden lovers. Round, emotionless
faces—the man's motif—stared blankly, as if the souls had been
nipped out of their smooth bodies.

The painter was never very successful, even after the most
ironclad of marketing ideas—his own suicide—and the bank
foreclosed on the building several years ago.

Shhhhh. . . .

The bone collector had stumbled across the place last year and
he'd known immediately that this was home. The desolation of
the neighborhood was certainly important to him—it was obviously practical. But there was another appeal, more personal: the
lot across the street. During some excavation several years ago a
backhoe had unearthed a load of human bones. It turned out this

had been one of the city's old cemeteries. Newspaper articles about it suggested the graves might contain the remains not only of Federal and Colonial New Yorkers but Manate and Lenape Indians as well.

He now set aside what he'd been smoothing with the emery paper—a carpal, the delicate palm bone—and picked up the wrist, which he'd carefully detached from the radius and ulna last night just before leaving for Kennedy Airport to collect the first victims. It had been drying for over a week and most of the flesh was gone but it still took some effort to separate the elaborate cluster of bones. They snapped apart with faint plops, like fish breaking the surface of a lake.

Oh, the constables, they were a lot better than he'd anticipated. He'd been watching them search along Pearl Street, wondering if they'd ever figure out where he'd left the woman from the airport. Astonished when they suddenly ran toward the right building. He'd guessed it would take two or three victims until they got a feel for the clues. They hadn't saved her of course. But they might have. A minute or two earlier would have made all the difference.

As with so much in life.

The navicular, the lunate, the hamate, the capitate ... the bones, intertwined like a Greek puzzle ring, came apart under his strong fingers. He picked bits of flesh and tendon off them. He selected the greater multangulum—at the base of where the thumb had once been—and began to sand once more.

Shhhhh, shhhhhhh.

The bone collector squinted as he looked outside and imagined he saw a man standing beside one of the old graves. It *must* have been his imagination because the man wore a bowler hat and was dressed in mustard-colored gabardine. He rested some dark roses beside the tombstone and then turned away from it, dodging the horses and carriages on his way to the elegantly arched bridge over the Collect Pond outlet at Canal Street. Who'd he been visiting? Parents? A brother? Family who'd died of consumption or in one of the terrible influenza epidemics that'd been ravaging the city recently—

Recently?

No, not recently of course. A hundred years ago—*that's* what he meant.

He squinted and looked again. No sign of the carriages or the horses. Or the man with the bowler hat. Though they'd seemed as real as flesh and blood.

However real *they* are.

Shhhhh, shhhhhh.

It was intruding again, the past. He was seeing things that'd happened *before*, that had happened *then*, as if they were now. He could control it. He *knew* he could.

But as he gazed out the window he realized that of course there was no before or after. Not for him. He drifted back and forth through time, a day, five years, a hundred years or two, like a dried leaf on a windy day.

He looked at his watch. It was time to leave.

Setting the bone on the mantel, he washed his hands carefully—like a surgeon. Then for five minutes he ran a pet-hair roller over his clothes to pick up any bone dust or dirt or body hairs that might lead the constables to him.

He walked into the carriage house past the half-finished painting of a moon-faced butcher in a bloody white apron. The bone collector started to get into the taxi but then changed his mind. Unpredictability is the best defense. This time he'd take the carriage . . . the *sedan*, the Ford. He started it, he drove into the street, closed and locked the garage door behind him.

No before or after . . .

As he passed the cemetery the pack of dogs glanced up at the Ford then returned to scuffling through the brush, looking for rats and nosing madly for water in the unbearable heat.

No then or now . . .

He took the ski mask and gloves from his pocket, set them on the seat beside him as he sped out of the old neighborhood. The bone collector was going hunting.

TEN

Something had changed about the room but she couldn't quite decide what.

Lincoln Rhyme saw it in her eyes.

"We missed you, Amelia," he said coyly. "Errands?"

She looked away from him. "Apparently nobody'd told my new commander I wouldn't be showing up for work today. I thought somebody ought to."

"Ah, yes."

She was gazing at the wall, slowly figuring it out. In addition to the basic instruments that Mel Cooper had brought with him, there was now a scanning electron microscope fitted with the X-ray unit, flotation and hot-stage 'scope setups for testing glass, a comparison microscope, a density-gradient tube for soil testing and a hundred beakers, jars and bottles of chemicals.

And in the middle of the room, Cooper's pride—the computerized gas chromatograph and mass spectrometer. Along with another computer, on-line with Cooper's own terminal at the IRD lab.

Sachs stepped over the thick cables snaking downstairs—house current worked, yes, but the amperage was too taxed for the bedroom outlets alone. And in that slight sidestep, an elegant, practiced maneuver, Rhyme observed how truly beautiful she was. Certainly the most beautiful woman he'd ever seen in the police department ranks.

For a brief instant he found her immeasurably appealing. People said that sex was all in the mind and Rhyme knew that this was true. Cutting the cord didn't stop the urge. He remembered, still with a faint crunch of horror, a night six months after the accident. He and Blaine had tried. Just to see what happened, they'd disclaimed, trying to be casual. No big deal.

But it *had* been a big deal. Sex is a messy business to start with and when you add catheters and bags to the equation you need a lot of stamina and humor and a better foundation than they'd had. Mostly, though, what killed the moment, and killed it fast, was her face. He saw in Blaine Chapman Rhyme's tough, game smile that she was doing it from pity and that stabbed him in the heart. He filed for divorce two weeks later. Blaine had protested but she signed the papers on the first go-round.

Sellitto and Banks had returned and were organizing the evidence Sachs had collected. She looked on, mildly interested.

Rhyme said to her, "The Latents Unit only found eight other recent partials and they belong to the two maintenance men in the building."

"Oh."

He nodded broadly. "Only *eight!*"

"He's complimenting you," Thom explained. "Enjoy it. That's the most you'll ever get out of him."

"No translations needed, please and thank you, Thom."

She responded, "I'm happy I could help." Pleasant as could be.

Well, what was *this?* Rhyme had fully expected her to storm into his room and fling the evidence bags onto his bed. Maybe the saw itself or even the plastic bag containing the vic's severed hands. He'd been looking forward to a real knock-down, dragout; people rarely take the gloves off when they fight with a crip. He'd been thinking of that look in her eyes when she'd met him, perhaps evidence of some ambiguous kinship between them.

But no, he saw now he was wrong. Amelia Sachs was like

everybody else—patting him on the head and looking for the nearest exit.

With a snap, his heart turned to ice. When he spoke it was to a cobweb high on the far wall. "We've been talking about the deadline for the next victim, officer. There doesn't seem to be specific time."

"What we think," Sellitto continued, "whatever this prick's got planned for the next one is something ongoing. He doesn't know exactly when the time of death will be. Lincoln thought maybe he's buried some poor SOB someplace where there's not much air."

Sachs's eye narrowed slightly at this. Rhyme noticed it. Burial alive. If you've got to have a phobia, that's as good as any.

They were interrupted by two men in gray suits who climbed the stairs and walked into the bedroom as if they lived here.

"We knocked," one of them said.

"We rang the bell," said the other.

"No answer."

They were in their forties, one taller than the other but both with the same sandy-colored hair. They bore identical smiles and before the Brooklyn drawl destroyed the image Rhyme had thought: Hayseed farm boys. One had an honest-to-God dusting of freckles along the bridge of his pale nose.

"Gentlemen."

Sellitto introduced the Hardy Boys: Detectives Bedding and Saul, the spadework team. Their skill was canvassing—interviewing people who live near a crime scene for wits and leads. It was a fine art but one that Rhyme had never learned, had no desire to. He was content to unearth hard facts and hand them off to officers like these, who, armed with the data, became living lie detectors who could shred perps' best cover stories. Neither of them seemed to think it was the least bit weird to be reporting to a bedridden civilian.

Saul, the taller of them, the frecklee, said, "We've found thirty-six—"

"-eight, if you count a couple of crack-heads. Which he doesn't. I do."

"—subjects. Interviewed all of them. Haven't had much luck."

"Most of 'em blind, deaf, amnesiacs. You know, the usual."

"No sign of the taxi. Combed the West Side. Zero. Zip."

Bedding: "But tell them the good news."

"We found a wit."

"A witness?" Banks asked eagerly. "Fan-tastic."

Rhyme, considerably less enthusiastic, said, "Go on."

" 'Round the TOD this morning at the train tracks."

"He saw a man walk down Eleventh Avenue, turn—"

" 'Suddenly,' he said," added no-freckle Bedding.

"—and go through an alley that led to the train underpass. He just stood there for a while—"

"Looking down."

Rhyme was troubled by this. "That doesn't sound like our boy. He's too smart to risk being seen like that."

"But—" Saul continued, raising a finger and glancing at his partner.

"There was only one window in the whole 'hood you could see the place from."

"Which is where our wit happened to be standing."

"Up early, bless his heart."

Before he remembered he was angry with her Rhyme asked, "Well, Amelia, how's it feel?"

"I'm sorry?" Her attention returned from the window.

"To be right," Rhyme said. "You pegged Eleventh Avenue. Not Thirty-seventh."

She didn't know how to respond but Rhyme turned immediately back to the twins. "Description?"

"Our wit couldn't say much."

"Was on the sauce. Already."

"He said it was a smallish guy. No hair color. Race—"

"Probably white."

"Wearing?" Rhyme asked.

"Something dark. Best he could say."

"And doing what?" Sellitto asked.

"I quote. 'He just like stood there, looking down. I thought he gonna jump. You know, in front of a train. Looked at his watch a couple times.' "

"And then finally left. Said he kept looking around. Like he didn't want to be seen."

What had he been doing? Rhyme wondered. Watching the victim die? Or was this before he planted the body, checking to see if the roadbed was deserted?

Sellitto asked, "Walked or drove?"

"Walked. We checked every parking lot—"

"And garage."

"—in the neighborhood. But that's near the convention center so you got parking coming out your ears. There're so many lots the attendants stand in the street with orange flags and wave cars in."

"And 'causa the expo half of them were full by seven. We got a list of about nine hundred tags."

Sellitto shook his head. "Follow up on it—"

"It's delegated," said Bedding.

"—but I betcha this's one unsub who ain't putting cars in lots," the detective continued. "Or getting parking tickets."

Rhyme nodded his agreement and asked, "The building at Pearl Street?"

One, or both, of the twins said, "That's next on our list. We're on our way."

Rhyme caught Sachs checking her watch, which sat on her white wrist near her ruddy fingers. He instructed Thom to add these new characteristics of the unsub to the profile chart.

"You want to interview that guy?" Banks asked. "The one by the railroad?"

"No. I don't trust witnesses," Rhyme said bombastically. "I want to get back to work." He glanced at Mel Cooper. "Hairs, blood, bone, and a sliver of wood. The bone first," Rhyme instructed.

———

Morgen . . .

Young Monelle Gerger opened her eyes and slowly sat up in the sagging bed. In her two years in east Greenwich Village she'd never gotten used to morning.

Her round, twenty-one-year-old body eased forward and she got a blast of unrelenting August sunlight in her bleary eyes. *"Mein Gott . . ."*

She'd left the club at five, home at six, made love with Brian until seven . . .

What time was it now?

Early morning, she was sure.

She squinted at the clock. Oh. Four-thirty in the afternoon.

Not so *früh morgens* after all.

Coffee or laundry?

It was around this time of day that she'd wander over to Dojo's for a veggie-burger breakfast and three cups of their tough coffee. There she'd meet people she knew, clubbies like herself— downtown people.

But she'd let a lot of things go lately, the domestic things. And so now she pulled on two baggy T-shirts to hide her chubby figure and jeans, hung five or six chains around her neck and grabbed the laundry basket, tossed the Wisk onto it.

Monelle undid the three dead bolts barring the door. She hefted the laundry basket and walked down the dark staircase of the residence hall. At the basement level she paused.

Irgendwas stimmt hier nicht.

Feeling uneasy, Monelle looked around the deserted stairway, the murky corridors.

What's different?

The light, that's it! The bulbs in the hall're burned out. No— she looked closely—they were *missing*. Fucking kids'll steal anything. She'd moved in here, the Deutsche Haus—because it was supposedly a haven for German artists and musicians. It turned out to be just another filthy, way-overpriced East Village walk-up, like all the other tenements around here. The only difference was that she could bitch to the manager in her native tongue.

She continued through the basement door into the incinerator room, which was so dark she had to grope her way along the wall to make sure she didn't trip over the junk on the floor.

Pushing open the door, she stepped into the corridor that led to the laundry room.

A shuffling. A skitter.

She turned quickly and saw nothing but motionless shadows. All she heard was the sound of traffic, the groans of an old, old building.

Through the dimness. Past stacks of boxes and discarded chairs and tables. Under wires caked with greasy dust. Monelle continued toward the laundry room. No bulbs here either. She was uneasy, recalling something that hadn't occurred to her for years. Walking with her father down a narrow alley off Lange Strasse, near the Obermain Brücke, on their way to the zoo. She must have been five or six. Her father had suddenly gripped her by the shoulder and pointed to the bridge and told her matter-of-factly that a hungry troll lived underneath it. When they crossed it on their way home, he warned, they'd have to walk quickly. She now felt a ripple of panic rise up her spine to her crew-cut blond hair.

Stupid. Trolls . . .

She continued down the dank corridor, listening to the humming of some electrical equipment. Far off she heard a song by the feuding brothers in Oasis.

The laundry room was dark.

Well, if *those* bulbs were gone, that was it. She'd go upstairs, and pound on Herr Neischen's door until he came running. She'd given him hell for the broken latches on the front and back doors and for the beer-guzzling kids he never kicked off the front stoop. She'd give him hell for the missing bulbs too.

She reached inside and flicked the switch.

Brilliant white light. Three large bulbs glowed like suns, revealing a room that was filthy but empty. Monelle strode up to the bank of four machines and dumped the whites in one, the colors in the next. She counted out quarters, dropped them into slots and shoved the levers forward.

Nothing.

Monelle jiggled the lever. Then hit the machine itself. No response.

"Shit. This *gottverdammte* building."

Then she saw the power cord. Some idiot had unplugged the machines. She knew who. Neischen had a twelve-year-old son who was responsible for most of the carnage around the building. When she'd complained about something last year the little shit'd tried to kick her.

She picked up the cord and crouched, reaching behind the machine to find the outlet. She plugged it in.

And felt the man's breath on her neck.

Nein!

He was sandwiched between the wall and the back of the washer. Barking a fast scream, she caught a glimpse of ski mask and dark clothes then his hand clamped down on her arm like an animal's jaws. She was off balance and he easily jerked her forward. She tumbled to the floor, hitting her face on the rough concrete, and swallowed the scream forming in her throat.

He was on her in an instant, pinning her arms to the concrete, slapping a piece of thick gray tape over her mouth.

Hilfe!

Nein, bitte nicht.

Bitte nicht.

He wasn't large but he was strong. He easily rolled her over onto her stomach and she heard the ratcheting of the handcuffs closing on her wrists.

Then he stood up. For a long moment, no sound but the drip of water, the rasp of Monelle's breath, the click of a small motor somewhere in the basement.

Waiting for the hands to touch her body, to tear off her clothes. She heard him walk to the doorway to make sure they were alone.

Oh, he had complete privacy, she knew, furious with herself; she was one of the few residents who used the laundry room.

Most of them avoided it because it was so deserted, so close to the back doors and windows, so far away from help.

He returned and rolled her over onto her back. Whispered something she couldn't make out. Then: "Hanna."

Hanna? It's a mistake! He thinks I'm somebody else. She shook her head broadly, trying to make him understand this.

But then, looking at his eyes, she stopped. Even though he wore a ski mask, it was clear that something was wrong. He was upset. He scanned her body, shaking his head. He closed his gloved fingers around her big arms. Squeezed her thick shoulders, grabbed a pinch of fat. She shivered in pain.

That's what she saw: disappointment. He'd caught her and now he wasn't sure he wanted her after all.

He reached into his pocket and slowly withdrew his hand. The click of the knife opening was like an electric shock. It started a jag of sobbing.

Nein, nein, nein!

A hiss of breath escaped from his teeth like wind through winter trees. He crouched over her, debating.

"Hanna," he whispered. "What am I going to do?"

Then, suddenly, he made a decision. He put the knife away and yanked her to her feet then led her out to the corridor and through the rear door—the one with the broken lock she'd been hounding Herr Neischen for weeks to fix.

ELEVEN

Acriminalist is a renaissance man.

He's got to know botany, geology, ballistics, medicine, chemistry, literature, engineering. If he knows facts—that ash with a high strontium content probably came from a highway flare, that *faca* is Portuguese for "knife," that Ethiopian diners use no utensils and eat with their right hands exclusively, that a slug with five land-and-groove rifling marks, right twist, could not have been fired by a Colt pistol—if he knows these things he may just make the connection that places an unsub at the crime scene.

One subject all criminalists know is anatomy. And this was certainly a specialty of Lincoln Rhyme's, for he had spent the past three and a half years enmeshed in the quirky logic of bone and nerve.

He now glanced at the evidence bag from the steam room, dangling in Jerry Banks's hand, and announced, "Leg bone. Not human. So it's not from the next vic."

It was a ring of bone about two inches around, sawn through evenly. There was blood in the tracks left by the saw blade.

"A medium-sized animal," Rhyme continued. "Large dog, sheep, goat. It'd support, I'd guess, a hundred to a hundred fifty pounds of weight. Let's make sure the blood's from an animal though. Still could be the vic's."

UNSUB 823

Appearance	Residence	Vehicle	Other
• Caucasian male, slight build • Dark clothing	• Prob. has safe house	• Yellow Cab	• knows CS proc. • possibly has record • knows FR prints • gun = .32 Colt

Perps had been known to beat or stab people to death with bones. Rhyme himself had had three such cases; the weapons had been a beef knuckle bone, a deer's leg bone, and in one disturbing case the victim's own ulna.

Mel Cooper ran a gel-diffusion test for blood origin. "We'll have to wait a bit for the results," he explained apologetically.

"Amelia," Rhyme said, "maybe you could help us here. Use the eye loupe and look the bone over carefully. Tell us what you see."

"Not the microscope?" she asked. He thought she'd protest but she stepped forward to the bone, peered at it with curiosity.

"Too much magnification," Rhyme explained.

She put on the goggles and bent over the white enamel tray. Cooper turned on a gooseneck lamp.

"The cutting marks," Rhyme said. "Is it hacked up or are they even?"

"They're pretty even."

"A power saw."

Rhyme wondered if the animal had been alive when he'd done this.

"See anything unusual?"

She pored over the bone for a moment, muttered, "I don't know. I don't think so. It just looks like a hunk of bone."

It was then that Thom walked past and glanced at the tray. "That's your clue? That's funny."

"Funny," Rhyme said. *"Funny?"*

Sellitto asked, "You got a theory?"

"No theory." He bent down and smelled it. "It's osso bucco."

"What?"

"Veal shank. I made it for you once, Lincoln. Osso bucco. Braised veal shank." He looked at Sachs and grimaced. "He said it needed more salt."

"Goddamn!" Sellitto cried. "He bought it at a grocery store!"

"If we're lucky," Rhyme said, "he bought it at *his* grocery store."

Cooper confirmed that the precipitin test showed negative for human blood on the samples Sachs had collected. "Probably bovine," he said.

"But what's he trying to tell us?" Banks asked.

Rhyme had no idea. "Let's keep going. Oh, anything on the chain and padlock?"

Cooper glanced at the hardware in a crisp plastic bag. "Nobody name-stamps chain anymore. So we're out of luck there. The lock's a Secure-Pro middle-of-the-line model. It isn't very secure and definitely not professional. How long d'it take to break it?"

"Three whole seconds," Sellitto said.

"See. No serial numbers and it's sold in every hardware and variety store in the country."

"Key or combination?" Rhyme asked.

"Combination."

"Call the manufacturer. Ask them if we take it apart and reconstruct the combination from the tumblers, will that tell us which shipment it was in and where it went to?"

Banks whistled. "Man, that's a long shot."

Rhyme's glare sent a ferocious blush across his face. "And the enthusiasm in your voice, detective, tells me you're just the one to handle the job."

"Yessir"—the young man held up his cellular phone defensively—"I'm on it."

Rhyme asked, "Is that blood on the chain?"

Sellitto said, "One of our boys. Cut himself pretty bad trying to break the lock off."

"So it's contaminated." Rhyme scowled.

"He was trying to save her," Sachs said to him.

"I understand. That was good of him. It's still contaminated." Rhyme glanced back at the table beside Cooper. "Prints?"

Cooper said he'd checked it and found only Sellitto's print on the links.

"All right, the splinter of wood Amelia found. Check for prints."

"I did," Sachs said quickly. "At the scene."

P.D., Rhyme reflected. She didn't seem to be the nickname sort. Beautiful people rarely were.

"Let's try the heavy guns, just to be sure," Rhyme said and instructed Cooper, "Use DFO or ninhydrin. Then hit it with the nit-yag."

"The what?" Banks asked.

"A neodymium:yttrium aluminum garnet laser."

The tech spritzed the splinter with liquid from a plastic spray bottle and trained the laser beam on the wood. He slipped on tinted goggles and examined it carefully. "Nothing."

He shut off the light and examined the splinter closely. It was about six inches long, dark wood. There were black smears on it, like tar, and it was impregnated with dirt. He held it with forceps.

"I know Lincoln likes the chopstick approach," Cooper said, "but I always ask for a fork when I go to Ming Wa's."

"You could be crushing the cells," the criminalist grumbled.

"I *could* be but I'm not," Cooper responded.

"What kind of wood?" Rhyme wondered. "Want to run a spodogram?"

"No, it's oak. No question."

"Saw or plane marks?" Rhyme leaned forward. Suddenly his neck spasmed and the cramp that bolted through the muscles was unbearable. He gasped, closed his eyes and twisted his neck, stretching. He felt Thom's strong hands massaging the muscles. The pain finally faded.

"Lincoln?" Sellitto asked. "You okay?"

Rhyme breathed deeply. "Fine. It's nothing."

"Here." Cooper brought the piece of wood over to the bed, lowered the magnifying goggles over Rhyme's eyes.

Rhyme examined the specimen. "Cut in the direction of the grain with a frame saw. There're big variations in the cuts. So I'd guess it was a post or beam milled over a hundred years ago. Steam saw probably. Hold it closer, Mel. I want to smell it."

He held the splinter under Rhyme's nose.

"Creosote—coal-tar distillation. Used for weatherproofing wood before lumber companies started pressure-treating. Piers, docks, railroad ties."

"Maybe we've got a train buff here," Sellitto said. "Remember the tracks this morning."

"Could be." Rhyme ordered, "Check for cellular compression, Mel."

The tech examined the splinter under the compound microscope. "It's compressed all right. But *with* the grain. Not against it. Not a railroad tie. This is from a post or column. Weight-bearing."

A bone . . . an old wooden post . . .

"I see dirt embedded in the wood. That tell us anything?"

Cooper set a large pad of newsprint on the table, tore the cover off. He held the splinter over the pad and brushed some dirt from cracks in the wood. He examined the speckles lying on the white paper—a reverse constellation.

"You have enough for a density-gradient test?" Rhyme asked.

In a D-G test, dirt is poured into a tube containing liquids of different specific gravities. The soil separates and each particle hangs suspended according to its own gravity. Rhyme had established a very extensive library of density-gradient profiles for dirt from all over the five boroughs. Unfortunately the test only worked with a fair amount of soil; Cooper didn't think they had enough. "We could try it but we'd have to use the entire sample. And if it didn't work we wouldn't have anything left for other tests."

Rhyme instructed him to do a visual then analyze it in the GC-MS—the chromatograph-spectrometer.

The technician brushed some dirt onto a slide. He gazed at it for a few minutes under the compound microscope. "This is strange, Lincoln. It's topsoil. With an unusually high level of vegetation in it. But it's in a curious form. Very deteriorated, verydecomposed." He looked up and Rhyme noticed the dark lines under his eyes from the eyepieces. He remembered that after hours of lab work the marks were quite pronounced and that occasionally a forensic tech would emerge from the IRD lab only to be greeted by a chorus of *Rocky Raccoon*.

"Burn it," Rhyme ordered.

Cooper mounted a sample in the GC-MS unit. The machine rumbled to life and there was a hiss. "A minute or two."

"While we're waiting," Rhyme said, "the bone . . . I keep wondering about the bone. 'Scope it, Mel."

Cooper carefully set the bone onto the examination stage of the compound microscope. He went over it carefully. "Whoa, got something here."

"What?"

"Very small. Transparent. Hand me the hemostat," Cooper said to Sachs, nodding at a pair of gripper tweezers. She handed them to him and he carefully probed in the marrow of the bone. He lifted something out.

"A tiny piece of regenerated cellulose," Cooper announced.

"Cellophane," Rhyme said. "Tell me more."

"Stretch and pinch marks. I'd say he didn't leave it intentionally; there are no cut edges. It's not inconsistent with heavy-duty cello," Cooper said.

" 'Not inconsistent.' " Rhyme scowled. "I don't like his hedges."

"We *have* to hedge, Lincoln," Cooper said cheerfully.

" 'Associate with.' 'Suggest.' I particularly hate 'not inconsistent.' "

"Very versatile," Cooper said. "The boldest I'll be is that it's probably commercial butcher or grocery store cellophane. Not Saran Wrap. Definitely not generic-brand wrap."

Jerry Banks walked inside from the hallway. "Bad news. The Secure-Pro company doesn't keep any records on combinations. A machine sets them at random."

"Ah."

"But interesting . . . they said they get calls from the police all the time about their products and you're the first one who's ever thought of tracing a lock through the combination."

"How 'interesting' can it be if it's a dead end?" Rhyme grumbled and turned to Mel Cooper, who was shaking his head as he stared at the GC-MS computer. "What?"

"Got that soil sample result. But I'm afraid the machine might be on the fritz. The nitrogen's off the charts. We should run it again, use more sample this time."

Rhyme instructed him to go ahead. His eyes turned back to the bone. "Mel, how recent was the kill?"

He examined some scrapings under the electron microscope.

"Minimal bacteria clusters. Bambi here was recently deceased, looks like. Or just out of the fridge about eight hours."

"So our perp just bought it," Rhyme said.

"Or a month ago and froze it," Sellitto suggested.

"No," Cooper said. "It hasn't been frozen. There's no evidence of tissue damage from ice crystals. And it hasn't been refrigerated that long. It's not desiccated; modern refrigerators dehydrate food."

"It's a good lead," Rhyme said. "Let's get to work on it."

" 'Get to work'?" Sachs laughed. "Are you saying we call up all the grocery stores in the city and find out who sold veal bones yesterday?"

"No," Rhyme countered. "In the past *two* days."

"You want the Hardy Boys?"

"Let them keep doing what they're doing. Call Emma, downtown, if she's still working. And if she isn't get her back to the office with the other dispatchers and put them on overtime. Get her a list of every grocery chain in town. I'll bet our boy isn't buying groceries for a family of four so have Emma limit the list to customers buying five items or less."

"Warrants?" Banks asked.

"Anybody balks, we'll get a warrant," Sellitto said. "But let's try without. Who knows? Some citizens might actually cooperate. I'm told it happens."

"But how are the stores going to know who bought veal shanks?" Sachs asked. She was no longer as aloof as she had been. There was an edge in her voice. Rhyme wondered if her frustration might be a symptom of what he himself had often felt—the burdensome weight of the evidence. The essential problem for the criminalist is not that there's too little evidence but that there's too much.

"Checkout scanners," Rhyme said. "They record purchases on computer. For inventory and restocking. Go ahead, Banks. I see something just crossed your mind. Speak up. I won't send you to Siberia this time."

"Well, only the chains have scanners, sir," the young detective offered. "There're hundreds of independents and butcher shops that don't."

"Good point. But I think he wouldn't go to a small shop. Anonymity's important to him. He'll be doing his buying at big stores. Impersonal."

Sellitto called Communications and explained to Emma what they needed.

"Let's get a polarized shot of the cellophane," Rhyme said to Cooper.

The technician put the minuscule fragment in a polarizing 'scope, then fitted the Polaroid camera to the eyepiece and took a shot. It was a colorful picture, a rainbow with gray streaks through it. Rhyme examined it. This pattern told them nothing by itself but it could be compared with other cello samples to see if they came from a common source.

Rhyme had a thought. "Lon, get a dozen Emergency Service officers over here. On the double."

"Here?" Sellitto asked.

"We're going to put an operation together."

"You're sure about that?" the detective asked.

"Yes! I want them now."

"All right." He nodded to Banks, who made the call to Haumann.

"Now, what about the other planted clue—those hairs Amelia found?"

Cooper poked through them with a probe then mounted several in the phase-contrast microscope. This instrument shot two light sources at a single subject, the second beam delayed slightly—out of phase—so the sample was both illuminated and set off by shadow.

"It's not human," Cooper said. "I'll tell you that right now. And they're guard hairs, not down."

Hairs from the animal's coat, he meant.

"What kind? Dog?"

"Veal calf?" Banks suggested, once again youthfully enthusiastic.

"Check the scales," Rhyme ordered. Meaning the microscopic flakes that make up the outer sheath of a strand of hair.

Cooper typed on his computer keyboard and a few seconds later thumbnail images of scaly rods popped onto the screen. "This is thanks to you, Lincoln. Remember the database?"

At IRD Rhyme had compiled a huge collection of micrographs of different types of hair. "I do, yes, Mel. But they were in three-ring binders when I saw 'em last. How'd you get them on the computer?"

"ScanMaster of course. JPEG compressed."

Jay-peg? What was that? In a few years technology had soared beyond Rhyme. Amazing . . .

And as Cooper examined the images, Lincoln Rhyme wondered again what he'd been wondering all day—the question that kept floating to the surface: Why the clues? The human creature is so astonishing but count on it before anything else to be just that—a creature. A laughing animal, a dangerous one, a clever one, a scared one, but always acting for a *reason*—a motive that will move the beast toward its desires. Scientist Lincoln Rhyme didn't believe in chance, or randomness, or frivolity. Even psychopaths had their own logic, twisted though it may have been, and he knew there was a reason Unsub 823 spoke to them only in this cryptic way.

Cooper called, "Got it. Rodent. Probably a rat. And the hairs were shaved off."

"That's a hell of a clue," Banks said. "There're a million rats in the city. That doesn't pin down anyplace. What's the point of telling us that?"

Sellitto closed his eyes momentarily and muttered something under his breath. Sachs didn't notice the look. She glanced at Rhyme curiously. He was surprised that she hadn't figured out what the kidnapper's message was but he said nothing. He saw no reason to share this horrifying bit of knowledge with anyone else for the time being.

James Schneider's seventh victim, or eighth, should you choose to number poor, angelic little Maggie O'Connor among them, was the wife of a hardworking immigrant, who had established the family's modest habitation near Hester Street on the Lower East Side of the City.

It was thanks to the courage of this unfortunate woman that the constables and the police discovered the identity of the criminal. Hanna Goldschmidt was of German-Jewish extraction and was held in high esteem by the close-knit community in which she, her husband and their six children (one had died at birth) lived.

The bone collector drove through the streets slowly, careful to remain under the speed limit though he knew perfectly well that the traffic cops in New York wouldn't stop you for something as minor as speeding.

He paused at a light and glanced up at another UN billboard. His eyes took in the bland, smiling faces—like the eerie faces painted on the walls of the mansion—and then looked beyond it, at the city around him. He was, occasionally, surprised to look up and find the buildings so massive, the stone cornices so high aloft, the glass so smooth, the cars so sleek, the people so scrubbed. The city he knew was dark, low, smoky, smelling of sweat and mud. Horses would trample you, roving gangs of hoodlums—some as young as ten or eleven—would knock you on the head with a shillelagh or sap and make off with your pocket watch and billfold. . . . *This* was the bone collector's city.

Sometimes, though, he found himself just like this—driving a spiffy silver Taurus XL along a smooth asphalt road, listening to WNYC and irritated, like all New Yorkers, when he missed a green light, wondering why the hell didn't the city let you make right turns on red.

He cocked his head, heard several thumps from the trunk of the car. But there was so much ambient noise that no one would hear Hanna's protests.

The light changed.

It is, of course, exceptional even in these enlightened times for a woman to venture forth into the city streets in the evening, unaccompanied by a gentleman; and in those days it was more exceptional still. Yet on this unfortunate night Hanna had no choice but to quit her abode for a brief time. Her youngest had a fever, and, with her husband praying devoutly at a nearby synagogue, she issued forth into the night to secure a poultice for the child's fiery forehead. As she closed the door she said to her eldest daughter,—

"Lock tight the bolt behind me. I shall return soon."

But, alas, she would not be true to those words. For only moments later she chanced to encounter James Schneider.

The bone collector looked around at the shabby streets here. This area—near where he'd buried the first victim—was Hell's Kitchen, on the West Side of the city, once the bastion of Irish gangs, now populated more and more with young professionals, ad agencies, photo studios and stylish restaurants.

He smelled manure and wasn't the least surprised when suddenly a horse reared in front of him.

Then he noticed that the animal wasn't an apparition from the 1800s but was being hitched to one of the hansom cabs that cruised Central Park charging very twentieth-century fees. Their stables were located here.

He laughed to himself. Though it was a hollow sound.

One can only speculate as to what occurred, for there were no witnesses. But we can picture the horror all too clearly. The villain drew the struggling woman into an alley and stabbed her with a dagger, his cruel intent not to kill but to subdue, as was his wont. But such was the strength in good Mrs. Goldschmidt's soul, thinking as she surely was of her fledglings back in the nest, that she surprised the monster by as-

saulting him ferociously:—she struck him repeatedly about the face and ripped hair from his head.

She freed herself momentarily and from her mouth issued an horrendous scream. The cowardly Schneider struck her several times more and fled.

The brave woman staggered to the sidewalk and collapsed, where she died in the arms of a constable who had responded to the alarm neighbors had raised.

This story appeared in a book, which was with the bone collector now, resting in his hip pocket. *Crime in Old New York.* He couldn't explain his overwhelming attraction to the slim volume. If he had to describe his relation to this book he would have to say he was addicted to it. Seventy-five years old and still in remarkable shape, a bookbinding jewel. It was his good-luck charm and his talisman. He'd found it at a small branch of the public library and committed one of the few larcenies of his life by slipping it into his raincoat one day and strolling out of the building.

He'd read the chapter on Schneider a hundred times and virtually had it memorized.

Driving slowly. They were almost there.

When Hanna's poor, weeping husband huddled over her lifeless body, he looked upon her face:—one last time before she was taken to the funeral home (for in the Jewish faith it is dictated that the dead must be interred as quickly as possible). And he noticed upon her porcelain cheek a bruise in the shape of a curious emblem. It was a round symbol and appeared to be a crescent moon and a cluster of what might be taken to be stars hovering over the same.

The constable exclaimed that this must have been an imprint made by the ring of the heinous butcher himself when he struck the poor victim. Detectives enlisted the aid of an artist and he sketched a picture of the impression. (The good reader is referred to plate XXII.) Rounds were made of jewelers in the city, and several names and addresses were secured of men who had bought such rings in the recent past. Two of the gentlemen purchasing these rings were beyond suspicion, being as they were a deacon of a church and another a learned professor at a fine uni-

versity. Yet the third was a man of whom the constables had long har-
bored suspicion of nefarious activity. To wit:—one James Schneider.

This gentleman had at one time been influential in several benevo-
lent organizations in the city of Manhattan: the Consumptives' Assis-
tance League and the Pensioners' Welfare Society, most notably. He
had come under the eye of the constabulary when several elderly charges
from said groups vanished not long after Schneider paid them calls. He
was never charged with any offense but soon after the investigations, he
dropped from sight.

In the aftermath of Hanna Goldschmidt's heinous murder, a still
search of the dubious haunts of the city revealed no abode where Schnei-
der might be found. The constables posted broadsides throughout the
down-town and River-front areas, setting forth the description of the
villain, but he could not be apprehended;—a true tragedy, to be sure, in
light of the carnage that was soon to befall the city at his vile hands.

The streets were clear. The bone collector drove into the
alley. He opened the warehouse door and drove down a wooden
ramp into a long tunnel.

After making sure the place was deserted, he walked to the
back of the car. He opened the trunk and pulled Hanna out. She
was fleshy, fat, like a bag of limp mulch. He grew angry again and
he carried her roughly down another wide tunnel. Traffic from
the West Side Highway sped over them. He listened to her
wheezing and was just reaching out to loosen the gag when he
felt her shudder and go completely limp. Gasping for breath with
the effort of carrying her, he rested her on the floor of the tunnel
and eased the tape off her mouth. Air dribbled in weakly. Had
she just fainted? He listened to her heart. It seemed to be beating fine.

He cut the clothesline binding her ankles, leaned forward
and whispered, "Hanna, *kommen Sie mit mir mit,* Hanna Goldschmidt . . ."

"*Nein,*" she muttered, her voice trailing to silence.

He leaned closer, lightly slapped her face. "Hanna, you must
come with me."

And she screamed: *"Mein Name ist nicht Hanna."* Then kicked him square in the jaw.

A burst of yellow light flashed through his head and he leapt sideways two or three feet, trying to keep his balance. Hanna sprang up, raced blindly down a dark corridor. But he was after her fast. He tackled her before she'd gotten ten yards away. She fell hard; he did too, grunting as he lost his breath.

He lay on his side for a minute, consumed with pain, struggling to breathe, gripping her T-shirts as she thrashed. Lying on her back, hands still cuffed, the girl used the only weapon she had—one of her feet, which she lifted in the air and brought down hard onto his hand. A spike of pain shot through him and his glove flew off. She lifted her strong leg again and only her bad aim saved him from her heel, which slammed so hard into the ground it would've broken bones if she'd connected.

"So nicht!" he growled madly and grabbed her by the throat with his bare hand and squeezed until she squirmed and whined and then stopped squirming and whining. She trembled several times and went still.

When he listened to her heart the beating was very faint. No tricks this time. He snatched up his glove, pulled it on and dragged her back through the tunnel to the post. Bound her feet once more and put a new piece of tape on her mouth. As she came to, his hand was straying over her body. She gasped at first and shrank away as he caressed the flesh behind her ear. Her elbow, her jaw. There weren't many other places he wanted to touch her. She was so *padded* . . . it disgusted him.

Yet *beneath* the skin . . . He gripped her leg firmly. Her wide eyes stared as he fumbled in his pocket and the knife appeared. Without a moment's hesitation he cut through her skin down to the yellow-white bone. She screamed through the tape, a manic wail, and kicked hard but he held her tight. Enjoying this, Hanna? The girl sobbed and groaned loudly. So he had to lower his ear to her leg to hear the delicious sound of the tip of the blade scraping back and forth on the bone. *Skrisssss.*

Then he took her arm.

They locked eyes for a moment and she shook her head pathetically, begging in silence. His gaze dropped to her pudgy forearm and again the cut was deep. Her whole body went rigid with the pain. Another wild, muted scream. Again he lowered his head like a musician, listening to the sound of the blade scraping the ulna. Back and forth. *Skrissss, skrisss* . . . It was some moments later that he realized she'd fainted.

Finally he pried himself away and returned to the car. He planted the next clues then took the broom from the trunk and carefully swept over their footsteps. He drove up the ramp, parked, left the engine running and climbed out once more, carefully sweeping away the tire tracks.

He paused and looked back down the tunnel. Staring at her, just staring. Suddenly a rare smile crossed the bone collector's lips. He was surprised that the first of the guests had already shown up. A dozen pairs of tiny red eyes, two dozen, then three . . . It seemed they were gazing at Hanna's bloody flesh with curiosity . . . and what might have been hunger. Though that could have been his imagination; Lord knew, it was vivid enough.

TWELVE

Mel, go through the Colfax woman's clothes. Amelia, would you help him?"

She offered him another pleasant nod, the sort meant for polite society. Rhyme realized he was really quite angry with her.

At the tech's direction she pulled on latex gloves, gently opened the clothing and ran a horsehair brush through the garments, above large sheets of clean newsprint. Tiny flecks fell out. Cooper picked them up on tape and examined them through the compound 'scope.

"Not much," he reported. "The steam took care of most of the trace. I see a little soil. Not enough to D-G. Wait . . . Excellent. I've got a couple of fibers. Look at these. . . ."

Well, I can't, Rhyme thought angrily.

"Navy blue, acrylic-and-wool blend, I'd guess. It isn't coarse enough to be carpet and it's not lobed. So it's clothing."

"In this heat he's not going to be wearing thick socks or a sweater. Ski mask?"

"That'd be my bet," Cooper said.

Rhyme reflected, "So he's serious about giving us a chance to save them. If he was bent on killing, it wouldn't matter if they saw him or not."

Sellitto added, "Also means the asshole thinks he can get away. Doesn't have suicide on his mind. Might just give us some bargaining power if he's got hostages when we nail him."

"I like that optimism of yours, Lon," Rhyme said.

Thom answered the buzzer and a moment later Jim Polling climbed the stairs, looking disheveled and harried. Well, shuttling between press conferences, the mayor's office and the federal building would do that to you.

"Too bad about the trout," Sellitto called to him. Then explained to Rhyme, "Jimmy here's one of those *real* fishermen. Ties his own flies and everything. Me, I go out on a party boat with a six-pack and I'm happy."

"We'll nail this fucker then worry about the fish," Polling said, helping himself to the coffee Thom had left by the window. He looked outside and blinked in surprise to find two large birds staring at him. He turned back to Rhyme and explained that because of the kidnapping he'd had to postpone a fishing trip to Vermont. Rhyme had never fished—never had the time or inclination for any hobbies—but he found he envied Polling. The serenity of fishing appealed to him. It was a sport you could practice in solitude. Crip sports tended to be in-your-face athletics. Competitive. Proving things to the world . . . and to yourself. Wheelchair basketball, tennis, marathons. Rhyme decided if he had to have a sport it'd be fishing. Though casting a line with a single finger was probably beyond modern technology.

Polling said, "The press is calling him a serial kidnapper."

If the bootie fits, Rhyme reflected.

"And the mayor's going nuts. Wants to call in the feds. I talked the chief into sitting tight on that one. But we can't lose another vic."

"We'll do our best," Rhyme said caustically.

Polling sipped the black coffee and stepped close to the bed. "You okay, Lincoln?"

Rhyme said, "Fine."

Polling appraised him for a moment longer then nodded to Sellitto. "Brief me. We got another press conference in a half hour. You see the last one? Hear what that reporter asked? What did we think the vic's family felt about her being scalded to death?"

Banks shook his head. "Man."

"I nearly decked the fucker," Polling said.

Three and a half years ago, Rhyme recalled, during the cop-killer investigation, the captain had smashed a news crew's videocam when the reporter wondered if Polling was being too aggressive in his investigations just because the suspect, Dan Shepherd, was a member of the force.

Polling and Sellitto retired to a corner of Rhyme's room and the detective filled him in. When the captain descended the stairs this time, Rhyme noticed, he wasn't half as buoyant as he had been.

"Okay," Cooper announced. "We've got a hair. It was in her pocket."

"The whole shaft?" Rhyme asked, without much hope, and was not surprised when Cooper sighed. "Sorry. No bulb."

Without a bulb attached, hair isn't individuated evidence; it's merely class evidence. You can't run a DNA test and link it to a specific person. Still, it has good probative value. The famous Canadian Mounties study a few years ago concluded that if a hair found at the scene matches a suspect's hair the odds are around 4,500 to 1 that he's the one who left it. The problem with hair, though, is that you can't deduce much about the person it belonged to. Sex is almost impossible to determine, and race can't be reliably established. Age can be estimated only with infant hair. Color is deceptive because of wide pigmentation variations and cosmetic dyes, and since everybody loses dozens of hairs every day you can't even tell if the suspect is going bald.

"Check it against the vic's. Do a scale count and medulla pigmentation comparison," Rhyme ordered.

A moment later Cooper looked up from the 'scope. "It's not hers, the Colfax woman's."

"Description?" asked Rhyme.

"Light brown. No kink so I'd say not Negroid. Pigmentation suggests it's not Mongoloid."

"So Caucasian," Rhyme said, nodding at the chart on the wall. "Confirms what the wit said. Head or body hair?"

"There's little diameter variation and a uniform pigment distribution. It's head hair."

"Length?"

"Three centimeters."

Thom asked if he should add to the profile that the kidnapper had brown hair.

Rhyme said no. "We'll wait for some corroboration. Just write down that we know he wears a ski mask, navy blue. Fingernail scrapings, Mel?"

Cooper examined the trace but found nothing useful.

"The print you found. The one on the wall. Let's take a look at it. Could you show it to me, Amelia?"

Sachs hesitated then carried the Polaroid over to him.

"Your monster," Rhyme said. It was a large deformed palm, indeed grotesque, not with the elegant swirls and bifurcations of friction ridges but a mottled pattern of tiny lines.

"It's a wonderful picture—you're a virtual Edward Weston, Amelia. But unfortunately it's not a hand. Those aren't ridges. It's a glove. Leather. Old. Right, Mel?"

The technician nodded.

"Thom, write down that he has an old pair of gloves." Rhyme said to the others, "We're starting to get some ideas about him. He's not leaving *his* FR prints at the scene. But he is leaving glove prints. If we find the glove in his possession we can still place him at the scene. He's smart. But not brilliant."

Sachs asked, "And what do brilliant criminals wear?"

"Cotton-lined suede," Rhyme said. Then asked, "Where's the filter? From the vacuum?"

The technician emptied the cone filter—like one from a coffee-maker—onto a sheet of white paper.

Trace evidence . . .

DAs and reporters and juries loved obvious clues. Bloody gloves, knives, recently fired guns, love letters, semen and finger-prints. But Lincoln Rhyme's favorite evidence was trace—the dust and effluence at crime scenes, so easily overlooked by perps.

But the vacuum had captured nothing helpful.

"All right," Rhyme said, "let's move on. Let's look at the handcuffs."

Sachs stiffened as Cooper opened the plastic bag and slid the cuffs out onto a sheet of newsprint. There was, as Rhyme had predicted, minimal blood. The tour doctor from the medical ex-aminer's office had done the honors with the razor saw, after an NYPD lawyer had faxed a release to the ME.

Cooper examined the cuffs carefully. "Boyd & Keller. Bottom of the line. No serial number." He sprayed the chrome with DFO and hit the PoliLight. "No prints, just a smudge from the glove."

"Let's open them up."

Cooper used a generic cuff key to click them open. With a lens-cleaning air puffer he blew into the mechanism.

"You're still mad at me, Amelia," Rhyme said. "About the hands."

The question caught her off guard. "I wasn't mad," she said after a moment. "I thought it was unprofessional. What you were suggesting."

"Do you know who Edmond Locard was?"

She shook her head.

"A Frenchman. Born in 1877. He founded the University of Lyons' Institute of Criminalistics. He came up with the one rule I lived by when I ran IRD. Locard's Exchange Principle. He thought that whenever two human beings come into contact, something from one is exchanged to the other, and vice versa. Maybe dust, blood, skin cells, dirt, fibers, metallic residue. It might be tough to find exactly what's been exchanged, and even harder to figure out what it means. But an exchange *does* occur—and because of that we can catch our unsubs."

This bit of history didn't interest her in the least.

"You're lucky," Mel Cooper said to Sachs, not looking up.

"He was going to have you and the medic do a spot autopsy and examine the contents of her stomach."

"It would've been helpful," Rhyme said, avoiding her eyes.

"I talked him out of it," Cooper said.

"Autopsy," Sachs said, sighing, as if nothing about Rhyme could surprise her.

Why, she isn't even *here*, he thought angrily. Her mind's a thousand miles away.

"Ah," Cooper said. "Found something. I think it's a bit of the glove."

Cooper mounted a fleck on the compound microscope. Examined it.

"Leather. Reddish-colored. Polished on one side."

"Red, that's good," Sellitto said. To Sachs he explained, "The wilder their clothes, the easier it is to find the perp. They don't teach you that at the academy, bet. Sometime I'll tell you 'bout the time we collared Jimmy Plaid, from the Gambino crew. You remember that, Jerry?"

"You could spot those pants a mile away," the young detective said.

Cooper continued, "The leather's desiccated. Not much oil in the grain. You were right too about them being old."

"What kind of animal?"

"I'd say kidskin. High quality."

"If they were new it might mean he was rich," Rhyme grumbled. "But since they're old he might've found them on the street or bought them secondhand. No snappy deductions from 823's accessorizing, looks like. Okay. Thom, just add to the profile that the gloves are reddish kidskin. What else do we have?"

"He wears aftershave," Sachs reminded him.

"Forgot that. Good. Maybe to cover up another scent. Unsubs do that sometimes. Write it down, Thom. What did it smell like again, Amelia? You described it."

"Dry. Like gin."

"What about the clothesline?" Rhyme asked.

Cooper examined it. "I've seen this before. Plastic. Several dozen interior filaments composed of six to ten different plastic types and one—no, two—metallic filaments."

"I want a manufacturer and source."

Cooper shook his head. "Impossible. Too generic."

"Damn," Rhyme muttered. "And the knot?"

"Now *that's* unusual. Very efficient. See how it loops around twice? PVC is the hardest cord to tie and this knot ain't going anywhere."

"They have a knot file downtown?"

"No."

Inexcusable, he thought.

"Sir?"

Rhyme turned to Banks.

"I do some sailing . . ."

"Out of Westport," Rhyme said.

"Well, as a matter of fact, yeah. How'd you know?"

If there were a forensic test for location of origin Jerry Banks would turn up positive for Connecticut. "Lucky guess."

"It isn't nautical. I don't recognize it."

"That's good to know. Hang it up there." Rhyme nodded toward the wall, next to the Polaroid of the cellophane and the Monet poster. "We'll get to it later."

The doorbell rang and Thom disappeared to answer it. Rhyme had a bad moment thinking that perhaps it was Dr. Berger returning to tell him he was no longer interested in helping him with their "project."

But the heavy thud of boots told Rhyme who had come a-calling.

The Emergency Services officers, all large, all somber, dressed in combat gear, entered the room politely and nodded to Sellitto and Banks. They were men of action and Rhyme bet that behind the twenty still eyes were ten very bad reactions to the sight of a man laid up forever on his back.

"Gentlemen, you've heard about the kidnapping last night and the death of the victim this afternoon." He continued through the affirmative muttering, "Our unsub has another victim. We have a lead in the case and I need you to hit locations around the city and secure evidence. Immediately and simultaneously. One man, one location."

"You mean," one mustachioed officer asked uncertainly, "no backup."

"You won't need it."

"All due respect, sir, I'm not inclined to go into any tactical situation without backup. A partner at least."

"I don't think there'll be any firefights. The targets are the major chain grocery stores in town."

"Grocery stores?"

"Not every store. Just one of every chain. J&G's, ShopRite, Food Warehouse . . ."

"What exactly are we going to do?"

"Buy veal shanks."

"What?"

"One package at each store. I'm afraid I'll have to ask you to pay from your own pocket, gentlemen. But the city'll reimburse you. Oh, and we need them ASAP."

———

She lay on her side, immobile.

Her eyes had grown accustomed to the dimness of the old tunnel and she could see the little fuckers moving closer. One in particular she kept her eye on.

Monelle's leg stung like a bitch but most of the pain was in her arm, from where he'd cut deep into her skin. Because it was cuffed behind her she couldn't see the wound, didn't know how much she'd bled. But it must have been a lot; she was very faint and could feel the sticky ooze all over her arms and side.

The sound of scratching—needlish claws on concrete. The gray-brown lumps rustling in the shadows. The rats continued to twitch their way toward her. There must have been a hundred of them.

She forced herself to stay completely still and kept her eyes on the big black one. Schwarzie, she called him. He was in the front, moving back and forth, studying her.

Monelle Gerger had been around the world twice by the time she was nineteen. She'd hitched through Sri Lanka and Cambodia and Pakistan. Through Nebraska, where women stared at her eyebrow rings and braless boobs with contempt. Through Iran, where men stared at her bare arms like dogs in heat. She'd slept in city parks in Guatemala City and spent three days with rebel forces in Nicaragua after getting lost on the way to a wildlife refuge.

But she'd never been so scared as now.

Mein Gott.

And what scared her the most was what she was about to do to herself.

One rat ran close, a small one, its brown body zipping forward, backing up, moving forward again a few inches. Rats were scary, she decided, because they were more like reptiles than rodents. A snaky nose and snaky tail. And those fucking red eyes.

Behind him was Schwarzie, the size of a small cat. He rose up on his haunches and stared at what fascinated him. Watching. Waiting.

Then the little one attacked. Scurrying on his four needlish feet, ignoring her muffled scream, he darted fast and straight. Quick as a roach he tore a bite from her cut leg. The wound stung like fire. Monelle squealed—in pain, yes, but from anger too. I don't fucking want *you!* She slammed her heel into his back with a dull crunch. He quivered once and lay still.

Another one raced up to her neck, ripped away a bite then leapt back, staring at her, twitching his nose as if he were running his tongue around his little rat mouth, savoring her flavor.

Dieser Schmerz . . .

She shivered as the searing burn radiated from the bite. *Dieser Schmerz!* The pain! Monelle forced herself to lie still again.

The tiny attacker poised for another run but suddenly he twitched and turned away. Monelle saw why. Schwarzie was finally easing to the front of the pack. He was coming after what he wanted.

Good, good.

He was the one she'd been waiting for. Because he hadn't

seemed interested in the blood or her flesh; he'd padded up close twenty minutes before, fascinated by the silver tape across her mouth.

The smaller rat scurried back into the swarming bodies as Schwarzie eased forward, on his obscenely tiny feet. Paused. Then advanced again. Six feet, five.

Then three.

She remained completely still. Breathing as shallowly as she dared, afraid the inhalation would scare him off.

Schwarzie paused. Padded forward again. Then stopped. Two feet away from her head.

Don't move a muscle.

His back was humped high and his lips kept retracting over his brown and yellow teeth. He moved another foot closer and stopped, eyes darting. Sat up, rubbed his clawed paws together, eased forward again.

Monelle Gerger played dead.

Another six inches. *Vorwärts!*

Come on!

Then he was at her face. She smelled garbage and oil on his body, feces, rotten meat. He sniffed and she felt the unbearable tickle of whiskers on her nose as his tiny teeth emerged from his mouth and began to chew the tape.

For five minutes he gnawed around her mouth. Once another rat scooted in, sank his teeth into her ankle. She closed her eyes to the pain and tried to ignore it. Schwarzie chased him away then stood in the shadows studying her.

Vorwärts, Schwarzie! Come on!

Slowly he padded back to her. Tears running down her cheek, Monelle reluctantly lowered her mouth to him.

Chewing, chewing . . .

Come on!

She felt his vile, hot breath in her mouth as he broke through the tape and began to rip off larger chunks of the shiny plastic. He pulled the pieces from his mouth and squeezed them greedily in his front claws.

Big enough now? she wondered.

It would have to be. She couldn't take any more.

Slowly she lifted her head up, one millimeter at a time. Schwarzie blinked and leaned forward, curiously.

Monelle spread her jaws and heard the wonderful sound of the ripping tape. She sucked air deep into her lungs. She could breathe again!

And she could shout for help.

"*Bitte, helfen Sie mir!* Please help me!"

Schwarzie backed away, startled by her ragged howl, dropping his precious silver tape. But he didn't go very far. He stopped and turned back, rose on his pudgy haunches.

Ignoring his black, humped body she kicked the post she was tied to. Dust and dirt floated down like gray snow but the wood didn't give a bit. She screamed until her throat burned.

"*Bitte.* Help me!"

The sticky rush of traffic swallowed the sound.

Stillness for a moment. Then Schwarzie started toward her again. He wasn't alone this time. The slimy pack followed his lead. Twitching, nervous. But drawn steadily by the tempting smell of her blood.

Bone and wood, wood and bone.

"Mel, what do you have there?" Rhyme was nodding toward the computer attached to the chromatograph-spectrometer. Cooper had once more retested the dirt they'd found in the splinter of wood.

"It's still nitrogen-rich. Off the charts."

Three separate tests, the results all the same. A diagnostic check of the unit showed it was working fine. Cooper reflected and said, "That much nitrogen—maybe a firearms or ammunition manufacturer."

"That'd be Connecticut, not Manhattan." Rhyme looked at the clock. 6:30. How fast time had raced past today. How slowly it had moved for the past three and a half years. He felt as if he'd been awake for days and days.

The young detective pored over the map of Manhattan, moving aside the pale vertebra that had fallen to the floor earlier.

The disk had been left here by Rhyme's SCI specialist, Peter Taylor. An early appointment with the man. The doctor had examined him expertly then sat back in the rustling rattan chair and pulled something out of his pocket.

"Show-and-tell time," the doctor had said.

Rhyme had glanced at Taylor's open hand.

"This's a fourth cervical vertebra. Just like the one in your neck. The one that broke. See the little tails on the end?" The doctor turned it over and over for a moment then asked, "What do you think of when you see it?"

Rhyme respected Taylor—who didn't treat him like a child or a moron or a major inconvenience—but that day he hadn't been in the mood to play the inspiration game. He hadn't answered.

Taylor continued anyway, "Some of my patients think it looks like a stingray. Some say it's a spaceship. Or an airplane. Or a truck. Whenever I ask that question people usually compare it to something big. Nobody ever says, 'Oh, a hunk of calcium and magnesium.' See, they don't like the idea that something so insignificant has made their lives pure hell."

Rhyme had glanced back at the doctor skeptically but the placid, gray-haired medico was an old hand at SCI patients and he said kindly, "Don't tune me out, Lincoln."

Taylor had held the disk up close to Rhyme's face. "You're thinking it's unfair this little thing causing you so much grief. But forget that. *Forget* it. I want you to remember what it was like before the accident. The good and bad in your life. Happiness, sadness . . . You can feel that again." The doctor's face had grown still. "But frankly all I see now is somebody who's given up."

Taylor had left the vertebra on the bedside table. Accidentally, it seemed. But then Rhyme realized the act was calculated. Over the past months while Rhyme was trying to decide whether or not to kill himself he'd stared at the tiny disk. It became an emblem for Taylor's argument—the pro-living argument. But in the end that side lost; the doctor's words, as valid as they might be, couldn't overcome the burden of pain and heartache and exhaustion Lincoln Rhyme felt day after day after day.

He now looked away from the disk—to Amelia Sachs—and said, "I want you to think about the scene again."

"I told you everything I saw."

"Not *saw*, I want to know what you felt."

Rhyme remembered the thousands of times he'd run crime scenes. Sometimes a miracle would happen. He'd be looking around and somehow ideas about the unsub would come to him. He couldn't explain how. The behaviorists talked about profiling as if they'd invented it. But criminalists had been profiling for hundreds of years. Walk the grid, walk where *he's* walked, find what *he's* left behind, figure out what *he's* taken with him—and you'll come away from the scene with a profile as clear as a portrait.

"Tell me," he prodded. "What did you feel?"

"Uneasy. Tense. Hot." She shrugged. "I don't know. I really don't. Sorry."

If he'd been mobile Rhyme would have leapt from the bed, grabbed her shoulders and shaken her. Shouted: *But you know what I'm talking about! I know you do. Why won't you work with me? . . . Why are you ignoring me?*

Then he understood something. . . . That she *was* there, in the steamy basement. Hovering over T.J.'s ruined body. Smelling the vile smell. He saw it in the way her thumb flicked a bloody cuticle, he saw it in the way she maintained the no-man's-land of politeness between the two of them. She detested being in that vile basement, and she hated him for reminding her that part of her was still there.

"You're walking through the room," he said.

"I really don't think I can be any more help."

"Play along," he said, forcing his temper down. He smiled. "Tell me what you thought."

Her face went still and she said, "It's . . . just thoughts. Impressions everybody'd have."

"But *you* were there. *Everybody* wasn't. Tell us."

"It was scary or something. . . ." She seemed to regret the clumsy word.

Unprofessional.

"I felt—"

"Somebody watching you?" he asked.

This surprised her. "Yes. That's exactly it."

Rhyme had felt it himself. Many times. He'd felt it three and a half years ago, bending down over the decomposing body of the young policeman, picking a fiber off the uniform. He'd been *positive* that someone was nearby. But there was no one—just a large oak beam that chose that moment to groan and splinter and come crashing down on the fulcrum of Lincoln Rhyme's fourth cervical vertebra with the weight of the earth.

"What else did you think, Amelia?"

She wasn't resisting anymore. Her lips were relaxed, her eyes drifting over the curled *Nighthawks* poster—the diners, lonely or contentedly alone. She said, "Well, I remember saying to myself, 'Man, this place is old.' It was like those pictures you see of turn-of-the-century factories and things. And I—"

"Wait," Rhyme barked. "Let's think about that. Old . . ."

His eyes strayed to the Randel Survey map. He'd commented before on the unsub's interest in historical New York. The building where T.J. Colfax had died was old too. And so was the tunnel for the railroad where they'd found the first body. The New York Central trains used to run aboveground. There'd been so many crossing fatalities that Eleventh Avenue had earned the name Death Avenue and the railroad had finally been forced to move the tracks belowground.

"And Pearl Street," he mused to himself, "was a major byway in early New York. Why's he so interested in old things?" He asked Sellitto, "Is Terry Dobyns still with us?"

"Oh, the shrink? Yeah. We worked a case last year. Come to

think of it, he asked about you. Said he called you a couple times and you never—"

"Right, right, right," Rhyme said. "Get him over here. I want his thoughts on 823's patterns. Now, Amelia, what else did you think?"

She shrugged but far too nonchalantly. "Nothing."

"No?"

And where *did* she keep her feelings? he wondered, recalling something Blaine had said once, seeing a gorgeous woman walking down Fifth Avenue: *The more beautiful the package, the harder it is to unwrap.*

"I don't know. . . . All right, I remember one thing I thought. But it doesn't mean anything. It's not, like a professional observation."

Professional . . .

It's a bitch when you set your own standards, ain't it, Amelia?

"Let's hear it," he said to her.

"When you were having me pretend to be him? And I found where he stood to look back at her?"

"Keep going."

"Well, I thought . . ." For a moment it seemed that tears threatened to fill her beautiful eyes. They were iridescent blue, he noticed. Instantly she controlled herself. "I wondered, did she have a dog. The Colfax woman."

"A dog? Why'd you wonder that?"

She hesitated a moment then said, "This friend of mine . . . a few years ago. We were talking about getting a dog when, well, if we moved in together. I always wanted one. A collie. It was funny. That was the kind my friend wanted too. Even before we knew each other."

"A dog." Rhyme's heart popped like beetles on a summer screen door. "And?"

"I thought that woman—"

"T.J.," Rhyme said.

"T.J.," Sachs continued. "I just thought how sad it was—if she had any pets she wouldn't be coming home to them and playing with them anymore. I didn't think about her boyfriends or husbands. I thought about pets."

"But why *that* thought? Dogs, pets. Why?"

"I don't know why."

Silence.

Finally she said, "I suppose seeing her tied up there . . . And I was thinking how he stood to the side to watch her. Just standing between the oil tanks. It was like he was watching an animal in a pen."

Rhyme glanced at the sine waves on the GC-MS computer screen.

Animals . . .

Nitrogen . . .

"Shit!" Rhyme blurted.

Heads turned toward him.

"It's shit." Staring at the screen.

"Yes, of course!" Cooper said, replastering his strands of hair. "All the nitrogen. It's manure. And it's old manure at that."

Suddenly Lincoln Rhyme had one of those moments he'd reflected on earlier. The thought just burst into his mind. The image was of lambs.

Sellitto asked, "Lincoln, you okay?"

A lamb, sauntering down the street.

It was like he was watching an animal . . .

"Thom," Sellitto was saying, "is he all right?"

. . . in a pen.

Rhyme could picture the carefree animal. A bell around its neck, a dozen others behind.

"Lincoln," Thom said urgently. "You're sweating. Are you all right?"

"Shhhhh," the criminalist ordered.

He felt the tickle running down his face. Inspiration and heart failure; the symptoms are oddly similar. Think, think . . .

Bones, wooden posts and manure . . .

"Yes!" he whispered. A Judas lamb, leading the flock to slaughter.

"Stockyards," Rhyme announced to the room. "She's being held in a stockyard."

THIRTEEN

T here are no stockyards in Manhattan."

"The *past*, Lon," Rhyme reminded him. "Old things turn him on. Get his juices flowing. We should think of *old* stockyards. The older the better."

In researching his book, Rhyme had read about a murder that gentleman mobster Owney Madden was accused of committing: gunning down a rival bootlegger outside his Hell's Kitchen townhouse. Madden was never convicted—not for this particular murder, at any rate. He took the stand and, in his melodious British-accented voice, lectured the courtroom about betrayal. "This entire case has been trumped up by my rivals, who are speaking lies about me. Your honor, do you know what they remind me of? In my neighborhood, in Hell's Kitchen, the flocks of lambs were led through the streets from the stockyards to the slaughterhouses on Forty-second Street. And you know who led them? Not a dog, not a man. But one of theirs. A Judas lamb with a bell around its neck. He'd lead the flock up that ramp. But then he'd stop and the rest of them would go on inside. I'm an innocent lamb and those witnesses against me, they're the Judases."

Rhyme continued. "Call the library, Banks. They must have a historian."

UNSUB 823

Appearance	Residence	Vehicle	Other
• Caucasian male, slight build • Dark clothing • Old gloves, reddish kidskin • Aftershave; to cover up other scent? • Ski mask? Navy blue?	• Prob. has safe house	• Yellow Cab	• knows CS proc. • possibly has record • knows FR prints • gun = .32 Colt • Ties vics w/ unusual knots • "Old" appeals to him

The young detective flipped open his cellular phone and called. His voice dropped a tone or two as he spoke. After he explained what they needed he stopped speaking and gazed at the map of the city.

"Well?" Rhyme asked.

"They're finding someone. They've got—" He lowered his head as someone answered and the young man repeated his request. He started nodding and announced to the room, "I've got two locations . . . no, three."

"Who is it?" Rhyme barked. "Who're you talking to?"

"The curator of the city archives. . . . He says there've been three major stockyard areas in Manhattan. One on the West Side, around Sixtieth Street . . . One in Harlem in the 1930s or '40s. And on the Lower East Side during the Revolution."

"We need addresses, Banks. Addresses!"

Listening.

"He's not sure."

"Why can't he look it up? Tell him to look it up!"

Banks responded, "He heard you, sir. . . . He says, in what? Look them up in what? They didn't have Yellow Pages back then. He's looking at old—"

"Demographic maps of commercial neighborhoods without street names," Rhyme groused. "Obviously. Have him *guess*."

"That's what he's doing. He's guessing."

Rhyme called, "Well, we need him to guess *fast*."

Banks listened, nodding.

"What, what, what, *what?*"

"Around Sixtieth Street and Tenth," the young officer said. A moment later: "Lexington near the Harlem River . . . And then . . . where the Delancey farm was. Is that near Delancey Street?—"

"Of *course* it is. From Little Italy all the way to the East River. Lots of territory. *Miles.* Can't he narrow it down?"

"Around Catherine Street. Lafayette . . . Walker. He's not sure."

"Near the courthouses," Sellitto said and told Banks, "Get Haumann's teams moving. Divide 'em up. Hit all three neighborhoods."

The young detective made the call, then looked up. "What now?"

"We wait," Rhyme said.

Sellitto muttered, "I fucking hate waiting."

Sachs asked Rhyme, "Can I use your phone."

Rhyme nodded toward the one on his bedside table.

She hesitated. "You have one in there?" She pointed to the hallway.

Rhyme nodded.

With perfect posture she walked out of the bedroom. In the hallway mirror he could see her, solemn, making the precious phone call. Who? he wondered. Boyfriend, husband? Day-care center? Why had she hesitated before mentioning her "friend" when she told them about the collie? There was a story behind that, Rhyme bet.

Whomever she was calling wasn't there. He noticed her eyes turn to dark-blue pebbles when there was no answer. She looked up and caught Rhyme gazing at her in the dusty glass. She turned her back. The phone slipped to the cradle and she returned to his room.

There was silence for a full five minutes. Rhyme lacked the mechanism most people have for bleeding off tension. He'd been a manic pacer when he was mobile, drove the officers in IRD crazy. Now, his eyes energetically scanned the Randel map of the city as Sachs dug beneath her Patrol cap and scratched at her scalp. Invisible Mel Cooper cataloged evidence, calm as a surgeon.

All but one of the people in the room jumped inordinately when Sellitto's phone brayed. He listened; his face broke into a grin.

"Got it!" One of Haumann's squads is at Eleventh and Sixtieth. They can hear a woman's screams coming from somewhere around there. They dunno where for sure. They're doing a door-to-door."

"Get your running shoes on," Rhyme ordered Sachs.

He saw her face sag. She glanced at Rhyme's phone, as if it might be ringing with a reprieve call from the governor at any minute. Then a look at Sellitto, who was poring over the ESU tactical map of the West Side.

"Amelia," Rhyme said, "we lost one. That's too bad. But we don't have to lose any more."

"If you saw her," she whispered. "If you only saw what he did to her—"

"Oh, but I have, Amelia," he said evenly, his eyes relentless and challenging. "I've seen what happened to T.J. I've seen what happens to bodies left in hot trunks for a month. I've seen what a pound of C4 does to arms and legs and faces. I worked the Happy Land social club fire. Over eighty people burned to death. We took Polaroids of the vics' faces, or what was left of them, for their families to identify—because there's no way in hell a human being could walk past those rows of bodies and stay sane. Except us. We didn't have any choice." He inhaled against the excruciating pain that swept through his neck. "See, if you're going to get by in this business, Amelia . . . If you're going to get by in *life*, you're going to have to learn to give up the dead."

One by one the others in the room had stopped what they were doing and were looking at the two of them.

No pleasantries now from Amelia Sachs. No polite smiles. She tried for a moment to make her gaze cryptic. But it was transparent as glass. Her fury at him—out of proportion to his comment—roiled through her; her long face folded under the dark energy. She swept aside a lock of lazy red hair and snatched the headset from the table. At the top of the stairs she paused and looked at him with a withering glance, reminding Rhyme that there was nothing colder than a beautiful woman's cold smile.

And for some reason he found himself thinking: Welcome back, Amelia.

———

"Whatcha got? You got goodies, you got a story, you got pictures?"

The Scruff sat in a bar on the East Side of Manhattan, Third Avenue—which is to the city what strip malls are to the 'burbs.

This was a dingy tavern, soon to be rockin' with Yuppies on the make. But now it was the refuge of badly dressed locals, eating suppers of questionable fish and limp salads.

The lean man, skin like knotty ebony, wore a very white shirt and a very green suit. He leaned closer to the Scruff. "You got news, you got secret codes, you got letters? You got shit?"

"Man. Ha."

"You're not laughing when you say ha," said Fred Dellray, really D'Ellret but that had been generations ago. He was six foot four, rarely smiled despite the Jabberwocky banter, and was a star special agent in the Manhattan office of the FBI.

"No, man. I'm not laughing."

"So what've you *got?*" Dellray squeezed the end of a cigarette, which perched over his left ear.

"It takes time, man." The Scruff, a short man, scratched his greasy hair.

"But you ain't got time. Time is precious, time is fleeing, and time is one thing you. Ain't. Got."

Dellray put his huge hand under the table, on which sat two coffees, and squeezed the Scruff's thigh until he whined.

Six months ago the skinny little guy had been caught trying to sell automatic M-16s to a couple of right-wing crazies, who— whether they actually were or not—also happened to be under- cover BATF agents.

The feds hadn't wanted the Scruff himself of course, the greasy little wild-eyed *thing*. They wanted whoever was supplying the guns. ATF swam upstream a ways but no great busts were forth- coming and so they gave him to Dellray, the Bureau's Número Uno snitch handler, to see if he might be some use. So far, though, he'd proved to be just an irritating, mousy little skel who didn't, apparently, have news, secret codes or even shit for the feds.

"The only way we're dropping down a charge, any charge, is you give us something beautiful and sticky. Are we all together on that?"

"I don't have nothing for youse guys right *now* is what I'm say- ing. Just *now*."

"Not true, not true. You gotchaself somethin'. I can see it in your face. You're knowing something, mon."

A bus pulled up outside, with a hiss of brake air. A crowd of Pakistanis climbed from the open door.

"Man, that fucking UN conference," the Scruff muttered, "what the fuck they coming here for? This city's too crowded already. All them foreigners."

" 'Fucking conference.' You little skel, you little turd," Dellray snapped. "Whatcha got against world peace?"

"Nothin'."

"Now, tell me something good."

"I don't know nothin' good."

"Who you talking to here?" Dellray grinning devilishly. "I'm the Chameleon. I can smile'n be happy or I can frown and play squeezie."

"No, man, no," the Scruff squealed. "Shit, that hurts. Cut it out."

The bartender looked over at them and a short glance from Dellray sent him back to polishing polished glasses.

"All right, maybe I know one thing. But I need help. I need—"

"Squeezie time again."

"Fuck you, man. Just fuck you!"

"Oh, that's mighty smart dialogue," Dellray shot back. "You sound like in those bad movies, you know, the bad guy and the good guy finally meet. Like Stallone and somebody. And all they can say to each other is, 'Fuck you, man.' 'No, fuck you.' 'No, fuck *you*.' Now, you're gonna tell me something useful. Are we all together on that?"

And just stared at the Scruff until he gave up.

"Okay, here's what it is. I'm trusting you, man. I'm—"

"Yeah, yeah, yeah. Whatcha got?"

"I was talking to Jackie, you know Jackie?"

"I know Jackie."

"An' he was telling me."

"What was he telling you?"

"He was telling me he heard anything anybody got coming in or going out this week, don't do it the airports."

"So what was coming in or going out? More 16s?"

"I told you, man, there wasn't nothing *I* had. I'm telling you what Jackie—"

"Told you."

"Right, man. Just in general, you know?" The Scruff turned big brown eyes on Dellray. "Would I lie to you?"

"Don't ever lose your dignity," the agent warned solemnly, pointing a stern finger at the Scruff's chest. "Now what's this about airports. Which one? Kennedy, La Guardia?"

"I don't know. All I know is word's up that somebody was gonna be at a airport here. Somebody who was pretty bad."

"Gimme a name."

"Don't got a name."

"Where's Jackie?"

"Dunno. South Africa, I think. Maybe Liberia."

"What's all this *mean?*" Dellray squeezed his cigarette again.

"I guess just there was a chance something was going down, you know, so nobody should be having shipments coming in then."

"You guess." The Scruff cringed but Dellray wasn't thinking about tormenting the little man any longer. He was hearing alarm bells: Jackie—an arms broker both Bureaus had known about for a year—might have heard something from one of his clients, soldiers in Africa and Central Europe and militia cells in America, about some terrorist hit at the airports. Dellray normally wouldn't've thought anything about this, except for that kidnapping at JFK last night. He hadn't paid much attention to it—it was NYPD's case. But now he was also thinking about that botched fragging at the UNESCO meeting in London the other day.

"Yo boy dint tell you anything more?"

"No, man. Nothing more. Hey, I'm hungry. Can we eat somethin'?"

"Remember what I told you about dignity? Quit moaning." Dellray stood up. "I gotta make a call."

———

The RRV skidded to a stop on Sixtieth Street.

Sachs snagged the crime-scene suitcase, the PoliLight and the big twelve-volt flashlight.

"Did you get her in time?" Sachs called to an ESU trooper. "Is she all right?"

No one answered at first. Then she heard the screams.

"What's going on?" she muttered, running breathless up to the large door, which had been battered in by Emergency Services. It opened onto a wide driveway that descended underneath an abandoned brick building. "She's still *there?*"

"That's right."

"Why?" demanded a shocked Amelia Sachs.

"They told us not to go in."

"Not to go in? She's screaming. Can't you hear her?"

An ESU cop said, "They told us to wait for you."

They. No, not *they* at all. Lincoln Rhyme. That son of a bitch.

"We were supposed to find her," the officer said. "*You're* supposed to go in."

She clicked the headset on. "Rhyme!" she barked. "Are you there?"

No answer . . . You goddamn coward.

Give up the dead . . . Sonofabitch! As furious as she'd been storming down the stairs in his townhouse a few minutes ago, she was twice as angry now.

Sachs glanced behind her and noticed a medic standing beside an EMS bus.

"You, come with me."

He took a step forward and saw her draw her weapon. He stopped.

"Whoa, time out," the medic said. "I don't have to go in until the area's secure."

"Now! Move!" She spun around and he must have seen more muzzle than he wanted. He grimaced and hurried after her.

From underground they heard: "Aiiiii! *Hilfe!*" Then sobbing.

Jesus. Sachs started to run toward the looming doorway, twelve feet high, smoky blackness inside.

She heard in her head: *You're him, Amelia. What are you thinking?*

Go away, she said silently.

But Lincoln Rhyme didn't go away.

You're a killer and a kidnapper, Amelia. Where would you walk, what would you touch?

Forget it! I'm going to save her. Hell with the crime scene . . .

"Mein Gott! Pleece! Some-von, pleece help!"

Go, Sachs shouted to herself. Sprint! He's not in here. You're safe. Get her, go . . .

She picked up the pace, her utility belt clanking as she ran. Then, twenty feet down the tunnel, she pulled up. Debating. She didn't like which side won.

"Oh, fuck," she spat out. She set down the suitcase and opened it up. She blurted to the medic, "You, what's your name?"

The uneasy young man answered, "Tad Walsh. I mean, what's going on?" He glanced down into the murk.

"Oh . . . *Bitte, helfen Sie mir!"*

"Cover me," Sachs whispered.

"Cover you? Wait a minute, I don't do that."

"Take the gun, all right?"

"What'm I supposed to cover you *from?"*

Thrusting the automatic into his hand, she dropped to her knees. "Safety's off. Be careful."

She grabbed two rubber bands and slipped them over her shoes. Taking the pistol back she ordered him to do the same.

With unsteady hands he slipped the bands on.

"I'm just thinking—"

"Quiet. He could still be here."

"Wait a minute now, ma'am," the medic whispered. "This ain't in my job description."

"It's not in mine either. Hold the light." She handed him the flashlight.

"But if he's here he's probably gonna shoot at the light. I mean, that's what *I'd* shoot at."

"Then hold it up high. Over my shoulder. I'll go in front. If anybody gets shot it'll be me."

"Then whatta I do?" Tad sounded like a teenager.

"I myself'd run like hell," Sachs muttered. "Now follow me. And keep that beam steady."

Lugging the black CS suitcase in her left hand, holding her weapon in front of her, she gazed at the floor as they moved into the darkness. She saw the familiar broom marks again, just like at the other scene.

"*Bitte nicht, bitte nicht, bitte . . .*" There was a brief scream, then silence.

"What the hell's going on down there?" Tad whispered.

"Shhhh," Sachs hissed.

They walked slowly. Sachs blew on her fingers gripping the Glock—to dry the slick sweat—and carefully eyed the random targets of wooden pillars, shadows and discarded machinery picked out by the flashlight held unsteadily in Tad's hand.

She found no footprints.

Of course not. He's smart.

But we're smart too, she heard Lincoln Rhyme say in her thoughts. And she told him to shut up.

Slower now.

Five more feet. A pause. Then moving slowly forward. Trying to ignore the girl's moans. She felt it again—that sensation of being watched, the slippery crawl of the iron sights tracking you. The body armor, she reflected, wouldn't stop a full-metal jacket. Half the bad guys used Black Talons anyway—so a leg or arm shot would kill you just as efficiently as a chest hit. And a lot more painfully. Nick had told her how one of those bullets could open up a human body; one of his partners, hit by two of the vicious slugs, had died in his arms.

Above and behind . . .

Thinking of him, she remembered one night, lying against Nick's solid chest, gazing at the silhouette of his handsome Italian face on her pillow as he told her about hostage-rescue entry—"Somebody inside wants to nail you when you go in they'll do it from above and behind . . ."

"Shit." She dropped to a crouch, spinning around and aiming the Glock toward the ceiling, ready to empty the entire clip.

"What?" Tad whispered, cowering. *"What?"*

The emptiness gaped at her.

"Nothing." And breathed deeply, stood up.

"Don't *do* that."

There was a gurgling noise ahead of them.

"Jesus," came Tad's high voice again. "I hate this."

This guy's a pussy, she thought. I know that 'cause he's saying everything *I* want to.

She stopped. "Shine the light up there. Ahead."

"Oh, my everloving . . ."

Sachs finally understood the hairs she'd found at the last scene. She remembered the look that had passed between Sellitto and Rhyme. He'd known then what the unsub had planned. He'd known this was what was happening to her—and *still* he'd told ESU to wait. She hated him that much more.

In front of them a pudgy girl lolled on the floor, in a pool of blood. She glanced toward the light with glazed eyes and passed out. Just as a huge black rat—big as a housecat—crawled up onto her belly and moved toward the girl's fleshy throat. It bared its dingy teeth to take a bite from the girl's chin.

Sachs smoothly lifted the chunky black Glock, her left palm circling under the butt for support. She aimed carefully.

Shooting is breathing.

Inhale, out. Squeeze.

Sachs fired her weapon for the first time in the line of duty. Four shots. The huge black rat standing on the girl's chest exploded. She hit one more on the floor behind and another one that, panicking, raced toward Sachs and the medic. The others vanished silently, fast as water on sand.

"Jesus," the medic said. "You could've hit the girl."

"From thirty feet?" Sachs snorted. "Not hardly."

The radio burst to life and Haumann asked if they were under fire.

"Negative," Sachs replied. "Just shooing a few rats."

"Roger, K."

She took the flashlight from the medic and shining it low, started forward.

"It's all right, miss," Sachs called. "You'll be all right."

The girl's eyes opened, head flipping from side to side.

"*Bitte, bitte* . . ."

She was very pale. Her blue eyes clung to Sachs, as if she was afraid to look away. "*Bitte, bitte* . . . Pleece . . ." Her voice rose to a wild keening and she began to sob and thrash in terror as the medic pressed bandages on her wounds.

Sachs cradled her bloody blond head, whispering, "You'll be all right, honey, you'll be all right, you'll be all right. . . ."

FOURTEEN

The office, high above downtown Manhattan, looked out over Jersey. The crap in the air made the sunset absolutely beautiful.

"We gotta."

"We can't."

"Gotta," Fred Dellray repeated and sipped his coffee—even worse than in the restaurant where the Scruff and he'd been sitting not long before. "Take it away from 'em. They'll live with it."

"It's a local case," responded the FBI's assistant special agent in charge of the Manhattan office. The ASAC was a meticulous man who could never work undercover—because when you saw him you thought, Oh, look, an FBI agent.

"It's not local. They're *treating* it local. But it's a big case."

"We're down eighty men because of the UN thing."

"And this's related to it," Dellray said. "I'm positive."

"Then we'll tell UN Security. Let everybody . . . Oh, don't give me that look."

"UN Security? UN *Security*? Say, you ever heara the words oxy-moron? . . . Billy, you see that picture? Of the scene this morning? The hand comin' outa the dirt, and all the skin cut offa that finger? That's a sick fuck out there."

"NYPD's keeping us informed," the ASAC said smartly. "We've got Behavioral on call if they want."

"Oh, Jesus Christ on the merry cross. 'Behavioral on call'? We gotta catch this ripper, Billy. *Catch* him. Not figger out his tick-tocky workings."

"Tell me what your snitch said again."

Dellray knew a crack in a rock when he saw one. Wasn't going to let it seal up again. Rapid fire now: about the Scruff and Jackie in Johannesburg or Monrovia and the hushed word throughout the illicit arms trade that something was going down at a New York airport this week so stay clear. "It's *him*," Dellray said. "Gotta be."

"NYPD's got a task force together."

"Not Anti-Terror. I made calls. Nobody at A-T there knows zippo about it. To NYPD it's 'dead tourists equal bad public relations.' I want this case, Billy." And Fred Dellray said the one word he'd never uttered in his eight years of undercover work. "Please."

"What grounds're you talking?"

"Oh-oh, bullshit question," Dellray said, stroking his index finger like a scolding teacher. "Lessee. We got ourselves that spiffy new anti-terrorism bill. But that's not enough for you, you want jurisdiction? I'll give you jurisdiction. A Port Authority felony. Kidnapping. I can fucking argue that this prick's driving a taxi so he's affecting interstate commerce. We don't want to play *those* games, do we, Billy?"

"You're not listening, Dellray. I can recite the U.S. Code in my sleep, thank you. I want to know if we're going to take over, what we tell people and make *everybody* happy. 'Cause remember, after this unsub's bagged and tagged we're going to have to keep working with NYPD. I'm not going to send my big brother to beat up their big brother even though I can. Anytime I want. Lon Sellitto's running the case and he's a good man."

"A lieutenant?" Dellray snorted. He tugged the cigarette out from behind his ear and held it under his nostrils for a moment.

"Jim Polling's in charge."

Dellray reared back with mock horror. "Polling? Little Adolph? The 'You-have-the-right-to-remain-silent-'cause-I'ma-hit-you-upside-the-motherfuckin'-head' Polling? *Him?*"

The ASAC had no response for that. He said, "Sellitto's good. A real workhorse. I've been with him on two OC task forces."

"That unsub's grabbing bodies right and left and this here boy's betting he's going to work his way up."

"Meaning?"

"We got senators in town. We got congressmen, we got heads of state. I think these folk he's grabbing now're just for practice."

"*You* been talking to Behavioral and not telling me?"

"It's what I smell." Dellray couldn't resist touching his lean nose.

The ASAC blew air from his clean-shaven-federal-agent cheeks. "Who's the CI?"

Dellray had trouble thinking of the Scruff as a confidential informant, which sounded like something out of a Dashiell Hammett novel. Most *CIs* were skels, short for skeletons, meaning scrawny, disgusting little hustlers. Which fit the Scruff to a T.

"He's a tick," Dellray admitted. "But Jackie, this guy he heard it from's solid."

"I know you want it, Fred. I understand." The ASAC said this with some sympathy. Because he knew exactly what was behind Dellray's request.

Even as a boy in Brooklyn, Dellray had wanted to be a cop. It hadn't mattered much to him what kind of cop as long as he could spend twenty-four hours a day doing it. But soon after joining the Bureau he found his calling—undercover work.

Teamed with his straight man and guardian angel Toby Do-little, Dellray was responsible for sending a large number of perps away for a very long time—the sentences totaled close to a thousand years. ("They kin call us the Millennium Team, Toby-o," he declared to his partner once.) The clue to Dellray's success was his nickname: "the Chameleon." Bestowed after—in the space of twenty-four hours—he played a brain-dead cluckhead in a

Harlem crack house and a Haitian dignitary at a dinner in the Panamanian consulate, complete with diagonal red ribbon on his chest and impenetrable accent. The two of them were regularly loaned out to ATF or DEA and, occasionally, city police departments. Drugs and guns were their specialty though they had a minor in 'jacked merchandise.

The irony of undercover work is that the better you are, the earlier the retirement. Word gets around and the big boys, the perps worth going after, become harder to fox. Dolittle and Dellray found themselves working less in the field and more as handlers of informants and other undercover agents. And while it wasn't Dellray's first choice—nothing excited him like the street—it still got him out of the office more often than most SAs in the Bureau. It had never occurred to him to request a transfer.

Until two years ago—a warm April morning in New York. Dellray was just about to leave the office to catch a plane at La Guardia when he got a phone call from the assistant director of the Bureau in Washington. The FBI is a nest of hierarchy and Dellray couldn't imagine why the big man himself was calling. Until he heard the AD's somber voice break the news that Toby Dolittle, along with an assistant U.S. attorney from Manhattan, had been on the ground floor of the Oklahoma City federal building that morning, preparing for the deposition session that Dellray himself was just about to depart for.

Their bodies were being flown back to New York the next day.

Which was the same day that Dellray put in the first of his RFT-2230 forms, requesting a transfer to the Bureau's Anti-Terror Division.

The bombing had been the crime of crimes to Fred Dellray, who, when no one was looking, devoured books on politics and philosophy. He believed there was nothing essentially un-American about greed or lust—hey, those qualities were encouraged everywhere from Wall Street to Capitol Hill. And if people making a business of greed or lust sometimes stepped over the border of legality, Dellray was pleased to track them down—but he never did so with personal animosity. But to murder people for their beliefs—hell, to murder children before they even knew *what* they believed—my God, that was a stab at the heart of the country. Sitting in his two-room, sparsely furnished Brooklyn apartment after Toby's funeral, Dellray decided that this was the kind of crime he wanted a crack at.

But unfortunately the Chameleon's reputation preceded him. The Bureau's best undercover agent was now their best handler, running agents and CIs throughout the East Coast. His bosses simply couldn't afford to let him go to one of the more quiescent departments of the FBI. Dellray was a minor legend, personally responsible for some of the Bureau's greatest recent successes. So it was with considerable regret that his persistent requests were turned down.

The ASAC was well aware of this history and he now added a sincere, "I wish I could help out, Fred. I'm sorry."

But all Dellray heard in these words was the rock cracking a little further. And so the Chameleon pulled a persona off the rack and stared down his boss. He wished he still had his fake gold tooth. Street man Dellray was a tough hombre with one mother-fucker of a mean stare. And in that look was the unmistakable message anybody on the street would know instinctively: I done for you, now you do for me.

Finally the smarmy ASAC said lamely, "It's just that we need *something.*"

"Somethin'?"

"A hook," the ASAC said. "We don't have a hook."

A reason to take the case away from NYPD, he meant.

Politics, politics, polifuckingtics.

Dellray lowered his head but the eyes, brown as polish, didn't waver a millimeter from the ASAC. "He cut the skin off that vic's finger this morning, Billy. Clean down to the bone. Then buried him alive."

Two scrubbed, federal-agent hands met beneath a crisp jaw. The ASAC said slowly, "Here's a thought. There's a deputy com-missioner at NYPD. Name's Eckert. You know him? He's a friend of mine."

The girl lay on her back on a stretcher, eyes closed, conscious but groggy. Still pale. An IV of glucose ran into her arm. Now that she'd been rehydrated she was coherent and surprisingly calm, all things considered.

Sachs walked back to the gates of hell and stood looking down into the black doorway. She clicked on the radio and called Lincoln Rhyme. This time he answered.

"How's the scene look?" Rhyme asked casually.

Her answer was a curt: "We got her out. If you're interested."

"Ah, good. How is she?"

"Not good."

"But alive, right."

"Barely."

"You're upset because of the rats, aren't you, Amelia?"

She didn't answer.

"Because I didn't let Bo's men get her right away. Are you there, Amelia?"

"I'm here."

"There are five contaminants of crime scenes," Rhyme explained. She noticed he'd gone into his low, seductive tone again. "The weather, the victim's family, the suspect, souvenir hunters. The last is the worst. Guess what it is?"

"You tell me."

"Other cops. If I'd let ESU in they could've destroyed all the trace. You know how to handle a scene now. And I'll bet you preserved everything just fine."

Sachs needed to say, "I don't think she'll ever be the same after this. The rats were all over her."

"Yes, I imagine they were. That's their nature."

Their nature . . .

"But five minutes or ten wasn't going to make any difference. She—"

Click.

She shut off the radio and walked to Walsh, the medic.

"I want to interview her. Is she too groggy?"

"Not yet. We gave her locals—to stitch the lacerations and the bites. She'll want some Demerol in a half hour or so."

Sachs smiled and crouched down beside her. "Hi, how you doing?"

The girl, fat but very pretty, nodded.

"Can I ask you some questions?"

"Yes, pleece. I want you get him."

Sellitto arrived and ambled up to them. He smiled down at the girl, who gazed at him blankly. He proffered a badge she had no interest in and identified himself.

"You all right, miss?"

The girl shrugged.

Sweating fiercely in the muggy heat, Sellitto nodded Sachs aside. "Polling been here?"

"Haven't seen him. Maybe he's at Lincoln's."

"No, I just called there. He's gotta get to City Hall pronto."

"What's the problem?"

Sellitto lowered his voice, his doughy face twisted up. "A fuckup—our transmissions're supposed to be secure. But those fucking reporters, somebody's got an unscrambler or something. They heard we didn't go in right away to get her." He nodded toward the girl.

"Well, we *didn't*," Sachs said harshly. "Rhyme told ESU to wait until I got here."

The detective winced. "Man, I hope they don't have *that* on tape. We need Polling for damage control." He nodded to the girl. "Interviewed her yet?"

"No. Just about to." With some regret Sachs clicked on the radio and heard Rhyme's urgent voice.

". . . you there? This goddamn thing doesn't—"

"I'm here," Sachs said coolly.

"What happened?"

"Interference, I guess. I'm with the vic."

The girl blinked at the exchange and Sachs smiled. "I'm not

talking to myself." Gestured toward the mike. "Police head-quarters. What's your name?"

"Monelle. Monelle Gerger." She looked at her bitten arm, pulled up a dressing and examined a wound.

"Interview her fast," Rhyme instructed, "then work the scene."

Hand covering the microphone stalk, Sachs whispered fiercely to Sellitto, "This man is a pain in the ass to work for. Sir."

"Humor him, officer."

"Amelia!" Rhyme barked. "Answer me!"

"We're interviewing her, all right?" she snapped.

Sellitto asked, "Can you tell us what happened?"

Monelle began to talk, a disjointed story about being in the laundry room of a residence hall in the East Village. He'd been hiding, waiting for her.

"What residence hall?" Sellitto asked.

"The Deutsche Haus. It's, you know, mostly German expatriates and students."

"What happened then?" Sellitto continued. Sachs noted that although the big detective appeared gruffer, more ornery than Rhyme, he was really the more compassionate of the two.

"He threwed me in the trunk of car and drove here."

"Did you get a look at him?"

The woman closed her eyes. Sachs repeated the question and Monelle said she hadn't; he was, as Rhyme had guessed, wearing a navy-blue ski mask.

"*Und* gloves."

"Describe them."

They were dark. She didn't remember what color.

"Any unusual characteristics? The kidnapper?"

"No. He was white. I could tell that."

"Did you see the license plate of the taxi?" Sellitto asked.

"*Was?*" the girl asked, drifting into her native tongue.

"Did you see—"

Sachs jumped as Rhyme interrupted: "*Das Nummernschild.*"

Thinking: How the hell does he *know* all this? She repeated the word and the girl shook her head no then squinted. "What you mean, taxi?"

"Wasn't he driving a Yellow Cab?"

"Taxicab? *Nein.* No. It was regular car."

"Hear that, Lincoln?"

"Yup. Our boy's got another set of wheels. And he put her in the trunk so it's not a station wagon or hatchback."

Sachs repeated this. The girl nodded. "Like a sedan."

"Any idea of the make or color?" Sellitto continued.

Monelle answered, "Light, I think. Maybe silver or gray. Or that, you know, what is it? Light brown."

"Beige?"

She nodded.

"Maybe beige," Sachs added for Rhyme's benefit.

Sellitto asked, "Was there anything in the trunk? Anything at all? Tools, clothes, suitcases?"

Monelle said there wasn't. It was empty.

Rhyme had a question. "What did it smell like? The trunk."

Sachs relayed the query.

"I don't know."

"Oil and grease?"

"No. It smelled . . . clean."

"So maybe a new car," Rhyme reflected.

Monelle dissolved into tears for a moment. Then shook her head. Sachs took her hand and, finally, she continued. "We drove for long time. *Seemed* like long time."

"You're doing fine, honey," Sachs said.

Rhyme's voice interrupted. "Tell her to strip."

"What?"

"Take her clothes off."

"I will not."

"Have the medics give her a robe. We need her clothes, Amelia."

"But," Sachs whispered, "she's crying."

"Please," Rhyme said urgently. "It's important."

Sellitto nodded and Sachs, tight-lipped, explained to the girl about the clothes and was surprised when Monelle nodded. She was, it turned out, eager to get out of the bloody garments anyway. Giving her privacy, Sellitto walked away, to confer with Bo Haumann. Monelle put on a gown the medic offered her and one of the plain-clothes detectives covered her with his sportscoat. Sachs bagged the jeans and T-shirts.

"Got them," Sachs said into the radio.

"Now she's got to walk the scene with you," Rhyme said.

"What?"

"But make sure she's behind you. So she doesn't contaminate any PE."

Sachs looked at the young woman, huddling on a gurney beside the two EMS buses.

"She's in no shape to do that. He cut her. All the way to the bone. So she'd bleed and the rats'd get her."

"Is she mobile?"

"Probably. But you know what she's just been through?"

"She can give you the route they walked. She can tell you where he stood."

"She's going to the ER. She lost a lot of blood."

A hesitation. He said pleasantly, "Just ask her."

But his joviality was fake and Sachs heard just impatience. She could tell that Rhyme was a man who wasn't used to coddling people, who didn't *have* to. He was someone used to having his own way.

He persisted, "Just once around the grid."

You can go fuck yourself, Lincoln Rhyme.

"It's—"

"Important. I know."

Nothing from the other end of the line.

She was looking at Monelle. Then she heard a voice, no, *her* voice say to the girl, "I'm going down there to look for evidence. Will you come with me?"

The girl's eyes nailed Sachs deep in her heart. Tears burst. "No, no, no. I am not doing that. *Bitte nicht, oh, bitte nicht . . .*"

Sachs nodded, squeezed the woman's arm. She began to speak into the mike, steeling herself for his reaction, but Rhyme surprised her by saying, "All right, Amelia. Let it go. Just ask her what happened when they arrived."

The girl explained how she'd kicked him and escaped into an adjoining tunnel.

"I kick him again," she said with some satisfaction. "Knock off his glove. Then he get all pissed and strangle me. He—"

"Without the glove on?" Rhyme blurted.

Sachs repeated the question and Monelle said, "Yes."

"Prints, excellent!" Rhyme shouted, his voice distorting in the mike. "When did it happen? How long ago?"

Monelle guessed about an hour and a half.

"Hell," Rhyme muttered. "Prints on skin last an hour, ninety minutes, tops. Can you print skin, Amelia?"

"I never have before."

"Well, you're about to. But fast. In the CS suitcase there'll be a packet labeled Kromekote. Pull out a card."

She found a stack of glossy five-by-seven cards, similar to photographic paper.

"Got it. Do I dust her neck?"

"No. Press the card, glossy side down, against her skin where she thinks he touched her. Press for about three seconds."

Sachs did this, as Monelle stoically gazed at the sky. Then, as Rhyme instructed, she dusted the card with metallic powder, using a puffy Magna-Brush.

"Well?" Rhyme asked eagerly.

"It's no good. A shape of a finger. But no visible ridges. Should I pitch it?"

"Never throw away *anything* at a crime scene, Sachs," he lectured sternly. "Bring it back. I want to see it anyway."

"One thing, I am thinking I forget," said Monelle. "He touch me."

"You mean he molested you?" Sachs asked gently. "Rape?"

"No, no. Not in a sex way. He touch my shoulder, face, behind my ear. Elbow. He squeezed me. I don't know why."

"You hear that, Lincoln? He touched her. But it didn't seem like he was getting off on it."

"Yes."

"*Und* . . . And one thing I am forgetting," Monelle said. "He spoke German. Not good. Like he only study it in school. And he call me Hanna."

"Called her what?"

"Hanna," Sachs repeated into the mike. "Do you know why?" she asked the girl.

"No. But that's all he call me. He seemed to like saying the name."

"Did you get that, Lincoln."

"Yes, I did. Now do the scene. Time's awasting."

As Sachs stood, Monelle suddenly reached up and gripped her wrist.

"Miss . . . Sachs. You are German?"

She smiled and answered, "A long time ago. A couple generations."

Monelle nodded. She pressed Sachs's palm to her cheek. "*Vielen Dank.* Thank you, Miss Sachs. *Danke schön.*"

FIFTEEN

The three ESU halogens clicked to light, bringing an eerie tide of white glare to the grim tunnel.

Alone now at the scene Sachs gazed at the floor for a moment. Something had changed. What?

She drew her weapon again, dropped into a crouch. "He's here," she whispered, stepping behind one of the posts.

"What?" Rhyme asked.

"He's come back. There were some dead rats here. They're gone."

She heard Rhyme's laughter.

"What's so funny?"

"No, Amelia. Their friends took the bodies away."

"Their friends?"

"Had a case up in Harlem once. Dismembered, decomposed body. A lot of the bones were hidden in a big circle around the torso. The skull was in an oil drum, toes underneath piles of leaves . . . Had the borough in an uproar. The press was talking about Satanists, serial killers. Guess who the perp turned out to be?"

"No idea," she said stiffly.

"The vic himself. It was a suicide. Raccoons, rats and squirrels made off with the remains. Like trophies. Nobody knows why but they love their souvenirs. Now, where are you?"

UNSUB 823

Appearance	Residence	Vehicle	Other
• Caucasian male, slight build • Dark clothing • Old gloves, reddish kidskin • Aftershave; to cover up other scent? • Ski mask? Navy blue? • Gloves are dark	• Prob. has safe house	• Yellow Cab • Recent model sedan • Lt. gray, silver, beige	• knows CS proc. • possibly has record • knows FR prints • gun = .32 Colt • Ties vics w/ unusual knots • "Old" appeals to him • Called one vic "Hanna" • Knows basic German

"At the foot of the ramp."

"What do you see?"

"A wide tunnel. Two side tunnels, narrower. Flat ceiling, supported by wooden posts. The posts're all battered and nicked. The floor's old concrete, covered with dirt."

"And manure?"

"Looks like it. In the center, right in front of me's the post she was tied to."

"Windows?"

"None. No doors either." She looked over the wide tunnel, the floor disappearing into a black universe a thousand miles away. She felt the crawl of hopelessness. "It's too big! There's too much space to cover."

"Amelia, relax."

"I'll never find *anything* here."

"I know it seems overwhelming. But just keep in mind that there're only three types of PE that we're concerned about. Objects, body materials and impressions. That's all. It's less daunting if you think of it that way."

Easy for you to say.

"And the scene isn't as big as it looks. Just concentrate on the places they walked. Go to the post."

Sachs walked the path. Staring down.

The ESU lights were brilliant but they also made the shadows starker, revealing a dozen places the kidnapper could hide. A chill trickled down her spine. Stay close, Lincoln, she thought reluctantly. I'm pissed, sure, but I wanna hear you. Breathe or something.

She paused, shone the PoliLight over the ground.

"Is it all swept?" he asked.

"Yes. Just like before."

The body armor chafed her breasts despite the sports bra and undershirt and as hot as it was outside it was unbearable down here. Her skin prickled and she felt a ravenous desire to scratch under her vest.

"I'm at the post."

"Vacuum the area for trace."

Sachs ran the Dustbuster. Hating the noise. It covered up any sound of approaching footsteps, guns cocking, knives being drawn. Involuntarily she looked behind her once, twice. Nearly dropped the vacuum as her hand strayed to her gun.

Sachs looked at the impression in the dust of where Monelle's body had lain. *I'm him. I'm dragging her along. She kicks me. I stumble . . .*

Monelle could have kicked in only one direction, away from the ramp. The unsub didn't fall, she'd said. Which meant he must've landed on his feet. Sachs walked a yard or two into the gloom.

"Bingo!" Sachs shouted.

"What? Tell me?"

"Footprints. He missed a spot sweeping up."

"Not hers?"

"No. She was wearing running shoes. These are smooth soles. Like dress shoes. Two good prints. We'll know what size feet he's got."

"No, they won't tell us that. Soles can be larger or smaller than the uppers. But it may tell us something. In the CS bag there's an electrostatic printer. It's a small box with a wand on it. There'll be some sheets of acetate next to it. Separate the paper, lay the acetate on the print and run the wand over it."

She found the device and made two images of the prints. Carefully slipped them into a paper envelope.

Sachs returned to the post. "And here's a bit of straw from the broom."

"From?—"

"Sorry," Sachs said quickly. "We don't know where it's from. A bit of straw. I'm picking it up and bagging it."

Getting good with these pencils. Hey, Lincoln, you son of a bitch, know what I'm doing to celebrate my permanent retirement from crime scene detail? I'm going out for Chinese.

The ESU halogens didn't reach into the side tunnel where Monelle had run. Sachs paused at the day–night line then plunged forward into the shadows. The flashlight beam swept the floor in front of her.

"Talk to me, Amelia."

"There isn't much to see. He swept up here too. Jesus, he thinks of everything."

"What *do* you see?"

"Just marks in the dust."

I tackle her, I bring her down. I'm mad. Furious. I try to strangle her.

Sachs stared at the ground.

"Here's something—knee prints! When he was strangling her he must have straddled her waist. He left knee prints and he missed them when he swept."

"Electrostatic them."

She did, quicker this time. Getting the hang of the equipment. She was slipping the print into the envelope when something caught her eye. Another mark in the dust.

What is that?

"Lincoln . . . I'm looking at the spot where . . . it looks like the glove fell here. When they were struggling."

She clicked on the PoliLight. And couldn't believe what she saw.

"A print. I've got a fingerprint!"

"What?" Rhyme asked, incredulous. "It's not hers?"

"Nope, couldn't be. I can see the dust where she was lying. Her hands were cuffed the whole time. It's where he picked up the glove. He probably thought he'd swept here but missed it. It's a big, fat beautiful one!"

"Stain it, light it and shoot the son of a bitch on the one-to-one."

It took her only two tries to get a crisp Polaroid. She felt like she'd found a hundred-dollar bill in the street.

"Vacuum the area and then go back to the post. Walk the grid," he told her.

She slowly walked the floor, back and forth. One foot at a time.

"Don't forget to look up," he reminded her. "I once caught an unsub because of a single hair on the ceiling. He'd loaded a .357 round in a true .38 and the blowback pasted a hair from his hand on the crown molding."

"I'm looking. It's a tile ceiling. Dirty. Nothing else. Nowhere to stash anything. No ledges or doorways."

"Where're the staged clues?" he asked.

"I don't see anything."

Back and forth. Five minutes passed. Six, seven.

"Maybe he didn't leave any this time," Sachs suggested. "Maybe Monelle's the last."

"No," Rhyme said with certainty.

Then behind one of the wooden pillars a flash caught her eye.

"Here's something in the corner . . . Yep. Here they are."

"Shoot it 'fore you touch it."

She took a photograph and then picked up a wad of white cloth with the pencils. "Women's underwear. Wet."

"Semen?"

"I don't know," she said. Wondering if he was going to ask her to smell it.

Rhyme ordered, "Try the PoliLight. Proteins will fluoresce."

She fetched the light, turned it on. It illuminated the cloth but the liquid didn't glow. "No."

"Bag it. In plastic. What else?" he asked eagerly.

"A leaf. Long, thin, pointed at one end."

It had been cut sometime ago and was dry and turning brown.

She heard Rhyme sigh in frustration. "There're about eight thousand varieties of deciduous vegetation in Manhattan," he explained. "Not very helpful. What's underneath the leaf?"

Why does he think there's anything there?

But there was. A scrap of newsprint. Blank on one side, the other was printed with a drawing of the phases of the moon.

"The moon?" Rhyme mused. "Any prints? Spray it with ninhydrin and scan it fast with the light."

A blast of the PoliLight revealed nothing.

"That's all."

Silence for a moment. "What're the clues sitting on?"

"Oh, I don't know."

"You *have* to know."

"Well, the ground," she answered testily. "Dirt." What else would they be sitting on?

"Is it like all the rest of the dirt around there?"

"Yes." Then she looked closely. Hell, it was different. "Well, not exactly. It's a different color."

Was he *always* right?

Rhyme instructed, "Bag it. In paper."

As she scooped up the grains he said, "Amelia?"

"Yeah?"

"He's not there," Rhyme said reassuringly.

"I guess."

"I heard something in your voice."

"I'm fine," she said shortly. "I'm smelling the air. I smell blood. Mold and mildew. And the aftershave again."

"The same as before?"

"Yes."

"Where's it coming from?"

Sniffing the air, Sachs walked in a spiral, the Maypole again, until she came to another wooden post.

"Here. It's strongest right here."

"What's 'here,' Amelia? You're my legs *and* my eyes, remember."

"One of these wooden columns. Like the kind she was tied to. About fifteen feet away."

"So he might have rested against it. Any prints?"

She sprayed it with ninhydrin and shone the light on it.

"No. But the smell's very strong."

"Sample a portion of the post where it's the strongest. There's a MotoTool in the case. Black. A portable drill. Take a sampling bit—it's like a hollow drill bit—and mount it in the tool. There's something called a chuck. It's a—"

"I own a drill press," she said tersely.

"Oh," Rhyme said.

She drilled a piece of the post out, then flicked sweat from her forehead. "Bag it in plastic?" she asked. He told her yes. She felt faint, lowered her head and caught her breath. No fucking air in here.

"Anything else?" Rhyme asked.

"Nothing that I can see."

"I'm proud of you, Amelia. Come on back and bring your treasures with you."

SIXTEEN

Careful," Rhyme barked.

"I'm an expert at this."

"Is it new or old?"

"Shhh," Thom said.

"Oh, for Christ's sake. The blade, is it old or new?"

"Don't breathe. . . . Ah, there we go. Smooth as a baby's butt."

The procedure was not forensic but cosmetic.

Thom was giving Rhyme his first shave in a week. He had also washed his hair and combed it straight back.

A half hour before, waiting for Sachs and the evidence to arrive, Rhyme had sent Cooper out of the room while Thom slicked up a catheter with K-Y and wielded the tube. After that business had been completed Thom had looked at him and said, "You look like shit. You realize that?"

"I don't care. Why would I care?"

Realizing suddenly that he did.

"How 'bout a shave?" the young man had asked.

"We don't have time."

Rhyme's real concern was that if Dr. Berger saw him groomed he'd be less inclined to go ahead with the suicide. A disheveled patient is a despondent patient.

"And a wash."

"No."

"We've got company now, Lincoln."

Finally Rhyme had grumbled, "All right."

"And let's lose those pajamas, what do you say?"

"There's nothing wrong with them."

But that meant all right too.

Now, scrubbed and shaved, dressed in jeans and a white shirt, Rhyme ignored the mirror his aide held in front of him.

"Take that away."

"Remarkable improvement."

Lincoln Rhyme snorted derisively. "I'm going for a walk until they get back," he announced and settled his head back into the pillow. Mel Cooper turned to him with a perplexed expression.

"In his head," Thom explained.

"Your head?"

"I imagine it," Rhyme continued.

"That's quite a trick," Cooper said.

"I can walk through any neighborhood I want and never get mugged. Hike in the mountains and never get tired. *Climb* a mountain if I want. Go window-shopping on Fifth Avenue. Of course the things I see aren't necessarily there. But so what? Neither are the stars."

"How's that?" Cooper asked.

"The starlight we see is thousands or millions of years old. By the time it gets to Earth the stars themselves've moved. They're not where we see them." Rhyme sighed as the exhaustion flooded over him. "I suppose some of them have already burned out and disappeared." He closed his eyes.

———

"He's making it harder."

"Not necessarily," Rhyme answered Lon Sellitto.

Sellitto, Banks and Sachs had just returned from the stock-yard scene.

"Underwear, the moon and a plant," cheerfully pessimistic Jerry Banks said. "That's not exactly a road map."

"Dirt too," Rhyme reminded, ever appreciative of soil.

"Have any idea what they mean?" Sellitto asked.

"Not yet," Rhyme said.

"Where's Polling?" Sellitto muttered. "He *still* hasn't answered his page."

"Haven't seen him," Rhyme said.

A figure appeared in the doorway.

"As I live and breathe," rumbled the stranger's smooth baritone.

Rhyme nodded the lanky man inside. He was somber-looking but his lean face suddenly cracked into a warm smile, as it tended to do at odd moments. Terry Dobyns was the sum total of the NYPD's behavioral science department. He'd studied with the FBI behaviorists down at Quantico and had degrees in forensic science and psychology.

The psychologist loved opera and touch football and when Lincoln Rhyme had awakened in the hospital after the accident three and a half years ago Dobyns had been sitting beside him listening to *Aïda* on a Walkman. He'd then spent the next three hours conducting what turned out to be the first of many counseling sessions about Rhyme's injury.

"Now what's this I recall the textbooks sayin' 'bout people who don't return phone calls?"

"Analyze me later, Terry. You hear about our unsub?"

"A bit," Dobyns said, looking Rhyme over. He wasn't an M.D. but he knew physiology. "You all right, Lincoln? Looking a little peaked."

"I'm getting a bit of a workout today," Rhyme admitted. "And I could use a nap. You know what a lazy SOB I am."

"Yeah, right. You're the man'd call me at three in the morning with some question about a perp and couldn't understand why I was in the sack. So what's up? You fishin' for a profile?"

"Whatever you can tell us'll help."

Sellitto briefed Dobyns, who—as Rhyme recalled from the days they worked together—never took notes but managed to retain everything he heard inside a head crowned with dark-red hair.

The psychologist paced in front of the wall chart, glancing up at it occasionally as he listened to the detective's rumbling voice.

He held up a finger, interrupting Sellitto. "The victims, the victims . . . They've all been found underground. Buried, in a basement, in the stockyard tunnel."

"Right," Rhyme confirmed.

"Go on."

Sellitto continued, explaining about the rescue of Monelle Gerger.

"Fine, all right," Dobyns said absently. Then braked to a halt and turned to the wall again. He spread his legs and, hands on hips, gazed at the sparse facts about Unsub 823. "Tell me more about this idea of yours, Lincoln. That he likes old things."

"I don't know what to make of it. So far his clues have something to do with historical New York. Building materials from the turn of the century, the stockyards, the steam system."

Dobyns stepped forward suddenly and tapped the profile. "Hanna. Tell me about Hanna."

"Amelia?" Rhyme asked.

She told Dobyns how the unsub had referred to Monelle Gerger as Hanna for no apparent reason. "She said he seemed to like saying the name. And speaking to her in German."

"And he took a bit of a chance to 'nap her, didn't he?" Dobyns noted. "The cab, at the airport—that was safe for him. But hiding in a laundry room . . . He must've been real motivated to snatch somebody German."

Dobyns twined some ruddy hair around a lengthy finger and flopped down in one of the squeaky rattan chairs, stretched his feet out in front of him.

"Okay, try this on for size. The underground . . . that's the key. It tells me he's somebody who's hiding something and when I hear that I start thinking hysteria."

"He's not acting hysterical," Sellitto said. "He's pretty damn calm and calculating."

"Not hysteria in that sense. It's a category of mental disorders.

The condition manifests when something traumatic happens in a patient's life and the subconscious *converts* that trauma into something else. It's an attempt to protect the patient. With traditional conversion hysteria you see physical symptoms—nausea, pain, paralysis. But I think here we're dealing with a related problem. Dissociation—that's what we call it when the reaction to the trauma affects the mind, not the physical body. Hysterical amnesia, fugue states. And multiple personalities."

"Jekyll and Hyde?" Mel Cooper played straight man this time, beating Banks to the punch.

"Well, I don't think he's got true multiple personalities," Dobyns continued. "That's a very rare diagnosis and the classic mult pers is young and has a lower IQ than your boy." He nodded at the profile chart. "He's slick and he's smart. Clearly an organized offender." Dobyns stared out the window for a moment. "This is interesting, Lincoln. I think your unsub pulls on his other personality when it suits him—when he wants to kill—and that's important."

"Why?"

"Two reasons. First, it tells us something about his main personality. He's someone who's been trained—maybe at his job, maybe his upbringing—to help people, not hurt them. A priest, a counselor, politician, social worker. And, two, I think it means he's found himself a blueprint. If you can find out what it is, maybe you can get a lead to him."

"What kind of blueprint?"

"He may have wanted to kill for a long time. But he didn't act until he found himself a role model. Maybe from a book or movie. Or somebody he actually knows. It's someone he can identify with, someone whose own crimes in effect give him permission to kill. Now, I'm going out on a limb here—"

"Climb," Rhyme said. "Climb."

"His obsession with history tells me that his personality is a character from the past."

"Real life?"

"That I couldn't say. Maybe fictional, maybe not. Hanna, who-ever she is, figures in the story somewhere. Germany too. Or German Americans."

"Any idea what might've set him off?"

"Freud felt it was caused by—what else?—sexual conflict at the Oedipal stage. Nowadays, the consensus is that developmental glitches're only one cause—any trauma can trigger it. And it doesn't have to be a single event. It could be a personality flaw, a long series of personal or professional disappointments. Hard to say." His eyes glowed as they gazed at the profile. "But I sure hope you bag him alive, Lincoln. I'd love the chance to get him on the couch for a few hours."

"Thom, are you writing this down?"

"Yes, bwana."

"But one question," Rhyme began.

Dobyns whirled around. "I'd say it's *the* question, Lincoln: Why is he leaving the clues? Right?"

"Yep. Why the clues?"

"Think about what he's done. . . . He's talking to you. Not rambling incoherently like Son of Sam or the Zodiac killer. He's not schizophrenic. He's communicating—in *your* language. The language of forensics. Why?" More pacing, eyes flipping over the chart. "All I can think of is that he wants to share the guilt. See, it's hard for him to kill. It becomes easier if he makes us accom-plices. If we don't save the vics in time their deaths are partly *our* fault."

"But that's good, isn't it?" Rhyme asked. "It means he'll keep giving us clues that are solvable. Otherwise, if the puzzle's too hard, he's not sharing the burden."

"Well, that's true," Dobyns said, smiling no longer. "But there's another factor at work too."

Sellitto supplied the answer. "Serial activity escalates."

"Right," Dobyns confirmed.

"How can he strike more often?" Banks muttered. "Every three hours isn't fast enough?"

"Oh, he'll find a way," the psychologist continued. "Most

likely, he'll start targeting multiple victims." The psychologist's eyes narrowed. "Say, you all right, Lincoln?"

There were beads of sweat on the criminalist's forehead and he'd been squinting his eyes hard. "Just tired. A lot of excitement for an old crip."

"One last thing. The profile of the victims's vital in serial crimes. But here we've got different sexes, ages and economic classes. All white but he's been preying in a predominantly white pool so that's not statistically significant. With what we know so far we can't figure out why he's taken these particular people. If you can, you might just get ahead of him."

"Thanks, Terry," Rhyme said. "Stick around for a while."

"Sure, Lincoln. If you'd like."

Then Rhyme ordered, "Let's look at the PE from the stock-yard scene. What've we got? The underwear?"

Mel Cooper assembled the bags that Sachs had brought back from the scene. He glanced at the one containing the underwear. "Katrina Fashion's D'Amore line," he announced. "One hundred percent cotton, elastic band. Cloth made in the U.S. They were cut and sewn in Taiwan."

"You can tell that just by looking at them?" Sachs asked, incredulous.

"Naw, I was reading," he answered, pointing at the label.

"Oh."

The cops laughed.

"He's telling us he's got another woman then?" Sachs asked.

"Probably," Rhyme said.

Cooper opened the bag. "Don't know what the liquid is. I'll do a chromatograph."

Rhyme asked Thom to hold up the scrap of paper with the phases of the moon on it. He studied it closely. A scrap like this was wonderful individuated evidence. You could fit it to the sheet it'd been torn from and link the two as closely as fingerprints. The problem here of course was that they had no original piece of paper. He wondered if they'd ever find it. The unsub might have destroyed it once he'd torn this bit out. Yet Lincoln Rhyme preferred to think not. He liked to picture it somewhere. Just waiting to be found. The way he always pictured source evidence: the automobile the paint chip had scraped off of, the finger that had lost the nail, the gun barrel that had discharged the rifled slug found in the victim's body. These sources—always close to the unsub—took on personalities of their own in Rhyme's mind. They could be imperious or cruel.

Or mysterious.

Phases of the moon.

Rhyme asked Dobyns if their unsub could be driven to act cyclically.

"No. The moon isn't in a major phase right now. We're four days past new."

"So the moons mean something else."

"If they're even moons in the first place," Sachs said. Pleased with herself, and rightly so, Rhyme thought. He said, "Good point, Amelia. Maybe he's talking about circles. About ink. About paper. About geometry. The planetarium . . ."

Rhyme realized that she was staring at him. Maybe just realizing now that he'd shaved and his hair was combed, his clothes changed.

And what was her mood now? he wondered. Angry at him, or disengaged? He couldn't tell. At the moment Amelia Sachs was as cryptic as Unsub 823.

The beeping of the fax machine sounded in the hallway. Thom went to get it and returned a moment later with two sheets of paper.

"It's from Emma Rollins," he announced. He held the sheets up for Rhyme to see.

"Our grocery scanner survey. Eleven stores in Manhattan sold veal shanks to customers buying fewer than five items in the last two days." He started to write on the poster then glanced at Rhyme. "The names of the stores?"

"Of course. We'll need them for cross-referencing later."

Thom wrote them down on the profile chart.

B'way & 82nd,
  ShopRite
B'way & 96th,
  Anderson Foods
Greenwich & Bank,
  ShopRite
2nd Ave., 72nd–73rd,
  Grocery World
Battery Park City,
  J&G's Emporium
1709 2nd Ave.,
  Anderson Foods
34th & Lex.,
  Food Warehouse
8th Ave. & 24th,
  ShopRite
Houston & Lafayette,
  ShopRite
6th Ave. & Houston,
  J&G's Emporium
Greenwich & Franklin,
  Grocery World

"That narrows it down," Sachs said, "to the entire city."

"Patience," said restless Lincoln Rhyme.

Mel Cooper was examining the straw that Sachs had found. "Nothing unique here." He tossed it aside.

"Is it new?" Rhyme asked. If it was they might cross-reference stores that had sold brooms and veal shanks on the same day.

But Cooper said, "Thought of that. It's six months old or older." He began shaking the trace evidence in the German girl's clothing out over a piece of newsprint.

"Several things here," he said, poring over the sheet. "Dirt."

"Enough for a density-gradient?"

"Nope. Just dust really. Probably from the scene."

Cooper looked over the rest of the effluence he'd brushed off the bloodstained clothing.

"Brick dust. Why's there so much brick?"

"From the rats I shot. The wall was brick."

"You shot them? At the scene?" Rhyme winced.

Sachs said defensively, "Well, yes. They were all over her."

He was angry but he let it go. Adding just, "All *kinds* of contaminants from gunfire. Lead, arsenic, carbon, silver."

"And here . . . another bit of reddish leather. From the glove. And . . . We've got another fiber. A different one."

Criminalists love fibers. This was a tiny gray tuft barely visible to the naked eye.

"Excellent," Rhyme announced. "And what else?"

"And here's the photo of the scene," Sachs said, "and the fingerprints. The one from her throat and from where he picked up the glove." She held them up.

"Good," Rhyme said, looking them over carefully.

There was a sheen of reluctant triumph on her face—the rush of winning, which is the flip side of hating yourself for being unprofessional.

Rhyme was studying the Polaroids of the prints when he heard footsteps on the stairs and Jim Polling arrived. He entered the room, did a double-take at the spiffed-up Lincoln Rhyme and strode to Sellitto.

"I was just at the scene," he said. "You saved the vic. Great job, guys." He nodded toward Sachs to show the noun included her too. "But the prick's 'napped another one?"

"Or's about to," Rhyme muttered, gazing at the prints.

"We're working on the clues right now," Banks said.

"Jim, I've been trying to track you down," Sellitto said. "I tried the mayor's office."

"I was with the chief. Had to fucking beg for some extra searchers. Got another fifty men pulled off UN security detail."

"Captain, there's something we got to talk about. We gotta problem. Something happened at the last scene . . ."

A voice as yet unheard from boomed through the room, "Problem? Who got a *problem?* We don't got no problems here, do we? None ay-tall."

Rhyme looked up at the tall, thin man in the doorway. He was jet black and wore a ridiculous green suit and shoes that shone like brown mirrors. Rhyme's heart plummeted. "Dellray."

"Lincoln Rhyme. New York's own Ironside. Hey, Lon. And Jim Polling, how's it hangin', buddy?"

Behind Dellray were a half-dozen other men and a woman. Rhyme knew in a heartbeat why the federal agents were here. Dellray scanned the officers in the room, his attention alighting momentarily on Sachs then flying away.

"What do you want?" Polling asked.

Dellray said, "Haven't you guessed, gemmuns. You're outa business. We closin' you up. Yessir. Just like a bookie."

SEVENTEEN

One of us.

That's how Dellray was looking at Lincoln Rhyme as he walked around the bed. Some people did this. Paralysis was a club and they crashed the party with jokes, nods, winks. You know I love you, man, 'cause I'm makin' funna you.

Lincoln Rhyme had learned that this attitude got tiring very, very quickly.

"Lookit that," Dellray said, poking at the Clinitron. "That's something outa *Star Trek*. Commander Riker, get your ass in the shuttle."

"Go away, Dellray," Polling said. "It's our case."

"And how's dis here patient doing, Dr. Crusher?"

The captain was stepping forward, a rooster the lanky FBI agent towered over. "Dellray, you listening? Go away."

"Man, I'ma get me one of those, Rhyme. Lay my ass down in it, watcha game. Seriously, Lincoln, how you doin'? Been a few years."

"Did they knock?" Rhyme asked Thom.

"No, they didn't knock."

"You didn't knock," Rhyme said. "So may I suggest that you leave?"

"Gotta warrant," Dellray murmured, flicking papers in his breast pocket.

UNSUB 823

Appearance	Residence	Vehicle	Other
• Caucasian male, slight build • Dark clothing • Old gloves, reddish kidskin • Aftershave; to cover up other scent? • Ski mask? Navy blue? • Gloves are dark	• Prob. has safe house • Located near: B'way & 82nd, ShopRite B'way & 96th, Anderson Foods Greenwich & Bank, ShopRite 2nd Ave., 72nd–73rd, Grocery World Battery Park City, J&G's Emporium 1709 2nd Ave., Anderson Foods 34th & Lex., Food Warehouse 8th Ave. & 24th, ShopRite Houston & Lafayette, ShopRite 6th Ave. & Houston, J&G's Emporium Greenwich & Franklin, Grocery World	• Yellow Cab • Recent model sedan • Lt. gray, silver, beige	• knows CS proc. • possibly has record • knows FR prints • gun = .32 Colt • Ties vics w/ unusual knots • "Old" appeals to him • Called one vic "Hanna" • Knows basic German • Underground appeals to him • Dual personalities • Maybe priest, soc. worker, counselor

Amelia Sachs's right index fingernail worried her thumb, which was on the verge of bleeding.

Dellray looked around the room. He was clearly impressed at their impromptu lab but strangled the feeling fast. "We're taking over. Sorry."

In twenty years of policing, Rhyme had never seen a peremptory takeover like this.

"Fuck this, Dellray," Sellitto began, "you passed on the case."

The agent swiveled his glossy black face around until he was looking down at the detective.

"Passed? Passed? I never got no ring-a-ling about it. D'jou call me?"

"No."

"Then who dropped the dime?"

"Well . . ." Sellitto, surprised, glanced at Polling, who said, "You got an advisory. That's all we've gotta send you." On the defensive now too.

"An advisory. Yeah. And, hey, how 'xactly was that delivered? Would that have been by Pony *Ex*-press? Book-rate mail? Tell me, Jim, what's the good of an overnight advisory when there's an ongoing operation?"

Polling said, "We didn't see the need."

"We?" Dellray asked quickly. Like a surgeon spotting a microscopic tumor.

"*I* didn't see the need," Polling snapped. "I told the mayor to keep it a local operation. We've got it under control. Now fuck off, Dellray."

"And you thought you could wrap it up in time for the eleven o'clock news."

Rhyme was startled when Polling shouted, "What we thought was none of your goddamn business. It's our fucking case." He knew about the captain's legendary temper but he'd never seen it in action.

"Ac-tu-ally, it's ou-ur fuck-ing case now." Dellray strolled past the table that held Cooper's equipment.

Rhyme said, "Don't do this, Fred. We're getting a handle on

this guy. Work with us but don't take it away. This unsub isn't like anything you've ever seen."

Dellray smiled. "Let's see, what's the latest I hear about this 'fuck-ing' case? That you've got a civvy doin' the 'rensics." The agent forewent a glance at the Clinitron bed. "You got a portable doing crime scene. You got soldiers out buying groceries."

"Evidence standards, Frederick," Rhyme reminded stridently. "That's SOP."

Dellray looked disappointed. "But ESU, Lincoln? All those taxpayer dollars. Then there's cutting up people like *Texas Chainsaw* . . ."

How had *that* news got out? Everyone was sworn to secrecy on the dismemberment issue.

"And whatsis I hear 'bout Haumann's boys found the vic but dint go in and save her right away? Channel Five had a Big Ear mike on it. Got her screaming for a good five minutes 'fore you sent somebody in." He glanced at Sellitto with a wry grin. "Lon, my man, would that've been the *problem* you were just talking about?"

They'd come so far, Rhyme was thinking. They *were* getting a feel for him, starting to learn the unsub's language. Starting to see him. With a burst of surprise he understood that he was once again doing what he loved. After all these years. And now somebody was going to take it away from him. Anger rippled inside him.

"Take the case, Fred," Rhyme grumbled. "But don't cut us out. Don't do it."

"You lost two vics," Dellray reminded.

"We lost *one*," Sellitto corrected, looking uneasily at Polling, who was still fuming. "Nothing we coulda done about the first. He was a calling card."

Dobyns, arms crossed, merely observed the argument. But Jerry Banks leapt in. "We've got his routine down now. We aren't going to lose any more."

"You are if ESU's gonna sit around listenin' to vics scream their heads off."

Sellitto said, "It was my—"

"*My* decision," Rhyme sang out. "Mine."

"But you're civvy, Lincoln. So it couldn't have been your decision. It mighta been your *suggestion*. It mighta been your *recommendation*. But I don't think it was your decision."

Dellray's attention had turned to Sachs again. His eyes on her, he said to Rhyme, "You told Peretti not to run the scene? That's mighty curious, Lincoln. Why'd you go and do something like that?"

Rhyme said, "I'm better than he is."

"Peretti's not a happy boy scout. Nosir. He and I had a chin wag with Eckert."

Eckert? The Dep Com? How was he involved?

And with one glance at Sachs, at the evasive blue eyes, framed by strands of mussed red hair, he knew how.

Rhyme nailed her with a look, which she promptly avoided, and he said to Dellray, "Let's see . . . Peretti? Wasn't he the one opened up traffic on the spot where the unsub'd stood to watch the first vic? Wasn't he the one released the scene before we'd had a chance to pick up any serious trace? The scene my own Sachs here had the foresight to seal off. *My* Sachs had it right and Vince Peretti and everybody *else* had it wrong. Yes, she did."

She was gazing at her thumb, a look that bespoke seeing a familiar sight, and slipped a Kleenex from her pocket, wrapped it around the bloody digit.

Dellray summarized, "You shoulda called us at the beginning."

"Just get out," Polling muttered. Something snapped in his eyes and his voice rose. "Get the hell out!" he screamed.

Even cool Dellray blinked and eased back as the spittle flew from the captain's mouth.

Rhyme frowned at Polling. There was a chance they might salvage something of the case but not if Polling had a tantrum. "Jim . . ."

The captain ignored him. "Out!" he shouted again. "You are not taking over our case!" And startling everyone in the room, Polling leapt forward, grabbed the agent by his green lapels and shoved him against the wall. After a moment of stunned silence

Dellray simply pushed the captain back with his fingertips and took out a cellular phone. He offered it to Polling.

"Call the mayor. Or Chief Wilson."

Polling eased instinctively away from Dellray—a short man putting some distance between himself and a tall one. "You want the case, you fucking got it." The captain strode to the stairs and then down them. The front door slammed.

"Jesus, Fred," Sellitto said, "work with us. We can nail this scumbag."

"We need the Bureau's A-T," said Dellray, now sounding like reason itself. "You're not set up for the terrorist angle."

"What terrorist angle?" Rhyme asked.

"The UN peace conference. Snitch o' mine said word was up that something was gonna go down at the airport. Where he snatched the vics."

"I wouldn't profile him as a terrorist," Dobyns said. "Whatever's going on inside him's psychologically motivated. It's not ideological."

"Well, fact is, Quantico and us're pegging him one way. 'Preciate that you feel different. But this's how we're handling it."

Rhyme gave up. Fatigue was spiriting him away. He wished Sellitto and his scar-faced assistant had never shown up this morning. He wished he'd never met Amelia Sachs. Wished he wasn't wearing the ridiculous crisp white shirt, which felt stiff at his neck and felt like nothing below it.

He realized that Dellray was speaking to him.

"I'm sorry?" Rhyme cocked a muscular eyebrow.

Dellray asked, "I mean, *couldn't* politics be a motive too?"

"Motive doesn't interest me," Rhyme said. "Evidence interests me."

Dellray glanced again at Cooper's table. "So. The case's ours. We all together on that?"

"What're our options?" Sellitto asked.

"You back us up with searchers. Or you can drop out altogether. That's about all that's left. We'll take the PE now, you don't mind."

Banks hesitated.

"Give 'em it," Sellitto ordered.

The young cop picked up the evidence bags from the most recent scene, slipped them into a large plastic bag. Dellray held his hands out. Banks glanced at the lean fingers and tossed the bag onto the table, walking back to the far side of the room—the cop side. Lincoln Rhyme was a demilitarized zone between them and Amelia Sachs stood riveted at the foot of Rhyme's bed.

Dellray said to her, "Officer Sachs?"

After a pause, her eyes on Rhyme, she responded, "Yes?"

"Commissioner Eckert wants ya t'come with us for debriefing 'bout the crime scenes. He said something about starting your new assignment on Monday."

She nodded.

Dellray turned to Rhyme and said sincerely, "Don'tcha worry, Lincoln. We're gonna git him. Next you hear, his head gonna be on a stake at the gates to the city."

He nodded to his fellow agents, who packed up the evidence and headed downstairs. From the hallway Dellray called to Sachs, "You coming, officer?"

She stood with her hands together, like a schoolgirl at a party she regretted she'd come to.

"In a minute."

Dellray vanished down the stairs.

"Those pricks," Banks muttered, flinging his watchbook onto the table. "Can you believe that?"

Sachs rocked on her heels.

"Better get going, Amelia," Rhyme said. "Your carriage awaits."

"Lincoln." Walking closer to the bed.

"It's all right," he said. "You did what you had to do."

"I have no business doing CS work," she blurted. "I never wanted to."

"And you won't be doing it anymore. That works out well, doesn't it?"

She started to walk to the door then turned and blurted, "You don't care about anything but the evidence, do you?"

Sellitto and Banks stirred but she ignored them.

"Say, Thom, could you show Amelia out?"

Sachs continued, "This is all just a game to you, isn't it? Monelle—"

"Who?"

Her eyes flared, "There! See? You don't even remember her name. Monelle Gerger. The girl in the tunnel . . . she was just a part of the puzzle to you. There were rats crawling all over her and you said, 'That's their nature'? That's their *nature?* She's never going to be the same again and all you cared about was your precious evidence."

"In living victims," he droned, lecturing, "rodent wounds are always superficial. As soon as the first li'l critter drooled on her she needed rabies vaccine. What did a few more bites matter?"

"Why don't we ask her opinion?" Sachs's smile was different now. It had turned pernicious, like those of the nurses and therapy aides who hated crips. They walked around rehab wards with smiles like this. Well, he hadn't been happy with the polite Amelia Sachs; he'd wanted the feisty one. . . .

"Answer me something, Rhyme. Why did you really want me?"

"Thom, our guest has overstayed her welcome. Would you—?"

"Lincoln," the aide began.

"Thom," Rhyme snapped, "believe I asked you to do something."

"Because I don't know shit," Sachs blurted. "That's why! You didn't want a real CS tech because then you wouldn't be in charge. But me . . . you can send me here, send me there. I'll do exactly what you want, and I won't bitch and moan."

"Ah, the troops mutiny . . ." Rhyme said, lifting his eyes to the ceiling.

"But I'm not one of the troops. I never wanted this in the first place."

"I didn't want it either. But here we are. In bed together. Well, one of us." And he knew his cold smile was far, far icier than any she could muster.

"Why, you're just a spoiled brat, Rhyme."

"Hey, officer, time out here," Sellitto barked.

But she kept going. "You can't walk your crime scenes any-more and I'm sorry about that. But you're risking an investiga-tion just to massage your ego and I say fuck that." She grabbed her Patrol hat and stormed out of the room.

He expected to hear a slamming door from downstairs, maybe breaking glass. But there was a faint click and then silence.

As Jerry Banks retrieved his watchbook and thumbed through it with more concentration than was needed, Sellitto said, "Lin-coln, I'm sorry. I—"

"Nothing to it," Rhyme said, yawning excessively in the false hope that it would calm his stinging heart. "Nothing at all."

The cops stood beside the half-empty table for a few mo-ments, difficult silence, then Cooper said, "Better get packed up." He hefted a black 'scope case onto the table and began to un-screw an eyepiece with the loving care of a musician disassem-bling his saxophone.

"Well, Thom," Rhyme said, "it's after sunset. You know what that tells me? Bar's open."

———

Their war room was impressive. It beat Lincoln Rhyme's bed-room hands down.

Half a floor at the federal building, three dozen agents, com-puters and electronic panels out of some Tom Clancy movie. The agents looked like lawyers or investment bankers. White shirts, ties. *Crisp* was the word that came to mind. And Amelia Sachs in the center, conspicuous in her navy-blue uniform, soiled with rat blood, dust and grainy shit from cattle dead a hun-dred years.

She was no longer shaking from her blowup with Rhyme and though her mind kept reeling with a hundred things she wanted to say, wished she *had* said, she forced herself to concentrate on what was happening around her.

A tall agent in an immaculate gray suit was conferring with Dellray—two large men, heads down, solemn. She believed he

was the special agent in charge of the Manhattan office, Thomas
Perkins, but she didn't know for certain; a Patrol officer has as
much contact with the FBI as a dry cleaner or insurance salesman
does. He seemed humorless, efficient, and kept glancing at a
large map of Manhattan pinned to the wall. Perkins nodded several times as Dellray briefed him then he stepped up to a fiber-
board table filled with manila folders, looked over the agents and
began to speak.

"If I could have your attention . . . I've just been in communi-
cation with the director and the AG in Washington. You've all
heard about the Kennedy Airport unsub by now. It's an unusual
profile. Kidnapping, absent a sexual element, is rarely the basis
for serial activity. In fact this's the first unsub of the sort we've
had in the Southern District. In light of the possible connection
with the events at the UN this week we're coordinating with
headquarters, Quantico and the secretary-general's office. We've
been told to be completely proactive on this case. It's getting pri-
oritization at the highest level."

The SAC glanced at Dellray, who said, "We've taken over the
case from the NYPD but we'll be using them for backup and
personpower. We have the crime scene officer here to brief us on
the scenes." Dellray sounded completely different here. Not a
shred of Superfly.

"Have you vouchered the PE?" Perkins asked Sachs.

Sachs admitted that she hadn't. "We were working on saving
the vics."

The SAC was troubled by this. At trial, otherwise solid cases
tanked regularly because of slipups in recording the chain of custody of the physical evidence. It was the first thing the perps' defense lawyers wailed on.

"Make sure you do that before you leave."

"Yessir."

What a look on Rhyme's face when he guessed I bitched to
Eckert and got them shut down. What a look . . .

My Sachs figured it out, my Sachs preserved the scene.

She worried a nail again. Stop it, she told herself, as she always did, and continued to dig into the flesh. The pain felt good. That's what the therapists never understood.

The SAC said, "Agent Dellray? Could you brief the room as regards the approach we'll be taking."

Dellray looked from the SAC to the other agents and continued, "At this moment we have field agents hitting every major terrorist cell in the city and pursuing whatever leads we can find that'll get us to the unsub's residence. *All* CIs, *all* undercover agents. It'll mean compromising some existing operations but we've decided it's worth the risk.

"Our job here is to be rapid response. You'll break out into groups of six agents each and be ready to move on any lead. You'll have complete hostage-rescue and barricade-entry support."

"Sir," Sachs said.

Perkins looked up, frowning. Apparently one didn't interrupt briefings until the approved Q&A break. "Yes, what is it, officer?"

"Well, I'm just wondering, sir. What about the victim?"

"Who, that German girl? You think we should interview her again?"

"No, sir. I meant the *next* victim."

Perkins responded, "Oh, we'll certainly stay cognizant of the fact that there may be other targets."

Sachs continued, "He's got one now."

"He does?" The SAC glanced at Dellray, who shrugged. Perkins asked Sachs, "How do you know?"

"Well, I don't exactly know, sir. But he left clues at the last scene and he wouldn't've done that if he didn't have another vic. Or was just about to snatch one."

"Noted, officer," the SAC continued. "We're going to mobilize as fast as we can to make sure nothing happens to them."

Dellray said to her, "We think it's best to focus on the beast himself."

"Detective Sachs—" Perkins began.

"I'm not a detective, sir. I'm assigned to Patrol."

"Yes, well," the SAC continued, looking at the stacks of files.

"If you could just give us some of your bullet points, that would be helpful."

Thirty agents watching her. Two women among them.

"Just tell us whatcha saw," Dellray said, gripping an unlit cigarette between prominent teeth.

She gave them a synopsis of her searches of the crime scenes and the conclusions Rhyme and Terry Dobyns had come to. Most of the agents were troubled by the unsub's curious MO.

"Like a goddamn game," an agent muttered.

One asked if the clues had any political messages they could decipher.

"Well, sir, we really don't think he's a terrorist," Sachs persisted.

Perkins turned his high-powered attention toward her. "Let me ask you, officer, you concede he's smart, this unsub?"

"Very smart."

"Couldn't he be double-bluffing?"

"How do you mean?"

"You . . . I should say the NYPD's thinking is that he's just a nutcase. I mean, a criminal personality. But isn't it possible he's smart enough to make you *think* that. When something else's going on."

"Like what?"

"Take those clues he left. Couldn't they be diversions?"

"No, sir, they're directions," Sachs said. "Leading us to the vics."

"I understand that," quick Thomas Perkins said. "But by doing that he's also leading us *away* from other targets, right?"

She hadn't considered that. "I suppose it's possible."

"And Chief Wilson's been pulling men off UN security detail right and left to work the kidnapping. This unsub might be keeping everyone distracted, which leaves him free for his real mission."

Sachs remembered that she'd had a similar thought herself earlier in the day, watching all the searchers along Pearl Street. "And that'd be the UN?"

"We think so," Dellray said. "The perps behind the UNESCO bombing attempt in London might want to try again."

Meaning Rhyme was going off in the completely wrong direction. It eased the weight of her guilt somewhat.

"Now, officer, could you itemize the evidence for us?" Perkins asked.

Dellray gave her an inventory sheet of everything she'd found and she went through it item by item. As she spoke Sachs was aware of bustling activity around her—some agents taking calls, some standing and whispering to other agents, some taking notes. But when, glancing down at the sheet, she added, "Then I picked up this fingerprint of his at the last scene," she realized that the room had fallen utterly silent. She looked up. Every face in the office was staring at her in what could pass for shock—if federal agents were capable of that.

She glanced helplessly at Dellray, who cocked his head, "You saying you gotchaself a print?"

"Well, yes. His glove fell off in a struggle with the last vic and when he picked it up he brushed against the floor."

"Where is it?" Dellray asked quickly.

"Jesus," one agent called. "Why didn't you *say* anything?"

"Well, I—"

"Find it, find it!" somebody else called.

A murmur ran through the room.

Her hands shaking, Sachs dug through the evidence bags and handed Dellray the Polaroid of the fingerprint. He held it up, looked carefully. Showed it to someone who, she guessed, was a friction-ridge expert. "Good," the agent offered. "It's definitely A-grade."

Sachs knew that prints were rated A, B and C, the lower category being unacceptable to most law enforcement agencies. But whatever pride she felt in her evidence-gathering skills was crushed by their collective dismay that she hadn't mentioned it before this.

Then everything started to happen at once. Dellray handed off to an agent who jogged to an elaborate computer in the corner of the office and rested the Polaroid on a large, curved bed of something called an Opti-Scan. Another agent turned on the computer and started typing in commands as Dellray snatched up the phone. He tapped his foot impatiently and then lowered his head as, somewhere, the call was answered.

"Ginnie, s'Dellray. This's gonna be a true-blue pain but I needya to shut down all AFIS Northeast Region requests and give the one I'm sending priority. . . . I got Perkins here. He'll okay it and if that ain't enough I'll call the man in Washington himself. . . . It's the UN thing."

Sachs knew the Bureau's Automated Fingerprint Identification System was used by police departments throughout the country. That's what Dellray would be braking to a halt at the moment.

The agent at the computer said, "It's scanned. We're transmitting now."

"How long's it gonna take?"

"Ten, fifteen minutes."

Dellray pressed his dusty fingers together. "Please, please, please."

All around her was a cyclone of activity. Sachs heard voices talking about weapons, helicopters, vehicles, anti-terror negotiators. Phone calls, clattering keyboards, maps unrolling, pistols being checked.

Perkins was on the phone, talking to the hostage-rescue people, or the director, or the mayor. Maybe the president. Who knew? Sachs said to Dellray, "I didn't know the print was that big a deal."

"S'always a big deal. Least, with AFIS now it is. Used to be you dusted for prints mostly for show. Let the vics and the press know you were doing *something*."

"You're kidding."

"Naw, not a bit. Take New York City. You do a cold search— that's when you don't have any suspects—you do a cold search manually, it'd take a tech fifty years to go through all the print cards. No foolin'. An automated search? Fifteen minutes. Used to be you'd ID a suspect maybe two, three percent of the time. Now we're running close to twenty, twenty-two percent. Oh, yup, prints're golden. Dincha tell Rhyme about it?"

"He knew, sure."

"And he didn't get all hands on board? My oh my, the man's slipping."

"Say, officer," SAC Perkins called, holding his hand over the phone, "I'll ask you to complete those chain-of-custody cards now. I want to get the PE off to PERT."

The Physical Evidence Response Team. Sachs remembered that Lincoln Rhyme had been the one the feds hired to help put it together.

"I'll do that. Sure."

"Mallory, Kemple, take that PE to an office and get our guest some COC cards. You have a pen, officer?"

"Yes, I do."

She followed the two men into a small office, clicking her ballpoint nervously while they hunted down and returned with a pack of federal-issue chain-of-custody cards. She sat down and broke the package open.

The voice behind her was the hip Dellray, the persona that seemed the eagerest to break out. In the car on the way here someone had referred to him as the Chameleon and she was beginning to see why.

"We call Perkins the Big Dict. Nyup—not 'dick' like you're thinking. 'Dict' like *dictionary*. But don' worry over him. He's smarter'n an agent sandwich. And better'n that he's pulled strings all the way to D.C., which is where strings gotta be pulled in cases like this." Dellray ran his cigarette beneath his nose as if it were a fine cigar. "You know, officer, you're foxy smart doing whatch're doing."

"Which is?"

"Getting out of Major Crimes. You don't want it." The lean black face, glossy and wrinkled only about the eyes, seemed sincere for the first time since she'd met him. "Best thing you ever did, going into Public Affairs. You'll do some good there and it won't turn you to dust. That's what happens, you bet. This job turns you to dust."

One of the last victims of James Schneider's mad compulsion, a young man named Ortega, had come to Manhattan from Mexico City, where political unrest (the much-heralded populist uprising, which had begun the year before) had made commerce difficult at best. Yet the ambitious entrepreneur had been in the city no more than one week when he vanished from sight. It was learned that he was last seen in front of a West Side tavern and authorities immediately suspected that he was yet another victim of Schneider's. Sadly, this was discovered to be the case.

The bone collector cruised the streets for fifteen minutes around NYU, Washington Square. Plenty of people hanging out. But kids mostly. Students in summer school. Skateboarders. It was festive, weird. Singers, jugglers, acrobats. It reminded him of the "museums," down on the Bowery, popular in the 1800s. They weren't museums at all of course but arcades, teeming with burlesque shows, exhibits of freaks and daredevils, and vendors selling everything from French postcards to splinters of the True Cross.

He slowed once or twice but nobody wanted a cab, or could afford one. He turned south.

Schneider tied bricks to Señor Ortega's feet and rolled him under a pier into the Hudson River so the foul water and the fish might reduce his body to mere bone. The corpse was found two weeks after he had vanished and so it was never known whether or not the unfortunate victim was alive or had full use of his senses when he was thrown into the drink. Yet it is suspected that this was so. For Schneider cruelly shortened the rope so that Señor Ortega's face was inches below the surface of Davy Jones's locker;—his hands undoubtedly thrashed madly about as he gazed upward at the air that would have been his salvation.

The bone collector saw a sickly young man standing by the curb. AIDS, he thought. But your bones are healthy—and *so* prominent. Your bones'll last forever. . . . The man didn't want a cab and the taxi cruised past, the bone collector hungrily gazing at his thin frame in the rearview mirror.

He looked back to the street just in time to swerve around an elderly man who'd stepped off the curb, his thin arm raised to flag down the cab. The man leapt back, as best he could, and the cab skidded to a stop just past him.

The man opened the back door and leaned inside. "You should look where you're going." He said this instructionally. Not with anger.

"Sorry," the bone collector muttered contritely.

The elderly man hesitated for a moment, looked up the street but saw no other taxis. He climbed in.

The door slammed shut.

Thinking: Old and thin. The skin would ride on his bones like silk.

"So, where to?" he called.

"East Side."

"You got it," he said as he pulled on the ski mask and spun the wheel sharply right. The cab sped west.

III
THE PORTABLE'S DAUGHTER

Overturn, overturn, overturn! is the maxim of
New York. . . . The very bones of our ancestors
are not permitted to lie quiet a quarter of a century,
and one generation of men seem studious to remove
all relics of those which preceded them.

—PHILIP HONE,
MAYOR OF NEW YORK, DIARY, 1845

EIGHTEEN

Hit me again, Lon."

Rhyme drank through a straw, Sellitto from a glass. Both took the smoky liquor neat. The detective sank down in the squeaky rattan chair and Rhyme decided he looked a little like Peter Lorre in *Casablanca*.

Terry Dobyns was gone—after offering some acerbic psychological insights about narcissism and those employed by the federal government. Jerry Banks had left too. Mel Cooper continued to painstakingly disassemble and pack up his equipment.

"This is good, Lincoln." Sellitto sipped his Scotch. "God-damn. I can't afford this shit. How old's it?"

"I think that one's twenty."

The detective eyed the tawny liquor. "Hell, this was a woman, she'd be legal and then some."

"Tell me something, Lon. Polling? That little tantrum of his. What was that all about?"

"Little Jimmy?" Sellitto laughed. "He's in trouble now. He's the one ran interference to take Peretti off the case and keep it out of the feds' hands. Really went out on a limb. Asking for you too, that took some doing. There were noses outa joint over that. I don't mean you personally. Just a civilian in on a hot case like this."

"Polling asked for me? I thought it was the chief."

"Yeah, but it was Polling put the bug in his ear in the first place. He called soon as he heard there'd been a taking and there was some bogus PE on the scene."

And wanted me? Rhyme wondered. This was curious. Rhyme hadn't had any contact with Polling over the past few years—not since the cop-killer case in which Rhyme had been hurt. It had been Polling who'd run the case and eventually collared Dan Shepherd.

"You seem surprised," Sellitto said.

"That he asked for me? I am. We weren't on the best of terms. Didn't used to be anyway."

"Why's that?"

"I 14-43'd him."

An NYPD complaint form.

"Five, six years ago, when he was a lieutenant, I found him interrogating a suspect right in the middle of a secure scene. Contaminated it. I blew my stack. Put in a report and it got cited at one of his IA reviews—the one where he popped the unarmed suspect."

"Well, I guess all's forgiven, 'cause he wanted you bad."

"Lon, make a phone call for me, would you?"

"Sure."

"No," Thom said, lifting the phone out of the detective's hand. "Make him do it himself."

"I didn't have time to learn how it works," Rhyme said, nodding toward the dialing ECU Thom had hooked up earlier.

"You didn't *spend* the time. Big difference. Who're you calling?"

"Berger."

"No, you're not," Thom said. "It's late."

"I've been reading clocks for a while now," Rhyme replied coolly. "Call him. He's staying at the Plaza."

"No."

"I asked you to call him."

"Here." The aide slapped a slip of paper down on the far edge of the table but Rhyme read it easily. God may have taken much from Lincoln Rhyme but He'd given him the eyesight of a young man. He went through the process of dialing with his cheek on the control stalk. It was easier than he'd thought but he purposely took a long time and muttered as he did it. Infuriatingly, Thom ignored him and went downstairs.

Berger wasn't in his hotel room. Rhyme disconnected, mad that he wasn't able to slam the phone down.

"Problem?" Sellitto asked.

"No," Rhyme grumbled.

Where is he? Rhyme thought testily. It *was* late. Berger ought to be at his hotel room by now. Rhyme was stabbed with an odd feeling—jealousy that *his* death doctor was out helping someone else die.

Sellitto suddenly chuckled softly. Rhyme looked up. The cop was eating a candy bar. He'd forgotten that junk food'd been the staple of the big man's diet when they were working together. "I was thinking. Remember Bennie Ponzo?"

"The OC Task Force ten, twelve years ago?"

"Yeah."

Rhyme had enjoyed organized-crime work. The perps were pros. The crime scenes challenging. And the vics were rarely innocent.

"Who was that?" Mel Cooper asked.

"Hitman outa Bay Ridge," Sellitto said. "Remember after we booked him, the candy sandwich?"

Rhyme laughed, nodding.

"What's the story?" Cooper asked.

Sellitto said, "Okay, we're down at Central Booking, Lincoln and me and a couple other guys. And Bennie, remember, he was a big guy, he was sitting all hunched over, feeling his stomach. All of a sudden he goes, 'Yo, I'm hungry, I wanna candy sandwich.' And we're like looking at each other and I go, 'What's a candy sandwich?' And he looks at me like I'm from Mars and goes, 'What the fuck you think it is? Ya take a Hershey bar, ya put it between two slices of bread and ya eat it. That's a fucking candy sandwich.' "

They laughed. Sellitto held out the bar to Cooper, who shook his head, then to Rhyme, who felt a sudden impulse to take a bite. It'd been over a year since he'd had chocolate. He avoided food like that—sugar, candy. Troublesome food. The little things about life were the biggest burdens, the ones that saddened and exhausted you the most. Okay, you'll never scuba-dive or hike the Alps. So what? A lot of people don't. But everybody brushes their teeth. And goes to the dentist, gets a filling, takes the train home. Everybody picks a hunk of peanut from out behind a molar when nobody's looking.

Everybody except Lincoln Rhyme.

He shook his head to Sellitto and drank a long swallow of Scotch. His eyes slid back to the computer screen, recalling the goodbye letter to Blaine he'd been composing when Sellitto and Banks had interrupted him that morning. There were some other letters he wanted to write as well.

The one he was putting off writing was to Pete Taylor, the spinal cord trauma specialist. Most of the time Taylor and Rhyme had talked not about the patient's condition but about death. The doctor was an ardent opponent of euthanasia. Rhyme felt he owed him a letter to explain why he'd decided to go ahead with the suicide.

And Amelia Sachs?

The Portable's Daughter would get a note too, he decided.

Crips are generous, crips are kind, crips are iron . . .

Crips are nothing if not forgiving.

> *Dear Amelia:*
> *My Dear Amelia:*
> *Amelia:*
> *Dear Officer Sachs:*
>
> *Inasmuch as we have had the pleasure of working together, I would like to take this opportunity to state that although I consider you a betraying Judas, I've forgiven you. Furthermore I wish you well in your future career as a kisser of the media's ass. . . .*

THE BONE COLLECTOR · 219

"What's her story, Lon? Sachs."

"Aside from the fact she's got a ball-buster temper I didn't know about?"

"She married?"

"Naw. A face and bod like that, you'da thought some good-lookin' hunk woulda snagged her by now. But she doesn't even date. We heard she was going with somebody a few years ago but she never talks about it." He lowered his voice. "Lipstick lesbos's what the rumor is. But I don't know from that—*my* social life's picking up women at the laundromat on Saturday night. Hey, it works. What can I say?"

You'll have to learn to give up the dead. . . .

Rhyme was thinking about the look on her face when he'd said that to her. What was that all about? Then he grew angry with himself for spending any time thinking about her. And took a good slug of Scotch.

The doorbell rang, then footsteps on the stairs. Rhyme and Sellitto glanced toward the doorway. The sound was from the boots of a tall man, wearing city-issue jodhpurs and a blue helmet. One of NYPD's elite mounted police. He handed a bulky envelope to Sellitto and returned down the stairs.

The detective opened it. "Lookit what we got here." He poured the contents onto the table. Rhyme glanced up with irritation. Three or four dozen plastic evidence bags, all labeled. Each contained a patch of cellophane from the packages of veal shanks they'd sent ESU to buy.

"A note from Haumann." He read: " 'To: L. Rhyme. L. Sellitto. From: B. Haumann, TSRF.' "

"What's 'at?" Cooper asked. The police department is a nest of initials and acronyms. RMP—remote mobile patrol—is a squad car. IED—improvised explosive device—is a bomb. But TSRF was a new one. Rhyme shrugged.

Sellitto continued to read, chuckling. " 'Tactical Supermarket Response Force. Re: Veal shanks. Citywide search discovered forty-six subjects, all of which were apprehended and neutralized with minimal force. We read them their rights and have transported same to detention facility in the kitchen of Officer T. P. Giancarlo's mother. Upon completion of interrogation, a half-dozen suspects will be transferred to your custody. Heat at 350 for thirty minutes.' "

Rhyme laughed. Then sipped more Scotch, savoring the flavor. This was one thing he'd miss, the smoky breath of the liquor. (Though in the peace of senseless sleep, how could you miss anything? Just like evidence, take away the baseline standard and you have nothing to judge the loss against; you're safe for all eternity.)

Cooper fanned out some of the samples. "Forty-six samples of the cello. One from each chain and the major independents."

Rhyme gazed at the samples. The odds were good for class identification. Individuation of cellophane'd be a bitch—the scrap found on the veal bone clue wouldn't of course exactly match one of these. But, because parent companies buy identical supplies for all their stores, you might learn in which *chain* 823 bought the veal and narrow down the neighborhoods he might live in. Maybe he should call the Bureau's physical-evidence team and—

No, no. Remember: it's their *fuck-ing* case now.

Rhyme commanded Cooper, "Bundle them up and ship them to our federal brethren."

Rhyme tried shutting down his computer and hit the wrong button with his sometimes ornery ring finger. The speakerphone came on with a loud wail of squelch.

"Shit," Rhyme muttered darkly. "Fucking machinery."

Uneasy with Rhyme's sudden anger, Sellitto glanced at his glass and joked, "Hell, Linc, Scotch this good's supposed to make you mellow."

"Got news," Thom replied sourly. "He *is* mellow."

He parked close to the huge drainpipe.

Climbing from the cab he could smell the fetid water, slimy and ripe. They were in a cul-de-sac leading to the wide runoff pipe that ran from the West Side Highway down to the Hudson River. No one could see them here.

The bone collector walked to the back of the cab, enjoying the sight of his elderly captive. Just like he'd enjoyed staring at the girl he'd tied in front of the steam pipe. And the wiggling hand by the railroad tracks early this morning.

Gazing at the frightened eyes. The man was thinner than he'd thought. Grayer. Hair disheveled.

Old in the flesh but young in the bone . . .

The man cowered away from him, arms folded defensively across his narrow chest.

Opening the door, the bone collector pressed his pistol against the man's breastbone.

"Please," his captive whispered, his voice quavering. "I don't have much money but you can have it all. We can go to an ATM. I'll—"

"Get out."

"Please don't hurt me."

The bone collector gestured with his head. The frail man looked around miserably then scooted forward. He stood beside the car, cowering, his arms still crossed, shivering despite the relentless heat.

"Why are you doing this?"

The bone collector stepped back and fished the cuffs from his pocket. Because he wore the thick gloves it took a few seconds to find the chrome links. As he dug them out he thought he saw a four-rigger tacking up the Hudson. The opposing current here wasn't as strong as in the East River, where sailing ships had a hell of a time making their way from the East, Montgomery and Out Ward wharves north. He squinted. No, wait—it wasn't a sailboat, it was just a cabin cruiser, Yuppies lounging on the long front deck.

As he reached forward with the cuffs, the man grabbed his captor's shirt, gripped it hard. "Please. I was going to the hospital. That's why I flagged you down. I've been having chest pains."

"Shut up."

And the man suddenly reached for the bone collector's face, the liver-spotted hands gripping his neck and shoulder and squeezing hard. A jolt of pain radiated from the spot where the yellow nails dug into him. With a burst of temper, he pulled his victim's hands off and cuffed him roughly.

Slapping a piece of tape on the man's mouth, the bone collector dragged him down the gravel embankment toward the mouth of the pipe, four feet in diameter. He stopped, examined the old man.

It'd be so easy to take you down to the bone.

The bone . . . Touching it. Hearing it.

He lifted the man's hand. The terrified eyes gazed back, his lips trembling. The bone collector caressed the man's fingers, squeezed the phalanges between his own (wished he could take his glove off but didn't dare). Then he lifted the man's palm and pressed it hard against his own ear.

"What?—"

His left hand curled around his mystified captive's little finger and slowly pulled until he heard the deep *thonk* of brittle bone snapping. A satisfying sound. The man screamed, a muted cry stuttering through the tape. And slumped to the ground.

The bone collector pulled him upright and led the stumbling man into the mouth of the pipe. He prodded the man forward.

They emerged underneath the old, rotting pier. It was a disgusting place, strewn with the decomposed bodies of animals and fish, trash on the wet rocks, a gray-green sludge of kelp. A mound of seaweed rose and fell in the water, humping like a fat lover. Despite the evening heat in the rest of the city, down here it was cold as a March day.

Señor Ortega . . .

He lowered the man into the river, cuffed him to a pier post, ratcheting the bracelet tight around his wrist again. The captive's grayish face was about three feet above the surface of the water. The bone collector walked carefully over the slick rocks to the drainpipe. He turned and paused for a moment, watching, watching. He hadn't cared much whether the constables found the others or not. Hanna, the woman in the taxi. But this one . . . The bone collector hoped they didn't find him in time. Indeed, that they didn't find him at all. So he could come back in a month or two and see if the clever river had scrubbed the skeleton clean.

Back on the gravel drive he pulled the mask off and left the clues to the next scene not far from where he'd parked. He was angry, furious at the constables, and so this time he hid the clues. And he also included a special surprise. Something he'd been saving for them. The bone collector returned to the taxi.

The breeze was gentle, carrying the fragrance of the sour river with it. And the rustle of grass and, as always in the city, the *shushhhh* of traffic.

Like emery paper on bone.

He stopped and listened to this sound, head cocked as he looked out over the billion lights of the buildings, stretching to the north like an oblong galaxy. It was then that a woman, running fast, emerged on a jogging path beside the drainpipe and nearly collided with him.

In purple shorts and top, the thin brunette danced out of his way. Gasping, she stopped, flicked sweat from her face. In good shape—taut muscles—but not pretty. A hook of a nose, broad lips, blotchy skin.

But beneath that . . .

"You're not supposed . . . You shouldn't park here. This's a jogging path. . . ."

Her words fading and fear rising into her eyes, which flicked from his face to the taxi to the wad of ski mask in his hand.

She knew who he was. He smiled, noting her remarkably pronounced clavicle.

Her right ankle shifted slightly, ready to take her weight when she sprinted away. But he got her first. He ducked low, to tackle her, and when she gave a fast scream and dropped her arms to block him the bone collector straightened up fast from his feint and swung his elbow into her temple. There was a crack like a snapping belt.

She went down on the gravel, hard, and lay still. Horrified, the bone collector dropped to his knees and cradled her head. He moaned, "No, no, no . . ." Furious with himself for striking so hard, sick at heart that he might've broken what seemed to be a perfect skull beneath the tentacles of stringy hair and the unremarkable face.

————

Amelia Sachs finished another COC card and took a break. She paused, found a vending machine and bought a paper cup of vile coffee. She returned to the windowless office, looked over the evidence she'd gathered.

She felt a curious fondness for the macabre collection. Maybe because of what she'd gone through to collect it—her fiery joints ached and she still shuddered when she thought of the buried body at the first scene this morning, the bloody branch of a hand, and of T. J. Colfax's dangling flesh. Until today physical evidence hadn't meant anything to her. PE was boring lectures on drowsy spring afternoons at the academy. PE was math, it was charts and graphs, it was science. It was dead.

No, Amie Sachs was going to be a people cop. Walking beats, dissing back the dissers, outing druggies. Spreading respect for the law—like her father. Or pounding it into them. Like handsome Nick Carelli, a five-year vet, the star of Street Crimes, grinning at the world with his *yo-you-gotta-problem?* smile.

That's just who *she* was going to be.

She looked at the crisp brown leaf she'd found in the stockyard tunnel. One of the clues 823 had left for them. And here was the underwear too. She remembered that the feebies had snagged the PE before Cooper'd finished the test on the . . . what was that machine? The chromatograph? She wondered what the liquid soaking the cotton was.

But these thoughts led to Lincoln Rhyme and he was the one person she didn't want to think about just now.

She began to voucher the rest of the PE. Each COC card had a series of blank lines that would list the custodians of the evidence, in sequence, from the initial discovery at the scene all the way to trial. Sachs had transported evidence several times and her name had appeared on COC cards. But this was the first time *A. Sachs, NYPD 5885* had occupied the first slot.

Once again she lifted the plastic bag containing the leaf.

He'd actually touched it. *Him.* The man who'd killed T.J. Colfax. Who'd held Monelle Gerger's pudgy arm and cut deep into it. Who was out searching for another vic right now—if he hadn't already snatched one.

Who'd buried that poor man this morning, waving for mercy he never got.

She thought of Locard's Exchange Principle. People coming into contact, each transferring something to the other. Something big, something small. Most likely they didn't even know what.

Had something of 823 come off on this leaf? A cell of skin? A dot of sweat? It was a stunning thought. She felt a trill of excitement, of fear, as if the killer were right here in this tiny airless room with her.

Back to the COC cards. For ten minutes she filled them out and was just finishing the last one when the door burst open, startling her. She spun around.

Fred Dellray stood in the doorway, his green jacket abandoned, his starched shirt rumpled. Fingers pinching the cigarette behind his ear. "Step inside a minute'r two, officer. It's payoff time. Thought you might wanna be there."

Sachs followed him down the short corridor, two steps behind his lope.

"The AFIS results're comin' in," Dellray said.

The war room was even busier than before. Jacketless agents hovered over desks. They were armed with their on-duty weapons—the big Sig-Sauer and Smith & Wesson automatics, 10mm and .45s. A half-dozen agents were clustered around the computer terminal beside the Opti-Scan.

Sachs hadn't liked the way Dellray'd taken the case away from them, but she had to admit that beneath the slick-talking hipster Dellray was one hell of a good cop. Agents—young and old—

would come up to him with questions and he'd patiently answer them. He'd yank a phone from the cradle and cajole or berate whoever was on the other end to get him what he needed. Sometimes, he'd look up across the bustling room and roar, "We gonna nail this prick-dick? Yep, you betcha we are." And the straight-arrows'd look at him uneasily but with the obvious thought in mind that if anybody could nail him it'd be Dellray.

"Here, it's coming in now," an agent called.

Dellray barked, "I want open lines to New York, Jersey and Connecticut DMVs. And Corrections and Parole. INS too. Tell 'em to stand by for an incoming ID request. Put everything else on hold."

Agents peeled off and began making phone calls.

The computer screen filled.

She couldn't believe that Dellray actually crossed his stickish fingers.

Utter silence throughout the room.

"Got him!" the agent at the keyboard shouted.

"Ain't no unsub anymore," Dellray sang melodically, bending over the screen. "Listen up, people. We gotta name: Victor Pietrs. Born here, 1948. His parents were from Belgrade. So, we got a Serbian connection. ID brought to us courtesy of New York D of C. Convictions for drugs, assault, one with a deadly. Two sentences served. Okay, listen to this—psychiatric history, committed three times on involuntary orders. Intake at Bellevue and Manhattan Psychiatric. Last release date three years ago. LKA Washington Heights."

He looked up. "Who's got the phone companies?"

Several agents raised their hands.

"Make the calls," Dellray ordered.

An interminable five minutes.

"Not there. No current New York Telephone listing."

"Nothing in Jersey," another agent echoed.

"Negative, Connecticut."

"Fuck-all," Dellray muttered. "Mix the names up. Try variations. An' lookit phone-service accounts canceled in the past year for nonpayment."

For several minutes voices rose and fell like the tide.

Dellray paced manically and Sachs understood why his frame was so scrawny.

Suddenly an agent shouted, "Found him!"

Everyone turned to look.

"I'm on with NY DMV," another agent called. "They've got him. It's coming through now. . . . He's a cabbie. Got a hack license."

"Why don' that s'prise me," Dellray muttered. "Shoulda thoughta that. Where's home sweet home?"

"Morningside Heights. A block from the river." The agent wrote down the address and held it aloft as Dellray swept past and took it. "Know the neighborhood. Pretty deserted. Lotta druggies."

Another agent typed the address into his computer terminal. "Okay, checking deeds . . . Property's an old house. A bank's got title. He must be renting."

"You want HRT?" one agent called across the bustling room. "I got Quantico on the line."

"No time," Dellray announced. "Use the field office SWAT. Get 'em suited up."

Sachs asked, "And what about the next victim?"

"What next victim?"

"He's already taken somebody. He knows we've had the clues for an hour or two. He'd've planted the vic awhile ago. He had to."

"No reports of anybody missing," the agent said. "And if he did snatch 'em they're probably at his house."

"No, they wouldn't be."

"Why not?"

"They'd pick up too much PE," she said. "Lincoln Rhyme said he has a safe house."

"Well, then we'll get him to tell us where they are."

Another agent said, "We can be real persuasive."

228 · *Jeffery Deaver*

"Let's move it," Dellray called. "Yo, ever'body, let's thank Officer Amelia Sachs here. She's the one found that print and lifted it."

She was blushing. Could feel it, hated it. But she couldn't help herself. As she glanced down she noticed strange lines on her shoes. Squinting, she realized she was still wearing the rubber bands.

When she looked up she saw a room full of unsmiling federal agents checking weapons and heading for the door as they glanced at her. The same way, she thought, lumberjacks look at logs.

NINETEEN

*I*n 1911 a tragedy of massive dimension befell our fair city.

On March 25, hundreds of industrious young women were hard at work in a garment factory, one of the many, known notoriously as "sweat-shops", in Greenwich Village in down-town Manhattan.

So enamored of profits were the owners of this company that they denied the poor girls in their employ even the rudimentary facilities that slaves might enjoy. They believed the laborers could not be trusted to make expeditious visits to the rest-room facilities and so kept the doors to the cutting and sewing rooms under lock and key.

The bone collector was driving back to his building. He passed a squad car but he kept his eyes forward and the constables never noticed him.

On the day in question a fire started on the eighth floor of the building and within minutes swept through the factory, from which the young employees tried to flee. They were unable to escape, however, owing to the chained state of the door. Many died on the spot and many more, some horribly afire, leapt into the air a hundred feet above the cobblestones and died from the collision with unyielding Mother Earth.

There numbered 146 victims of the Triangle Shirtwaist fire. The police, however, were confounded by the inability to locate one of the victims, a young woman, Esther Weinraub, whom several witnesses had seen leap in desperation from the eighth floor window. None of the other girls who similarly leapt survived the fall. Was it possible that she, miraculously, had? For when the bodies were laid out in the street for bereaved family members to identify, poor Miss Weinraub's was not to be found.

Reports began to circulate of a ghoul, a man seen carting off a large bundle from the scene of the fire. So incensed were the constables that someone might violate the sacred remains of an innocent young woman that they put on a still search for the man.

After several weeks, their diligent efforts bore fruit. Two residents of Greenwich Village reported seeing a man leaving the scene of the fire and carrying a heavy bundle "like a carpet" over his shoulder. The constables picked up his trail and tracked him to the West Side of the city, where they interviewed neighbors and learned that the man fit the description of James Schneider, who was still at large.

They narrowed their search to a decrepit abode in an alley in Hell's Kitchen, not far from the 60th Street stock-yards. As they entered the alleyway they were greeted with a revolting stench. . . .

He was now driving past the very site of the Triangle fire itself—maybe he'd even been subconsciously prompted to come here. The Asch Building—the ironic name of the structure that had housed the doomed factory—was gone and the site was now a part of NYU. *Then and now . . .* The bone collector would not have been surprised to see white-bloused working girls, trailing sparks and faint smoke, tumbling gracefully to their deaths, falling around him like snow.

Upon breaking into Schneider's habitation, the authorities found a sight that sent even the most seasoned of them reeling with horror. The body of wretched Esther Weinraub—(or what remained of it)—was found in the basement. Schneider was bent on completing the work of the tragic fire and was slowly removing the woman's flesh through means too shocking to recount here.

A search of this loathsome place revealed a secret room, off the basement, filled with bones that had been stripped clean of flesh.

Beneath Schneider's bed, a constable found a diary, in which the madman chronicled his history of evil. "Bone"—(Schneider wrote)—"is the ultimate core of a human being. It alters not, deceives not, yields not. Once the facade of our intemperate ways of the flesh, the flaws of the lesser Races, and the weaker gender, are burnt or boiled away, we are—all of us—noble bone. Bone does not lie. It is immortal."

The lunatic writings set forth a chronicle of gruesome experimentation as he sought to ascertain the most effective way of cleansing his victims of their flesh. He tried boiling the bodies, burning them, rendering with lye, staking them out for animals, and immersing them in water.

But one method above all he favored for this macabre sport. "It is best, I have concluded"—(his diary continues)—"simply to bury the body in rich earth and let Nature do the tedious work. This is the most time-consuming method but the least likely to arouse suspicion as the odors are kept to a minimum. I prefer to inter the individuals while still alive, though why that might be I cannot say with any certainty."

In his heretofore secret room three more bodies were discovered in this very condition. The splayed hands and agog faces of the poor victims attest that they were indeed alive when Schneider piled the last shovelful of dirt upon their tormented crowns.

It was these dark designs that prompted the journalists of the day to christen Schneider with the name by which he was forever after known:—"The Bone Collector."

He drove on, his mind returning to the woman in the trunk, Esther Weinraub. Her thin elbow, her collarbone delicate as a bird's wing. He sped the cab forward, even risked running two red lights. He couldn't wait much longer.

———

"I'm not tired," Rhyme snapped.

"Tired or not, you need to rest."

"No, I need another drink."

Black suitcases lined the wall, awaiting the help of officers from the Twentieth Precinct to transport them back to the IRD lab. Mel Cooper was carting a microscope case downstairs. Lon Sellitto was still sitting in the rattan chair but he wasn't saying much. Just coming to the obvious conclusion that Lincoln Rhyme was not a mellow drunk at all.

Thom said, "I'm sure your blood pressure's up. You need rest."

"I need a drink."

Goddamn you, Amelia Sachs, Rhyme thought. And didn't know why.

"You should give it up. Drinking's never been any good for you."

Well, I *am* giving it up, Rhyme responded silently. For good. Monday. And no twelve-step plan for me; it's a one-stepper.

"Pour me another drink," he ordered.

Not really wanting one.

"No."

"Pour me a drink *now!*" Rhyme snapped.

"No way."

"Lon, would you please pour me another drink?"

"I—"

Thom said, "He doesn't get any more. When he's in a mood like this he's insufferable and we're not going to put up with him."

"You're going to withhold something from me? I could fire you."

"Fire away."

"Crip abuse! I'll get you indicted. Arrest him, Lon."

"Lincoln," Sellitto said placatingly.

"Arrest him!"

The detective was taken aback by the viciousness of Rhyme's words.

"Hey, buddy, maybe you should go a little light," Sellitto said.

"Oh, Christ," Rhyme groaned. He started to moan loudly.

Sellitto blurted, "What is it?" Thom was silent, looking on cautiously.

"My liver." Rhyme's face broke into a cruel grin. "Cirrhosis probably."

Thom swung around, furious. "I will *not* put up with this crap. Okay?"

"No, It's not oh-kay—"

A woman's voice, from the doorway: "We don't have much time."

"—at all."

Amelia Sachs walked into the room, glanced at the empty tables. Rhyme felt spittle on his lip. He was overwhelmed with fury. Because she saw the drool. Because he wore a crisp white shirt he'd changed into just for her. And because he wanted desperately to be alone, forever, alone in the dark of motionless peace—where he was king. Not king for a day. But king for eternity.

The spit tickled. He cramped his already sore neck muscles trying to wipe his lip dry. Thom deftly swiped a Kleenex from a box and dried his boss's mouth and chin.

"Officer Sachs," Thom said. "Welcome. A shining example of maturity. We aren't seeing much of *that* right at the moment."

She wasn't wearing her hat and her navy blouse was open at the collar. Her long red hair tumbled to her shoulders. Nobody'd have any trouble differentiating *that* hair under a comparison 'scope.

"Mel let me in," she said, nodding toward the stairs.

"Isn't it past your bedtime, Sachs?"

Thom tapped a shoulder. *Behave yourself*, the gesture meant.

"I was just at the federal building," she said to Sellitto.

"How are our tax dollars doing?"

"They've caught him."

"*What?*" Sellitto asked. "Just like that? Jesus. They know about it downtown?"

"Perkins called the mayor. The guy's a cabbie. He was born here but his father's Serbian. So they're thinking he's trying to get even with the UN, or something. Got a yellow sheet. Oh, and a history of mental problems too. Dellray and feebie SWAT're on their way there right now."

"How'd they do it?" Rhyme asked. "Betcha it was the fingerprint."

She nodded.

"I suspected that would figure prominently. And, tell me, how concerned were they about the next victim?"

"They're concerned," she said evenly. "But mostly they want to nail the unsub."

"Well, that's *their* nature. And let me guess. They're figuring they'll sweat the location of the vic out of him after they take him down."

"You got it."

"That may take some doing," Rhyme said. "I'll venture that opinion without the benefit of our Dr. Dobyns and the Behavioral mavens. So, a change of heart, Amelia? Why'd you come back?"

"Because whether Dellray collars him or not I don't think we have time to wait. To save the next vic, I mean."

"Oh, but we're dismantled, haven't you heard? Shut down, done gone outa business." Rhyme was looking in the dark computer screen, trying to see if his hair had stayed combed.

"You giving up?" she asked.

"Officer," Sellitto began, "even if we wanted to do somethin' we don't have any of the PE. That's the only link—"

"I've got it."

"What?"

"All of it. It's downstairs in the RRV."

The detective glanced out the window.

Sachs continued, "From the last scene. From all the scenes."

"You have it?" Rhyme asked. "How?"

But Sellitto was laughing. "She 'jacked it, Lincoln. Gawdamn!"

"Dellray doesn't need it," Sachs pointed out. "Except for the trial. They've got the unsub, we'll save the victim. Works out nice, hm?"

"But Mel Cooper just left."

"Naw, he's downstairs. I asked him to wait." Sachs crossed her arms. She glanced at the clock. After eleven. "We don't have much time," she repeated.

His eyes too were on the clock. Lord, he was tired. Thom was right; he'd been awake longer than in years. But, he was surprised—no, *shocked*—to find, that, while he might have been furious or embarrassed or stabbed with heartless frustration today, the passing minutes had not lain like hot, unbearable weights on his soul. As they had for the past three and a half years.

"Well, church mice in heaven." Rhyme barked a laugh. "Thom?

Thom! We need coffee. On the double. Sachs, get those cello samples to the lab along with the Polaroid of the bit Mel lifted from the veal bone. I want a polarization-comparison report in an hour. And none of this 'most probably' crap. I want an answer—*which* grocery chain did our unsub buy the veal bone at. And get that little shadow of yours back here, Lon. The one named after the baseball player."

The black vans sped through side streets.

This was a more circuitous route to the perp's location but Dellray knew what he was doing; anti-terror operations were supposed to avoid major city streets, which were often monitored by accomplices. Dellray, in the back of the lead van, tightened the Velcro strap on the body armor. They were less than ten minutes away.

He looked at the failing apartments, the trash-filled lots as they sped along. The last time he'd been in this decrepit neighborhood he'd been Rastafarian Peter Haile Thomas from Queens. He'd bought 137 pounds of cocaine from a shriveled little Puerto Rican, who decided at the last minute to 'jack his buyer. He took Dellray's buy-and-bust money and aimed a gun at Dellray's groin, pulling the trigger as calmly as if he were picking vegetables at the A&P. Click, click, click. Misfire. Toby Dolittle and the backup team took the fucker and his minders down before the scumbag found his other piece, leaving one shook-up Dellray to reflect on the irony of nearly getting killed because the perp truly bought the agent's performance—that he was a dealer not a cop.

"ETA, four minutes," the driver called.

For some reason Dellray's thoughts flipped to Lincoln Rhyme. He regretted he'd been such a shit when he took over the case. But there hadn't been much choice. Sellitto was a bulldog and Polling was a psycho—though Dellray could handle them. Rhyme was the one who made him uneasy. Sharp as a razor (hell, it *had* been his team that found Pietrs's print, even if they didn't jump on it as fast as they should've). In the old days, before his accident, you couldn't beat Rhyme if he didn't want to get beat. And you couldn't fool him either.

Now, Rhyme was a busted toy. It was a sad thing what could happen to a man, how you could die and still be alive. Dellray had walked into his room—his *bedroom*, no less—and hit him hard. Harder than he needed to.

Maybe he'd call. He could—

"Show time," the driver called, and Dellray forgot all about Lincoln Rhyme.

The vans turned onto the street where Pietrs lived. Most of the other streets they'd passed had been filled with sweating residents, clutching beer bottles and cigarettes, hoping for a breath or two of cool air. But this one was dark, empty.

The vans cruised slowly to a stop. Two dozen agents climbed out, in black tactical outfits, carrying their H&Ks equipped with muzzle lights and laser sights. Two homeless men stared at them; one quickly hid his bottle of Colt 44 malt liquor under his shirt.

Dellray gazed at a window in Pietrs's building; it gave off a faint yellow glow.

The driver backed the first van into a shadowy parking space and whispered to Dellray, "It's Perkins." Tapping his headset. "He's got the director on the horn. They want to know who's leading the assault."

"I am," snapped the Chameleon. He turned to his team. "I want surveillance across the street and in the alleys. Snipers, there, there and there. An' I want ever'body in place fi' minutes ago. Are we all together on that?"

Down the stairs, the old wood creaking.

His arm around her, he guided the woman, half-conscious from the blow to her head, into the basement. At the foot of the stairs, he shoved her to the dirt floor and gazed down at her.

Esther . . .

Her eyes rose to meet his. Hopeless, begging. He didn't notice. All he saw was her body. He began to remove her clothing, the purple jogging outfit. It was unthinkable that a woman would actually go outside in this day and age wearing what was no more than, well, undergarments. He hadn't thought that Esther Weinraub was a whore. She'd been a working girl, stitching shirts, five for a penny.

The bone collector observed how her collarbone showed at her throat. And where some other man might glance over her breasts and dark areolae *he* stared at the indentation at the manubrium and the ribs blossoming from it like spider's legs.

"What're you doing?" she asked, groggy from the blow to her head.

The bone collector looked her over carefully but what he saw wasn't a young, anorectic woman, nose too broad, lips too full, with skin like dirty sand. He saw beneath those imperfections the perfect beauty of her *structure*.

He caressed her temple, stroked it gently. Don't let it be cracked, please. . . .

She coughed and her nostrils flared—the fumes *were* very strong down here though he hardly noticed them anymore.

"Don't hurt me again," she whispered, her head lolling. "Just don't hurt me. Please."

He took the knife from his pocket and bent down, cut her underwear off. She looked down at her naked body.

"You want that?" she said breathlessly. "Okay, you can fuck me. Okay."

The pleasure of the flesh, he thought . . . it just doesn't come close.

He pulled her to her feet and madly she pushed away from him and began stumbling toward a small doorway in the corner of the basement. Not running, not really trying to escape. Just sobbing, reaching out a hand, weaving toward the door.

The bone collector watched her, entranced by her slow, pathetic gait.

The doorway, which had once opened onto a coal chute, now led to a narrow tunnel that connected to the basement of the abandoned building next door.

Esther struggled to the metal door and pulled it open. She climbed inside.

It was no more than a minute later that he heard the wailing scream. Followed by a breathless, wrenching, "God, no, no, no . . ." Other words too, lost in her boiling howls of terror.

Then she was coming back through the tunnel, moving faster now, whipping her hands around her, as if she was trying to shake off what she'd just seen.

Come to me, Esther.

Stumbling over the dirt floor, sobbing.

Come to me.

Running straight into his patient, waiting arms, which wrapped around her. He squeezed the woman tight as a lover, felt that marvelous collarbone beneath his fingers, and slowly dragged the frantic woman back toward the tunnel doorway.

TWENTY

The phases of the moon, the leaf, the damp underwear, dirt. Their team was back in Rhyme's bedroom—all except Polling and Haumann; it was straining NYPD loyalty to bring captains in on what was, no two ways about it, an unauthorized operation.

"You G-C'd the liquid in the underwear, right, Mel?"

"Have to do it again. They shut us down before we got the results."

He blotted out a sample and injected it into the chromatograph. As he ran the machine Sachs jockeyed to look at the peaks and valleys of the profile appearing on the screen. Like a stock index. Rhyme realized she was standing close to him, as if she'd edged near when he wasn't looking. She spoke in a low voice. "I was . . ."

"Yes?"

"I was blunter than I meant to be. Before, I mean. I have a temper. I don't know where I got it from. But I have it."

"You were right," Rhyme said.

They easily held each other's eyes and Rhyme thought of the times he and Blaine had had serious discussions. As they talked they always focused on an object between them—one of the ceramic horses she collected, a book, a nearly empty bottle of Merlot or Chardonnay.

He said, "I work scenes differently than most criminalists. I needed somebody without any preconceived ideas. But I also needed somebody with a mind of her own."

The contradictory qualities we seek in that elusive perfect lover. Strength and vulnerability, in equal measures.

"When I talked to Commissioner Eckert," she said, "it was just to get my transfer through. That's all I wanted. It never occurred to me that word'd get back to the feds and they'd take the case away."

"I know that."

"I still let my temper go. I'm sorry for that."

"Don't backpedal, Sachs. I need somebody to tell me I'm a jerk when I act like one. Thom does. That's why I love him."

"Don't get sentimental on me, Lincoln," Thom called from across the room.

Rhyme continued, "Nobody else ever tells me to go to hell. They're always walking on eggshells. I hate it."

"It doesn't seem like there've been many people around here to say much of anything to you lately."

After a moment he said, "That's true."

On the screen of the chromatograph-spectrometer the peaks and valleys stopped moving and became one of nature's infinite signatures. Mel Cooper tapped on the computer keys and read the results. "Water, diesel oil, phosphate, sodium, trace minerals . . . No idea what it means."

What, Rhyme wondered, was the message? The underwear itself? The liquid? He said, "Let's move on. I want to see the dirt."

Sachs brought him the bag. It contained pinkish sand, laced with chunks of clay and pebbles.

"Bull's liver," he announced. "Rock-and-sand mixture. Found just above the bedrock in Manhattan. Sodium silicate mixed in?"

Cooper ran the chromatograph. "Yep. Plenty of it."

"Then we're looking for a downtown location within fifty yards of the water—" Rhyme laughed at the astonished gaze on Sachs's face. "It's not magic, Sachs. I've just done my homework, that's all. Contractors mix sodium silicate with bull's liver to stabilize the earth when they dig foundations in deep-bedrock areas near the water. That means it's got to be downtown. Now, let's take a look at the leaf."

She held up the bag.

"No clue what it is," Rhyme said. "I don't think I've ever seen one like that. Not in Manhattan."

"I've got a list of horticulture web sites," Cooper said, staring at his computer screen. "I'll do some surfing."

Rhyme himself had spent some time on-line, cruising the Internet. As it had with books, movies and posters, his interest in the cyberworld had eventually paled. Perhaps because so much of his own world was virtual, the net was, in the end, a forlorn place for Lincoln Rhyme.

Cooper's screen flicked and danced as he clicked on hyperlinks and disappeared deeper into the web. "I'm downloading some files. Should take ten, twenty minutes."

Rhyme said, "All right. The rest of the clues Sachs found . . . Not the planted ones. The others. They might tell us about where he's been. Let's look at our secret weapon, Mel."

"Secret weapon?" Sachs asked.

"The trace evidence."

Special Agent Fred Dellray had put together a ten-man entry operation. Two teams plus search and surveillance. The flak-jacketed agents stood in the bushes, sweating madly. Across the street, upstairs in an abandoned brownstone, the S&S team had their Big Ears and video infrareds trained on the perp's house.

The three snipers, with their big Remingtons strapped, loaded and locked, lay prone on rooftops. Their binoculared spotters crouched beside them like Lamaze coaches.

Dellray—wearing an FBI windbreaker and jeans instead of his Leprechaun-green outfit—listened through his clip-on earphone.

"Surveillance to Command. We've got infrared on the basement. Somebody moving down there."

"What'sa view like?" Dellray asked.

"No view. Windows're too dirty."

"He all by his humble self? Maybe got a vic with him?" Knowing somehow that Officer Sachs was probably right; that he'd already 'napped somebody else now.

"Can't tell. We've just got motion and heat."

Dellray had sent other officers around to the sides of the house. They reported in. "No sign of anyone on the first or second floor. Garage is locked."

"Snipers?" Dellray asked. "Report."

"Shooter One to Command. I've acquired on front door. Over."

The others were covering the hallway and a room on the first floor. "Loaded and locked," they radioed in.

Dellray drew his large automatic.

"Okay, we got paper," Dellray said. Meaning a warrant. They wouldn't have to knock. "Lessgo! Teams one and two, deploy, deploy, deploy."

The first team took out the front door with a battering ram while the second used the slightly more civilized approach of breaking in the back-door window and unlocking the dead bolt. They streamed inside, Dellray following the last of Team One's officers into the old, filthy house. The smell of rotting flesh was overwhelming and Dellray, no stranger to crime scenes, swallowed hard, struggling to keep from vomiting.

The second team secured the ground floor and then charged up the stairs toward the bedroom while the first sped down the basement stairs, boots thumping loudly on the old wood.

Dellray raced down into the foul-smelling basement. He heard a door being kicked in somewhere below and the shout of, "Don't move! Federal agents. Freeze, freeze, freeze!"

But when he reached the basement doorway he heard the same agent blurt in a very different tone, "What the hell's this? Oh, Jesus."

"Fuck," another one called. "That's gross."

"Shit in a flaming pile," Dellray spat out, choking, as he stepped inside. Swallowing hard at the vile smell.

The man's body lay on the floor, leaching black fluid. Throat cut. His dead, glazed eyes stared at the ceiling but his torso seemed to be moving—swelling and shifting. Dellray shuddered; he'd never developed much immunity to the sight of insect infestation. The number of bugs and worms suggested the vic'd been dead for at least three days.

"Why'd we get positive on the infrared?" one agent asked.

Dellray pointed out the rat and mouse teeth marks along the vic's bloated leg and side. "They're around here someplace. We interrupted dinner hour."

"So what happened? One of the vics get *him?*"

"Watcha talkin' about?" Dellray snapped.

"Isn't that him?"

"No, it's not *him*," Dellray exploded, gazing at one particular wound on the corpse.

One of the team was frowning. "Naw, Dellray. This's the guy. We got mug shots. That's Pietrs."

"Of course it's fucking Pietrs. But he ain't the unsub. Don'tcha get it?"

"No? What do you mean?"

It was all clear to him now. "Sumvabitch."

Dellray's phone chirped and made him jump. He flipped it open, listened for a minute. "She did *what?* Oh, like I really need this too. . . . No, we don't have the fucking perp in fucking custody."

He jammed the OFF button, pointed an angry finger at two SWAT agents. "You're coming with me."

"What's up, Dellray?"

"We gonna pay ourselves a visit. And what ain't we gonna be when we do it?" The agents looked at each other, frowning. But Dellray supplied the answer. "We ain't gonna be very nice at all."

Mel Cooper shook the contents of the envelopes out onto newsprint. Examined the dust with an eye loupe. "Well, there's the brick dust. And some other kind of stone. Marble, I think."

He put a sample on the slide and examined it under the compound 'scope. "Yep, marble. Rose-colored."

"Was there any marble at the stockyard tunnel? Where you found the German girl?"

"None," Sachs responded.

Cooper suggested it might have come from Monelle's residence hall when Unsub 823 grabbed her.

"No, I know the block the Deutsche Haus is in. It's just a converted East Village tenement. The best stone you'd find there'd be polished granite. Maybe, just maybe, it's a fleck of his hidey-hole. Anything notable about it?"

"Chisel marks," Cooper said, bending over the 'scope.

"Ah, good. How clean?"

"Not very. Ragged."

"So an old steam stonecutter?"

"Yes, I'd guess."

"Write, Thom," Rhyme instructed, nodding at the poster. "There's marble in his safe house. And it's old."

"But why do we care about his safe house?" Banks asked, looking at his watch. "The feds'll be there by now."

"You can never have too much information, Banks. Remember that. Now, what else've we got?"

"Another bit of the glove. That red leather. And what's this?" he asked Sachs, holding up a plastic bag containing a plug of wood.

"The sample of the aftershave. Where he brushed up against a post."

"Should I run an olfactory profile?" Cooper wondered.

"Let me smell it first," Rhyme said.

Sachs brought the bag over to him. Inside was a tiny disk of wood. She opened it up and he inhaled the air.

"Brut. How could you miss it? Thom, add that our man uses drugstore cologne."

Cooper announced, "Here's that other hair." The technician mounted it in a comparison 'scope. "Very similar to the one we found earlier. Probably the same source. Oh, hell, Lincoln, for you, I'll say it *is* the same. Brown."

"Are the ends cut or fractured naturally?"

"Cut."

"Good, we're closing in on hair color," Rhyme said.

Thom wrote *brown* just as Sellitto said, "Don't write that!"

"What?"

"Obviously it's not brown," Rhyme continued.

"I thought—"

"It's anything *but* brown. Blond, sandy, black, red . . ."

The detective explained, " 'S'an old trick. You go into an alley behind a barbershop, cop some hairs from the garbage. Drop 'em around the scene."

"Oh." Banks filed this somewhere in his enthusiastic brain.

Rhyme said, "Okay. The fiber."

Cooper mounted it in the polarizing 'scope. As he adjusted knobs he said, "Birefringence of .053."

Rhyme blurted, "Nylon 6. What's it look like, Mel?"

"Very coarse. Lobed cross-section. Light gray."

"Carpet."

"Right. I'll check the database." A moment later he looked up from the computer. "It's a Hampstead Textile 118B fiber."

Rhyme exhaled a disgusted sigh.

"What?" Sachs asked.

"The most common trunk liner used by U.S. automakers. Found in over two hundred different makes going back fifteen years. Hopeless . . . Mel, is there anything *on* the fiber? Use the SEM."

The tech cranked up the scanning electron microscope. The screen burst to life with an eerie blue-green glow. The strand of fiber looked like a huge rope.

"Got something here. Crystals. A lot of 'em. They use titanium dioxide to deluster shiny carpet. That might be it."

"Gas it. It's important."

"There's not enough here, Lincoln. I'd have to burn the whole fiber."

"So, burn it."

Sellitto said delicately, "Borrowing federal evidence is one thing. Destroying it? I don't know 'bout that, Lincoln. If there's a trial . . ."

"We have to."

"Oh, man," Banks said.

Sellitto nodded reluctantly and Cooper mounted the sample. The machine hissed. A moment later the screen flickered and columns appeared. "There, that's the long-chained polymer molecule. The nylon. But that small wave, that's something else. Chlorine, detergent . . . It's cleanser."

"Remember," Rhyme said, "the German girl said the car smelled clean. Find out what kind it is."

Cooper ran the information through a brand-name database. "Pfizer Chemicals makes it. It's sold under the name Tidi-Kleen by Baer Automotive Products in Teterboro."

"Perfect!" cried Lincoln Rhyme. "I know the company. They sell in bulk to fleets. Mostly rental-car companies. Our unsub's driving a rental."

"He wouldn't be crazy enough to drive a rental car to crime scenes, would he?" Banks asked.

"It's stolen," Rhyme muttered, as if the young man had asked what was two plus two. "And it'll have stolen tags on it. Is Emma still with us?"

"She's probably home by now."

"Wake her up and have her start canvassing Hertz, Avis, National, Budget for thefts."

"Will do," Sellitto said, though uneasily, perhaps smelling the faint stench of burned federal evidence wafting through the air.

"The footprints?" Sachs asked.

Rhyme looked over the electrostatic impressions she'd lifted.

"Unusual wear on the soles. See the rubbed-down portion on the outsides of each shoe at the ball of the foot?"

"Pigeon-toed?" Thom wondered aloud.

"Possibly but there's no corresponding heel wear, which you'd expect to see." Rhyme studied the prints. "What I think is, he's a reader."

"A reader?"

"Sit in a chair there," Rhyme said to Sachs. "And hunch over the table, pretend you're reading."

She sat, then looked up. "And?"

"Pretend you're turning pages."

She did, several times. Looked up again.

"Keep going. You're reading *War and Peace*."

The pages kept turning, her head was bowed. After a moment, without thinking, she crossed her ankles. The outside edges of her shoes were the only part that met the floor.

Rhyme pointed this out. "Put *that* in the profile, Thom. But add a question mark.

"Now let's look at the friction ridges."

Sachs said she didn't have the good fingerprint, the one they'd ID'd the unsub with. "It's still at the federal building."

But Rhyme wasn't interested in that print. It was the other one, the Kromekote Sachs had lifted from the German girl's skin, he wanted to look at.

"Not scannable," Cooper announced. "Isn't even C grade. I wouldn't give an opinion about this if I had to."

Rhyme said, "I'm not interested in identity. I'm interested in that line there." It was crescent-shaped and sat right in the middle of the pad of the finger.

"What is it?" Sachs asked.

"A scar, I think," Cooper said. "From an old cut. A bad one. Looks like it went all the way to the bone."

Rhyme thought back to other markings and defects he'd seen on skin over the years. In the days before jobs became mostly paper shuffling and computer keyboarding it was far easier to tell people's jobs by examining their hands: distorted finger pads from manual typewriters, punctures from sewing machines and cobbler's needles, indentations and ink stains from stenographers' and accountants' pens, paper cuts from printing presses, scars from die cutters, distinctive calluses from various types of manual labor. . . .

But a scar like this told them nothing.

Not yet at any rate. Not until they had a suspect whose hands they might examine.

"What else? The knee print. This is good. Give us an idea of what he's wearing. Hold it up, Sachs. Higher! Baggy slacks. It retained that deep crease there so it's natural fiber. In this weather, I'll bet cotton. Not wool. You don't see silk slacks much nowadays."

"Lightweight, not denim," Cooper said.

"Sports clothes," Rhyme concluded. "Add that to our profile, Thom."

Cooper looked back at the computer screen and typed some more. "No luck with the leaf. Doesn't match anything at the Smithsonian."

Rhyme stretched back into his pillow. How much time would they have? An hour? Two?

The moon. Dirt. Brine . . .

He glanced at Sachs who was standing by herself in the corner. Her head was down and her long red hair fell dramatically toward the floor. She was looking into an evidence bag, a frown on her face, lost in concentration. How many times had Rhyme himself stood in the same pose, trying to—

"A newspaper!" she cried, looking up. "Where's a newspaper?" Her eyes were frantic as she looked from table to table. "Today's paper?"

"What is it, Sachs?" Rhyme asked.

She grabbed *The New York Times* from Jerry Banks and leafed quickly through it.

"That liquid . . . in the underwear," she said to Rhyme. "Could it be salt water?"

"Salt water?" Cooper pored over the GC-MS chart. "Of course! Water and sodium and other minerals. And the oil, phosphates. It's polluted seawater."

Her eyes met Rhyme's and they said simultaneously, "High tide!"

She held up the paper, open to the weather map. It contained a phases-of-the-moon diagram identical to the one found at the scene. Below it was a tidal chart. "High tide's in forty minutes."

Rhyme's face curled in disgust. He was never angrier than when he was angry with himself. "He's going to drown the vic. They're under a pier downtown." He looked hopelessly at the map of Manhattan, with its miles of shoreline. "Sachs, time to play race-car driver again. You and Banks go west. Lon, why don't you take the East Side? Around the South Street Seaport. And Mel, figure out what the hell that leaf is!"

———

A fluke of wave slapped his sagging head.

William Everett opened his eyes and snorted the shivery water from his nose. It was icy cold and he felt his questionable heart stutter as it struggled to send warming blood through his body.

He almost fainted again, like when the son of a bitch'd broken his finger. Then he floated back to waking, his thoughts on his late wife—and for some reason, on their travels. They'd been to Giza. And to Guatemala. Nepal. Teheran (one week before the embassy takeover).

Their Southeast China Airlines plane had lost one of two engines an hour out of Beijing and Evelyn had lowered her head, the crash position, preparing to die and staring at an article in the in-flight magazine. It warned that drinking hot tea right after a meal was dangerous for you. She told him about it afterwards, at the Raffles bar in Singapore, and they'd laughed hysterically until tears came to their eyes.

Thinking of the kidnapper's cold eyes. His teeth, the bulky gloves.

Now, in this horrid wet tomb the unbearable pain rolled up his arm and into his jaw.

Broken finger or heart attack? he wondered.

Maybe a little of both.

Everett closed his eyes until the pain subsided. He looked around him. The chamber where he was handcuffed was beneath a rotting pier. A lip of wood dipped from the edge toward the churning water, which was about six inches below the bottom of the rim. Lights from boats on the river and the industrial sites of Jersey reflected through the narrow slit. The water was up to his neck now and although the roof of the pier was several feet above his head the cuffs were extended as far as they'd go.

The pain swept up from his finger again and Everett's head roared with the agony and dipped toward the water as he passed out. A noseful of water and the racking cough that followed revived him.

Then the moon tugged the plane of water slightly higher and with a sodden gulp the chamber was sealed off from the river outside. The room went dark. He was aware of the sounds of groaning waves and his own moaning from the pain.

He knew he was dead, knew he couldn't keep his head above the greasy surface for more than a few minutes. He closed his eyes, pressed his face against the slick, black column.

TWENTY-ONE

Ａll the way downtown, Sachs," Rhyme's voice clattered from the radio.

She punched the accelerator of the RRV, red lights flashing, as they screamed downtown along the West Side Highway. Ice-cool, she goosed the wagon up to eighty.

"Okay, whoa," said Jerry Banks.

Counting down. Twenty-third Street, Twentieth, the skidding jog at the Fourteenth Street garbage-barge dock. As they roared through the Village, the meatpacking district, a semi pulled out of a side street directly into her path. Instead of braking she nudged the wagon over the center curb like a steeplechaser, drawing breathless oaths from Banks and a wail from the air horn of the big White, which jackknifed spectacularly.

"Oops," said Amelia Sachs and swung back into the southbound lane. To Rhyme she added, "Say again. Missed that."

Rhyme's tinny voice popped through her earphones. "Downtown is all I can tell you. Until we figure out what the leaf means."

"We're coming up on Battery Park City."

"Twenty-five minutes to high tide," Banks called.

Maybe Dellray's team could get the exact location out of him. They could drag Mr. 823 into an alley somewhere with a bag of

UNSUB 823

Appearance	Residence	Vehicle	Other

• Caucasian male, slight build
• Dark clothing
• Old gloves, reddish kidskin
• Aftershave; to cover up other scent?
• Ski mask? Navy blue?
• Gloves are dark
• Aftershave = Brut
• Hair color not brown
• Deep scar, index finger
• Casual clothes
	• Prob. has safe house
	• Located near:
	    B'way & 82nd, ShopRite
	    B'way & 96th, Anderson Foods
	    Greenwich & Bank, ShopRite
	    2nd Ave., 72nd–73rd, Grocery World
	    Battery Park City, J&G's Emporium
	    1709 2nd Ave., Anderson Foods
	    34th & Lex., Food Warehouse
	    8th Ave. & 24th, ShopRite
	    Houston & Lafayette, ShopRite
	    6th Ave. & Houston, J&G's Emporium
	    Greenwich & Franklin, Grocery World
	• Old building, pink marble
		• Yellow Cab
		• Recent model sedan
		• Lt. gray, silver, beige
		• Rental car; prob. stolen
			• knows CS proc.
			• possibly has record
			• knows FR prints
			• gun = .32 Colt
			• Ties vics w/ unusual knots
			• "Old" appeals to him
			• Called one vic "Hanna"
			• Knows basic German
			• Underground appeals to him
			• Dual personalities
			• Maybe priest, soc. worker, counselor
			• Unusual wear on shoes, reads a lot?

apples. Nick had told her that was the way they talked perps into "cooperating." Whack 'em in the gut with a bag of fruit. Really painful. No marks. When she was growing up she wouldn't have thought cops did that. Now she knew different.

Banks tapped her shoulder. "There. A bunch of old piers."

Rotten wood, filthy. Spooky places.

They skidded to a stop and climbed out, running toward the water.

"You there, Rhyme?"

"Talk to me, Sachs. Where are you?"

"A pier just north of Battery Park City."

"I just heard from Lon, on the East Side. He hasn't found anything."

"It's hopeless," she said. "There're a dozen piers. Then the whole promenade . . . And the fireboat house and ferry docks and the pier at Battery Park . . . We need ESU."

"We don't *have* ESU, Sachs. They're not on our side anymore."

Twenty minutes to high tide.

Her eyes darted along the waterfront. Her shoulders sagged with helplessness. Hand on her weapon, she sprinted to the river, Jerry Banks not far behind.

———

"Get me *something* on that leaf, Mel. A guess, anything. Wing it."

Fidgeting, Cooper looked from the microscope to the computer screen.

Eight thousand varieties of leafy plants in Manhattan.

"It doesn't fit the cell structure of *anything*."

"It's old," Rhyme said. "How old?"

Cooper looked at the leaf again. "Mummified. I'd put it at a hundred years, little less maybe."

"What's gone extinct in the last hundred years?"

"Plants don't go extinct in an ecosystem like Manhattan. They always show up again."

A ping in Rhyme's mind. He was close to remembering something. He both loved and hated this feeling. He might grab the thought like a slow pop-up fly. Or it might vanish completely, leaving him with only the sting of lost inspiration.

Sixteen minutes to high tide.

What *was* the thought? He grappled with it, closed his eyes . . .

Pier, he was thinking. The vic's under a pier.

What about it? *Think!*

Pier . . . ships . . . unloading . . . cargo.

Unloading cargo!

His eyes snapped open. "Mel, is it a crop?"

"Oh, hell. I've been looking at general-horticulture pages, not cultivated crops." He typed for what seemed like hours.

"Well?"

"Hold on, hold on. Here's a list of the encoded binaries." He scanned it. "Alfalfa, barley, beets, corn, oats, tobacco . . ."

"Tobacco! Try that."

Cooper double clicked his mouse and the image slowly unfurled on the screen.

"That's it!"

"The World Trade Towers," Rhyme announced. "The land from there north used to be tobacco plantations. Thom, the research for my book—I want the map from the 1740s. And that modern map Bo Haumann was using for the asbestos-cleanup sites. Put them up there on the wall, next to each other."

The aide found the old map in Rhyme's files. He taped them both onto the wall near his bed. Crudely drawn, the older map showed the northern part of the settled city—a cluster on the lower portion of the isle—covered with plantations. There were three commercial wharves along the river, which was then called not the Hudson but the West River. Rhyme glanced at the recent map of the city. The farmland was gone of course, as were the original wharves, but the contemporary map showed an abandoned wharf in the exact location of one of the tobacco exporter's old piers.

Rhyme strained forward, struggling to see the street name it was near. He was about to shout for Thom to come hold the map closer when, from downstairs, he heard a loud snap and the door crashed inward. Glass shattered.

Thom started down the stairs.

"I want to see him." The terse voice filled the hallway.

"Just a—" the aide began.

"No. Not inaminute, not in a hour. But right. Fucking. Now."

"Mel," Rhyme whispered, "ditch the evidence, shut the systems down."

"But—"

"Do it!"

Rhyme shook his head violently, dislodging the headset microphone. It fell onto the side of the Clinitron. Footsteps pounded up the stairs.

Thom did the best he could to stall but the visitors were three federal agents and two of the three were holding large guns. Slowly they backed him up the stairs.

Bless him, Mel Cooper pulled apart a compound microscope in five seconds flat and was calmly replacing the components with meticulous care as the FBI crested the stairs and stormed into Rhyme's room. The evidence bags were stuffed under a table and covered with *National Geographic*s.

"Ah, Dellray," Rhyme asked. "Find our unsub, did you?"

"Why didn't you tell us?"

"Tell you what?"

"That the fingerprint was bogus."

"No one asked me."

"Bogus?" Cooper asked, mystified.

"Well, it was a real print," Rhyme said, as if it were obvious. "But it wasn't the unsub's. Our boy needed a taxi to catch his fish with. So he met—what *was* his name?"

"Victor Pietrs," Dellray muttered and gave the cabbie's history.

"Nice touch," Rhyme said with some genuine admiration. "Picked a Serb with a rap sheet and mental problems. Wonder how long he looked for a candidate. Anyway, 823 killed poor Mr. Pietrs and stole his cab. Cut off his finger. He kept it and figured if we were getting too close he'd leave a nice obvious print at a scene to throw us off. I guess it worked."

Rhyme glanced at the clock. Fourteen minutes left.

"How'd you know?" Dellray glanced at the maps on Rhyme's wall but, thank God, wasn't interested in them.

"The print showed signs of dehydration and shriveling. Bet the body was a mess. And you found it in the basement? Am I right? Where our boy likes to stow his victims."

Dellray ignored him and nosed around the room like a giant terrier. "Where you hidin' our evidence?"

"Evidence? I don't know what you're talking about. Say, did you break my door? Last time you walked in without knocking. Now you just kicked it in."

"You know, Lincoln, I was thinking of apologizing to you for before—"

"That's big of you, Fred."

"But now I'm a inch away from collaring your ass."

Rhyme glanced down at the microphone headset, dangling on the floor. He imagined Sachs's voice bleating from the earphones.

"Gimme that evidence, Rhyme. You don't realize what kind of pissy-bad trouble you're in."

"Thom," Rhyme asked slowly, "Agent Dellray startled me and I dropped my Walkman headset. Could you hook it on the bedframe?"

The aide didn't miss a beat. He rested the mike next to Rhyme's head, out of Dellray's sight.

"Thank you," Rhyme said to Thom. Then added, "You know, I haven't had my bath yet. I think it's about time, wouldn't you say?"

"I've been wondering when you were going to ask," said Thom, with the ability of a natural-born actor.

"Come in, Rhyme. For Christ's sake. Where are you?"

Then she heard a voice in her headset. Thom's. It sounded stilted, exaggerated. Something was wrong.

"I've got the new sponge," the voice said.

"Looks like a good one," Rhyme answered.

"Rhyme?" Sachs blurted. "What the hell's going on?"

"Cost seventeen dollars. It ought to be good. I'm going to turn you over."

More voices sounded through the earphone but she couldn't make them out.

Sachs and Banks were jogging along the waterfront, peering over the wharves into the gray-brown water of the Hudson. She motioned to Banks to stop, leaned away from the cramp below her breastbone, spit into the river. Tried to catch her breath.

Through the headset she heard: ". . . won't take long. You'll have to excuse us, gentlemen."

". . . we'll just wait, you don't mind."

"I do mind," Rhyme said. "Can't I get a little privacy here?"

"Rhyme, can you hear me?" Sachs called desperately. What the hell was he doing?

"Nup. No privacy for them that steal evidence."

Dellray! He was in Rhyme's room. Well, that's the end of it. The vic's as good as dead.

"I want that evidence," the agent barked.

"Well, what you're going to *get* is a panoramic view of a man taking a sponge bath, Dellray."

Banks started to speak but she waved him quiet.

Some muttered words she couldn't hear.

The agent's angry shout.

Then Rhyme's calm voice again. ". . . You know, Dellray, I used to be a swimmer. Swam every day."

"We've got less than ten minutes," Sachs whispered. The water lapped calmly. Two placid boats cruised past.

Dellray muttered something.

"I'd go down to the Hudson River and swim. It was a lot cleaner then. The water, I mean."

A garbled transmission. He was breaking up.

". . . old pier. My favorite one's gone now. Used to be the home of the Hudson Dusters. That gang, you ever hear of them?

In the 1890s. North of where Battery Park City is now. You look bored. Tired of looking at a crip's flabby ass? No? Suit yourself. That pier was between North Moore and Chambers. I'd dive in, swim around the piers . . ."

"North Moore and Chambers!" Sachs shouted. Spinning around. They'd missed it because they'd gone too far south. It was a quarter mile from where they were. She could see the brown scabby wood, a large drainpipe backing up with tidal water. How much time was left? Hardly any. There was no way they could save him.

She ripped the headset off and started sprinting to the car, Banks close behind.

"Can you swim?" she asked.

"Me? A lap or two at the Health and Racquet Club."

They'd never make it.

Sachs stopped suddenly, spun around in a fast circle, gazing at the deserted streets.

———

The water was nearly to his nose.

A small wave washed over William Everett's face just as he inhaled and the foul, salty liquid streamed into his throat. He began to choke, a deep, horrible sound. Racking. The water filled his lungs. He lost his grip on the pier piling and sank under the surface, stiffened and rose once more, then sank again.

No, Lord, no . . . please don't let—

He shook the cuffs, kicked hard, trying to get some play. As if some miracle might happen and his puny muscles could bend the huge bolt he was cuffed to.

Snorting water from his nose, swiping his head back and forth in panic. He cleared his lungs momentarily. Neck muscles on fire—as painful as his shattered finger—from bending his head back to find the faint layer of air just above his face.

He had a moment's respite.

Then another wave, slightly higher.

And that was it.

He couldn't fight anymore. Surrender. Join Evelyn, say good-bye . . .

And William Everett let go. He floated beneath the surface into the drecky water, full of junk and tendrils of seaweed.

Then jerked back in horror. No, no . . .

He was here. The kidnapper! He'd come back.

Everett kicked to the surface, sneezing more water, trying desperately to get away. The man shone a brilliant light into Everett's eyes and reached toward him with a knife.

No, no . . .

It wasn't enough to drown him, he had to slash him to death. Without thinking Everett kicked out toward him. But the kidnapper vanished under the water . . . and then, *snap*, Everett's hands were free.

The old man forgot his placid goodbyes and kicked like hell to the surface, sucking sour air through his nose and ripping the tape from his mouth. Gasping, spitting the foul water. His head banged solidly into the underside of the oak pier and he laughed out loud. "Oh, God, God, God . . ."

Then another face appeared . . . Also hooded, with another blindingly bright lamp attached, and Everett could just make out the NYFD emblem on the man's wetsuit. They weren't knives the men held but metal cutters. One of them thrust a bitter rubber mouthpiece between Everett's lips and he inhaled a dazzling breath of oxygen.

The diver slipped his arm around him and together they swam to the lip of the pier.

"Take a deep breath, we'll be out in a minute."

He filled his narrow lungs to bursting and, eyes closed, sailed with the diver deep into the water, lit eerily by the man's yellow light. It was a short but harrowing trip, straight down then up again through cloudy, flecked water. Once he slipped out of the diver's hands and they separated momentarily. But William Everett took the glitch in stride. After this evening, a solo swim in the choppy Hudson River was a piece of cake.

———

She hadn't planned on taking a cab. The airport bus would've been fine.

But Pammy was wired from too little sleep—they'd both been up since five that morning—and she was getting restless. The little girl needed to be in bed soon, tucked away with her blanket and her bottle of Hawaiian Punch. Besides, Carole herself couldn't wait to get to Manhattan—she was just a skinny Midwest gal who'd never been farther east than Ohio in all her forty-one years, and she was dying for her first look at the Big Apple.

Carole collected her luggage and they started toward the exit. She checked to make sure she had everything they'd left Kate and Eddie's house with that afternoon.

Pammy, Pooh, purse, blanket, suitcase, yellow knapsack.

Everything accounted for.

Her friends had warned her about the city. "They'll hustle you," Eddie'd said. "Purse snatchers, pickpockets."

"And don't play those card games on the street," maternal Kate had added.

"I don't play cards in my *living* room," Carole reminded her, laughing. "Why'm I going to start playing on the streets of Manhattan?"

But she appreciated their concern. After all, here she was, a widow with a three-year-old, heading to the toughest city on earth for the UN conference—more foreigners, hell, more *people* than she'd ever seen at one time.

Carole found a pay phone and called the residence hotel to check on their reservations. The night manager said the room was ready and waiting for them. He'd see them in forty-five minutes or so.

They walked through automatic doors and were socked breathless by the scalding summer air. Carole paused, looking around. Gripping Pammy firmly with one hand, the handle of the battered suitcase with the other. The heavy yellow knapsack was snug on her shoulder.

They joined the line of passengers waiting at the taxi starter's booth.

Carole glanced at a huge billboard across the highway. *Welcome U.N. Delegates!* it announced. The artwork was terrible, but she stared at it for a long moment; one of the men on the billboard looked like Ronnie.

For a time, after he died, two years ago, virtually everything reminded her of her handsome, crew-cut husband. She'd drive past McDonald's and remember that he liked Big Macs. Actors in movies who didn't look a thing like him might cock their heads the way he used to. She'd see a flyer for a lawn-mower sale and remember how much he loved to cut their tiny square of grass in Arlington Heights.

Then the tears would come. And she'd go back on Prozac or imipramine. She'd spend a week in bed. Reluctantly acquiesce in Kate's offer that she stay with her and Eddie for a night. Or a week. Or a month.

But no tears anymore. She was here to jump-start her life. The sorrow was behind her now.

Tossing her mass of dark-blond hair off her sweaty shoulders, Carole ushered Pammy forward and kicked the luggage ahead of them as the taxi queue moved up several places. She looked all around, trying to catch a glimpse of Manhattan. But she could see nothing except traffic and the tails of airplanes and a sea of people and cabs and cars. Steam rose like frantic ghosts from manholes and the night sky was black and yellow and hazy.

Well, she'd see the city soon enough, she guessed. She hoped that Pammy was old enough to keep her first memory of the sight.

"How do you like our adventure so far, honey?"

"Adventure. I like adventures. I want some 'Waiin Punch. Can I please have some?"

Please . . . That was new. The three-year-old was learning all the keys and buttons. Carole laughed. "We'll get you some soon."

Finally they got their cab. The trunk popped open and Carole dumped the luggage inside, slammed the lid. They climbed into the back seat and closed the door.

Pammy, Pooh, purse . . .

The driver asked, "Where to?" And Carole gave him the address of the Midtown Residence Hotel, shouting through the Plexiglas divider.

The driver pulled into traffic. Carole sat back and settled Pammy on her lap.

"Will we go past the UN?" she called.

But the man was concentrating on changing lanes and didn't hear her.

"I'm here for the conference," she explained. "The UN conference."

Still no answer.

She wondered if he had trouble with English. Kate had warned her that the taxi drivers in New York were all foreigners. ("Taking American jobs," Eddie grumbled. "But don't get me started on *that*.") She couldn't see him clearly through the scuffed divider.

Maybe he just doesn't want to talk.

They swung onto another highway—and, suddenly, there it was in front of her, the jagged skyline of the city. Brilliant. Like the crystals that Kate and Eddie collected. A huge cluster of blue and gold and silver buildings in the middle of the island and another cluster way to the left. It was bigger than anything Carole had ever seen in her life and for a moment the island seemed like a massive ship.

"Look, Pammy, that's where we're going. Is that beeaaautiful or what?"

A moment later, though, the view was cut off as the driver turned off the expressway and made a fast turn at the bottom of the ramp. Then they were moving through hot, deserted streets, lined with dark brick buildings.

Carole leaned forward. "Is this the right way to the city?"

Again, no answer.

She rapped hard on the Plexiglas. "Are you going the right way? Answer me. *Answer me!*"

"Mommy, what's wrong?" Pammy said and started to cry.

"Where are you going?" Carole shouted.

But the man just kept driving—leisurely, stopping at all the red lights, never going over the speed limit. And when he pulled into the deserted parking lot behind a dark, abandoned factory he made sure he signaled properly.

Oh no . . . no!

He pulled on a ski mask and climbed from the cab. Walking to the back, he reached for the door. But he hesitated and his hand dropped. He leaned forward, face against the window, and tapped on the glass. Once, twice, three times. Getting the attention of lizards in the reptile room at a zoo. He stared at the mother and daughter for a long moment before he opened the door.

TWENTY-TWO

How'd you do it, Sachs?"

Standing beside the pungent Hudson River, she spoke into her stalk mike. "I remembered seeing the fireboat station at Battery Park. They scrambled a couple divers and were at the pier in about three minutes. Man, you should've seen that boat move! I want to try one of those someday."

Rhyme explained to her about the fingerless cabbie.

"Son of a bitch!" she said, clicking her tongue in disgust. "The weasel tricked us all."

"Not all of us," Rhyme reminded her coyly.

"So Dellray knows I boosted the evidence. Is he looking for me?"

"He said he was heading back to the federal building. Probably to decide which one of us to collar first. How's the scene there, Sachs?"

"Pretty bad," she reported. "He parked on gravel—"

"So no footprints."

"But it's worse than that. The tide backed out of this big drainpipe and where he parked's underwater."

"Hell," Rhyme muttered. "No trace, no prints, no nothing. How's the vic?"

"Not so good. Exposure, broken finger. He's had heart problems. They're going to keep him in the hospital for a day or two."

"Can he tell us anything?"

Sachs walked over to Banks, who was interviewing William Everett.

"He wasn't big," the man said matter-of-factly, carefully examining the splint the medic was putting on his hand. "And he wasn't really strong, not a muscle man. But he was stronger'n me. I grabbed him and he just pulled my hands away."

"Description?" Banks asked.

Everett recounted the dark clothes and ski mask. That was all he could remember.

"One thing I should tell you," Everett held up his bandaged hand. "He's got a mean streak. I grabbed him, like I said. I wasn't thinking—I just panicked. But he got real mad. That's when he busted my finger."

"Retaliation, hm?" Banks asked.

"I guess. But that's not the strange part."

"No?"

"The strange part is he listened to it."

The young detective had stopped writing. Looked at Sachs.

"He held my hand against his ear, real tight, and bent the finger until it broke. Like he was listening. And liking it."

"Did you hear that, Rhyme?"

"Yes. Thom's added it to our profile. I don't know what it means, though. We'll have to think about it."

"Any sign of the planted PE?"

"Not yet."

"Grid it, Sachs. Oh, and get the vic's—"

"Clothes? I've already asked him. I—Rhyme, you all right?" She heard a fit of coughing.

The transmission was shut off momentarily. He came back on a moment later. "You there, Rhyme? Everything okay?"

"Fine," he said quickly. "Get going. Walk the grid."

She surveyed the scene, lit starkly by the ESU halogens. It was so frustrating. He'd *been* here. He'd walked on the gravel just a few feet away. But whatever PE he'd inadvertently left behind was lying inches below the surface of the dim water. She covered the ground slowly. Back and forth.

"I can't see *anything*. The clues might've been washed away."

"No, he's too smart not to've taken the tide into account. They'll be on dry land somewhere."

"I've got an idea," she said suddenly. "Come on down here."

"What?"

"Work the scene with me, Rhyme."

Silence.

"Rhyme, did you hear me?"

"Are you talking to me?" he asked.

"You *look* like De Niro. You can't act as good as De Niro. You know? That scene from *Taxi Driver?*"

Rhyme didn't laugh. He said, "The line's 'Are you looking at me?' Not 'talking to me.' "

Sachs continued, unfazed, "Come on down. Work the scene with me."

"I'll spread my wings. No, better yet, I'll project myself there. Telepathy, you know."

"Quit joking. I'm serious."

"I—"

"We need you. I can't find the planted clues."

"But they'll be there. You just have to try a little harder."

"I've walked the entire grid twice."

"Then you've defined the perimeter too narrowly. Add another few feet and keep going. Eight twenty-three's not finished yet, not by a long shot."

"You're changing the subject. Come on down and help me."

"How?" Rhyme asked. "How'm I supposed to do that?"

"I had a friend who was challenged," she began. "And he—"

"You mean he was a *crip*," Rhyme corrected. Softly but firmly.

She continued, "His aide'd put him into this fancy wheelchair every morning and he drove himself all over the place. To the movies, to—"

"Those chairs ..." Rhyme's voice sounded hollow. "They don't work for me."

She stopped speaking.

He continued, "The problem's how I was injured. It'd be dan-

gerous for me to be in a wheelchair. It could"—he hesitated—
"make things worse."

"I'm sorry. I didn't know."

After a moment he said, "Of course you didn't."

Blew that one. Oh, boy. Brother . . .

But Rhyme didn't seem any the worse for her faux pas. His
voice was smooth, unemotional. "Listen, you've got to get on
with the search. Our unsub's making it trickier. But it won't be
impossible. . . . Here's an idea. He's the underground man, right?
Maybe he buried them."

She looked over the scene.

Maybe there . . . She saw a mound of earth and leaves in a
patch of tall grass near the gravel. It didn't look right; the mound
seemed too assembled.

Sachs crouched beside it, lowered her head and, using the pencils, began to clear away leaves.

She turned her face slightly to the left and found she was staring at a rearing head, bared fangs. . . .

"Jesus Lord," she shouted, stumbling backwards, falling hard
on her butt, scrambling to draw her weapon.

No . . .

Rhyme shouted, "You all right?"

Sachs drew a target and tried to steady the gun with very
unsteady hands. Jerry Banks came running up, his own Glock
drawn. He stopped. Sachs climbed to her feet, looking at what
was in front of them.

"Man," Banks whispered.

"It's a snake—well, a snake's skeleton," Sachs told Rhyme. "A
rattlesnake. Fuck." Holstered the Glock. "It's mounted on a board."

"A snake? Interesting." Rhyme sounded intrigued.

"Yeah, real interesting," she muttered. She pulled on latex
gloves and lifted the coiled bones. She turned it over. " 'Metamorphosis.' "

"What?"

"A label on the bottom. The name of the store it came from,
I'd guess. 604 Broadway."

Rhyme said, "I'll have the Hardy Boys check it out. What've we got? Tell me the clues."

They were underneath the snake. In a Baggie. Her heart pounded as she crouched down over the bag.

"A book of matches," she said.

"Okay, maybe he's thinking arson. Anything printed on them?"

"Nope. But there's a smear of something. Like Vaseline. Only stinky."

"Good, Sachs—always smell evidence you're not sure about. Only be more precise."

She bent close. "Yuck."

"That's not precise."

"Sulfur maybe."

"Could be nitrate-based. Explosive. Tovex. Is it blue?"

"No, it's milky clear."

"Even if it could go bang I imagine it's a secondary explosive. They're the stable ones. Anything else?"

"Another scrap of paper. Something on it."

"What, Sachs? His name, his address, e-mail handle?"

"Looks like it's from a magazine. I can see a small black-and-white photo. Looks like part of a building but you can't see which one. And underneath that, all you can read is a date. May 20, 1906."

"Five, twenty, oh-six. I wonder if it's a code. Or an address. I'll have to think about it. Anything else?"

"Nope."

She heard him sigh. "All right, come on back, Sachs. What time is it? My God, almost one a.m. I haven't been up this late in years. Come on back and let's see what we have."

Of all the neighborhoods in Manhattan, the Lower East Side has remained the most unchanged over the course of the city's history.

Much of it's gone of course: The rolling pastoral fields. The solid mansions of John Hancock and early government luminaries.

Der Kolek, the large freshwater lake (its Dutch name eventually corrupted to "The Collect," which more accurately described the grossly polluted pond). The notorious Five Points neighborhood—in the early 1800s the most dangerous square mile on earth—where a single tenement, like the decrepit Gates of Hell, might be the site of two or three hundred murders every year.

But thousands of the old buildings remained—tenements from the nineteenth century and Colonial frame houses and Federal brick townhomes from the prior one, Baroque meeting halls, several of the Egyptian-style public buildings constructed by order of the regally corrupt Congressman Fernando Wood. Some were abandoned, their facades overgrown with weeds and floors cracked by persistent saplings. But many were still in use; this had been the land of Tammany Hall iniquity, of pushcarts and sweatshops, of the Henry Street Settlement house, Minsky's burlesque and the notorious Yiddish Gomorra—the Jewish Mafia. A neighborhood that gives birth to institutions like these does not die easily.

It was toward this neighborhood that the bone collector now piloted the taxi containing the thin woman and her young daughter.

Observing that the constabulary was on to him, James Schneider went once again to ground like the serpent that he was, seeking accommodations—it is speculated—in the cellars of the city's many tenant-houses (which the reader may perchance recognize as the still-prevalent "tenements"). And so he remained, quiescent for some months.

As he drove home, the bone collector saw around him not the Manhattan of the 1990s—the Korean delis, the dank bagel shops, the X-rated-video stores, the empty clothing boutiques—but a dreamy world of bowler-clad men, women in rustling crinoline, hems and cuffs filthy with street refuse. Hordes of buggies and wagons, the air filled with the sometimes pleasant, sometimes repulsive scent of methane.

But such was the foul, indefatigable drive within him to start his collection anew that he was soon forced from his lair to waylay yet another good citizen;—this, a young man newly arrived in town to attend university.

Driving through the notorious Eighteenth Ward, once the home of nearly fifty thousand people crammed into a thousand decrepit tenements. When most people thought of the nineteenth century they thought in sepia—because of old photographs. But this was wrong. Old Manhattan was the color of stone. With choking industrial smoke, paint prohibitively expensive and dim lighting, the city was many shades of gray and yellow.

Schneider snuck up behind the fellow and was about to strike when Fortune's conscience, at last, cried out. Two constables chanced upon the assault. They recognized Schneider and gave chase. The killer fled east, across that engineering marvel, the Manhattan Bridge, completed in 1909, two years before these events. But he stopped halfway across, seeing that three constables were approaching from Brooklyn, having heard the alarm raised by the whistles and pistol reports of their confederates from Manhattan.

Schneider, unarmed, as chance would have it, climbed onto the railing of the bridge as he was surrounded by the law. He shouted maniacal diatribes against the constables, condemning them for having ruined his life. His words grew ever madder. As the constabulary moved closer, he leapt from the rail into the River. A week later a pilot discovered his body on the shore of Welfare Island, near Hell Gate. There was little left, for the crabs and turtles had been diligently working to reduce Schneider to the very bone which he, in his madness, cherished.

He turned the taxi onto his deserted cobblestoned street, East Van Brevoort, and paused in front of the building. He checked the two filthy strings he'd run low across the doors to make certain that no one had entered. A sudden motion startled him and he heard the guttural snarling of the dogs again, their eyes yellow, teeth brown, bodies dotted with scars and sores. His hand strayed to his pistol but they suddenly turned and, yelping, charged after a cat or rat in the alley.

He saw no one on the hot sidewalks and opened the padlock securing the carriage-house door then climbed back inside the car and drove into the garage, parked beside his Taurus.

After the villain's death his effects were secured and perused by detectives. His diary showed that he had murdered eight good citizens of the city. Nor was he above grave robbery, for it was ascertained from his pages (if his claims be true) that he had violated several holy resting places in cemeteries around the city. None of his victims had accorded him the least affront;—nay, most were upstanding citizens, industrious and innocent. And yet he felt not a modicum of guilt. Indeed, he seems to have labored under the mad delusion that he was doing his victims a favor.

He paused, wiped sweat from his mouth. The ski mask itched. He dragged the woman and her daughter out of the trunk and through the garage. She was strong and fought hard. At last he managed to get the cuffs on them.

"You prick!" she howled. "Don't you dare touch my daughter. You touch her and I'll kill you."

He gripped her hard around the chest and taped her mouth. Then he did the little girl's too.

"Flesh withers and can be weak,"—(the villain wrote in his ruthless yet steady hand)—"Bone is the strongest aspect of the body. As old as we may be in the flesh, we are always young in the bone. It is a noble goal I had, and it is beyond me why any-one might quarrel with it. I did a kindness to them all. They are immortal now. I freed them. I took them down to the bone."

He dragged them into the basement and pushed the woman down hard on the floor, her daughter beside her. Tied their cuffs to the wall with clothesline. Then returned upstairs.

He lifted her yellow knapsack from the back of the cab, the suitcases from the trunk, and pushed through a bolt-studded wooden door into the main room of the building. He was about to toss them into a corner but found that, for some reason, he was curious about these particular captives. He sat down in front of one of the murals—a painting of a butcher, placidly holding a knife in one hand, a slab of beef in the other.

He examined the luggage tag. Carole Ganz. Carole with an *E.* Why the extra letter? he wondered. The suitcase contained nothing but clothes. He started through the knapsack. He found the cash right away. There must have been four or five thousand. He put it back in the zippered compartment.

There were a dozen child's toys: a doll, a tin of watercolors, a package of modeling clay, a Mr. Potato Head kit. There were also an expensive Discman, a half-dozen CDs and a Sony travel clock radio.

He looked through some pictures. Photos of Carole and her girl. In most of the pictures the woman seemed very somber. In a few others, she seemed happier. There were no photos of Carole and her husband even though she wore a wedding ring. Many were of the mother and daughter with a couple—a heavyset woman wearing one of those old granny dresses and a bearded, balding man in a flannel shirt.

For a long time the bone collector gazed at a portrait of the little girl.

The fate of poor Maggie O'Connor, the young slip of a girl, merely eight years of age, was particularly sad. It was her misfortune, the police speculate, that she stumbled across the path of James Schneider as he was disposing of one of his victims.

The girl, a resident of the notorious "Hell's Kitchen," had gone out to pluck horsehairs from one of the many dead animals found in that impoverished part of the city. It was the custom of youngsters to wind tail-hairs into bracelets and rings—the only trinkets such urchins might have to adorn themselves with.

Skin and bone, skin and bone.

He propped the photo on the mantelpiece, beside the small pile of bones he'd been working on that morning and some that he'd stolen from the store where he'd found the snake.

It is surmised that Schneider found young Maggie near his lair, witnessing the macabre spectacle of his murdering one of his victims. Whether he dispatched her quickly or slowly we cannot guess. But unlike his other victims, whose remains were ultimately discovered,—of frail, becurled Maggie O'Connor, nought was ever found.

The bone collector walked downstairs.

He ripped the tape off the mother's mouth and the woman gasped for air, eyed him with cold fury. "What do you want?" she rasped. *"What?"*

She wasn't as thin as Esther but, thank God, she was nothing at all like fat Hanna Goldschmidt. He could see so *much* of her soul. The narrow mandible, the clavicle. And, through the thin blue skirt, the hint of the innominate bone—a fusion of the ilium, the ischium, the pubis. Names like Roman gods'.

The little girl squirmed. He leaned forward and placed his hand on her head. Skulls don't grow from a single piece of bone but from eight separate ones, and the crown rises up like the triangular slabs of the Astrodome roof. He touched the girl's occipital bone, the parietal bones of the cap of the skull. And two of his favorites, the sensuous bones around the eye sockets—the sphenoid and the ethmoid.

"Stop it!" Carole shook her head, furious. "Keep away from her."

"Shhhh," he said, holding his gloved finger to his lips. He looked at the little girl, who cried and pressed close to her mother.

"Maggie O'Connor," he cooed, looking at the shape of the girl's face. "My little Maggie."

The woman glared at him.

"You were in the wrong place at the wrong time, child. What did you see me do?"

Young in the bone.

"What are you talking about?" Carole whispered. He turned his attention to her.

The bone collector had always wondered about Maggie O'Connor's mother.

"Where's your husband?"

"He's dead," she spat out. Then glanced at the little girl and said more softly, "He was killed two years ago. Look, just let my daughter go. She can't tell them anything about you. Are you . . . listening to me? What are you doing?"

He gripped Carole's hands and lifted them.

He fondled the metacarpals of the wrists. The phalanges—the tiny fingers. Squeezing the bones.

"No, don't do that. I don't like that. Please!" Her voice crackled with panic.

He felt out of control and didn't like the sensation one bit. If he was going to succeed here, with the victims, with his plans, he had to fight down the encroaching lust—the madness was driving him further and further into the past, confusing the now with the then.

Before and after . . .

He needed all of his intelligence and craftiness to finish what he'd started.

And yet . . . yet . . .

She was *so* thin, she was so taut. He closed his eyes and imagined how a knife blade scraping over her tibia would sing like the bowing of an old violin.

His breathing was fast, he was sweating rivers.

When finally he opened his eyes he found he was looking at her sandals. He didn't have many foot bones in good condition. The homeless people he'd been preying on in the past months . . . well, they'd suffered from rickets and osteoporosis, their toes were impacted by badly fitting shoes.

"I'll make a deal with you," he heard himself saying.

She looked down at her daughter. Wriggled closer to her.

"I'll make a deal. I'll let you go if you let me do something."

"What?" Carole whispered.

"Let me take your skin off."

She blinked.

He whispered, "Let me. Please? A foot. Just one of your feet. If you do that I'll let you go."

"What . . . ?"

"Down to the bone."

She gazed at him with horror. Swallowed.

What would it matter? he thought. She was so nearly there anyway, so thin, so angular. Yes, there was something different about her—different from the other victims.

He put the pistol away and took the knife out of his pocket. Opened it with a startling click.

She didn't move, her eyes slid to the little girl. Back to him.

"You'll let us go?"

He nodded. "You haven't seen my face. You don't know where this place is."

A long moment. She stared around her at the basement. She muttered a word. A name, he thought. Ron or Rob.

And with her eyes firmly on his, she extended her legs

and pushed her feet toward him. He slipped her shoe off the right foot.

He took her toes. Kneaded the fragile twigs.

She leaned back, the cables of her tendons rising beautifully from her neck. Her eyes squeezed shut. He caressed her skin with the blade.

A firm grip on the knife.

She closed her eyes, inhaled and gave a faint whimper. "Go ahead," she whispered. And turned the girl's face away. Hugged her tightly.

The bone collector imagined her in a Victorian outfit, crinoline and black lace. He saw the three of them, sitting together at Delmonico's or strolling down Fifth Avenue. He saw little Maggie with them, dressed in frothy lace, rolling a hoop with a stick as they walked over the Canal bridge.

Then and now . . .

He nestled the stained blade in the arch of her foot.

"Mommy!" the girl screamed.

Something popped within him. For a moment he was overwhelmed with revulsion at what he was doing. At himself.

No! He couldn't do it. Not to *her.* Esther or Hanna, yes. Or the next one. But not her.

The bone collector shook his head sadly and touched her cheekbone with the back of his hand. He slapped the tape over Carole's mouth again and cut the cord binding her feet.

"Come on," he muttered.

She struggled fiercely but he gripped her head hard and pinched her nostrils till she passed out. Then he hefted her over his shoulder and started up the stairs, carefully lifting the bag that sat nearby. Very carefully. It was not the sort of thing he wanted to drop. Up the stairs. Pausing only once, to look at young, curly-haired Maggie O'Connor, sitting in the dirt, looking hopelessly up at him.

TWENTY-THREE

He snagged them both in front of Rhyme's townhouse.

Quick as the coiled snake that Jerry Banks was carrying at his side like a souvenir from Santa Fe.

Dellray and two agents stepped from an alley. He announced casually, "Got some news, honey dear. You're under arrest for the theft of evidence under custodial care of the U.S. government."

Lincoln Rhyme had been wrong. Dellray hadn't made it to the federal building after all. He'd been staking out Rhyme's digs.

Banks rolled his eyes. "Chill out, Dellray. We saved the vic."

"And a mighty good thing you did, sonny. If you hadn't we were gonna bring you up on homicide."

"But *we* saved 'im," Sachs said. "And you didn't."

"Thanks for that snappy recap, officer. Hold your wrists out."

"This is bullshit."

"Cuff this young lady," the Chameleon said dramatically to a burly agent beside him.

She began, "We found more clues, Agent Dellray. He's got another one. And I don't know how much time we have."

"Oh, and invite that thayre boy to ouah party too." Dellray nodded to Banks, who turned to the woman FBI agent approaching him and seemed to be thinking of decking her.

UNSUB 823

Appearance	Residence	Vehicle	Other
• Caucasian male, slight build • Dark clothing • Old gloves, reddish kidskin • Aftershave; to cover up other scent? • Ski mask? Navy blue? • Gloves are dark • Aftershave = Brut • Hair color not brown • Deep scar, index finger • Casual clothes	• Prob. has safe house • Located near: B'way & 82nd, ShopRite B'way & 96th, Anderson Foods Greenwich & Bank, ShopRite 2nd Ave., 72nd–73rd, Grocery World Battery Park City, J&G's Emporium 1709 2nd Ave., Anderson Foods 34th & Lex., Food Warehouse 8th Ave. & 24th, ShopRite Houston & Lafayette, ShopRite 6th Ave. & Houston, J&G's Emporium Greenwich & Franklin, Grocery World • Old building, pink marble	• Yellow Cab • Recent model sedan • Lt. gray, silver, beige • Rental car; prob. stolen	• knows CS proc. • possibly has record • knows FR prints • gun = .32 Colt • Ties vics w/ unusual knots • "Old" appeals to him • Called one vic "Hanna" • Knows basic German • Underground appeals to him • Dual personalities • Maybe priest, soc. worker, counselor • Unusual wear on shoes, reads a lot? • Listened as he broke vic's finger

Dellray said a cheerful, "No, no, no. You don' wanna."

Banks reluctantly held out his hands.

Sachs, angry, offered the agent a cold smile. "How was your trip to Morningside Heights?"

"He still killed that cabbie. Our PERT boys're crawling over that house now like beetles on dung."

"And that's all they're going to find," Sachs said. "This unsub knows crime scenes better than you and I do."

"Downtown," Dellray announced, nodding at Sachs, who winced as the cuffs ratcheted tight around her wrists.

"We can save the next one too. If you—"

"You know what you got, Officer Sachs? Take a guess. You gotchaself the right to *re*-main silent. You got—"

"All right," the voice called from behind them. Sachs looked around and saw Jim Polling striding along the sidewalk. His slacks and dark sports shirt were rumpled. It looked as if he'd napped in them, though his bleary face suggested he hadn't slept in days. You could see a day's growth of beard and his sandy hair was an unruly mess.

Dellray blinked uneasily though it wasn't the cop he was troubled by but the tall physique of the U.S. attorney for the Southern District behind Polling. And bringing up the rear, SAC Perkins.

"Okay, Fred. Let 'em go." From the U.S. attorney.

In the modulated baritone of an FM disk jockey the Chameleon said, "She stole evidence, sir. She—"

"I just expedited some forensic analysis," Sachs said.

"Listen—" Dellray began.

"Nope," Polling said, completely in control now. No temper tantrums. "No, we're *not* listening." He turned to Sachs and barked, "But don't you try to be funny."

"Nosir. Sorry, sir."

The U.S. attorney said to Dellray. "Fred, you made a judgment call and it went south. Facts of life."

"It was a good lead," Dellray said.

"Well, we're changing the direction of the investigation," the U.S. attorney continued.

SAC Perkins said, "We've been conferencing with the director and with Behavioral. We've decided that Detectives Rhyme and Sellitto's positioning is the approach to pursue."

"But my snitch was clear that *something* was going down at the airport. That's not the sorta thing he'd be wishy about."

"It comes down to this, Fred," the U.S. attorney said bluntly. "*Whatever* the fucker's up to, it was Rhyme's team that saved the vics."

Dellray's lengthy fingers folded into an uncertain fist, opened again. "I appreciate that fact, sir. But—"

"Agent Dellray, this's a decision that has already been made."

The glossy black face—so energized at the federal building when he was marshaling his troops—was now somber, reserved. For the moment, the hipster was gone. "Yessir."

"This most recent hostage would've died if Detective Sachs here hadn't intervened," the U.S. attorney said.

"That'd be *Officer* Sachs," she corrected. "And it was mostly Lincoln Rhyme. I was his legman. So to speak."

"The case is going back to the city," the U.S. attorney announced. "The Bureau's A-T is to continue to handle terrorist-informant liaison but with reduced manpower. Anything they learn should be conveyed to Detectives Sellitto and Rhyme. Dellray, you're gonna put bodies at their disposal for any search-and-surveillance or hostage-rescue effort. Or anything else they might need. Got that?"

"Yessir."

"Good. You want to remove those handcuffs from these officers now?"

Dellray placidly unlocked the cuffs and slipped them into his pocket. He walked to a large van parked nearby. As Sachs picked up the evidence bag she saw him standing by himself at the edge of a pool of streetlight, his index finger lifted, stroking the cigarette behind his ear. She wasted a moment's sympathy on the feebie then turned and ran up the stairs, two at a time, after Jerry Banks and his rattlesnake.

———

"I have it figured out. Well, almost."

Sachs had just walked into Rhyme's room when he made this pronouncement. He was quite pleased with himself.

"Everything except the rattler and the glop."

She delivered the new evidence to Mel Cooper. The room had been transformed yet again and the tables were covered with new vials and beakers and pillboxes and lab equipment and boxes. It wasn't much compared to the feds' headquarters but, to Amelia Sachs, it felt oddly like home.

"Tell me," she said.

"Tomorrow's Sunday . . . pardon me—today's Sunday. He's going to burn down a church."

"How do you figure?"

"The date."

"On the scrap of paper? What's it mean?"

"You ever hear of the anarchists?"

"Little Russians in trench coats carrying around those bombs that look like bowling balls?" Banks said.

"From the man who reads picture books," Rhyme commented dryly. "Your Saturday-morning-cartoon roots are showing, Banks. Anarchism was an old social movement calling for the abolition of government. One anarchist, Enrico Malatesta—his shtick was 'propaganda by deed.' Translated that means murder and mayhem. One of his followers, an American named Eugene Lockworthy, lived in New York. One Sunday morning he bolted the doors of a church on the Upper East Side just after the service began and set the place on fire. Killed eighteen parishioners."

"And that happened on May 20, 1906?" Sachs asked.

"Yep."

"I'm not going to ask how you figured that out."

Rhyme shrugged. "Obvious. Our unsub likes history, right? He gave us some matches so he's telling us he's planning arson. I just thought back to the city's famous fires—the Triangle Shirt-waist, Crystal Palace, the *General Slocum* excursion boat . . . I checked the dates—May twentieth was the First Methodist Church fire."

Sachs asked, "But where? Same location as that church?"

"Doubt it," Sellitto said. "There's a commercial high-rise there now. Eight twenty-three doesn't like new places. I've got a couple men on it just in case but we're sure he's going for a church."

"And we think," Rhyme added, "that he's going to wait till a service starts."

"Why?"

"For one thing, that's what Lockworthy did," Sellitto continued. "Also, we were thinking 'bout what Terry Dobyns was telling us—upping the ante. Going for multiple vics."

"So we've got a little more time. Until the service starts."

Rhyme looked up at the ceiling. "Now, how many churches are there in Manhattan?"

"Hundreds."

"That was rhetorical, Banks. I mean—let's keep looking over the clues. He'll have to narrow it down some."

Footsteps on the stair.

It was the twins once again.

"We passed Fred Dellray outside."

"He wasn't the least bit cordial."

"Or happy."

"Whoa, look at that." Saul—Rhyme believed it was Saul; he'd forgotten who had the freckles—nodded at the snake. "I've seen more of those in one night than I ever want to again."

"Snakes?" Rhyme asked.

"We were at Metamorphosis. It's a—"

"—very spooky place. Met the owner there. Weird guy. As you may've guessed."

"Long, long beard. Wish we hadn't gone at night," Bedding continued.

"They sell taxidermied bats and insects. You wouldn't believe some of the insects—"

"Five inches long."

"—and critters like that one." Saul nodded at the snake.

"Scorpions, a lot of scorpions."

"Anyway, they had a break-in a month ago and guess what got took? A rattler's skeleton."

"Reported?" Rhyme asked.

"Yep."

"But total value of the perped merch was only a hundred bucks or so. So Larceny wasn't like all-hands-on-board, you know."

"But tell them."

Saul nodded. "The snake wasn't the only thing missing. Whoever broke in took a couple dozen bones."

"Human bones?" Rhyme asked.

"Yep. That's what the owner thought was funny. Some of those insects—"

"Forget five inches, some of 'em were eight. Easy."

"—are worth three or four hundred. But all the perp boosted was the snake and some bones."

"Any particular ones?" Rhyme asked.

"An assortment. Like your Whitman's Sampler."

"His words, not ours."

"Mostly little ones. Hand and foot. And a rib, maybe two."

"The guy wasn't sure."

"Any CS report?"

"For 'jacked bones? Noooope."

The Hardy Boys departed once more, heading downtown to the last scene to start canvassing the neighborhood.

Rhyme wondered about the snake. Was it giving them a location? Did it relate to the First Methodist fire? If rattlers had been indigenous to Manhattan, urban development had long ago played Saint Patrick and purged the island of them. Was he making a play on the word *snake* or *rattler*?

Then Rhyme suddenly believed he understood. "The snake's for us."

"Us?" Banks laughed.

"It's a slap in the face."

"Whose face?"

"Everybody who's looking for him. I think it's a practical joke."

"I wasn't laughing very hard," Sachs said.

"Your expression *was* pretty funny." Banks grinned.

"I think we're better than he expected and he's not happy about it. He's mad and he's taking it out on us. Thom, add that to our profile, if you would. He's mocking us."

Sellitto's phone rang. He opened it and answered. "Emma darlin'. Whatcha got?" He nodded as he jotted notes. Then looked up and announced, "Rental-car thefts. Two Avises disappeared from their location in the Bronx in the past week, one in Midtown. They're out 'cause the colors're wrong: red, green and white. No Nationals. Four Hertz were 'jacked. Three in Manhattan—one from their downtown East Side location, from Midtown and from the Upper West Side. There were two green and—this could be it—one tan. But a silver Ford got boosted from White Plains. That's my vote."

"Agree," Rhyme announced. "White Plains."

"How do you know?" Sachs asked. "Monelle said it could've been either beige or silver."

"Because our boy's in the city," Rhyme explained, "and if he's going to boost something as obvious as a car he'll do it as far away from his safe house as he can. It's a Ford, you said?"

Sellitto asked Emma the question, then looked up. "Taurus. This year's model. Dark-gray interior. Tag's irrelevant."

Rhyme nodded. "The first thing he changed, the plates. Thank her and tell her to get some sleep. But not to wander too far from the phone."

"Got something here, Lincoln," Mel Cooper called.

"What's that?"

"The glop. I'm running it through the database of brand names now." He stared at the screen. "Cross-referencing . . . Let's see, the most likely match is Kink-Away. It's a retail hair straightener."

"Politically incorrect but helpful. That puts us up in Harlem, wouldn't you think? Narrows down the churches considerably."

Banks was looking through the religious-service directories of all three metro newspapers. "I count twenty-two."

"When's the earliest service?"

"Three have services at eight. Six at nine. One at nine-thirty. The rest at ten or eleven."

"He'll go for one of the first services. He's already giving us hours to find the place."

Sellitto said, "I've got Haumann getting the ESU boys together again."

"How 'bout Dellray?" Sachs said. She pictured the forlorn agent by himself on the street corner outside.

"What about him?" Sellitto muttered.

"Aw, let's cut him in. He wants a piece of this guy bad."

"Perkins said he was supposed to help," Banks offered.

"You really want him?" Sellitto asked, frowning.

Sachs was nodding. "Sure."

Rhyme agreed. "Okay, he can run the fed S&S teams. I want a team on each church right away. All entrances. But they should stay way back. I don't want to spook him. Maybe we can nail him in the act."

Sellitto took a phone call. He looked up, eyes closed. "Jesus."

"Oh, no," Rhyme muttered.

The detective wiped his sweating face and nodded. "Central got a 9-1-1 from the night manager at this place? The Midtown Residence Hotel? Woman and her little girl called him from La Guardia, said they were just about to get a cab. That was a while ago; they never showed up. With all the news about the 'nappings he thought he should call. Her name's Carole Ganz. From Chicago."

"Hell," Banks muttered. "A little girl, too? Oughta just pull all the cabs off the streets till we nail his butt."

Rhyme was drenched with weariness. His head raged. He remembered working a crime scene at a bomb factory. Nitroglycerin had bled out of some dynamite and seeped into an armchair Rhyme had to search for trace. Nitro gave you blinding headaches.

The screen of Cooper's computer flickered. "E-mail," he announced and called up the message. He read the fine type.

"They've polarized all the samples of cello that ESU collected. They think the scrap we found in the bone at the Pearl Street scene was from a ShopRite grocery store. It's closest to the cello they use."

"Good," Rhyme called. He nodded at the poster. "Cross off all the grocery stores but the ShopRites. What locations do we have?"

He watched Thom ink through the stores, leaving four.

> B'way & 82nd
> Greenwich & Bank
> 8th Ave. & 24th
> Houston & Lafayette

"That leaves us with the Upper West Side, West Village, Chelsea and the Lower East Side."

"But he could have gone anywhere to buy them."

"Oh, sure he could've, Sachs. He could've bought them in White Plains when he was stealing the car. Or in Cleveland visiting his mother. But see, there's a point when unsubs feel comfortable in their deception and they stop bothering to cover their tracks. The stupid—or lazy—ones toss the smoking gun in the Dumpster behind their building and go on their merry way. The smarter ones drop it in a bucket of Spackle and pitch it into Hell Gate. The brilliant ones sneak into a refinery and vaporize it in a five-thousand-degree-centigrade furnace. Our unsub's smart, sure. But he's like every other perp in the history of the world. He's got limits. I'm betting he thinks we won't have the time or inclination to look for him or his safe house because we'll be concentrating on the planted clues. And of course he's dead wrong. This is *exactly* how we'll find him. Now, let's see if we can't get a little closer to his lair. Mel, anything in the vic's clothes from the last scene?"

But the tidal water had washed away virtually everything from William Everett's clothing.

"You say they fought, Sachs? The unsub and this Everett?"

"Wasn't much of a fight. Everett grabbed his shirt."

Rhyme clicked his tongue. "I must be getting tired. If I'd thought about it I would have had you scrape under his nails. Even if he was underwater that's one place—"

"Here you go," she said, holding up two small plastic bags.

"You scraped?"

She nodded.

"But why're there two bags?"

Holding up one bag then the other she said, "Left hand, right hand."

Mel Cooper broke into a laugh. "Even *you* never thought about separate bags for scraping, Lincoln. It's a great idea."

Rhyme grunted. "Differentiating the hands *might* have some marginal forensic value."

"Whoa," Cooper said, laughing still. "That means he thinks it's a brilliant idea and he's sorry he didn't think of it first."

The tech examined the scrapings. "Got some brick here."

"There was no brick anywhere around the drainpipe or the field," Sachs said.

"It's fragments. But there's something attached to it. I can't tell what."

Banks asked, "Could it've come from the stockyard tunnel? There was a lotta brick there, right?"

"All *that* came from Annie Oakley here," Rhyme said, nodding ruefully at Sachs. "No, remember, the unsub'd left before she pulled out her six-gun." Then he frowned, found himself straining forward. "Mel, I want to see that brick. In the 'scope. Is there any way?"

Cooper looked over Rhyme's computer. "I think we can rig something up." He ran a cable from the video-output port on the compound 'scope to his own computer and then dug into a large suitcase. He pulled out a long, thick gray wire. "This's a serial cable." He connected the two computers and transferred some software to Rhyme's Compaq. In five minutes, Rhyme, delighted, was seeing exactly what Cooper was looking at through the eyepiece.

The criminalist's eyes scanned the chunk of brick—hugely magnified. He laughed out loud. "He outfoxed himself. See those white blobs attached to the brick?"

"What are they?" Sellitto asked.

"Looks like glue," Cooper offered.

"Exactly. From a pet-hair roller. Perps who're real cautious use them to clean trace off themselves. But it backfired. Some bits of adhesive must've come off the roller and stuck to his clothes. So we *know* it's from his safe house. Held the brick in place until Everett picked it up under his fingernails."

"Does the brick tell us anything?" Sachs asked.

"It's old. And it's expensive—cheap brick was very porous because they mixed in filler. I'd guess his place is either institutional or built by someone wealthy. At least a hundred years old. Maybe older."

"Ah, here we go," Cooper said. "Another bit of glove, it looks like. If the damn things keep disintegrating we'll be down to his friction ridges before too long."

Rhyme's screen flashed and a moment later what he recognized as a tiny fleck of leather came on the screen. "Something's funny here," Cooper said.

"It's not red," Rhyme observed. "Like the other particle. This fleck's black. Run it through the microspectrophotometer."

Cooper ran the test and then tapped his computer screen. "It's leather. But the dye is different. Maybe it's stained or faded."

Rhyme was leaning forward, straining, looking closely at the fleck on the screen when he realized he was in trouble. Serious trouble.

"Hey, you okay?" It was Sachs who'd spoken.

Rhyme didn't answer. His neck and jaw began to shiver violently. A feeling like panic rose from the crest of his shattered spine and moved up into his scalp. Then, as if a thermostat had clicked on, the chills and goose bumps vanished and he began to sweat. Perspiration poured from his face and tickled frantically.

"Thom!" he whispered. "Thom, it's happening."

Then he gasped as the headache seared through his face and

spread along the walls of his skull. He jammed his teeth together, swayed his head, anything to stop the unbearable agony. But nothing worked. The light in the room flickered. The pain was so bad his reaction was to flee from it, to run flat-out on legs that hadn't moved in years.

"Lincoln!" Sellitto was shouting.

"His face," Sachs gasped, "it's bright red."

And his hands were pale as ivory. All of his body below the magic latitude at C4 was turning white. Rhyme's blood, on its phony, desperate mission to get to where it thought it was needed, surged into the tiny capillaries of his brain, expanding them, threatening to burst the delicate filaments.

As the attack grew worse Rhyme was aware of Thom over him, ripping the blankets off the Clinitron. He was aware of Sachs stepping forward, her radiant blue eyes narrowed in concern. The last thing he saw before the blackness was the falcon pushing off the ledge on his huge wings, startled by the sudden flurry of activity in the room, seeking easy oblivion in the hot air over the empty streets of the city.

TWENTY-FOUR

When Rhyme passed out, Sellitto got to the phone first.

"Call 911 for EMS," Thom instructed. "Then hit that number there. Speed dial. It's Pete Taylor, our spinal cord specialist."

Sellitto made the calls.

Thom was shouting, "I'll need some help here. Somebody!"

Sachs was closest. She nodded, stepped up to Rhyme. The aide had grabbed the unconscious man under the arms and pulled him higher up in bed. He ripped open the shirt and prodded the pale chest, saying, "Everybody else, if you could just leave us."

Sellitto, Banks and Cooper hesitated for a moment then stepped through the doorway. Sellitto closed the door behind them.

A beige box appeared in the aide's hands. It had switches and dials on the top and sprouted a wire ending in a flat disk, which he placed over Rhyme's chest and taped down.

"Phrenic nerve stimulator. It'll keep him breathing." He clicked on the machine.

Thom slipped a blood-pressure cuff onto Rhyme's alabaster-white arm. Sachs realized with a start that his body was virtually wrinkle-free. He was in his forties but his body was that of a twenty-five-year-old.

"Why's his face so red? It looks like he's going to explode."

"He is," Thom said matter-of-factly, yanking a doctor's kit from underneath the bedside table. He opened it then he continued to take the pressure. "Dysreflexia . . . All the stress today. Mental *and* physical. He's not used to it."

"He kept saying he was tired."

"I know. And I wasn't paying careful enough attention. Shhhh. I have to listen." He plugged the stethoscope into his ears, inflated the cuff and let the air out slowly. Staring at his watch. His hands were rock-steady. "Shit. Diastolic's one twenty-five. Shit."

Father in heaven, Sachs thought. He's going to stroke out.

Thom nodded at the black bag. "Find the bottle of nifedipine. And open up one of those syringes." As she searched, Thom yanked down Rhyme's pajamas and grabbed a catheter from beside the bed, tore open its plastic wrapper too. He smeared the end with K-Y jelly and lifted Rhyme's pale penis, inserting the catheter gently but quickly into the tip.

"This's part of the problem. Bowel and urinary pressure can trigger an attack. He's been drinking way more than he should today."

She opened the hypodermic but said, "I don't know how to do the needle."

"I'll do it." He looked up at her. "Could I ask . . . would you mind doing this? I don't want the tube to get a kink in it."

"Okay. Sure."

"You want gloves?"

She pulled on a pair and carefully took Rhyme's penis in her left hand. She held the tube in her right. It had been a long, long time since she'd held a man here. The skin was soft and she thought how strange it was that this center of a man's being is, most of the time, as delicate as silk.

Thom expertly injected the drug.

"Come on, Lincoln . . ."

A siren sounded in the distance.

"They're almost here," she said glancing out the window.

"If we don't bring him back now there's nothing they can do."

"How long does it take the drug to work?"

Thom stared at the unresponsive Rhyme, said, "It should've by now. But too high a dose and he goes into shock." The aide bent down and lifted an eyelid. The blue pupil was glazed, unfocused.

"This isn't good." He took the pressure again. "One fifty. Christ."

"It'll kill him," she said.

"Oh. That's not the problem."

"What?" a shocked Amelia Sachs whispered.

"He doesn't mind dying." He looked at her briefly as if surprised she hadn't figured this out. "He just doesn't want to be any more paralyzed than he already is." He prepared another injection. "He may already've had one. A stroke, I mean. *That's* what terrifies him."

Thom leaned forward and injected more of the drug.

The siren was closer now. Honking too. Cars would be blocking the ambulance's way, in no hurry to pull aside—one of the things that infuriated Sachs about the city.

"You can take the catheter out now."

She carefully extracted the tube. "Should I . . ." Nodding toward the urine bag.

Thom managed a weak smile. "That's my job."

Several minutes passed. The ambulance seemed to make no progress then a voice crackled over a speaker and gradually the siren grew closer.

Suddenly Rhyme stirred. His head shook slightly. Then it lolled back and forth, pressed into the pillow. His skin lost some of its florid tone.

"Lincoln, can you hear me?"

He moaned, "Thom . . ."

Rhyme was shivering violently. Thom covered him with a sheet.

Sachs found herself smoothing Rhyme's mussed hair. She took a tissue and wiped his forehead.

Footsteps pounded on the stairs and two burly EMS medics appeared, radios crackling. They hurried into the room, took Rhyme's blood pressure and checked the nerve stimulator. A moment later Dr. Peter Taylor burst into the room.

"Peter," Thom said. "Dysreflexia."

"Pressure?"

"It's down. But it was bad. Crested at one fifty."

The doctor winced.

Thom introduced Taylor to the EMS techs. They seemed pleased an expert was there and stepped back as Taylor walked over to the bedside.

"Doctor," Rhyme said groggily.

"Let's look at those eyes." Taylor shone a light into Rhyme's pupils. Sachs scanned the doctor's face for a reaction and was troubled by his frown.

"Don't need the nerve stimulator," Rhyme whispered.

"You and your lungs, right?" the doctor asked wryly. "Well, let's keep it going for a little while, why don't we? Just till we see what exactly's going on here." He glanced at Sachs. "Maybe you could wait downstairs."

———

Taylor leaned close and Rhyme noticed the beads of sweat dotting the doctor's scalp under his thin hair.

The man's deft hands lifted a lid and gazed again into one pupil, then the next. He rigged up the sphygmomanometer and took Rhyme's blood pressure, his eyes distant with that concentration of medicos lost in their minute, vital tasks.

"Approaching normal," he announced. "How's the urine?"

"Eleven hundred ccs," Thom said.

Taylor glowered. "Been neglecting things? Or just drinking to excess?"

Rhyme glowered right back. "We were distracted, doctor. It's been a busy night."

Taylor followed Rhyme's nod and glanced around the room, surprised, as if someone had just sneaked the equipment in when he wasn't looking. "What's all this?"

"They hauled me out of retirement."

Taylor's perplexed frown grew into a smile. "About time. I've been after you for months to do something with your life. Now, what's the bowel situation?"

Thom said, "Probably twelve hours, fourteen."

"Careless of you," Taylor chided.

"It wasn't *his* fault," Rhyme snapped. "I've had a roomful of people here all day."

"I don't want to hear excuses," the doctor shot back. This was Pete Taylor, who never spoke *through* anyone when he talked to Rhyme and never let his bullying patient bully him.

"We better take care of things." He pulled on surgical gloves, leaned over Rhyme's torso. His fingers began manipulating the abdomen to trick the numb intestines into doing their work. Thom lifted the blankets and got the disposable diapers.

A moment later the job was done and Thom cleaned his boss.

Taylor said suddenly, "So you've given up that nonsense, I hope?" Studying Ryhme closely.

That nonsense . . .

He'd meant the suicide. With a glance at Thom, Rhyme said, "Haven't thought about that for a while."

"Good." Taylor looked over the instruments on the table. "This is what you ought to be doing. Maybe the department'll put you back on the payroll."

"Don't think I could pass the physical."

"How's the head?"

" 'A dozen sledgehammers' comes close to describing it. My neck too. Had two bad cramps so far today."

Taylor walked behind the Clinitron, pressed his fingers on either side of Rhyme's spine, where—Rhyme supposed, though he'd never seen the spot of course—there were prominent incision scars from the operations he'd had over the years. Taylor gave Rhyme an expert massage, digging deep into the taut straps of muscle in his shoulders and neck. The pain slowly vanished.

He felt the doctor's thumbs pause at what he guessed was the shattered vertebra.

The spaceship, the stingray . . .

"Someday they'll fix this," Taylor said. "Someday, it'll be no worse than breaking your leg. You listen to me. I predict it."

———

Fifteen minutes later Peter Taylor came down the stairs and joined the cops on the sidewalk.

"Is he all right?" Amelia Sachs asked anxiously.

"The pressure's down. He needs rest mostly."

The doctor, a plain-looking man, suddenly realized he was talking to a very beautiful woman. He smoothed his thinning gray hair and cast a discreet glance at her willowy figure. His eyes then went to the squad cars in front of the townhouse and he asked, "What's the case he's helping you with?"

Sellitto demurred, as all detectives will in the face of that question from civilians. But Sachs had guessed Taylor and Rhyme were close so she said, "The kidnappings? Have you heard about them?"

"The taxi-driver case? It's on all the news. Good for him. Work is the best thing that could happen to him. He needs friends and he needs purpose."

Thom appeared at the top of the stairs. "He said thanks, Pete. Well, he didn't actually say thanks. But he meant it. You know how he is."

"Level with me," Taylor asked, voice lower now, conspiratorial. "Is he still planning on talking to them?"

And when Thom said, "No, he's not," something in his tone told Sachs that he was lying. She didn't know about what or what significance it might have. But it rankled.

Planning on talking to them?

In any case Taylor seemed not to pick up on the aide's deceit. He said, "I'll come back tomorrow, see how he's doing."

Thom said he'd appreciate it and Taylor slung his bag over his shoulder and started up the sidewalk. The aide gestured to Sellitto. "He'd like to talk to you for a minute." The detective climbed the stairs quickly. He disappeared into the room and a few minutes later he and Thom walked outside. Sellitto, solemn himself now, glanced at her. "Your turn." And nodded toward the stairs.

———

Rhyme lay in the massive bed, hair mussed, face no longer red, hands no longer ivory. The room smelled ripe, visceral. There were clean sheets on the bed and his clothes had been changed again. This time the pajamas were as green as Dellray's suit.

"Those are the ugliest PJs I've ever seen," she said. "Your ex gave them to you, didn't she?"

"How'd you guess? An anniversary present . . . Sorry for the scare," he said, looking away from her. He seemed suddenly timid and that upset her. She thought of her father in the pre-op room at Sloan-Kettering before they took him down to the exploratory surgery he never awoke from.

"Sorry?" she asked ominously. "No more of that shit, Rhyme."

He appraised her for a minute then said, "You two'll do fine."

"We two?"

"You and Lon. Mel too of course. And Jim Polling."

"What do you mean?"

"I'm retiring."

"You're *what?*"

"Too taxing for the old system, I'm afraid."

"But you can't quit." She waved at the Monet poster. "Look at everything we've found about 823. We're so close."

"So you don't need me. All you need is a little luck."

"Luck? It took years to get Bundy. And what about the Zodiac killer? And the Werewolf?"

"We've got good information here. Hard information. You'll come up with some good leads. You'll nail him, Sachs. Your swan song before they lap you up into Public Affairs. I've got a feeling Unsub 823's getting cocky; they might even collar him at the church."

"You look fine," she said after a moment. Though he didn't.

Rhyme laughed. Then the smile faded. "I'm very tired. And I hurt. Hell, I think I hurt in places the docs'll say I *can't* hurt."

"Do what I do. Take a nap."

He tried to snort a derisive laugh but he sounded weak. She hated seeing him this way. He coughed briefly, glanced down at the nerve stimulator, and grimaced, as if he was embarrassed that he depended on the machine. "Sachs . . . I don't suppose we'll be working together again. I just wanted to say that you've got a good career ahead of you, you make the right choices."

"Well, I'll come back and see you after we snag his bad ass."

"I'd like that. I'm glad you were first officer yesterday morning. There's nobody else I'd rather've walked the grid with."

"I—"

"Lincoln," a voice said. She turned to see a man in the doorway. He looked around the room curiously, taking in all the equipment.

"Been some excitement around here, looks like."

"Doctor," Rhyme said. His face blossoming into a smile. "Please come in."

He stepped into the room. "I got Thom's message. Emergency, he said?"

"Dr. William Berger, this is Amelia Sachs."

But Sachs could see she'd already ceased to exist in Lincoln Rhyme's universe. Whatever else was left to be said—and she felt there were some things, maybe many things—would have to wait. She walked through the door. Thom, who stood in the large hallway outside, closed the door behind her and, ever proper, paused, nodding for her to precede him.

As Sachs walked out into the steamy night she heard a voice from nearby. "Excuse me."

She turned and found Dr. Peter Taylor standing by himself under a ginkgo tree. "Can I talk to you for a minute?"

Sachs followed Taylor up the sidewalk a few doors.

"Yes?" she asked. He leaned against a stone wall and gave another self-conscious swipe at his hair. Sachs recalled how many times she'd intimidated men with a single word or glance. She thought, as she often did: What a useless power beauty is.

"You're his friend, right?" the doctor asked her. "I mean, you work with him but you're a friend too."

"Sure. I guess I am."

"That man who just went inside. Do you know who he is?"

"Berger, I think. He's a doctor."

"Did he say where he was from?"

"No."

Taylor looked up at Rhyme's bedroom window for a moment. He asked, "You know the Lethe Society?"

"No, oh, wait . . . It's a euthanasia group, right?"

Taylor nodded. "I know all of Lincoln's doctors. And I've never heard of Berger. I was just thinking maybe he's with them."

"What?"

Is he still talking to them . . .

So *that's* what the conversation was about.

She felt weightless from the shock. "Has he . . . has he talked seriously about this before?"

"Oh, yes." Taylor sighed, gazed into the smoky night sky. "Oh, yes." Then glanced at her name badge. "Officer Sachs, I've spent hours trying to talk him out of it. Days. But I've also worked with quads for years and I know how stubborn they are. Maybe he'd listen to you. Just a few words. I was thinking . . . Could you?—"

"Oh, goddamn it, Rhyme," she muttered and started down the sidewalk at a run, leaving the doctor in midsentence.

She got to the front door of the townhouse just as Thom was closing it. She pushed past him. "Forgot my watchbook."

"Your?—"

"Be right back."

"You can't go up there. He's with his doctor."

"I'll just be a second."

She was at the landing before Thom started after her.

He must have known it was a scam because he took the stairs two at a time. But she had a good lead and had shoved open Rhyme's door before the aide got to the top of the stairs.

She pushed in, startling both Rhyme and the doctor, who was leaning against the table, arms crossed. She closed the door and locked it. Thom began pounding. Berger turned toward her with a frown of curiosity on his face.

"Sachs," Rhyme blurted.

"I have to talk to you."

"What about?"

"About you."

"Later."

"How much later, Rhyme?" she asked sarcastically. "Tomorrow? Next week?"

"What do you mean?"

"You want me to schedule a meeting for, maybe, a week from Wednesday? Will you be able to make it then? Will you be *around?*"

"Sachs—"

"I want to talk to you. Alone."

"No."

"Then we'll do it the hard way." She stepped up to Berger. "You're under arrest. The charge is attempted assisted suicide." And the handcuffs flashed, click, click, snapping onto his wrists in a silver blur.

She guessed the building was a church.

Carole Ganz lay in the basement, on the floor. A single shaft of cold, oblique light fell on the wall, illuminating a shabby picture of Jesus and a stack of mildewy Golden Book Bible stories. A half-dozen tiny chairs—for Sunday-school students, she guessed—were nested in the middle of the room.

The cuffs were still on and so was the gag. He'd also tied her to a pipe near the wall with a four-foot-long piece of clothesline.

On a tall table nearby she could see the top of a large glass jug.

If she could knock it off she might use a piece of glass to cut the clothesline. The table seemed out of reach but she rolled over onto her side and started to squirm, like a caterpillar, toward it.

This reminded her of Pammy when she was an infant, rolling on the bed between herself and Ron; she thought of her baby, alone in that horrible basement, and started to cry.

Pammy, Pooh, purse.

For a moment, for a brief moment, she weakened. Wished she'd never left Chicago.

No, stop thinking that way! Quit feeling sorry for yourself! This was the absolute right thing to do. You did it for Ron. And for yourself too. He'd be proud of you. Kate had told her that a thousand times, and she believed it.

Struggling once more. She moved a foot closer to the table.

Groggy, couldn't think straight.

Her throat stung from the terrible thirst. And the mold and mildew in the air.

She crawled a little farther then lay on her side, catching her breath, staring up at the table. It seemed hopeless. What's the use? she thought.

Wondering what was going through Pammy's mind.

You fucker! thought Carole. I'll *kill* you for this!

She squirmed, trying to move farther along the floor. But instead, she lost her balance and rolled onto her back. She gasped, knowing what was coming. No! With a loud pop, her wrist snapped. She screamed through the gag. Blacked out. When she came to a moment later she was overwhelmed with nausea.

No, no, no . . . If she vomited she'd die. With the gag on, that would be it.

Fight it down! Fight it. Come on. You can do it. Here I go. . . . She retched once. Then again.

No! Control it.

Rising in her throat.

Control . . .

Control it. . . .

And she did. Breathing through her nose, concentrating on Kate and Eddie and Pammy, on the yellow knapsack containing all her precious possessions. Seeing it, picturing it from every angle. Her whole life was in there. Her *new* life.

Ron, I don't want to blow it. I came here for you, honey . . .

She closed her eyes. Thought: Breathe deep. In, out.

Finally, the nausea subsided. And a moment later she was

feeling better and, though she was crying in pain from the snapped wrist, she managed to continue to caterpillar her way toward the table, one foot. Two.

She felt a thump as her head collided with the table leg. She'd just managed to connect with it and couldn't move any farther. She swung her head back and forth and jostled the table hard. She heard the bottle slosh as it shifted on the tabletop. She looked up.

A bit of the jug was showing beyond the edge of the table. Carole drew back her head and hit the table leg one last time.

No! She'd knocked the leg out of reach. The jug teetered for a moment but stayed upright. Carole strained to get more slack from the clothesline but couldn't.

Damn. Oh, damn! As she gazed hopelessly up at the filthy bottle she realized it was filled with a liquid and something floated inside. What *is* that?

She scrunched her way back toward the wall a foot or two and looked up.

It seemed like a lightbulb inside. No, not a whole bulb, just the filament and the base, screwed into a socket. A wire ran from the socket out of the jug to one of those timers that turn the lights on and off when you're away on vacation. It looked like—

A bomb! Now she recognized the faintest whiff of gasoline.

No, no . . .

Carole began to squirm away from the table as fast as she could, sobbing in desperation. There was a filing cabinet by the wall. It'd give her some protection. She drew her legs up then felt a chill of panic and unwound them furiously. The motion knocked her off balance. She realized, to her horror, that she was rolling onto her back once more. Oh, stop. Don't . . . She stayed poised, perfectly still, for a long moment, quivering as she tried to shift her weight forward. But then she continued to roll, collapsing onto her cuffed hand, her shattered wrist taking the weight of her body. There was a moment of incredible pain and, mercifully, she fainted once more.

TWENTY-FIVE

N o way, Rhyme. You can't do it."

Berger looked on uneasily. Rhyme supposed that in this line of work he'd seen all sorts of hysterical scenarios played out at moments like this. The biggest problem Berger'd have wasn't those wanting to die but those who wanted everyone else to live.

Thom pounded on the door.

"Thom," Rhyme called. "It's all right. You can leave us." Then to Sachs: "We've said our farewells. You and me. It's bad form to ruin a perfect exit."

"You can't do this."

Who'd blown the whistle? Pete Taylor maybe. The doctor must've guessed that he and Thom were lying.

Rhyme saw her eyes slip to the three items on the table. The gifts of the Magi: the brandy, the pills and the plastic bag. Also a rubber band, similar to the ones Sachs still wore on her shoes. (How many times had he come home from a crime scene to find Blaine staring at the bands on his shoes, horrified? "Everybody'll think my husband can't afford new shoes. He's keeping the soles on with rubber bands. Honestly, Lincoln!")

"Sachs, take the cuffs off the good doctor here. I'll have to ask you to leave one last time."

She barked a fast laugh. "Excuse me. This's a crime in New York. The DA could bootstrap it into murder, he wanted to."

Berger said, "I'm just having a conversation with a patient."

"That's why the charge's only attempt. So far. Maybe we should run your name and prints through NCIC. See what we come up with."

"Lincoln," Berger said quickly, alarmed. "I can't—"

"We'll get it worked out," Rhyme said. "Sachs, please."

Feet apart, hands on trim hips, her gorgeous face imperious. "Let's go," she barked to the doctor.

"Sachs, you have no idea how important this is."

"I won't let you kill yourself."

"Let me?" Rhyme snapped. "*Let* me? And why exactly do I need your permission?"

Berger said, "Miss . . . Officer Sachs, it's his decision and it's completely consensual. Lincoln's more informed than most of the patients I deal with."

"Patients? Victims, you mean."

"Sachs!" Rhyme blurted, trying to keep the desperation from his voice. "It's taken me a year to find someone to help me."

"Maybe because it's wrong. Ever consider *that?* Why now, Rhyme? Right in the middle of the case?"

"If I have another attack and a stroke, I might lose all ability to communicate. I could be conscious for forty years and completely unable to move. And if I'm not brain-dead, nobody in the universe is going to pull the plug. At least now I'm still able to communicate my decisions."

"But why?" she blurted.

"Why not?" Rhyme answered. "Tell me. Why not?"

"Well . . ." It seemed as if the arguments against suicide were so obvious she was having trouble articulating them. "Because . . ."

"Because *why*, Sachs?"

"For one thing, it's cowardly."

Rhyme laughed. "Do you want to debate it, Sachs? *Do* you? Fair enough. 'Cowardly,' you say. That leads us to Sir Thomas Browne: 'When life is more terrible than death, it's the truest

valor to live.' Courage in the face of insurmountable adversity . . .
A classic argument in favor of living. But if that's true then why
anesthetize patients before surgery? Why sell aspirin? Why fix
broken arms? Why is Prozac the most prescribed medicine in
America? Sorry, but there's nothing intrinsically good about pain."

"But you're not in pain."

"And how do you define pain, Sachs? Maybe the absence of all
feeling can be pain too."

"You can contribute so much. Look at all you know. All the
forensics, all the history."

"The social-contribution argument. That's a popular one."
He glanced at Berger but the medico remained silent. Rhyme
saw his interest dip to the bone sitting on the table—the pale disk
of spinal column. He picked it up, kneaded it in his cuffed hands.
He was a former orthopedics man, Rhyme recalled.

He continued to Sachs, "But who says we should contribute anything to life? Besides, the corollary is I might contribute something
bad. I might cause some harm too. To myself or someone else."

"That's what life is."

Rhyme smiled. "But I'm choosing death, not life."

Sachs looked uneasy as she thought hard. "It's just . . . death
isn't natural. Life is."

"No? Freud'd disagree with you. He gave up on the pleasure
principle and came to feel that there was another force—a non-
erotic primary aggression, he called it. Working to unbind the
connections we build in life. Our own destruction's a perfectly
natural force. Everything dies; what's more natural than that?"

Again she worried a portion of her scalp.

"All right," she said. "Life's more of a challenge to you than
most people. But I thought . . . everything I've seen about you
tells me you're somebody who likes challenges."

"Challenges? Let me tell you about challenges. I was on a ventilator for a year. See the tracheostomy scar on my neck? Well,
through positive-pressure breathing exercises—and the greatest
willpower I could muster—I managed to get off the machine. In
fact I've got lungs like nobody's business. They're as strong as

yours. In a C4 quad that's one for the books, Sachs. It consumed my life for eight months. Do you understand what I'm saying? Eight months just to handle a basic animal function. I'm not talking about painting the Sistine Chapel or playing the violin. I'm talking about fucking *breathing*."

"But you could get better. Next year, they might find a cure."

"No. Not next year. Not in ten years."

"You don't know that. They must be doing research—"

"Sure they are. Want to know what? I'm an expert. Transplanting embryonic nerve tissue onto damaged tissue to promote axonal regeneration." These words tripped easily from his handsome lips. "No significant effect. Some doctors are chemically treating the affected areas to create an environment where cells can regenerate. No significant effect—not in advanced species. Lower forms of life show pretty good success. If I were a frog I'd be walking again. Well, hopping."

"So there *are* people working on it?" Sachs asked.

"Sure. But no one expects any breakthroughs for twenty, thirty years."

"If they were expected," she shot back, "then they wouldn't be breakthroughs, now would they?"

Rhyme laughed. She was good.

Sachs tossed the veil of red hair from her eyes and said, "Your career was law enforcement, remember. Suicide's illegal."

"It's a sin too," he responded. "The Dakota Indians believed that the ghosts of those who committed suicide had to drag around the tree they'd hanged themselves from for all eternity. Did that stop suicide? Nope. They just used small trees."

"Tell you what, Rhyme. Here's my last argument." She nodded at Berger, grabbed the cuff chain. "I'm taking him in and booking him. Refute *that* one."

"Lincoln," Berger said uneasily, panic in his eyes.

Sachs took the doctor by the shoulder and led him to the door. "No," he said. "Please. Don't do this."

As Sachs opened the door Rhyme called out, "Sachs, before you do that, answer me something."

She paused. One hand on the knob.

"One question."

She looked back.

"Have you ever wanted to? Kill yourself?"

She unlocked the door with a loud snap.

He said, "Answer me!"

Sachs didn't open the door. She stood with her back to him. "No. Never."

"Are you happy with your life?"

"As much as anybody."

"You're never depressed?"

"I didn't say that. I said I've never wanted to kill myself."

"You like to drive, you were telling me. People who like to drive like to drive fast. You do, don't you?"

"Yes. Sometimes."

"What's the fastest you've done?"

"I don't know."

"Over eighty?"

A dismissing smile. "Yes."

"Over a hundred?"

She gestured upward with her thumb.

"One ten? One twenty?" he asked, smiling in astonishment.

"Clocked at 168."

"My, Sachs, you *are* impressive. Well, driving that fast, didn't you think that maybe, just maybe, something might happen. A rod or axle or something would break, a tire would blow, a spot of oil on the road?"

"It was pretty safe. I'm not crazy."

"*Pretty* safe. But driving as fast as a small plane, well, that's not *completely* safe, now, is it?"

"You're leading the witness."

"No, I'm not. Stay with me. You drive that fast, you have to accept that you could have an accident and die, right?"

"Maybe," she conceded.

Berger, cuffed hands in front of him, looked on nervously, as he kneaded the pale yellow disk of spinal column.

"So you've moved close to that line, right? Ah, you know what I'm talking about. I know you do—the line between the *risk* of dying and the *certainty* of dying. See, Sachs, if you carry the dead around with you it's a very short step over that line. A short step to joining them."

She lowered her head and her face went completely still, as the curtain of hair obscured her eyes.

"Giving up the dead," he whispered, praying she wouldn't leave with Berger, knowing he was so very close to pushing her over the edge. "I touched a nerve there. How much of you wants to follow the dead? More than a little, Sachs. Oh, much more than a little."

She was hesitating. He knew he was near her heart.

She turned angrily to Berger, gripped him by the cuffs. "Come on." Pushed through the door.

Rhyme called, "You know what I'm saying, don't you?"

Again she stopped.

"Sometimes . . . things happen, Sachs. Sometimes you just can't be what you ought to be, you can't have what you ought to have. And life changes. Maybe just a little, maybe a lot. And at some point it just isn't worth the fight to try to fix what went wrong."

He watched them standing, motionless, in the doorway. The room was utterly silent. She turned and looked back at him.

"Death cures loneliness," Rhyme continued. "It cures tension. It cures the itch." Just like she'd glanced at his legs earlier he now gave a fast look at her torn fingers.

She released Berger's cuffs and walked to the window. Tears glistened on her cheeks in the yellow radiance from the street-lights outside.

"Sachs, I'm tired," he said earnestly. "I can't tell you how tired I am. You know how hard life is to start with. Pile on a whole mountainful of . . . burdens. Washing, eating, crapping, making phone calls, buttoning shirts, scratching your nose . . . Then pile on a thousand more. And more after that."

He fell silent. After a long moment she said, "I'll make a deal with you."

"What's that?"

She nodded toward the poster. "Eight twenty-three's got that mother and her little girl . . . Help us save them. Just them. If you do that I'll give him an hour alone with you." She glanced at Berger. "Provided he gets the hell out of town afterwards."

Rhyme shook his head. "Sachs, if I have a stroke, if I can't communicate . . ."

"If that happens," she said evenly, "even if you can't say a word, the deal still holds. I'll make sure you have one hour together." She crossed her arms, spread her feet again, in what was now Rhyme's favorite image of Amelia Sachs. He wished he could've seen her on the railroad tracks that morning, stopping the train. She said, "That's the best I'll do."

A moment passed. Rhyme nodded. "Okay. It's a deal." To Berger he said, "Monday?"

"Okay, Lincoln. Fair enough." Berger, still shaken, watched Sachs cautiously as she unlocked the cuffs. Afraid, it seemed, that she might change her mind. When he was free he walked quickly to the door. He realized he was still holding the vertebra and returned, set it—almost reverently—next to Rhyme on the crime scene report for the first murder that morning.

"Happier'n hogs in red Virginia mud," Sachs remarked, slouching in the squeaky rattan chair. Meaning Sellitto and Polling, after she'd told them that Rhyme had agreed to remain on the case for another day.

"Polling particularly," she said. "I thought the little guy was going to hug me. Don't tell him I called him that. How are you feeling? You look better." She sipped some Scotch and set the glass back on the bedside table, beside Rhyme's tumbler.

"Not bad."

Thom was changing the bedclothes. "You were sweating like a fountain," he said.

"But only above my neck," Rhyme pointed out. "Sweating, I mean."

"That right?" Sachs asked.

"Yep. That's how it works. Thermostat's busted below that. I never need any axial deodorant."

"Axial?"

"Pit," Rhyme snorted. "*Armpit.* My first aide never said armpit. He'd say, 'I'm going to elevate you by your axials, Lincoln.' Oh, and: 'If you feel like regurgitating go right ahead, Lincoln.' He called himself a 'caregiver.' The word was actually on his résumé. I have no idea why I hired him. We're very superstitious, Sachs. We think calling something by a different name is going to change it. Unsub. Perpetrator. But that aide, he was just a nurse who was up to his own armpits in piss 'n' puke. Right, Thom? Nothing to be ashamed of. It's an honorable profession. Messy but honorable."

"I thrive on mess. That's why I work for you."

"What're you, Thom? An aide or a caregiver?"

"I'm a saint."

"Ha, fast with the comebacks. And fast with the needle too. He brought me back from the dead. Done it more than once."

Rhyme was suddenly pierced with a fear that Sachs had seen him naked. Eyes fixed firmly on the unsub profile, he asked, 'Say, do I owe you some thanks too, Sachs? Did you play Clara Barton here?" He uneasily waited for her answer, didn't know how he could look at her again if she had.

"Nup," Thom answered. "Saved you all by my lonesome. Didn't want any of these sensitive souls repulsed by the sight of your baggy rear end."

Thank you, Thom, he thought. Then barked, "Now go away. We have to talk about the case. Sachs and me."

"You need some sleep."

"Of course I do. But we still need to talk about the case. Good night, good night."

After Thom left, Sachs poured some Macallan in a glass. She lowered her head and inhaled the smoky vapors.

"Who snitched?" Rhyme asked. "Pete?"

"Who?" she asked.

"Dr. Taylor, the SCI man."

She hesitated long enough for him to know that Taylor was the one. She said finally, "He cares about you."

"Of course he does. That's the problem—I want him to care a little *less*. Does he know about Berger?"

"He suspects."

Rhyme grimaced. "Look, tell him that Berger's just an old friend. He . . . what?"

Sachs exhaled slowly, as if shooting cigarette smoke through her pursed lips. "You not only want me to let you kill yourself you want me to lie to the one person who could talk you out of it."

"He couldn't talk me out of it," Rhyme responded.

"Then why do you want me to lie?"

He laughed. "Let's just keep Dr. Taylor in the dark for a few more days."

"All right," she said. "Jesus, you're a tough person to deal with."

He examined her closely. "Why don't you tell me about it."

"About what?"

"Who's the dead? That you haven't given up?"

"There's plenty of them."

"Such as?"

"Read the newspaper."

"Come on, Sachs."

She shook her head, stared down at her Scotch with a faint smile on her lips. "No, I don't think so."

He put her silence down to reluctance about having an intimate conversation with someone she'd known only for one day. Which seemed ironic, considering she sat next to a dozen catheters, a tube of K-Y jelly and a box of Depends. Still he wasn't going to push it and said nothing more. So he was surprised when she suddenly looked up and blurted, "It's just . . . It's just . . . Oh, *hell*." And as the sobbing began she lifted her hands to her face, spilling a good two inches of Scotland's best all over the parquet.

TWENTY-SIX

I can't believe I'm telling you this." She sat huddled in the deep chair, legs drawn up, issue shoes kicked off. The tears were gone though her face was as ruddy as her hair.

"Go on," he encouraged.

"That guy I told you about? We were going to get an apartment together."

"Oh, with the collie. You didn't say it was a guy. Your boyfriend?"

The secret lover? Rhyme wondered.

"He *was* my boyfriend."

"I was thinking maybe it was your father you'd lost."

"Naw. Pop did pass away—three years ago. Cancer. But we knew it was coming. If that prepares you for it I guess we were prepared. But Nick . . ."

"He was killed?" Rhyme asked softly.

But she didn't answer. "Nick Carelli. One of us. A cop. Detective, third. Worked Street Crimes."

The name was familiar. Rhyme said nothing and let her continue.

"We lived together for a while. Talked about getting married." She paused, seemed to be lining up her thoughts like targets at a shooting range. "He worked undercover. So we were pretty secret about our relationship. He couldn't let word get around on the street that his gal was a cop." She cleared her throat. "It's hard to explain. See, we had this . . . thing between us. It was . . . it hasn't happened for me very often. Hell, it *never* happened before Nick. We clicked in some really deep way. He knew I had to be a cop and that wasn't a problem for him. Same with me and his working undercover. That kind of . . . wavelength. You know, where you just completely understand someone? You ever felt what I'm talking about? With your wife?"

Rhyme smiled faintly. "I did. Yes. But not with Blaine, my wife." And that was all he wanted to say on the subject. "How'd you meet?" he asked.

"The assignments lectures at the academy. Where somebody gets up and they tell you a little about what their division does. Nick was lecturing on undercover work. He asked me out on the spot. Our first date was at Rodman's Neck."

"The gun range?"

She nodded, sniffing. "Afterwards, we went to his mom's in Brooklyn and had pasta and a bottle of Chianti. She pinched me hard and said I was too skinny to have babies. Made me eat two cannoli. We went back to my place and he stayed over that night. Quite a first date, huh? From then on we saw each other all the time. It was gonna work, Rhyme. I felt it. It was gonna work just fine."

Rhyme said, "What happened?"

"He was . . ."

Another bolstering hit of old liquor. "He was on the take is what happened. The whole time I knew him."

"He was?"

"Crooked. Oh, way crooked. I never had a clue. Not a single goddamn clue. He socked it away in banks around the city. He dusted close to two hundred thousand."

Lincoln was silent a moment. "I'm sorry, Sachs. Drugs?"

"No. Merch, mostly. Appliances, TVs. 'Jackings. They called it the Brooklyn Connection. The papers did."

Rhyme was nodding. "That's why I remember it. There were a dozen of them in the ring, right? All cops?"

"Mostly. A few ICC people too."

"What happened to him? Nick?"

"You know what happens when cops bust cops. They beat the crap out of him. Said he resisted but I know he didn't. Broke three ribs, a couple fingers, smashed his face all up. Pleaded guilty but he still got twenty to thirty."

"For hijacking?" Rhyme was astonished.

"He worked a couple of the jobs himself. Pistol-whipped one driver, took a shot at another one. Just to scare him. I *know* it was just to scare him. But the judge threw him away." She closed her eyes, pressed her lips together hard.

"When he got collared, Internal Affairs went after him like they were in heat. They checked pen registers. We were real careful about calling each other. He said perps sometimes tapped his line. But there were *some* calls to my place. IA came after me too. So Nick just cut me off. I mean, he *had* to. Otherwise I would've gone down with him. You know IA—it's always a god-damn witch-hunt."

"What happened?"

"To convince them that I wasn't anything to him . . . Well, he said some things about me." She swallowed, her eyes fixed on the floor. "At the IA inquest they wanted to know about me. Nick said, 'Oh, P.D. Sachs? I just fucked her a few times. Turned out she was lousy. So I dumped her.' " She tilted her head back and mopped tears with her sleeve. "The nickname? P.D."

"Lon told me."

She frowned. "Did he tell you what it means?"

"The Portable's Daughter. After your father."

She smiled wanly. "That's how it started. But that's not how it ended up. At the inquest Nick said I was such a lousy fuck it really stood for 'Pussy Diver' 'cause I probably liked girls better. Guess how fast *that* went through the department."

"It's a low common denominator out there, Sachs."

She took a deep breath. "I saw him in court toward the end of the inquest. He looked at me once and . . . I can't even describe what was in his eyes. Just pure heartbreak. Oh, he did it to protect me. But still . . . You were right, you know. About the lonely stuff."

"I didn't mean—"

"No," she said, unsmiling. "I hit you, you hit me. That was fair. And you were right. I hate being alone. I *want* to go out, I *want* to meet somebody. But after Nick I lost my taste for sex." Sachs gave a sour laugh. "Everybody thinks looking like me's wonderful. I could have my pick of guys, right? Bullshit. The only ones with the balls to ask me out're the ones who want to screw all the time. So I just gave up. It's easier by myself. I hate it, but it's easier."

At last Rhyme understood her reaction at seeing him for the first time. She was at ease with him because here was a man who was no threat to her. No sexual come-ons. Someone she wouldn't have to fend off. And perhaps a certain camaraderie too—as if they were both missing the same, crucial gene.

"You know," he joked, "you and me, we ought to get together and *not* have an affair."

She laughed. "So tell me about your wife. How long were you married?"

"Seven years. Six before the accident, one after."

"And she left you?"

"Nope. I left her. I didn't want her to feel guilty about it."

"Good of you."

"I'd have driven her out eventually. I'm a prick. You've only seen my good side." After a moment he asked, "This thing with Nick . . . it have anything to do with why you're leaving Patrol?"

"No. Well, yes."

"Gunshy?"

Finally she nodded. "Life on the street's different now. That's what did it to Nick, you know. What turned him. It's not like it was when Pop was walking his beat. Things were better then."

"You mean it's not like the *stories* your dad told you."

"Maybe," she conceded. Sachs slumped the chair. "The arthritis? That's true but it's not as serious as I pretend it is."

"I know," Rhyme said.

"You know? How?"

"I just looked at the evidence and drew some conclusions."

"Is that why you've been on my case all day? You knew I was faking?"

"I've been on your case," he said, "because you're better than you think you are."

She gave him a screwy look.

"Ah, Sachs, you remind me of me."

"I do?"

"Let me tell you a story. I'd been on crime scene detail maybe a year when we got a call from Homicide there was a guy found dead in an alley in Greenwich Village. All the sergeants were out and so I got elected to run the scene. I was twenty-six years old, remember. I go up there and check it out and it turns out the dead guy's the head of the City Health and Human Services. Now, what's he got all around him but a load of Polaroids? You should've seen some of those snaps—he'd been to one of those S&M clubs off Washington Street. Oh, and I forgot to mention, when they found him he was dressed in a stunning little black minidress and fishnet stockings.

"So, I secure the scene. All of a sudden a captain shows up and starts to cross the tape. I know he's planning to have those pictures disappear on the way to the evidence room but I was so naive I didn't care much about the pictures—I was just worried about somebody walking through the scene."

"P is for Protect the crime scene."

Rhyme chuckled. "So I didn't let him in. While he was standing at the tape screaming at me a dep com tried an end run. I told him no. *He* started screaming at me. The scene stays virgin till IRD's through with it, I told them. Guess who finally showed up?"

"The mayor?"

"Well, deputy mayor."

"And you held 'em all off?"

"Nobody got into that scene except Latents and Photography. Of course my payback was spending six months printing floaters.

But we nailed the perp with some trace and a print off one of those Polaroids—happened to be the same snap the *Post* used on page one, as a matter of fact. Just like what you did yesterday morning, Sachs. Closing off the tracks and Eleventh Avenue."

"I didn't think about it," she said. "I just did it. Why're you looking at me that way?"

"Come on, Sachs. You *know* where you ought to be. On the street. Patrol, Major Crimes, IRD, doesn't matter . . . But Public Affairs? You'll rot there. It's a good job for some people but not you. Don't give up so fast."

"Oh, and you're *not* giving up? What about Berger?"

"Things're a little different with me."

Her glance questioned, They are? And she went prowling for a Kleenex. When she returned to the chair she asked, "You don't carry any corpses around with you?"

"I have in my day. They're all buried now."

"Tell me."

"Really, there's nothing—"

"Not true. I can tell. Come on—I showed you mine."

He felt an odd chill. He knew it wasn't dysreflexia. His smile faded.

"Rhyme, go on," she persisted. "I'd like to hear."

"Well, there was a case a few years ago," he said, "I made a mistake. A bad mistake."

"Tell me." She poured them each another finger of the Scotch.

"It was a domestic murder-suicide call. Husband and wife in a Chinatown apartment. He shot her, killed himself. I didn't have much time for the scene; I worked it fast. And I committed a classic error—I'd made up my mind about what I was going to find before I started looking. I found some fibers that I couldn't place but I assumed that the husband and wife'd tracked them in. I found the bullet fragments but didn't check them against the gun we found at the scene. I noticed the blowback pattern but didn't grid it to double-check the exact position of the gun. I did the search, signed off and went back to the office."

"What happened?"

"The scene had been staged. It was really a burglary-murder. And the perp had never left the apartment."

"What? He was still there?"

"After I left he crawled out from under the bed and started shooting. He killed one forensic tech and wounded an assistant ME. He got out on the street and there was a shootout with a couple of portables who'd heard the 10-13. The perp was shot up—he died later—but he killed one of the cops and wounded the other. He also shot up a family that'd just come out of a Chinese restaurant across the street. Used one of the kids as a shield."

"Oh, my God."

"Colin Stanton was the father's name. He wasn't hurt at all and he'd been an army medic—EMS said he probably could've saved his wife or one or both of the kids if he'd tried to stop the bleeding but he panicked and froze. He just stood there, watching them all die in front of him."

"Jesus, Rhyme. But it wasn't your fault. You—"

"Let me finish. That wasn't the end of it."

"No?"

"The husband went back home—upstate New York. Had a breakdown and went into a mental hospital for a while. He tried to kill himself. They put him under a suicide watch. First he tried to cut his wrist with a piece of paper—a magazine cover. Then he sneaked into the library and found a water glass in the librarian's bathroom, shattered it and slashed his wrists. They stitched him up okay and kept him in the mental hospital for another year or so. Finally they released him. A month or so after he was out he tried again. Used a knife." Rhyme added coolly, "That time it worked."

He'd learned about Stanton's death in an obituary faxed from the Albany County coroner to NYPD Public Affairs. Someone there had sent it to Rhyme via interoffice mail with a Post-It attached: *FYI—thought you'd be interested*, the officer had written.

"There was an IA investigation. Professional incompetence. They slapped my wrist. I think they should've fired me."

She sighed and closed her eyes for a moment. "And you're telling me you don't feel guilty about that?"

"Not anymore."

"I don't believe you."

"I served my time, Sachs. I lived with those bodies for a while. But I gave 'em up. If I hadn't, how could I have kept on working?"

After a long moment she said, "When I was eighteen I got a ticket. Speeding. I was doing ninety in a forty zone."

"Well."

"Dad said he'd front me the money for the fine but I'd have to pay him back. With interest. But you know what else he told me? He said he would've tanned my hide for running a red light or reckless driving. But going fast he understood. He told me, 'I know how you feel, honey. When you move they can't getcha.' " Sachs said to Rhyme, "If I couldn't drive, if I couldn't move, then maybe I'd do it too. Kill myself."

"I used to walk everywhere," Rhyme said. "I never did drive much. Haven't owned a car in twenty years. What kind do you have?"

"Nothing a snooty Manhattanite like you'd drive. A Chevy. Camaro. It was my father's."

"Who gave you the drill press. For working on cars, I assume?"

She nodded. "And a torque wrench. And spark-gap set. And my first set of ratcheting sockets—my thirteenth-birthday present." Laughing softly. "That Chevy, it's a wobbly-knob car. You know what that is? An American car. The radio and vents and light switches are all loose and cheesy. But the suspension's like a rock, it's light as an egg crate and I'll take on a BMW any day."

"And I'll bet you have."

"Once or twice."

"Cars are status in the crip world," Rhyme explained. "We'd sit—or lie—around the ward in rehab and talk about what we could get out of our insurance companies. Wheelchair vans were the top of the heap. Next are hand-control cars. Which wouldn't do me any good of course." He squinted, testing his supple memory. "I haven't been in a car in years. I can't remember the last time."

"Got an idea," Sachs said suddenly. "Before your friend—Dr. Berger—comes back, let me take you for a ride. Or is that a problem? Sitting up? You were saying that wheelchairs don't work for you."

"Well, no, wheelchairs're a problem. But a car? I think that'd be okay." He laughed. "A hundred and sixty-eight? Miles per hour?"

"That was a special day," Sachs said, nodding at the memory. "Good conditions. And no highway patrol."

The phone buzzed and Rhyme answered it himself. It was Lon Sellitto.

"We got S&S on all the target churches in Harlem. Dellray's in charge of that—man's become a true believer, Lincoln. You wouldn't recognize him. Oh, and I've got thirty portables and a ton of UN security cruising for any other churches we might've missed. If he doesn't show up, we're going to do a sweep of all of them at seven-thirty. Just in case he snuck in without us seeing him. I think we're going to nail him, Linc," the detective said, suspiciously enthusiastic for a New York City homicide cop.

"Okay, Lon, I'll send Amelia up to your CP around eight."

They hung up.

Thom knocked on the door before coming into the room.

As if he'd catch us in a compromising position, Rhyme laughed to himself.

"No more excuses," he said testily. "Bed. Now."

It was after 3:00 a.m. and Rhyme had left exhaustion far behind long ago. He was floating somewhere else. Above his body. He wondered if he'd start to hallucinate.

"Yes, Mother," he said. "Officer Sachs's staying over, Thom. Could you get her a blanket, please?"

"What did you say?" Thom turned to face him.

"A blanket."

"No, after that," the aide said. "That word?"

"I don't know. 'Please'?"

Thom's eyes went wide with alarm. "Are you all right? You

want me to get Pete Taylor back here? The head of Columbia-Presbyterian? The surgeon general?"

"See how this son of a bitch torments me?" Rhyme said to Sachs. "He never knows how close he comes to getting fired."

"A wake-up call for when?"

"Six-thirty should be fine," Rhyme said.

When he was gone, Rhyme asked, "Hey, Sachs, you like music?"

"Love it."

"What kind?"

"Oldies, doo-wop, Motown . . . How 'bout you? You seem like a classical kind of guy."

"See that closet there?"

"This one?"

"No, no, the other one. To the right. Open it up."

She did and gasped in amazement. The closet was a small room filled with close to a thousand CDs.

"It's like Tower Records."

"That stereo, see it on the shelf?"

She ran her hand over the dusty black Harmon Kardon.

"It cost more than my first car," Rhyme said. "I don't use it anymore."

"Why not?"

He didn't answer but said instead, "Put something on. Is it plugged in? It is? Good. Pick something."

A moment later she stepped out of the closet and walked over to the couch as Levi Stubbs and the Four Tops started singing about love.

It had been a year since there'd been a note of music in this room, Rhyme estimated. Silently he tried to answer Sachs's question about why he'd stopped listening. He couldn't.

Sachs lifted files and books off the couch. Lay back on it and thumbed through a copy of *Scenes of the Crime*.

"Can I have one?" she asked.

"Take ten."

"Will you . . ." Her voice braked to a halt.

"Sign it for you?" He laughed. She joined him. "How 'bout if I put my thumbprint on it? Graphoanalysts'll never give you more than an eighty-five percent probability of a handwriting match. But a thumbprint? Any friction-ridge expert'll certify it's mine."

He watched her read the first chapter. Her eyes drooped. She closed the book.

"Will you do something for me?" she asked.

"What?"

"Read to me. Something from the book. When Nick and I were together . . ." Her voice faded.

"What?"

"When we were together, a lot of times Nick'd read out loud before we went to sleep. Books, the paper, magazines . . . It's one of the things I miss the most."

"I'm a terrible reader," Rhyme confessed. "I sound like I'm reciting crime scene reports. But I've got this memory . . . It's pretty good. How 'bout if I just tell you about some scenes?"

"Would you?" She turned her back, pulled her navy blouse off and unstrapped the thin American Body Armor vest, tossed it aside. Beneath it she wore a mesh T-shirt and under that a sports bra. She pulled the blouse back on and lay on the couch, pulling the blanket over her, and curled up on her side, closed her eyes.

With the environmental-control unit Rhyme dimmed the lights.

"I always found the sites of death fascinating," he began. "They're like shrines. We're a lot more interested in where people bought the big one than where they were born. Take John Kennedy. A thousand people a day visit the Texas Book Depository in Dallas. How many you think make pilgrimages to some obstetrics ward in Boston?"

Rhyme nestled his head in the luxurious softness of the pillow. "Is this boring you?"

"No," she said. "Please don't stop."

"You know what I've always wondered about, Sachs?"

"Tell me."

"It's fascinated me for years—Calvary. Two thousand years

ago. Now, *there's* a crime scene I'd like to've worked. I know what you're going to say: But we know the perps. Well, do we? All we really know is what the witnesses tell us. Remember what I say— never trust a wit. Maybe those Bible accounts aren't what happened at all. Where's the *proof?* The PE. The nails, blood, sweat, the spear, the cross, the vinegar. Sandal prints and friction ridges."

Rhyme turned his head slightly to the left and he continued to talk about crime scenes and evidence until Sachs's chest rose and fell steadily and faint strands of her fiery red hair blew back and forth under her shallow breath. With his left index finger he flipped through the ECU control and shut off the light. He too was soon asleep.

———

A faint light of dawn was in the sky.

Awakening, Carole Ganz could see it through the chicken-wire-impregnated glass above her head. Pammy. Oh, baby . . . Then she thought of Ron. And all her possessions sitting in that terrible basement. The money, the yellow knapsack . . .

Mostly, though, she was thinking about Pammy.

Something had wakened her from a light, troubled sleep. What was it?

The pain from her wrist? It throbbed horribly. She adjusted herself slightly. She—

The tubular howl of a pipe organ and a rising chorus of voices filled the room again.

That's what had wakened her. Music. A crashing wave of music. The church wasn't abandoned. There were people around! She laughed to herself. Somebody would—

And that was when she remembered the bomb.

Carole peered around the filing cabinet. It was still there, teetering on the edge of the table. It had the crude look of real bombs and murder weapons—not the slick, shiny gadgets you see in movies. Sloppy tape, badly stripped wires, dirty gasoline . . . Maybe it's a dud, she thought. In the daylight it didn't look so dangerous.

Another burst of music. It came from directly over her head. Accompanied by a shuffling of footsteps. A door closed. Creaks and groans as people moved around the old, dry wood floors. Plumes of dust fell from the joists.

The soaring voices were cut off in mid-passage. A moment later they started singing again.

Carole banged with her feet but the floor was concrete, the walls brick. She tried to scream but the sound was swallowed by the gag. The rehearsal continued, the solemn, vigorous music rattling through the basement.

After ten minutes Carole collapsed on the floor in exhaustion. Her eyes were drawn back to the bomb again. Now the light was better and she could see the timer clearly.

Carole squinted. The timer!

It wasn't a dud at all. The arrow was set for 6:15 a.m. The dial showed the time was now 5:30.

Squirming her way farther behind the filing cabinet, Carole began to kick the metal sides with her knee. But whatever faint noises the blows made immediately vanished in the booming, mournful rendition of "Swing Low, Sweet Chariot" filling the church basement from above.

IV
DOWN TO THE BONE

This only is denied the Gods:
the power to remake the past.

—ARISTOTLE

Sunday, 5:45 a.m., to Monday, 7:00 p.m.

TWENTY-SEVEN

He awoke to a scent. As he often did.

And—as on many mornings—he didn't at first open his eyes but just remained in his half-seated position, trying to figure out what the unfamiliar smell might be:

The gassy scent of dawn air? The dew on the oil-slick streets? Damp plaster? He tried to detect the scent of Amelia Sachs but could not.

His thoughts skipped over her and continued. What *was* it?

Cleanser? No.

A chemical from Cooper's impromptu lab?

No, he recognized all of those.

It was . . . Ah, yes . . . marking pen.

Now he could open his eyes and—after a glance at sleeping Sachs to make certain she hadn't deserted him—found himself gazing at the Monet poster on the wall. That's where the smell was coming from. The hot, humid air of this August morning had wilted the paper and brought the scent out.

- knows CS proc.
- possibly has record
- knows FR prints
- gun = .32 Colt

UNSUB 823

Appearance	Residence	Vehicle	Other
• Caucasian male, slight build • Dark clothing • Old gloves, reddish kidskin • Aftershave; to cover up other scent? • Ski mask? Navy blue? • Gloves are dark • Aftershave = Brut • Hair color not brown • Deep scar, index finger • Casual clothes • Gloves faded? Stained?	• Prob. has safe house • Located near: B'way & 82nd, ShopRite Greenwich & Bank, ShopRite 8th Ave. & 24th, ShopRite Houston & Lafayette, ShopRite • Old building, pink marble • At least 100 years old, prob. mansion or institutional	• Yellow Cab • Recent model sedan • Lt. gray, silver, beige • Rental car; prob. stolen • Hertz, silver Taurus, this year's model	• knows CS proc. • possibly has record • knows FR prints • gun = .32 Colt • Ties vics w/ unusual knots • "Old" appeals to him • Called one vic "Hanna" • Knows basic German • Underground appeals to him • Dual personalities • Maybe priest, soc. worker, counselor • Unusual wear on shoes, reads a lot? • Listened as he broke vic's finger • Left snake as slap at investigators

- Ties vics w/ unusual
  knots
- "Old" appeals to him
- Called one vic "Hanna"
- Knows basic German
- Underground appeals
  to him

The wall clock's pale numbers glowed: 5:45 a.m. His eyes returned to the poster. He couldn't see it clearly, just a ghostly pattern of pure white against a lesser white. But there was enough light from the dawn sky to make out most of the words.

- Dual personalities
- Maybe priest, soc.
  worker, counselor
- Unusual wear on shoes,
  reads a lot?
- Listened as he broke
  vic's finger
- Left snake as slap at
  investigators

The falcons were waking. He was aware of a flutter at the window. Rhyme's eyes skipped over the chart again. In his office at IRD he'd nailed up a dozen erasable marker boards and on them he'd keep a tally of the characteristics of the unsubs in major cases. He remembered: pacing, staring at them, wondering about the people they described.

Molecules of paint, mud, pollen, leaf . . .

- Old building, pink marble

Thinking about a clever jewel thief he and Lon had collared ten years ago. At Central Booking the perp had coyly said they'd never find the loot from the prior jobs but if they'd consider a plea he'd tell them where he'd hidden it. Rhyme had responded, "Well, we *have* been having some trouble figuring out where it is."

"I'm sure you have," the snide crook said.

"See," Rhyme continued, "we've narrowed it down to the stone wall in the coal bin of a Colonial farmhouse on the Connecticut River. About five miles north of Long Island Sound. I just can't tell whether the house is on the east bank or the west bank of the river."

When the story made the rounds the phrase everybody used to describe the expression on the perp's face was: You had to fucking be there.

Maybe it *is* magic, Sachs, he thought.

- At least 100 years old,
  prob. mansion or
  institutional

He scanned the poster once again and closed his eyes, leaning back into his glorious pillow. It was then that he felt the jolt. Almost like a slap on his face. The shock rose to his scalp like spreading fire. Eyes wide, locked onto the poster.

- "Old" appeals to him

"Sachs!" he cried. "Wake up!"

She stirred and sat up. "What? What's . . . ?"

Old, old, old . . .

"I made a mistake," he said tersely. "There's a problem."

She thought at first it was something medical and she leapt from the couch, reaching for Thom's medical bag.

"No, the clues, Sachs, the *clues* . . . I got it wrong." His breathing was rapid and he ground his teeth together as he thought.

She pulled her clothes on, sat back, her fingers disappearing automatically into her scalp, scratching. "What, Rhyme? What is it?"

"The church. It might not be in Harlem." He repeated, "I made a mistake."

Just like with the perp who killed Colin Stanton's family. In criminalistics you can nail down a hundred clues perfectly and it's the one you miss that gets people killed.

"What time is it?" she asked.

"Quarter to six, a little after. Get the newspaper. The church-services schedule."

Sachs found the paper, thumbed through it. Then looked up. "What're you thinking?"

"Eight twenty-three's obsessed with what's old. If he's after an old black church then he might not mean uptown. Philip Payton started the Afro-American Realty Company in Harlem in 1900. There were two other black settlements in the city. Downtown where the courthouses are now and San Juan Hill. They're mostly white now but . . . Oh, what the hell was I thinking of?"

"Where's San Juan Hill?"

"Just north of Hell's Kitchen. On the West Side. It was named in honor of all the black soldiers who fought in the Spanish-American War."

She read through the paper.

"Downtown churches," she said. "Well, in Battery Park there's the Seamen's Institute. A chapel there. They have services. Trinity. Saint Paul's."

"That wasn't the black area. Farther north and east."

"A Presbyterian church in Chinatown."

"Any Baptist. Evangelical?"

"No, nothing in that area at all. There's—Oh, hell." With resignation in her eyes she sighed. "Oh, no."

Rhyme understood. "Sunrise service!"

She was nodding. "Holy Tabernacle Baptist . . . Oh, Rhyme, there's a gospel service starting at six. Fifty-ninth and Eleventh Avenue."

"That's San Juan Hill! Call them!"

She grabbed the phone and dialed the number. She stood, head down, fiercely plucking an eyebrow and shaking her head. "Answer, answer . . . Hell. It's a recording. The minister must be out of his office." She said into the receiver, "This is the New York Police Department. We have reason to believe there's a firebomb in your church. Evacuate as fast as possible." She hung up, pulled her shoes on.

"Go, Sachs. You've got to get there. Now!"

"Me?"

"We're closer than the nearest precinct. You can be there in ten minutes."

She jogged toward the door, slinging her utility belt around her waist.

"I'll call the precinct," he yelled as she leapt down the stairs, hair a red cloud around her head. "And Sachs, if you ever wanted to drive fast, do it now."

The RRV wagon skidded into 81st Street, speeding west.

Sachs burst into the intersection at Broadway, skidded hard and whacked a *New York Post* vending machine, sending it through Zabar's window before she brought the wagon under control. She remembered all the crime scene equipment in the back. Rear-heavy vehicle, she thought; don't corner at fifty.

Then down Broadway. Brake at the intersections. Check left. Check right. Clear. Punch it!

She peeled off on Ninth Avenue at Lincoln Center and headed south. I'm only—

Oh, hell!

A mad stop on screaming tires.

The street was closed.

A row of blue sawhorses blocked Ninth for a street fair later that morning. A banner proclaimed, *Crafts and Delicacies of all Nations. Hand in hand, we are all one.*

Gaw ... *damn* UN! She backed up a half block and got the wagon up to fifty before she slammed into the first sawhorse. Spreading portable aluminum tables and wooden display racks in her wake, she tore a swath through the deserted fair. Two blocks later the wagon broke through the southern barricade and she skidded west on Fifty-ninth, using far more of the sidewalk than she meant to.

There was the church, a hundred yards away.

Parishioners on the steps—parents, little girls in frilly white and pink dresses, young boys in dark suits and white shirts, their hair in gangsta knobs or fades.

And from a basement window, a small puff of gray smoke.

Sachs slammed the accelerator to the floor, the engine roaring. Grabbing the radio. "RRV Two to Central, K?"

And in the instant it took her to glance down at the Motorola to make sure the volume was up, a big Mercedes slipped out of the alley directly into her path.

A fast glimpse of the family inside, eyes wide in horror, as the father slammed on the brakes.

Sachs instinctively spun the wheel hard to the left, putting the wagon into controlled skid. Come on, she was begging the tires, grip, grip, grip! But the oily asphalt was loose from the heat of the past few days and covered with dew. The wagon danced over the road like a hydrofoil.

The rear end met the Merc's front flat-on at fifty miles an hour. With an explosive boom the 560 sheared off the rear right side of the wagon. The black CS suitcases flew into the air, breaking open and strewing their contents along the street. Churchgoers dove for cover from the splinters of glass and plastic and sheet metal.

The air bag popped and deflated, stunning Sachs. She covered her face as the wagon tumbled over a row of cars and through a newsstand then skidded to a stop upside down. Newspapers and plastic evidence bags floated to the ground like tiny paratroopers.

Held upside down by the harness, blinded by her hair, Sachs wiped blood from her torn forehead and lip and tried to pop the belt release. It held tight. Hot gasoline flowed into the car and trickled along her arm. She pulled a switchblade from her back pocket, flicked the knife open and cut the seat belt. Falling, she nearly skewered herself on the knife and lay, gasping, choking on the gas fumes.

Come on, girl, get out. Out!

The doors were jammed closed and there was no escape through the crushed rear end of the wagon. Sachs began kicking the windows. The glass wouldn't break. She drew her foot back and slammed it hard into the cracked windshield. No effect, except that she nearly sprained her ankle.

Her gun!

She slapped her hip; the gun had been torn from the holster and tossed somewhere inside the car. Feeling the hot drizzle of gasoline on her arm and shoulder, she searched frantically through the papers and CS equipment littering the ceiling of the station wagon.

Then she saw the clunky Glock near the dome light. She swept it up and aimed at the side window.

Go ahead. Backdrop's clear, no spectators yet.

Then she hesitated. Would the muzzle flash ignite the gas?

She held the gun as far away from her soaked uniform blouse as she could, debating. Then squeezed the trigger.

TWENTY-EIGHT

Five shots, a star pattern, and even then the honest General Motors glass held firm.

Three more blasts, deafening her in the confines of the wagon. But at least the gas didn't explode.

She began to kick again. Finally the window burst outward in a cascade of blue-green ice. Just as she rolled out the interior of the wagon exploded with a breathless *woosh*.

Stripping down to her T-shirt, she flung away her gas-soaked uniform blouse and bulletproof vest and tossed aside the headset mike. Felt her ankle wobble but sprinted to the front door of the church, past the fleeing churchgoers and choir. The ground floor was filled with bubbling smoke. Nearby, a section of the floor rippled and steamed and then burst into flames.

The minister appeared suddenly, choking, tears streaming down his face. He was dragging an unconscious woman behind him. Sachs helped him get her to the door.

"Where's the basement?" she asked.

He coughed hard, shook his head.

"Where?" she cried, thinking of Carole Ganz and her little daughter. "The *basement?*"

"There. But . . ."

On the other side of the patch of burning floor.

Sachs could barely see it, the smoke was so thick. A wall collapsed in front of them, the old joists and posts behind it snapping and firing sparks and jets of hot gas, which hissed into the
cloudy room. She hesitated, then started for the basement door.

The minister took her arm. "Wait." He opened a closet and
grabbed a fire extinguisher, yanked the arming pin. "Let's go."

Sachs shook her head. "Not you. Keep checking up here. Tell
the fire department there's a police officer and another victim in
the basement."

Sachs was sprinting now.

When you move . . .

She jumped over the fiery patch of floor. But because of the
smoke she misjudged the distance to the wall; it was closer than
she'd thought and she slammed into the wood paneling then fell
backwards, rolling as her hair brushed the fire, some strands
igniting. Gagging on the stink, she crushed the flames out and
started to push herself to her feet. The floor, weakened by the
flames beneath, broke under her weight and her face crashed into
the oak. She felt the blaze in the basement lick her hands and
arms as she yanked her hands back.

Rolling away from the edge she climbed to her feet and reached
for the knob to the basement door. She stopped suddenly.

Come on, girl, think better! Feel a door before opening it. If
it's too hot and you let oxygen into a superheated room it'll ignite
and the backdraft'll fry your ass good. She touched the wood. It
was scorching hot.

Then thought: But what the hell else can I do?

Spitting on her hand, she gripped the knob fast, twisting it
open and releasing it just before the burn seared her palm.

The door burst open and a cloud of smoke and sparks shot
outward.

"Anybody down there?" she called and started down.

The lower stairs were burning. She blasted them with a short
burst of carbon dioxide and leapt into the murky basement. She
broke through the second-to-last step, pitching forward. The ex-

tinguisher clattered to the floor as she grabbed the railing just in time to save her leg from snapping.

Pulling herself out of the broken step, Sachs squinted through the haze. The smoke wasn't as bad down here—it was rising— but the flames were raging all around her. The extinguisher had rolled under a burning table. Forget it! She ran through the smoke.

"Hello?" she shouted.

No answer.

Then remembered that Unsub 823 used duct tape; he liked his vics silent.

She kicked in a small doorway and looked inside the boiler room. There was a door leading outside but burning debris blocked it completely. Beside it stood the fuel tank, which was now surrounded by flames.

It won't explode, Sachs remembered from the academy—the lecture on arson. Fuel oil doesn't explode. Kick aside the debris and push the door open. Clear your escape route. *Then* go look for the woman and the girl.

She hesitated, watching the flames roll over the side of the oil tank.

It won't explode, it won't explode.

She started forward, edging toward the door.

It won't—

The tank suddenly puffed out like a heated soda can and split down the middle. The oil squirted into the air, igniting in a huge orange spume. A fiery pool formed on the floor and flowed toward Sachs.

Won't explode. Okay. But it burns pretty fucking well. She leapt back through the door, slammed it shut. So much for her escape route.

Backing toward the stairs, choking now, keeping low, looking for any signs of Carole and Pammy. Could 823 have changed the rules? Could he have given up on basements and put these vics in the church attic?

Crack.

A fast look upward. She saw a large oak beam, rippling with flames, start to fall.

With a scream Sachs leapt aside, but tripped and landed hard on her back, staring at the huge falling bar of wood streaking directly at her face and chest. Instinctively she held her hands up.

A huge bang as the beam landed on a child's Sunday-school chair. It stopped inches from Sachs's head. She crawled out from underneath and rolled to her feet.

Looking around the room, peering through the darkening smoke.

Hell no, she thought suddenly. I'm not losing another one. Choking, Sachs turned back to the fire and staggered toward the one corner she hadn't checked.

As she jogged forward a leg shot out from behind a file cabinet and tripped her.

Hands flying outward, Sachs landed face down inches from a pool of burning oil. She rolled to her side, drawing her weapon and swinging it into the panicked face of a blond woman struggling to sit up.

Sachs pulled the gag off her mouth and the woman spit black mucus. She gagged for a moment, a deep, dying sound.

"Carole Ganz?"

She nodded.

"Your daughter?" Sachs cried.

"Not . . . here. My hands! The cuffs."

"No time. Come on." Sachs cut Carole's ankles free with her switchblade.

It was then that she saw, against the wall by the window, a melting plastic bag.

The planted clues! The ones that told where the little girl would be. She stepped toward it. But with a deafening bang the door to the boiler room cracked in half, spewing a six-inch tidal wave of burning oil over the floor, surrounding the bag, which disintegrated instantly.

Sachs stared for a moment and then heard the woman's scream.

All the stairs were blazing now. Sachs knocked the fire extinguisher out from under the smoldering table. The handle and nozzle had melted away and the metal canister was too hot to grasp. With her knife she cut a patch off her uniform blouse and lifted the crackling extinguisher by its neck, flung it to the top of the burning stairs. It staggered for a moment, like an uncertain bowling pin, and then started down.

Sachs drew her Glock and when the red cylinder was halfway down, fired one round.

The extinguisher erupted in a huge booming explosion; pieces of red shrapnel from the casing hissed over their heads. The mushroom cloud of carbon dioxide and powder settled over the stairs and momentarily dampened most of the flames.

"Now, move!" Sachs shouted.

Together they took the steps two at a time, Sachs carrying her own weight and half the woman's, and pushed through the doorway into the inferno on the first floor. They hugged the wall as they stumbled toward the exit, while above them stained-glass windows burst and rained hot shards—the colorful bodies of Jesus and Matthew and Mary and God Himself—down upon the bent backs of the escaping women.

TWENTY-NINE

Forty minutes later, Sachs had been salved and bandaged and stitched and had sucked so much pure oxygen she felt like she was tripping. She sat beside Carole Ganz. They stared at what was left of the church. Which was virtually nothing.

Only two walls remained and, curiously, a portion of the third floor, jutting into space above a lunar landscape of ash and debris piled in the basement.

"Pammy, Pammy . . ." Carole moaned, then retched and spit. She took her own oxygen mask to her face, leaned back, weary and in pain.

Sachs examined another alcohol-soaked rag with which she was wiping the blood from her face. The rags had started out brown and were now merely pink. The wounds weren't serious—a cut on her forehead, swatches of second-degree burns on her arm and hand. Her lips were no longer flawless, however; the lower one had been cut deeply in the crash, the tear requiring three stitches.

Carole was suffering from smoke inhalation and a broken wrist. An impromptu cast covered her left wrist and she cradled it, head down, speaking through clenched teeth. Every breath was an alarming wheeze. "That son of a bitch." Coughing. "Why . . . Pammy? Why on earth? A three-year-old child!" She wiped angry tears with the back of her uninjured arm.

"Maybe he doesn't want to hurt her. So he just brought you to the church."

"No," she spat out angrily. "He doesn't care about her. He's sick! I saw the way he looked at her. I'm going to kill him. I'm going to fucking kill him." The harsh words dissolved into a harsher bout of coughing.

Sachs winced in pain. She'd unconsciously dug a nail into a burned fingertip. She pulled out her watchbook. "Can you tell me what happened?"

Between bouts of sobbing and throaty coughs, Carole told her the story of the kidnapping.

"You want me to call anybody?" Sachs asked. "Your husband?"

Carole didn't answer. She drew her knees up to her chin, hugged herself, wheezing roughly.

With her scalded right hand Sachs squeezed the woman's biceps and repeated the question.

"My husband . . ." She stared at Sachs with an eerie look. "My husband's dead."

"Oh, I'm sorry."

Carole was getting groggy from the sedative and a woman medic helped her into the ambulance to rest.

Sachs looked up and saw Lon Sellitto and Jerry Banks running toward her from the burned-out church.

"Jesus, officer." Sellitto was surveying the carnage in the street. "What about the girl?"

Sachs nodded. "He's still got her."

Banks said, "You okay?"

"Nothing serious." Sachs glanced toward the ambulance. "The vic, Carole, she doesn't have any money, no place to stay. She's in town to work for the UN. Think you could make some calls, detective? See if they could set her up for a while?"

"Sure," Sellitto said.

"And the planted clues?" Banks asked. He winced as he touched a bandage over his right eyebrow.

"Gone," Sachs said. "I saw them. In the basement. Couldn't get to them in time. Burned up and buried."

"Oh, man," Banks muttered. "What's going to happen to the little girl?"

What does he *think's* going to happen to her?

She walked back toward the wreck of the IRD wagon, found the headset. She pulled it on and was about to call in a patch request to Rhyme but hesitated then lifted off the mike. What could he tell her anyway? She looked at the church. How can you work a crime scene when there *is* no scene?

She was standing with her hands on her hips, staring out onto the smoldering hulk of the building, when she heard a sound she couldn't place. A whining, mechanical sound. She paid no attention to it until she was aware of Lon Sellitto pausing as he dusted ash off his wrinkled shirt. He said, "I don't believe it."

She turned toward the street.

A large black van was parked a block away. A hydraulic ramp was protruding off the side and something sat on it. She squinted. One of those bomb squad robots, it seemed. The ramp lowered to the sidewalk and the robot rolled off.

Then she laughed out loud.

The contraption turned toward them and started to move. The wheelchair reminded her of a Pontiac Firebird, candy-apple red. It was one of those electric models, small rear wheels, a large battery and motor mounted underneath.

Thom walked along beside it but Lincoln Rhyme himself was driving—in control, she observed wryly—via a straw that he held in his mouth. His movements were oddly graceful. Rhyme pulled up to her and stopped.

"All right, I lied," he said abruptly.

She exhaled a sigh. "About your back? When you said you couldn't use a wheelchair."

"I'm confessing I lied. You're going to be mad, Amelia. So be mad and get it over with."

"You ever notice when you're in a good mood you call me Sachs, when you're in a bad mood, you call me Amelia?"

"I'm not in a bad mood," he snapped.

"He really isn't," Thom agreed. "He just hates to get caught at anything." The aide nodded toward the impressive wheelchair. She glanced at the side. It was made by the Action Company, a Storm Arrow model. "He had this in the closet downstairs all the while he spun his pathetic little tale of woe. Oh, I let him have it for that."

"No annotations, Thom, thank you. I'm apologizing, all right? I. Am. Sorry."

"He's had it for years," Thom continued. "Learned the sip-'n'-puff cold. That's the straw control. He's really very good at it. By the way, he always calls *me* Thom. I *never* get preferential last-name treatment."

"I got tired of being stared at," Rhyme said matter-of-factly. "So I stopped going for joyrides." Then glanced at her torn lip. "Hurt?"

She touched her mouth, which was bent into a grin. "Stings like hell."

Rhyme glanced sideways. "And what happened to you, Banks? Shaving your forehead now?"

"Walked into a fire truck." The young man grinned and touched the bandage again.

"Rhyme," Sachs began, smiling no longer. "There's nothing here. He's got the little girl and I couldn't get to the planted PE in time."

"Ah, Sachs, there's always *something*. Have faith in the teachings of Monsieur Locard."

"I saw them burn up, the clues. And if there was anything left at all, it's all buried under tons of debris."

"Then we'll look for the clues he didn't mean to leave. We'll do this scene together, Sachs. You and me. Come on."

He gave two short breaths into the straw and started forward. They'd got ten feet nearer the church when she said suddenly, "Wait."

He braked to a stop.

"You're getting careless, Rhyme. Get some rubber bands on those wheels. Wouldn't want to confuse your prints with the unsub's."

"Where do we start?"

"We need a sample of the ash," Rhyme said. "There were some clean paint cans in the back of the wagon. See if you can find one."

She collected a can from the remains of the RRV.

"You know where the fire started?" Rhyme asked.

"Pretty much."

"Take a sample of ash—a pint or two—as close to the point of origin as you can get."

"Right," she said, climbing up on a five-foot-high wall of brick—all that remained of the north side of the church. She peered down into the smoky pit at her feet.

A fire marshal called, "Hey, officer, we haven't secured the area yet. It's dangerous."

"Not as dangerous as the last time I was there," she answered. And holding the handle of the can in her teeth started down the wall.

Lincoln Rhyme watched her but he was really seeing himself, three and a half years ago, pull his suit jacket off and climb down into the construction site at the subway entrance near City Hall. "Sachs," Rhyme called. She turned. "Be careful. I saw what was left of the RRV. I don't want to lose you twice in one day."

She nodded and then disappeared over the edge of the wall.

After a few minutes Rhyme barked to Banks, "Where is she?"

"I don't know."

"What I'm saying is, could you go check on her?"

"Oh, sure." He walked to the wall, looked over.

"Well?" Rhyme asked.

"It's a mess."

"Of *course* it's a mess. Do you see her?"

"No."

"Sachs?" Rhyme shouted.

There was a long groan of wood then a crash. Dust rose.

"Sachs? Amelia?"

No answer.

Just as he was about to send ESU in after her they heard her voice. "Incoming."

"Jerry?" Rhyme called.

"Ready," the young detective called.

The can came flying up out of the basement. Banks caught it one-handed. Sachs climbed out of the basement, wiping her hands on her slacks, wincing.

"Okay?"

She nodded.

"Now, let's work the alley," Rhyme ordered. "There's traffic at all hours around here so he'd want the car off the street while he got her inside. That's where he parked. Used that door right there."

"How do you know?"

"There're two ways to open locked doors—without explosives, that is. Locks and hinges. This one'd be dead-bolted from the inside so he took the pins out of the hinges. See, he didn't bother to put them in very far again when he left."

They started at the door and worked their way to the back of the grim canyon, the smoldering building on their right. They moved a foot at a time, Sachs training the PoliLight on the cobblestones. "I want tire treads," Rhyme announced. "I want to know where his trunk was."

"Here," she said, examining the ground. "Treads. But I don't know whether these're the front or the rear tires. He might've backed in."

"Are they clear or fuzzy? The treadmarks?"

"A little fuzzy."

"Then those're the front." He laughed at her bewildered expression. "You're the automotive expert, Sachs. Next time you get in a car and start it see if you don't spin the wheel a little before you start moving. To see if the tires are pointed straight. The front treads're always fuzzier than the rear. Now, the stolen car was a '97 Ford Taurus. It measures 197.5 stem to stern, wheelbase 108.5. Approximately 45 inches from the center of the rear tire to the trunk. Measure that and vacuum."

"Come on, Rhyme. How'd you know that?"

"Looked it up this morning. You do the vic's clothing?"

"Yep. Nails and hair too. And, Rhyme, get this: the little girl's name is Pam but he called her Maggie. Just like he did with the German girl—he called her Hanna, remember?"

"You mean his other persona did," Rhyme said. "I wonder who the characters are in his little play."

"I'm going to vacuum around the door too," she announced. Rhyme watched her—face cut and hair uneven, singed short in spots. She vacuumed the base of the door and just as he was about to remind her that crime scenes were three-dimensional she ran the vacuum up and around the jamb.

"He probably looked inside before he took her in," she said and began vacuuming the windowsills too.

Which would have been Rhyme's next order.

He listened to the whine of the Dustbuster. But second by second he was fading away. Into the past, some hours before.

"I'm—" Sachs began.

"Shhh," he said.

Like the walks he now took, like the concerts he now attended, like so many of the conversations he had, Rhyme was slipping deeper and deeper into his consciousness. And when he got to a particular place—even he had no idea where—he found he wasn't alone. He was picturing a short man wearing gloves, dark sports clothes, a ski mask. Climbing out of the silver Ford Taurus sedan, which smelled of cleanser and new car. The woman— Carole Ganz—was in the trunk, her child captive in an old building made of pink marble and expensive brick. He saw the man dragging the woman from the car.

Almost a memory, it was that clear.

Popping the hinges, pulling open the door, dragging her inside, tying her up. He started to leave but paused. He walked to a place where he could look back and see Carole clearly. Just like he'd stared down at the man he'd buried at the railroad tracks yesterday morning.

Just like he'd chained Tammie Jean Colfax to the pipe in the center of the room. So he could get a good look at her.

But why? Rhyme wondered. Why does he look? To make sure the vics can't escape? To make sure he hasn't left anything behind? To—

His eyes sprang open; the indistinct apparition of Unsub 823 vanished. "Sachs! Remember the Colfax scene? When you found the glove print?"

"Sure."

"You said he was watching her, that's the reason he chained her out in the open. But you didn't know why. Well, I figured it out. He watches the vics because he *has to.*"

Because it's his nature.

"What do you mean?"

"Come on!"

Rhyme sipped twice into the straw control, which turned the Arrow wheelchair around. Then puffed hard and he started forward.

He wheeled to the sidewalk, sipped hard into the straw to stop. He squinted as he looked all around him. "He wants to see his victims. And I'm betting he wanted to see the parishioners too. From someplace he thought was safe. Where he didn't bother to sweep up afterwards."

He was gazing across the street at the only secluded vantage point on the block: the outdoor patio of a restaurant opposite the church.

"There! Sweep it clean, Sachs."

She nodded, slipped a new clip into her Glock, grabbed evidence bags, a pair of pencils and the Dustbuster. He saw her run across the street and work her way up the steps carefully, examining them. "He was here," she shouted. "There's a glove print. And the shoeprint—it's worn just like the other ones."

Yes! Rhyme thought. Oh, this felt good. The warm sun, the air, the spectators. And the excitement of the chase.

When you move they can't getcha.

Well, if *we* move faster, maybe we can.

Rhyme happened to glance at the crowd and saw that some people were staring at him. But far more were watching Amelia Sachs.

For fifteen minutes she pored over the scene and when she returned she held up a small evidence bag.

"What did you find, Sachs? His driver's license? His birth certificate?"

"Gold," she said, smiling. "I found some gold."

THIRTY

Come on, people," Rhyme called. "We've got to move on this one. Before he gets the girl to the next scene. I mean *move!*"

Thom did a sitting transfer to get Rhyme from the Storm Arrow back into bed, perching him momentarily on a sliding board and then easing him back into the Clinitron. Sachs glanced at the wheelchair elevator that had been built into one of the bedroom closets—it was the one he hadn't wanted her to open when he was directing her to the stereo and CDs.

Rhyme lay still for a moment, breathing deeply from the exertion.

"The clues're gone," he reminded them. "There's no way we can figure out where the next scene is. So we're going for the big one—his safe house."

"You think you can find it?" Sellitto asked.

Do we have a choice? Rhyme thought, and said nothing.

Banks hurried up the stairs. He hadn't even stepped into the bedroom before Rhyme blurted, "What did they say? Tell me. *Tell* me."

Rhyme knew that the tiny fleck of gold that Sachs had found was beyond the capabilities of Mel Cooper's impromptu lab. He'd asked the young detective to speed it down to the FBI's regional PERT office and have it analyzed.

"They'll call us in the next half hour."

"Half *hour?*" Rhyme muttered. "Didn't they give it priority?"

"You bet they did. Dellray was there. You should've seen him. He ordered every other case put on hold and said if the metallurgy report wasn't in your hands ASAP there'd be one mean mother—you get the picture—reaming their—you get the rest of the picture."

"Rhyme," Sachs said, "there's something else the Ganz woman said that might be important. He told her he'd let her go if she agreed to let him flail her foot."

"Flail?"

"Cut the skin off it."

"*Flay,*" Rhyme corrected.

"Oh. Anyway, he didn't do anything. She said it was—in the end—like he couldn't bring himself to cut her."

"Just like the first scene—the man by the railroad tracks," Sellitto offered.

"Interesting . . ." Rhyme reflected. "I thought he'd cut the vic's finger to discourage anybody from stealing the ring. But maybe not. Look at his behavior: Cutting the finger off the cabbie and carrying it around. Cutting the German girl's arm and leg. Stealing the bones and the snake skeleton. Listening while he broke Everett's finger . . . There's something about the way he sees his victims. Something . . ."

"Anatomical?"

"Exactly, Sachs."

"Except the Ganz woman," Sellitto said.

"My point," Rhyme said. "He could've cut her and still kept her alive for us. But something stopped him. What?"

Sellitto said, "What's different about her? Can't be that she's a woman. Or she's from out of town. So was the German girl."

"Maybe he didn't want to hurt her in front of her daughter," Banks said.

"No," Rhyme said, laughing grimly, "compassion isn't his thing."

Sachs said suddenly, "But that *is* one thing different about her—she's a mother."

Rhyme considered this. "That could be it. Mother and daughter. It didn't carry enough weight for him to let them go. But it stopped him from torturing her. Thom, jot that down. With a question mark." He then asked Sachs, "Did she say anything else about the way he looked?"

Sachs flipped through her notebook.

"Same as before." She read. "Ski mask, slight build, black gloves, he—"

"*Black* gloves?" Rhyme looked at the chart on the wall. "Not red?"

"She said black. I asked her if she was sure."

"And that other bit of leather was black too, wasn't it, Mel? Maybe *that* was from the gloves. So what's the red leather from?"

Cooper shrugged. "I don't know but we found a couple pieces of it. So it's something close to him."

Rhyme looked over the evidence bags. "What else did we find?"

"The trace we vacuumed in the alley and by the doorway." Sachs tapped the filter over a sheet of newsprint and Cooper went over it with a loupe. "Plenty o' nothin'," he announced. "Mostly soil. Bits of minerals. Manhattan mica schist. Feldspar."

Which was found throughout the city.

"Keep going."

"Decomposed leaves. That's about it."

"How about the Ganz woman's clothes?"

Cooper and Sachs opened the newspaper and examined the trace.

"Mostly soil," Cooper said. "And a few bits of what look like stone."

"Where did he keep her at his safe house? Exactly?"

"On the floor in the basement. She said it was a dirt floor."

"Excellent!" Rhyme shouted. To Cooper: "Burn it. The soil."

Cooper placed a sample in the GC-MS. They waited impatiently for the results. Finally the computer screen blinked. The grid resembled a lunar landscape.

"All right, Lincoln. Interesting. I'm reading off-the-charts for tannin and—"

"Sodium carbonate?"

"Ain't he amazin'?" Cooper laughed. "How'd you know?"

"They were used in tanneries in the eighteenth and nineteenth centuries. The tannic acid cures the hide and the alkaline fixes it. So, his safe house is near the site of an old tannery."

He smiled. Couldn't help himself. He thought: You hear footsteps, 823? That's us behind you.

His eyes slipped to the Randel Survey map. "Because of the smell no one wanted tanneries in their neighborhoods so the commissioners restricted them. I know there were some on the Lower East Side. And in West Greenwich Village—when it literally *was* a village, a suburb of the city. And then on the far West Side in the Fifties—near the stockyard tunnel where we found the German girl. Oh, and in Harlem in the early 1900s."

Rhyme glanced at the list of grocery stores—the locations of the ShopRites that sold veal shanks. "Chelsea's out. No tanning there. Harlem too—no *ShopRites* there. So, it's the West Village, Lower East Side or Midtown West Side—Hell's Kitchen again. Which he seems to like."

Only about ten square miles, Rhyme estimated cynically. He'd figured out on his first day on the job that it was easier to hide in Manhattan than in the North Woods.

"Let's keep going. What about the stone in Carole's clothes?"

Cooper was bent over the microscope. "Okay. Got it."

"Patch it in to me, Mel."

Rhyme's computer screen burst to life and he watched the flecks of stone and crystal, like brilliant asteroids.

"Move it around," Rhyme instructed. Three substances were bonded together.

"The one on the left is marble, pinkish," Cooper said. "Like what we found before. And in between, that gray stuff . . ."

"It's mortar. And the other is brownstone," Rhyme announced. "It's from a Federal-style building, like the 1812 City Hall. Only the front facade was marble; the rest was brownstone. They did it to save money. Well, they *did* it so the money appropriated for marble could find its way into various pockets. Now, what else do we have? The ash. Let's find the arson accelerant."

Cooper ran the ash sample through the GC-MS. He stared at the curve that appeared on the screen.

Newly refined gasoline, containing its manufacturer's dyes and additives, was unique and could be traced back to a single source, as long as different batches of gas weren't mixed together at the service station where the perp bought it. Cooper announced that the gasoline matched perfectly the brand sold by the Gas Exchange service stations.

Banks grabbed the Yellow Pages and flipped them open. "We've got six stations in Manhattan. Three downtown. One at Sixth Avenue and Houston. One on Delancey, 503 East. And one at Nineteenth and Eighth."

"Nineteenth's too far north," Rhyme said. He stared at the profile chart. "East Side or West. Which is it?"

Grocery stores, gasoline . . .

A lanky figure suddenly filled the doorway.

"I still invited to this here party?" Frederick Dellray asked.

"Depends," Rhyme countered. "You bearing gifts?"

"Ah got presents galore," the agent said, waving a folder emblazoned with the familiar disk of the FBI emblem.

"You *ever* knock, Dellray?" Sellitto asked.

"Got outa the habit, you know."

"Come on in," Rhyme said. "What've you got?"

"Dunno for sure. Doesn't make any sense to this boy. But then, whatta I know?"

Dellray read from the report for a moment then said, "We had Tony Farco at PERT—said 'Hey' to you by the way, Lincoln—analyze that bit of PE you found. Turns out it's gold leaf. Probably sixty to eighty years old. He found a few cellulose fibers attached so he thinks it's from a book."

"Of *course!* Gold topstain from a page," Rhyme said.

"Now he also found some particles of ink on it. He said, I'm quotin' the boy now: 'It's not inconsistent with the type of ink the New York Public Library uses to stamp the ends of their books.' Don't he talk funny?"

"A library book," Rhyme mused.

Amelia Sachs said, "A *red-leather-bound* library book."

Rhyme stared at her. "Right!" he shouted. "*That's* what the bits of red leather're from. Not the glove. It's a book he carries around with him. Could be his bible."

"Bible?" Dellray asked. "You thinkin' he's some kinda religious nutzo?"

"Not *the* Bible, Fred. Call the library again, Banks. Maybe that's how he wore down his shoes—in the reading room. I know, it's a long shot. But we don't have a lot of options here. I want a list of all the antiquarian books stolen from Manhattan locations in the past year."

"Will do." The young man rubbed a shaving scar as he called the mayor at home and bluntly asked hizzoner to contact the director of the public library and tell them what they needed.

A half hour later the fax machine buzzed and spewed out two pages. Thom ripped the transmission out of the machine. "Whoa, readers sure have sticky fingers in this city," he said as he brought it to Rhyme.

Eighty-four books fifty years old or older had disappeared from the public library branches in the past twelve months, thirty-five of them in Manhattan.

Rhyme scanned the list. Dickens, Austen, Hemingway, Dreiser . . . Books about music, philosophy, wine, literary criticism, fairy tales. Their value was surprisingly low. Twenty, thirty dollars. He supposed that none of them were first editions but perhaps the thieves hadn't known that.

He continued to scan the list.

Nothing, nothing. Maybe—

And then he saw it.

Crime in Old New York, by Richard Wille Stephans, published by Bountiful Press in 1919. Its value was listed at sixty-five dollars, and it had been stolen from the Delancey Street branch of the New York Public Library nine months earlier. It was described as five by seven inches in size, bound in red kidskin, with marbleized endpapers, gilded edges.

"I want a copy of it. I don't care how. Get somebody to the Library of Congress if you have to."

Dellray said, "I'll take care of that one."

Grocery stores, gasoline, the library . . .

Rhyme had to make a decision. There were three hundred searchers available—cops and state troopers and federal agents—but they'd be spread microscopically thin if they had to search both the West and East sides of downtown New York.

Gazing at the profile chart.

Is your house in the West Village? Rhyme silently asked 823. Did you buy the gas and steal the book on the East Side to fox us? Or is that your real neighborhood? How clever are you? No, no, the question's not how clever you are but how clever you *think* you are. How confident were you that we'd never find those minuscule bits of yourself that M. Locard assures us you'd leave behind?

Finally Rhyme ordered, "Go with the Lower East. Forget the Village. Get everybody down there. All of Bo's troops, all of yours, Fred. Here's what you're looking for: A large Federal-style building, close to two hundred years old, rose-colored marble front, brownstone sides and back. May have been a mansion or a public building at one time. With a garage or carriage house attached. A Taurus sedan and a Yellow Cab coming and going for the past few weeks. More often in the last few days."

Rhyme glanced at Sachs.

Giving up the dead . . .

Sellitto and Dellray made their calls.

Sachs said to Rhyme, "I'm going too."

"I hadn't expected anything else."

When the door had closed downstairs he whispered, "Godspeed, Sachs. Godspeed."

THIRTY-ONE

Three squad cars cruised slowly through the streets of the Lower East Side. Two constables in each. Eyes searching. And a moment later two black broughams appeared . . . two *sedans*, he meant. Unmarked, but their telltale search-lights next to the left side-view mirrors left no doubt who they were.

He'd known they were narrowing the search, of course, and that it was only a matter of time until they found his house. But he was shocked that they were this close. And he was particularly upset to see the cops get out and examine a silver Taurus parked on Canal Street.

How the hell had they found out about his carriage? He'd known that stealing a car was a huge risk but he thought it would take Hertz days to notice the missing vehicle. And even if they did he was sure the constables would never connect him with the theft. Oh, they were good.

One of the mean-eyed cops happened to glance at his cab.

Staring forward, the bone collector turned slowly onto Houston Street, lost himself in a crowd of other cabs. A half hour later, he'd ditched the taxi and the Hertz Taurus and had returned on foot to the mansion.

Young Maggie looked up at him.

UNSUB 823

Appearance	Residence	Vehicle	Other
• Caucasian male, slight build • Dark clothing • Old gloves, reddish kidskin • Aftershave; to cover up other scent? • Ski mask? Navy blue? • Gloves are dark • Aftershave = Brut • Hair color not brown • Deep scar, index finger • Casual clothes • Gloves are black	• Prob. has safe house • Located near: B'way & 82nd, ShopRite Greenwich & Bank, ShopRite 8th Ave. & 24th, ShopRite Houston & Lafayette, ShopRite • Old building, pink marble • At least 100 years old, prob. mansion or institutional • Federal-style building, Lower East Side	• Yellow Cab • Recent model sedan • Lt. gray, silver, beige • Rental car; prob. stolen • Hertz, silver Taurus, this year's model	• knows CS proc. • possibly has record • knows FR prints • gun = .32 Colt • Ties vics w/ unusual knots • "Old" appeals to him • Called one vic "Hanna" • Knows basic German • Underground appeals to him • Dual personalities • Maybe priest, soc. worker, counselor • Unusual wear on shoes, reads a lot? • Listened as he broke vic's finger • Left snake as slap at investigators • Wanted to flay vic's foot • Called one vic "Maggie" • Mother & child, special meaning to him? • Book "Crime in Old NY," his model?

She was scared, yes, but she'd stopped crying. He wondered if he should just keep her. Take himself a daughter. Raise her. The idea glowed within him for a moment or two then it faded.

No, there'd be too many questions. Also, there was something eerie about the way the girl was looking at him. She seemed older than her years. She'd always remember what he'd done. Oh, for a while she might think it had been a dream. But then someday the truth would come out. It always did. Repress what you will, someday the truth comes out.

No, he couldn't trust her any more than he trusted anyone else. Every human soul would let you down in the end. You could trust hate. You could trust bone. Everything else was betrayal.

He crouched beside Maggie and eased the tape off her mouth.

"Mommy!" she howled. "I want my mommy!"

He said nothing, just stood and looked down at her. At her delicate skull. At her twigs of arms.

She screamed like a siren.

He took off his glove. His fingers hovered over her for a moment. Then he caressed the soft hair on her head. (*"Fingerprints can be lifted from flesh, if taken within 90 minutes of contact [See KROMEKOTE] but no one has as yet successfully lifted and reconstructed friction-ridge prints from human hair."* Lincoln Rhyme, *Physical Evidence*, 4th ed. [New York: Forensic Press, 1994].)

The bone collector slowly rose and walked upstairs, into the large living room of the building, past the paintings on the walls—the workers, the staring women and children. He cocked his head at a faint noise outside. Then louder—a clatter of metal. He grabbed his weapon and hurried to the back of the building. Unbolting the door he pushed it open suddenly, dropping into a two-handed shooting stance.

The pack of wild dogs glanced at him. They returned quickly to the trash can they'd knocked over. He slipped the gun into his pocket and returned to the living room.

He found himself next to the bottle-glass window again, looking out at the old graveyard. Oh, yes. There! There was the man again, wearing black, standing in the cemetery. In the distance the sky was spiked by the black masts of clipper ships and sloops docked in the East River along the Out Ward's shore.

The bone collector felt an overwhelming sense of sorrow. He wondered if some tragedy had just occurred. Maybe the Great Fire of 1776 had just destroyed most of the buildings along Broadway. Or the yellow fever epidemic of 1795 had decimated the Irish community. Or the *General Slocum* excursion-boat fire in 1904 had killed over a thousand women and children, destroying the Lower East Side's German neighborhood.

Or maybe he was sensing tragedies soon to occur.

After a few minutes Maggie's screams grew quiet, replaced by the sounds of the old city, the roar of steam engines, the clang of bells, the pops of black-powder gunshots, the clop of hooves on resonant cobblestones.

He continued to stare, forgetting the constables who pursued him, forgetting Maggie, just watching the ghostly form stroll down the street.

Then and now.

His eyes remained focused out the window for a long moment, lost in a different time. And so he didn't notice the wild dogs, who'd pushed through the back door he'd left ajar. They looked at him through the doorway of the living room and paused only momentarily before turning around and loping quietly into the back of the building.

Noses lifted at the smells, ears pricked at the sounds of the strange place. Particularly the faint wailing that rose from somewhere beneath them.

───────

It was a sign of their desperation that even the Hardy Boys split up.

Bedding was working a half-dozen blocks around Delancey, Saul was farther south. Sellitto and Banks each had their search areas, and the hundreds of other officers, FBI agents and troopers made the door-to-door rounds, asking about a slight man, a young child crying, a silver Ford Taurus, a deserted Federal-style building, fronted in rose marble, the rest of it dark brownstone.

Huh? What the hell you mean, Federal? . . . Seen a kid? You asking if I ever seen a kid on the Lower East? Yo, Jimmy, you ever see any kids 'round here? Like not in the last, what, sixty seconds?

Amelia Sachs was flexing her muscle. She insisted that she be on Sellitto's crew, the one hitting the ShopRite on East Houston that had sold Unsub 823 the veal chop. And the gas station that had sold him the gasoline. The library from which he'd stolen *Crime in Old New York.*

But they'd found no leads there and scattered like wolves smelling a dozen different scents. Each picked a chunk of neighborhood to call his or her own.

As Sachs gunned the engine of the new RRV and tried another block she felt the same frustration she'd known when working the crime scenes over the past several days: too damn much evidence, too much turf to cover. The hopelessness of it. Here, on the hot, damp streets, branching into a hundred other streets and alleys running past a thousand buildings—all old—finding the safe house seemed as impossible as finding that hair that Rhyme had told her about, pasted to the ceiling by the blowback from a .38 revolver.

She'd intended to hit every street but as time wore on and she thought of the child buried underground, near death, she began to search more quickly, speeding down streets, glancing right and left for the rosy-marble building. Doubt stabbed her. Had she missed the building in her haste? Or should she drive like lightning and cover more streets?

On and on. Another block, another. And still nothing.

———

After the villain's death his effects were secured and perused by detectives. His diary showed that he had murdered eight good citizens of the city. Nor was he above grave robbery, for it was ascertained from his pages (if his claims be true) that he had violated several holy resting places in cemeteries around the city. None of his victims had accorded him the least affront;—nay, most were upstanding citizens, industrious and innocent. And yet he felt not a modicum of guilt. Indeed, he seems to have labored under the mad delusion that he was doing his victims a favor.

Lincoln Rhyme's left ring finger twitched slightly and the frame turned the onion-skin page of *Crime in Old New York*, which had been delivered by two federal officers ten minutes earlier, service expedited thanks to Fred Dellray's inimitable style.

"Flesh withers and can be weak,"—(the villain wrote in his ruthless yet steady hand)—"Bone is the strongest aspect of the body. As old as we may be in the flesh, we are always young in the bone. It is a noble goal I had, and it is beyond me why any-one might quarrel with it. I did a kindness to them all. They are immortal now. I freed them. I took them down to the bone."

Terry Dobyns had been right. Chapter 10, "James Schneider: the 'Bone Collector,' " was a virtual blueprint for Unsub 823's behavior. The MOs were the same—fire, animals, water, boiling alive. Eight twenty-three prowled the same haunts Schneider had. He'd confused a German tourist with Hanna Goldschmidt, a turn-of-the-century immigrant, and had been drawn to a German residence hall to find a victim. And he'd called little Pammy Ganz by a different name too—Maggie. Apparently thinking she was the young O'Connor girl, one of Schneider's victims.

A very bad etching in the book, covered by tissue, showed a demonic James Schneider, sitting in a basement, examining a leg bone.

Rhyme stared at the Randel Survey map of the city.

Bones . . .

Rhyme was recalling a crime scene he'd run once. He'd been called to a construction site in lower Manhattan where some excavators had discovered a skull a few feet below the surface of a vacant lot. Rhyme saw immediately that the skull was very old and brought a forensic anthropologist into the case. They continued to dig and discovered a number of bones and skeletons.

A little research revealed that in 1741 there'd been a slave rebellion in Manhattan and a number of slaves—and militant white abolitionists—had been hanged on a small island in the Collect. The island became a popular site for hangings and several informal cemeteries and potter's fields sprang up in the area.

Where had the Collect been? Rhyme tried to recall. Near where Chinatown and the Lower East Side meet. But it was hard to say for certain because the pond had been filled in so long ago. It had been—

Yes! he thought, his heart thudding: The Collect had been filled in because it had grown so polluted the city commissioners considered it a major health risk. And among the main polluters were the tanneries on the eastern shore!

Pretty good with the dialer now, Rhyme didn't flub a single number and got put through to the mayor on the first try. Hizzoner, though, the man's personal secretary said, was at a brunch at the UN. But when Rhyme identified himself the secretary said, "One minute, sir," and in much less time than that he found himself on the line with a man who said, through a mouthful of food, "Talk to me, detective. How the fuck're we doing?"

"Five-eight-eight-five, K," Amelia Sachs said, answering the radio. Rhyme heard the edginess in her voice.

"Sachs."

"This isn't good," she told him. "We're not having any luck."

"I think I've got him."

"*What?*"

"The six-hundred block, East Van Brevoort. Near Chinatown."

"How'd you know?"

"The mayor put me in touch with the head of the Historical Society. There's an archaeologic dig down there. An old graveyard. Across the street from where a big tannery used to be. And there were some big Federal mansions in the area at one time. I think he's nearby."

"I'm rolling."

Through the speakerphone he heard a squeal of tires, then the siren cut in.

"I've called Lon and Haumann," he added. "They're on their way over now."

"Rhyme," her urgent voice crackled. "I'll get her out."

Ah, you've got a cop's good heart, Amelia, a *professional* heart, Rhyme thought. But you're still just a rookie. "Sachs?" he said.

"Yes?"

"I've been reading this book. Eight twenty-three's picked a bad one for this role model of his. Really bad."

She said nothing.

"What I'm saying is," he continued, "whether the girl's there or not, if you find him and he so much as flinches, you nail him."

"But we get him alive, he can lead us to her. We can—"

"No, Sachs. Listen to me. You take him out. Any sign he's going for a weapon, anything . . . you take him out."

Static clattered. Then he heard her steady voice, "I'm at Van Brevoort, Rhyme. You were right. Looks like his place."

———

Eighteen unmarkeds, two ESU vans and Amelia Sachs's RRV were clustered near a short, deserted street on the Lower East Side.

East Van Brevoort looked like it was in Sarajevo. The buildings were abandoned—two of them burned to the ground. On the east side of the street was a dilapidated hospital of some kind, its roof caved in. Next to it was a large hole in the ground, roped off, with a No Trespassing sign emblazoned with the County Court seal—the archaeologic dig Rhyme had mentioned. A scrawny dog had died and lay in the gutter, its corpse picked over by rats.

In the middle of the other side of the street was a marble-fronted townhouse, faintly pink, with an attached carriage house, marginally nicer than the other decrepit tenements along Van Brevoort.

Sellitto, Banks and Haumann stood beside the ESU van, as a dozen officers suited up in Kevlar and racked their M-16s. Sachs joined them and, without asking, tucked her hair under a helmet and started to vest up.

Sellitto said, "Sachs, you're not tactical."

Slapping the Velcro strap down, she stared at the detective, eyebrow lifted high, until he relented and said, "Okay. But you're rear guard. That's an order."

Haumann said, "You'll be Team Two."

"Yessir. I can live with that."

One ESU cop offered her an MP-5 machine gun. She thought about Nick—their date on the range at Rodman's Neck. They'd spent two hours practicing with automatic weapons, firing Z-patterns through doors, flip-reloading with taped banana clips and field-stripping M-16s to clear the sand jams that plagued the Colts. Nick loved the staccato clutter but Sachs didn't much like the messy firepower of the big weapons. She'd suggested a match between them with Glocks and had whupped him three straight at fifty feet. He laughed and kissed her hard as the last of her empty casings spun, ringing, onto the firing range.

"I'll just use my sidearm," she told the ESU officer.

The Hardy Boys ran up, crouching as if they were mindful of snipers.

"Here's what we've got. There's nobody around. Block is—"

"Completely empty."

"The windows of his building're all barred. A back entrance—"

"Leading into the alley. The door's open."

"Open?" Haumann asked, glancing at several of his officers.

Saul confirmed, "Not just unlocked but open."

"Booby traps?"

"Not that we could see. Which isn't to say—"

"There aren't any."

Sellitto asked, "Any vehicles in the alley?"

"Nope."

"Two front entrances. Main front door—"

"Which looks painted shut. The second's the carriage-house doors. Double, wide enough for two vehicles. There's a padlock and chain."

"But they're lying on the ground."

Haumann nodded, "So maybe he's inside."

"Maybe," Saul said, then added, "And tell him what we think we heard."

"Very faint. Could have been crying."

"Could have been screaming."

Sachs asked, "The little girl?"

"Maybe. But then it just stopped. How'd Rhyme figure this place?"

"You tell *me* how his mind works," Sellitto said.

Haumann called one of his commanders and issued a series of orders. A moment later two ESU vans pulled into the intersection and blocked the other end of the street.

"Team One, front door. Blow it with cutting charges. It's wood and it's old so keep the plastic down, okay? Team Two, into the alley. On my three, you go. Got it? Neutralize but we're assuming the girl's in there so check your backdrops 'fore you squeeze. Officer Sachs, you're sure you want to do this?"

A firm nod.

"Okay, boys and girls. Go get him."

THIRTY-TWO

Sachs and the five other officers of Team Two ran into the torrid alley, which had been blocked off by ESU trucks. Renegade weeds grew profusely through the cobblestones and cracked foundations and the desolation reminded Sachs of the train-track grave yesterday morning.

He hoped the victim was dead. For his sake . . .

Haumann had ordered troopers onto the roofs of the surrounding buildings, and she saw the muzzles of their black Colts bristling like antennae.

The team paused at the rear doorway. Her fellow cops glanced at Sachs as she checked the rubber bands over her shoes. Heard one of them whisper to another something about superstition.

Then she heard through her earphone:

"Team One leader at front door, charge mounted and armed. We are clear, K."

"Roger, Team One leader. Team Two?"

"Team Two, in position, K."

"Roger, Team Two leader. Both teams, dynamic entry. On my three."

Checked her weapon one last time.

"One . . ."

Her tongue touched a dot of sweat hanging from the swollen wound on her lip.

"Two . . ."

Okay, Rhyme, here we go . . .

"Three!"

The explosion was very sedate, a distant pop, and then the teams were moving. Fast. She sprinted along behind the ESU troopers as they slipped inside and scattered, their muzzle-mounted flashlights crisscrossing the shafts of brilliant sunlight that streamed through the windows. Sachs found herself alone as the rest of the team dispersed, checking out armoires and closets and the shadows behind the grotesque statues the place was filled with.

She turned the corner. A pale face loomed. A knife . . .

A thud in her heart. Combat stance, gun up. She laid five pounds of pressure on the slick trigger before she realized she was staring at a painting on the wall. An eerie, moon-faced butcher, holding a knife in one hand, a slab of meat in the other.

Brother . . .

He picked a great place for home.

The ESU troops clopped upstairs, searching the first and second floors.

But Sachs was looking for something else.

She found the door leading down to the basement. Partly open. Okay. Halogen off. You've got to take a look first. But she remembered what Nick had said: never look around corners at head or chest level—that's where he's expecting you. Down on one knee. A deep breath. Go!

Nothing. Blackness.

Back to cover.

Listen . . .

At first she heard nothing. Then there was a definite scratching. A clatter. The sound of a fast breath or grunt.

He's there and he's digging his way out!

Into her mike she said, "I've got activity in the basement. Backup."

"Roger."

But she couldn't wait. She thought of the little girl down there with him. And she started down the stairs. Paused and listened again. Then she realized she was standing with her body fully exposed from the waist down. She practically leapt down to the floor, dropped into a crouch in the darkness.

Breathe deep.

Now, do it!

The halogen in her left hand stabbed a brilliant rod of light through the room. The muzzle of her weapon targeted the center of the white disk as it swung left to right. Keep the beam down. He'd be at crotch level too. Remembering what Nick had told her: Perps don't fly.

Nothing. No sign of him.

"Officer Sachs?"

An ESU trooper was at the top of the stairs.

"Oh, no," she muttered, as her beam fell on Pammy Ganz, frozen in the corner of the basement.

"Don't move," she called to the trooper.

Inches away from the girl stood the pack of emaciated wild dogs, sniffing at her face, her fingers, her legs. The girl's wide eyes darted from one animal to the other. Her tiny chest rose and fell and tears streamed down her face. Her mouth was open and the dot of her pink tongue seemed glued to the right arc of her lip.

"Stay up there," she said to the ESU trooper. "Don't spook 'em."

Sachs drew targets but didn't fire. She could kill two or three but the others might panic and grab the girl. One was big enough to snap her neck with a single flip of its scarred, mangy head.

"Is he down there?" the ESU cop asked.

"Don't know. Get a medic here. To the top of the stairs. Nobody come down."

"Roger."

Her weapon sights floating from one animal to another, Sachs slowly started forward. One by one the dogs became aware of her and turned away from Pammy. The little girl was merely food; Sachs was a predator. They growled and snarled, front legs quivering as their hindquarters tensed, ready to jump.

"I'm ascared," Pammy said shrilly, drawing their attention again.

"Shhhh, honey," Sachs cooed. "Don't say anything. Be quiet."

"Mommy. I want my *mommy!*" Her abrasive howl set the dogs off. They danced in place, and swung their battered noses from right to left, growling.

"Easy, easy . . ."

Sachs moved to the left. The dogs were facing her now, glancing from her eyes to her outstretched hand and the gun. They separated into two packs. One stayed close to Pammy. The other moved around Sachs, trying to flank her.

She eased between the little girl and the three dogs closest to her.

The Glock swinging back and forth, a pendulum. Their black eyes on the black gun.

One dog, with a scabby yellow coat, snarled and stepped forward on Sachs's right.

The little girl was whimpering, "Mommy . . ."

Sachs moved slowly. She leaned down, clamped her hand on the child's sweatshirt and dragged Pammy behind her. The yellow dog moved closer.

"Shoo," Sachs said.

Closer still.

"Go away!"

The dogs behind the yellow one tensed as he bared cracked brown teeth.

"Get the fuck outa here!" Sachs snarled and slammed the barrel of the Glock onto his nose. The dog blinked in dismay, yelped, skittered up the stairs.

Pammy screamed, sending the others into a frenzy. They started fighting among themselves, a whirlwind of snapping teeth and slaver. A scarred Rottweiler tossed a dustmop of a mutt to the floor in front of Sachs. She stamped her foot beside the scrawny brown thing and he skittered to his feet, raced up the stairs. The others chased him like greyhounds after a rabbit.

Pammy began to sob. Sachs crouched beside her and swept the basement again with her light. No sign of the unsub.

"It's okay, honey. We'll have you home soon. You'll be all right. That man here? You remember him?"

She nodded.

"Did he leave?"

"I don't know. I want my mommy."

She heard the other officers call in. The first and second floors were secure. "The car and taxi?" Sachs asked. "Any sign?"

A trooper transmitted, "They're gone. He's probably left."

He's not there, Amelia. That would be illogical.

From the top of the stairs an officer called, "Basement secure?"

She said, "I'm going to check. Hold on."

"We're coming down."

"Negative on that," she said. "We've got a pretty clean crime scene here and I want to keep it that way. Just get a medic down here to check out the little girl."

The young medic, a sandy-haired man, walked down the stairs and crouched beside Pammy.

It was then that Sachs saw the trail leading into the back of the basement—to a low, black-painted metal door. She walked to it, avoiding the path itself to save the prints, and crouched down. The door was partly open and there seemed to be a tunnel on the other side, dark but not completely black, leading to another building.

An escape route. The son of a bitch.

With the knuckles of her left hand she pushed the door open wider. It didn't squeak. She peered into the tunnel. Faint light, twenty, thirty feet away. No moving shadows.

If Sachs saw anything in the dimness it was T.J.'s contorted body dangling from the black pipe, Monelle Gerger's round, limp body as the black rat crawled toward her throat.

"Portable 5885 to CP," Sachs said into her mike.

"Go ahead, K," Haumann's terse voice responded.

"I've got a tunnel leading to the building south of the unsub's. Have somebody cover the doors and windows."

"Will do, K."

"I'm going in," she told him.

"The tunnel? We'll get you some backup, Sachs."

"Negative. I don't want the scene contaminated. Just have somebody keep an eye on the girl."

"Say again."

"No. No backup."

She clicked the light out and started crawling.

There'd been no courses in tunnel-rat work at the academy of course. But the things Nick had told her about securing a unfriendly scene came back to her. Weapon close to the body, not extended too far, where it could be knocked aside. Three steps—well, shuffles—forward, pause. Listen. Two more steps. Pause. Listen. Four steps next time. Don't do anything predictable.

Hell, it's dark.

And what's that *smell?* She shivered in disgust at the hot, foul stink.

The claustrophobia wrapped around her like a cloud of oil smoke and she had to stop for a moment, concentrating on anything but the closeness of the walls. The panic slipped away but the smell was worse. She gagged.

Quiet, girl. Quiet!

Sachs controlled the reflex and kept going.

And what's that noise? Something electrical. A buzzing. Rising and falling.

Ten feet from the end of the tunnel. Through the doorway she could see a second large basement. Murky though not quite as dark as the one Pammy had been in. Light leached in through a greasy window. She saw motes of dust pedaling through the gloom.

No, no, girl, the gun's too far in front of you. One kick and it's gone. Close to your face. Keep your weight low and back! Use your arms to aim, ass for support.

Then she was at the doorway.

She gagged again, tried to stifle the sound.

Is he waiting for me, or not?

Head out, a fast look. You've got a helmet. It'll deflect anything but a full-metal or Teflon and remember he's shooting a
.32. A girl gun.

All right. Think. Look which way first?

The *Patrolman's Guide* wasn't any help and Nick wasn't offering any advice at the moment. Flip a coin.

Left.

She stuck her head out fast, glancing to the left. Back into the
tunnel.

She'd seen nothing. A blank wall, shadows.

If he's the other way he's seen me and's got good target
positioning.

Okay, fuck. Just go. Fast.

When you move . . .

Sachs leapt.

. . . they can't getcha.

She hit the ground hard, rolling. Twisting around.

The figure was hidden in shadows against the wall to the right,
under the window. Drawing a target she started to fire. Then
froze.

Amelia Sachs gasped.

Oh, my God. . . .

Her eyes were inexorably drawn to the woman's body, propped
up against the wall.

From the waist up she was thin, with dark-brown hair, a gaunt
face, small breasts, bony arms. Her skin was covered with swarms
of flies—the buzzing Sachs had heard.

From the waist down, she was . . . nothing. Bloody hip bones,
femur, the whip of her spine, feet . . . All the flesh had been dissolved in the repulsive bath she rested next to—a horrible stew,
deep brown, chunks of flesh floating in it. Lye or acid of some
sort. The fumes stung Sachs's eyes, while horror—and fury too—
boiled in her heart.

Oh, you poor thing . . .

Sachs waved pointlessly at the flies that strafed the new intruder.

The woman's hands were relaxed, palms upward as if she were meditating. Eyes closed. A purple jogging outfit lay by her side.

She wasn't the only victim.

Another skeleton—completely stripped—lay beside a similar vat, older, empty of the terrible acid but coated with a dark sludge of blood and melted muscle. Its forearm and hand were missing. And beyond that was another one—this victim picked apart, the bones carefully scrubbed of all the flesh, cleaned, resting carefully on the floor. A stack of triple-ought sandpaper rested beside the skull. The elegant curve of the head shone like a trophy.

And then she heard it behind her.

A breath. Faint but unmistakable. The snap of air deep in a throat.

She spun around, furious at herself for her carelessness.

But the emptiness of the basement gaped back at her. She swept the light over the floor, which was stone and didn't show footprints as clearly as the dirt floor in 823's building next door.

Another inhalation.

Where was he? *Where?*

Sachs crouched further, sending the light sideways, up and down. . . . Nothing.

Where the fuck is he? Another tunnel? An exit to the street?

Looking at the floor again she spotted what she thought was a faint trail, leading into the shadows of the room. She moved along beside it.

Pause. Listen.

Breathing?

Yes. No.

Stupidly she spun around and looked at the dead woman once more.

Come *on!*

Eyes back again.

Moving along the floor.

Nothing. How can I hear him and not see him?

The wall ahead of her was solid. No doors or windows. She backed up, toward the skeletons.

From somewhere, Lincoln Rhyme's words came back. *"Crime scenes're three-dimensional."*

Sachs looked up suddenly, flashing the light in front of her. The huge Doberman's teeth shone back—dangling bits of gray flesh. Two feet away on a high ledge. He was waiting, like a wildcat, for her.

Neither of them moved for a moment. Absolutely frozen.

Then Sachs instinctively dropped her head and, before she could bring her weapon up, he launched himself toward her face. His teeth connected with the helmet. Gripping the strap in his mouth, he shook furiously, trying to break her neck as they fell backwards, onto the edge of an acid-filled pit. The pistol flew from her hand.

The dog kept his grip on her helmet while his hind legs galloped, his claws digging into her vest and belly and thighs. She hit him hard with her fists but it was like slugging wood; he didn't feel the blows at all.

Releasing the helmet, he reared back then lunged for her face. She flung her left arm over her eyes and, as he grabbed her forearm and she felt his teeth clamp down on her skin, she slipped the switchblade from her pocket and shoved the blade between his ribs. There was a yelp, a high sound, and he rolled off her, kept moving, speeding straight for the doorway.

Sachs snagged her pistol and was after him in an instant, scrabbling through the tunnel. She burst out to see the wounded animal sprinting straight toward Pammy and the medic, who stood frozen as the Doberman leapt into the air.

Sachs dropped into a crouch and squeezed off two rounds. One hit the back of the animal's head and the other streaked into the brick wall. The dog collapsed in a quivering pile at the medic's feet.

"Shots fired," she heard in her radio and a half-dozen troopers rushed down the stairs, pulled the dog away and deployed around the girl.

"It's all right!" Sachs shouted. "It was me!"

The team rose from their defensive positions.

Pammy was screaming, "Doggie dead . . . She made the doggie dead!"

Sachs holstered her weapon and hefted the girl onto her hip.

"Mommy!"

"You'll see your mommy soon," Sachs said. "We're going to call her right now."

Upstairs she set Pammy on the floor and turned to a young ESU officer standing nearby, "I lost my cuff key. Could you take those off her please? Open them over a piece of clean newspaper, wrap 'em up in the paper and put the whole thing in a plastic bag."

The officer rolled his eyes. "Listen, beautiful, go find yourself a rookie to order around." He started to walk away.

"Trooper," Bo Haumann barked, "you'll do what she says."

"Sir," he protested, "I'm ESU."

"Got news," Sachs muttered, "you're Crime Scene now."

———————

Carole Ganz was lying on her back in a very beige bedroom, staring at the ceiling, thinking about the time a few weeks ago when she and Pammy and a bunch of friends were sitting around a campfire in Wisconsin at Kate and Eddie's place, talking, telling stories, singing songs.

Kate's voice wasn't so hot but Eddie could've been a pro. He could even play barre chords. He sang Carole King's "Tapestry" just for her and Carole sang along softly through her tears. Thinking that maybe, just maybe, she really was putting Ron's death behind her and getting on with her life.

She remembered Kate's voice from that night: "When you're angry, the only way to deal with it is to wrap up that anger and give it away. Give it to somebody else. Do you hear me? Don't keep it inside you. Give it away."

Well, she was angry now. Furious.

Some young kid—a mindless little shit—had taken her husband away, shot him in the back. And now some crazy man had taken her daughter. She wanted to explode. And it took all her willpower not to start flinging things against the wall and howling like a coyote.

She lay back on the bed and gingerly placed her shattered wrist on her belly. She'd taken a Demerol, which had eased the pain, but she hadn't been able to sleep. She'd done nothing but stay inside all day long, trying to get in touch with Kate and Eddie and waiting for news about Pammy.

She kept picturing Ron, kept picturing her anger, actually imagining herself packing it up in a box, wrapping it carefully, sealing it up . . .

And then the phone rang. She stared for a moment then yanked it off the cradle.

"Hello?"

Carole listened to the policewoman tell her that they'd found Pammy, that she was in the hospital but that she was okay. A moment later Pammy herself came on the phone and they were both crying and laughing at the same time.

Ten minutes later she was on her way to Manhattan Hospital, in the back seat of a black police sedan.

Carole practically sprinted down the corridor to Pammy's room and was surprised to be stopped by the police guard. So they hadn't caught the fucker yet? But as soon as she saw her daughter she forgot about him, forgot the terror in the taxi and the fiery basement. She threw her arms around her little girl.

"Oh, honey, I missed you! Are you okay? Really okay?"

"That lady, she killed a doggie—"

Carole turned and saw the tall, red-haired policewoman standing nearby, the one who'd saved her from the church basement.

"—but it was all right because he was going to eat me."

Carole hugged Sachs. "I don't know what to say. . . . I just . . . Thank you, thank you."

"Pammy's fine," Sachs assured her. "Some scratches—nothing serious—and she's got a little cough."

"Mrs. Ganz?" A young man walked into the room, carrying

her suitcase and yellow knapsack. "I'm Detective Banks. We've got your things here."

"Oh, thank God."

"Is anything missing?" he asked her.

She looked through the knapsack carefully. It was all there. The money, Pammy's doll, the package of clay, the Mr. Potato Head, the CDs, the clock radio . . . He hadn't taken anything. Wait . . . "You know, I think there's a picture missing. I'm not sure. I thought I had more than these. But everything important's here."

The detective gave her a receipt to sign.

A young resident stepped into the room. He joked with Pammy about her Pooh bear as he took her blood pressure.

Carole asked him, "When can she leave?"

"Well, we'd like to keep her in for a few days. Just to make sure—"

"A few *days?* But she's fine."

"She's got a bit of bronchitis I want to keep an eye on. And . . ." He lowered his voice. "We're also going to bring in an abuse specialist. Just to make sure."

"But she was going to go with me tomorrow. To the UN ceremonies. I promised her."

The policewoman added, "It's easier to keep her guarded here. We don't know where the unsub—the kidnapper—is. We'll have an officer babysitting you too."

"Well, I guess. Can I stay with her for a while?"

"You bet," the resident said. "You can stay the night. We'll have a cot brought in."

Then Carole was alone with her daughter once more. She sat down on the bed and put her arm around the child's narrow shoulders. She had a bad moment remembering how *he*, that crazy man, had touched Pammy. How his eyes had looked when he'd asked if he could cut her own skin off . . . Carole shivered and began to cry.

It was Pammy who brought her back. "Mommy, tell me a

story. . . . No, no, sing me something. Sing me the friend song. Pleeeeease?"

Calming down, Carole asked, "You want to hear that one, hm?"

"Yes!"

Carole hoisted the girl onto her lap and, in a reedy voice, started to sing "You've Got a Friend." Pammy sang snatches of it along with her.

It had been one of Ron's favorites and, in the past couple years, after he was gone, she hadn't been able to listen to more than a few bars without breaking into tears.

Today, she and Pammy finished it together, pretty much on key, dry-eyed and laughing.

THIRTY-THREE

Amelia Sachs finally went home to her apartment in Carroll Gardens, Brooklyn.

Exactly six blocks from her parents' house, where her mother still lived. As soon as she walked in she hit the first speed-dial button on the kitchen phone.

"Mom. Me. I'm taking you to brunch at the Plaza. Wednesday. That's my day off."

"What for? To celebrate your new assignment? How *is* Public Affairs? You didn't call."

A fast laugh. Sachs realized her mother had no idea what she'd been doing for the past day and a half.

"You been following the news, Mom?"

"Me? I'm Brokaw's secret admirer, you know that."

"You hear about this kidnapper the last few days?"

"Who hasn't? . . . What're you telling me, honey?"

"I've got the inside scoop."

And she told her astonished mother the story—about saving the vics and about Lincoln Rhyme and, with some editing, about the crime scenes.

"Amie, your father'd be so proud."

"So, call in sick on Wednesday. The Plaza. OK?"

"Forget it, sweetheart. Save your money. I've got waffles and Bob Evans in the freezer. You can come here."

"It's not that expensive, Mom."

"Not that much? It's a *fortune*."

"Well, hey," Sachs said, trying to sound spontaneous, "you like the Pink Teacup, don't you?"

A little place in the West Village that served up platters of the best pancakes and eggs on the East Coast for next to nothing.

A pause.

"That might be nice."

This was a strategy Sachs had used successfully over the years.

"I've gotta get some rest, Mom. I'll call tomorrow."

"You work too hard. Amie, this case of yours . . . it wasn't dangerous, was it?"

"I was just doing the technical stuff, Mom. Crime scene. It doesn't get any safer than that."

"And they asked for *you* especially!" the woman said. Then repeated, "Your father'd be so proud."

They hung up and Sachs wandered into the bedroom, flopped down on the bed.

After she'd left Pammy's room Sachs had paid visits to the other two surviving victims of Unsub 823. Monelle Gerger, dotted with bandages and pumped full of anti-rabies serum, had been released and was returning to her family in Frankfurt "but just for rest of summer," she explained adamantly. "Not, you know, for good." And she'd pointed to her stereo and CD collection in the decrepit apartment in the Deutsche Haus by way of proving that no New World psycho was driving her permanently out of town.

William Everett was still in the hospital. The shattered finger was not a serious problem of course but his heart had been acting up again. Sachs was astonished to find that he'd owned a shop in Hell's Kitchen years ago and thought he might have known her father. "I knew all the beat cops," he said. She showed him her wallet picture of the man in his dress uniform. "I think so. Not sure. But I think so."

The calls had been social but Sachs had gone armed with her

watchbook. Neither of the vics, though, had been able to tell her anything more about Unsub 823.

In her apartment now Sachs glanced out her window. She saw the ginkgoes and maples shiver in the sharp wind. She stripped off her uniform, scratched under her boobs—where it always itched like mad from being squooshed under the body armor. She pulled on a bathrobe.

Unsub 823 hadn't had much warning but it had been enough. The safe house on Van Brevoort had been hosed completely. Even though the landlord said he'd moved in a long time ago— last January (with a phony ID, no one was very surprised to learn)—823 had left with everything he'd brought, trash included. After Sachs had worked the scene, NYPD Latents had descended and was dusting every surface in the place. So far the preliminary reports weren't encouraging.

"Looks like he even wore gloves when he crapped," young Banks had reported to her.

A Mobile unit had found the taxi and the sedan. Unsub 823'd cleverly parked them near Avenue D and Ninth Street. Sellitto guessed it probably took a local gang seven or eight minutes to strip them down to their chassis. Any physical evidence the vehicles might've yielded was now in a dozen chop shops around the city.

Sachs turned on the tube and found the news. Nothing about the kidnappings. All the stories were about the opening ceremonies of the UN peace conference.

She stared at Bryant Gumbel, stared at the UN secretary-general, stared at some ambassador from the Middle East, stared far more intently than her interest warranted. She even studied the ads as if she were memorizing them.

Because there was something she definitely *didn't* want to think about: her bargain with Lincoln Rhyme.

The deal was clear. Now that Carole and Pammy were safe, it was her turn to come through. To let him have his hour alone with Dr. Berger.

Now *him*, Berger . . . She hadn't liked the look of the doctor at all. You could see one big fucking ego in his compact, athletic frame, his evasive eyes. His black hair perfectly combed. Expensive clothes. Why couldn't Rhyme have found someone like Kevorkian? He may have been quirky but at least seemed like a wise old grandfather.

Her lids closed.

Giving up the dead . . .

A bargain was a bargain. But goddammit, Rhyme . . .

Well, she couldn't let him go without one last try. He'd caught her off guard in his bedroom. She was flustered. Hadn't thought of any really good arguments. Monday. She had until tomorrow to try to convince him not to do it. Or at least to wait awhile. A month. Hell, a day.

What could she say to him? She'd jot down her arguments. Write a little speech.

Opening her eyes, she climbed out of bed to find a pen and some paper. I could—

Sachs froze, her breath whistling into her lungs like the wind outside.

He wore dark clothes, the ski mask and gloves black as oil.

Unsub 823 stood in the middle of her bedroom.

Her hand instinctively went toward the bedside table—her Glock and knife. But he was ready. The shovel swung fast and caught her on the side of her head. A yellow light exploded in her eyes.

She was on her hands and knees when the foot slammed into her rib cage and she collapsed to her stomach, struggling for breath. She felt her hands being cuffed behind her, a strip of duct tape slapped onto her mouth. Moving fast, efficiently. He rolled her onto her back; her robe fell open.

Kicking furiously, struggling madly to pull the cuffs apart.

Another blow to her stomach. She gagged and fell still as he reached for her. Gripped her at the armpits, dragged her out the back door and into the large private garden behind the apartment.

His eyes remained on her face, not even looking at her tits, her flat belly, her mound with its few red curls. She could easily have given that up to him if it would have saved her life.

But, no, Rhyme's diagnosis was right. It wasn't lust that drove 823. He had something else in mind. He dropped her willowy figure, face up, into a patch of black-eyed Susans and pachysandra, out of sight of the neighbors. He looked around, catching his breath. He picked up the shovel and plunged the blade into the dirt.

Amelia Sachs began to cry.

Rubbing the back of his head into the pillow.

Compulsive, a doctor had once told him after observing this behavior—an opinion Rhyme hadn't asked for. Or wanted. His nestling, Rhyme reflected, was just a variation on Amelia Sachs's tearing her flesh with her own nails.

He stretched his neck muscles, rolling his head around, as he stared at the profile chart on the wall. Rhyme believed that the full story of the man's madness was here in front of him. In the black, swoopy handwriting—and the gaps between the words. But he couldn't see the story's ending. Not yet.

He looked over the clues again. There were only a few left unexplained.

The scar on the finger.

The knot.

The aftershave.

The scar was useless to them unless they had a suspect whose fingers they could examine. And there'd been no luck in identifying the knot—only preppy Banks's opinion that it wasn't nautical.

What about the cheap aftershave? Assuming that most unsubs wouldn't spritz themselves to go on a kidnapping spree, why had he worn it? Rhyme could only conclude again that he was trying to obscure another, a telltale scent. He ran through the possibilities: Food, liquor, chemicals, tobacco . . .

He felt eyes on him and looked to his right.

The black dots of the bony rattlesnake's eye sockets gazed toward the Clinitron. This was the one clue that was out of place. It had no purpose, except to taunt them.

Something occurred to him. Using the painstaking turning

frame Rhyme slowly flipped back through *Crime in Old New York*. To the chapter on James Schneider. He found the paragraphs he'd remembered.

> *It has been suggested by a well-known physician of the mind (a practitioner of the discipline of "psyche-logy," which has been much in the news of late) that James Schneider's ultimate intent had little to do with harming his victims. Rather—this learnèd doctor has suggested—the villain was seeking revenge against those that did him what he perceived to be harm: the city's constabulary, if not Society as a whole.*
>
> *Who can say where the source of this hate lay? Perhaps, like the Nile of old, its wellsprings were hidden to the world;—and possibly even to the villain himself. Yet one reason may be found in a little-known fact: Young James Schneider, at the tender age of ten, saw his father dragged away by constables only to die in prison for a robbery which, it was later ascertained, he did not commit. Following this unfortunate arrest, the boy's mother fell into life on the street and abandoned her son, who grew up a ward of the state.*
>
> *Did the madman perchance commit these crimes to fling derision into the face of the very constabulary which had inadvertently destroyed his family?*
>
> *We will undoubtedly never know.*
>
> *Yet what does seem clear is that by mocking the ineffectualness of the protectors of its citizenry, James Schneider—the "bone collector"—was wreaking his vengeance upon the city itself as much as upon his innocent victims.*

Lincoln Rhyme lay back in his pillow and looked at the profile chart again.

———

Dirt is heavier than anything.

It's the earth itself, the dust of an iron core, and it doesn't kill by strangling the air from the lungs but by compressing the cells until they die from the panic of immobility.

Sachs wished that she *had* died. She prayed that she would. Fast. From fear or a heart attack. Before the first shovelful hit her face. She prayed for this harder than Lincoln Rhyme had prayed for his pills and liquor.

Lying in the grave the unsub had dug in her own backyard Sachs felt the progress of the rich earth, dense and wormy, moving along her body.

Sadistically, he was burying her slowly, casting only a shallow scoop at a time, scattering it carefully around her. He'd started with her feet. He was now up to her chest, the dirt slipping into her robe and around her breasts like a lover's fingers.

Heavier and heavier, compressing, binding her lungs; she could suck only an ounce or two of air at a time. He paused once or twice to look at her then continued.

He likes to watch . . .

Hands beneath her, neck straining to keep her head above the tide.

Then her chest was buried completely. Her shoulders, her throat. The cold earth rose to the hot skin of her face, packing around her head so she couldn't move. Finally he bent down and ripped the tape off her mouth. As Sachs tried to scream he spilled a handful of dirt into her face. She shivered, choked on the black earth. Ears ringing, hearing for some reason an old song from her infancy—"The Green Leaves of Summer," a song her father played over and over again on the hi-fi. Sorrowful, haunting. She closed her eyes. Everything was going black. Opened her mouth once and got another cup's worth of soil.

Giving up the dead . . .

And then she was under.

Completely quiet. Not choking or gasping—the earth was a perfect seal. She had no air in her lungs, couldn't make any sounds. Silence, except for the haunting melody and the growing roar in her ears.

Then the pressure on her face ceased as her body went numb, as numb as Lincoln Rhyme's. Her mind began to shut down.

Blackness, blackness. No words from her father. Nothing from Nick . . . No dreams of downshifting from five to four to goose the speedometer into three digits.

Blackness.

Giving up the . . .

The mass sinking down onto her, pushing, pushing. Seeing only one image: The hand rising out of the grave yesterday morning, waving for mercy. When no mercy would be given.

Waving for her to follow.

Rhyme, I'll miss you.

Giving up . . .

THIRTY-FOUR

Something struck her forehead. Hard. She felt the thump but no pain.

What, what? His shovel? A brick? Maybe in an instant of compassion 823'd decided that this slow death was more than anyone could bear and was striking for her throat to sever her veins.

Another blow, and another. She couldn't open her eyes, but she was aware of light growing around her. Colors. And air. She forced the mass of dirt from her mouth and sucked in tiny breaths, all she could manage. Began coughing in a loud bray, retching, spitting.

Her lids sprang open and through tearing eyes she found herself looking up at the muddy vision of Lon Sellitto, kneeling over her, beside two EMS medics, one of whom dug into her mouth with latex-clad fingers and pulled out more gunk, while the other readied an oxygen mask and green tank.

Sellitto and Banks continued to uncover her body, shoving the dirt away with their muscular hands. They pulled her up, leaving the robe behind like a shed skin. Sellitto, old divorcé that he was, looked chastely away from her body as he put his jacket around her shoulders. Young Jerry Banks did look of course but she loved him anyway.

"Did . . . you . . . ?" she wheezed, then surrendered to a racking cough.

Sellitto glanced expectantly at Banks, who was the more breathless of the two. He must've done the most running after the unsub. The young detective shook his head. "Got away."

Sitting up, she inhaled oxygen for a moment.

"How?" she wheezed. "How'd you know?"

"Rhyme," he answered. "Don't ask me how. He called in 10-13s for everybody on the team. When he heard we were okay he sent us over here ASAP."

Then the numbness left, snap, in a flash. And for the first time she realized what had nearly happened. She dropped the oxygen mask, backed away in panic, tears streaming, her panicky keening growing louder and louder. "No, no, no . . ."

Slapping her arms and thighs, frantic, trying to shake off the horror clinging to her like a teeming swarm of bees.

"Oh God oh God . . . No . . ."

"Sachs?" Banks asked, alarmed. "Hey, Sachs?"

The older detective waved his partner away. "It's okay." He kept his arm around her shoulders as she dropped to all fours and vomited violently, sobbing, sobbing, gripping the dirt desperately between her fingers as if she wanted to strangle it.

Finally Sachs calmed and sat back on her naked haunches. She began laughing, softly at first then louder and louder, hysterical, astonished to find that the skies had opened and it had been raining—huge hot summer drops—and she hadn't even realized it.

Arm around his shoulders. Face pressed against his. They stayed that way for a long moment.

"Sachs . . . Oh, Sachs."

She stepped away from the Clinitron and scooted an old armchair from the corner of the room. Sachs—wearing navy sweatpants and a Hunter College T-shirt—flopped down into the chair and dangled her exquisite legs over the arm like a schoolgirl.

"Why us, Rhyme? Why'd he come after us?" Her voice was a raspy whisper from the dirt she'd swallowed.

"Because the people he kidnapped aren't the real victims. We are."

"Who's *we?*" she asked.

"I'm not sure. Society maybe. Or the city. Or the UN. Cops. I went back and reread his bible—the chapter on James Schneider. Remember Terry's theory about why the unsub'd been leaving the clues?"

Sellitto said, "Sort of making us accessories. To share the guilt. Make it easier for him to kill."

Rhyme nodded but said, "I don't think that's the reason though. I think the clues were a way to attack *us*. Every dead vic was a loss for us."

In her old clothes, hair pulled back in a ponytail, Sachs looked more beautiful than any time in the past two days. But her eyes were tin. She'd be reliving every shovelful of dirt, he supposed, and Rhyme found the thought of her living burial so disturbing he had to look away.

"What's he got against us?" she asked.

"I don't know. Schneider's father was arrested by mistake and died in prison. Our unsub? Who knows why? I only care about evidence—"

"—not motives." Amelia Sachs finished the sentence.

"Why'd he start going after us directly?" Banks asked, nodding at Sachs.

"We found his hidey-hole and saved the little girl. I don't think he expected us so soon. Maybe he just got pissed. Lon, we need twenty-four-hour babysitters for all of us. He could've just taken off after we saved the kid but he stuck around to do some damage. You and Jerry, me, Cooper, Haumann, Polling, we're all on his list, betcha. Meanwhile, get Peretti's boys over to Sachs's. I'm sure he kept it clean but there might be something there. He left a lot faster than he'd planned to."

"I better get over there," Sachs said.

"No," Rhyme said.

"I have to work the scene."

"You have to get some rest," he ordered. "*That's* what you have to do, Sachs. You don't mind my saying, you look lousy."

"Yeah, officer," Sellitto said. " 'S'an order. I told you to stand down for the rest of the day. We've got two hundred searchers looking for him. And Fred Dellray's got another hundred and twenty feebies."

"I got a crime scene in my own backyard and you're not gonna let me walk the grid?"

"That's it," Rhyme said, "in a nutshell."

Sellitto walked to the doorway. "Any problems with that, officer?"

"Nosir."

"Come on, Banks, we got work to do. You need a lift, Sachs? Or're they still trusting you with vehicles?"

"No thanks, got wheels downstairs," she said.

The two detectives left. Rhyme heard their voices echoing through the empty hall. Then the door closed and they were gone.

Rhyme realized the glaring overhead lights were on. He clicked through several commands and dimmed them.

Sachs stretched.

"Well," she said, just as Rhyme said, "So."

She glanced at the clock. "It's late."

"Sure is."

Rising, she walked to the table where her purse rested. She picked it up. Clicked it open, found her compact and examined her cut lip in the mirror.

"It doesn't look too bad," Rhyme said.

"Frankenstein," she said, prodding. "Why don't they use flesh-colored stitches?" She put the mirror away, slung the purse over her shoulder. "You moved the bed," she noticed. It was closer to the window.

"Thom did. I can look at the park. If I want to."

"Well, that's good."

She walked to the window. Looked down.

Oh, for Christ's sake, Rhyme thought to himself. Do it. What can happen? He blurted quickly, "You want to stay here? I mean, it's getting late. And Latents'll be dusting your place for hours."

He felt a mad bolt of anticipation deep within him. Well, kill *that*, he thought, furious with himself. Until her face blossomed into a smile. "I'd like that."

"Good." His jaw shivered from the adrenaline. "Wonderful. Thom!"

Listening to music, drinking some Scotch. Maybe he'd tell her more about famous crime scenes. The historian in him was also curious about her father, about police work in the '60s and '70s. About the infamous Midtown South Precinct in the old days.

Rhyme shouted, "Thom! Get some sheets. And a blanket. Thom! I don't know what the hell he's doing. *Thom!*"

Sachs started to say something but the aide appeared in the doorway and said testily, "One rude shout would've been enough, you know, Lincoln."

"Amelia's staying over again. Could you get some blankets and pillows for the couch?"

"No, not the couch again," she said. "It's like sleeping on rocks."

Rhyme was stabbed with a splinter of rejection. Thinking ruefully to himself: Been a few years since he'd felt *that* emotion. Resigned, he nonetheless smiled and said, "There's a bedroom downstairs. Thom can make it up for you."

But Sachs set down her purse. "That's okay, Thom. You don't have to."

"It's no bother."

"It's all right. Good night, Thom." She walked to the door.

"Well, I—"

She smiled.

"But—" he began, looking from her to Rhyme, who frowned, shook his head.

"Good *night*, Thom," she said firmly. "Watch your feet." And closed the door slowly, as he stepped back out of the way into the hall. It closed with a loud click.

Sachs kicked off her shoes, pulled off the sweats and T-shirt. She wore a lace bra and baggy cotton panties. She climbed into the Clinitron beside Rhyme, showing every bit of the authority beautiful women wield when it comes to climbing into bed with a man.

She wriggled down into the pellets and laughed. "This is one hell of a bed," she said, stretching like a cat. Eyes closed, Sachs asked, "You don't mind, do you?"

"I don't mind at all."

"Rhyme?"

"What?"

"Tell me more about your book, okay? Some more crime scenes?"

He started to describe a clever serial killer in Queens but in less than one minute she was asleep.

Rhyme glanced down and noted her breast against his chest, her knee resting on his thigh. A woman's hair was banked against his face for the first time in years. It tickled. He'd forgotten that this happened. For someone who lived so in the past, with such a good memory, he was surprised to find he couldn't exactly remember when he'd experienced this sensation last. What he could recall was an amalgam of evenings with Blaine, he supposed, before the accident. He *did* remember that he'd decided to endure the tickle, not push the strands away, so he wouldn't disturb his wife.

Now, of course, he couldn't brush away Sachs's hair if God Himself had asked. But he wouldn't think of moving it aside. Just the opposite; he wanted to prolong the sensation until the end of the universe.

THIRTY-FIVE

The next morning Lincoln Rhyme was alone again.

Thom had gone shopping and Mel Cooper was at the IRD lab downtown. Vince Peretti had completed the CS work at the mansion on East Van Brevoort and at Sachs's. They'd found woefully few clues though Rhyme put the lack of PE down to the unsub's ingenuity, not Peretti's derivative talents.

Rhyme was awaiting the crime scene report. But both Dobyns and Sellitto believed that 823 had gone to ground—temporarily at least. There'd been no more attacks on the police and no other victims had been kidnapped in the past twelve hours.

Sachs's minder—a large Patrol officer from MTS—had accompanied her to an appointment with an ear, nose and throat man at a hospital in Brooklyn; the dirt had done quite a number on her throat. Rhyme himself had a bodyguard too—a uniform from the Twentieth Precinct, stationed in front of his townhouse—a friendly cop he'd known for years and with whom Rhyme enjoyed a running argument on the merits of Irish peat versus Scottish in the production of whisky.

Rhyme was in a great mood. He called downstairs on the intercom. "I'm expecting a doctor in a couple of hours. You can let him up."

The cop said he would.

UNSUB 823

Appearance	Residence	Vehicle	Other
• Caucasian male, slight build • Dark clothing • Old gloves, reddish kidskin • Aftershave; to cover up other scent? • Ski mask? Navy blue? • Gloves are dark • Aftershave = Brut • Hair color not brown • Deep scar, index finger • Casual clothes • Gloves are black	• Prob. has safe house • Located near: Houston & Lafayette, ShopRite • Old building, pink marble • At least 100 years old, prob. mansion or institutional • Federal-style building, Lower East Side • Located near archaeologic dig	• Yellow Cab • Recent model sedan • Lt. gray, silver, beige • Rental car; prob. stolen • Hertz, silver Taurus, this year's model	• knows CS proc. • possibly has record • knows FR prints • gun = .32 Colt • Ties vics w/ unusual knots • "Old" appeals to him • Called one vic "Hanna" • Knows basic German • Underground appeals to him • Dual personalities • Maybe priest, soc. worker, counselor • Unusual wear on shoes, reads a lot? • Listened as he broke vic's finger • Left snake as slap at investigators • Wanted to flay vic's foot • Called one vic "Maggie" • Mother & child, special meaning to him? • Book "Crime in Old NY," his model? • Bases crimes on James Schneider, the "Bone Collector" • Has hatred of police

Dr. William Berger had assured Rhyme that today he'd be on time.

Rhyme leaned back in the pillow and realized he wasn't completely alone. On the windowsill, the falcons paced. Rarely skittish, they seemed uneasy. Another low front was approaching. Rhyme's window revealed a calm sky but he trusted the birds; they were infallible barometers.

He glanced at the clock on the wall. It was 11:00 a.m. Here he was, just like two days ago, awaiting Berger's arrival. That's life, he thought: postponement upon postponement but ultimately, with some luck, we get to where we're meant to be.

He watched television for twenty minutes, trolling for stories about the kidnappings. But all the stations were doing specials on the opening day of the UN conference. Rhyme found it boring and turned to a rerun of *Matlock*, flipped back to a gorgeous CNN reporter standing outside UN headquarters and then shut the damn set off.

The telephone rang and he went through the complicated gestures of answering it. "Hello."

There was a pause before a man's voice said, "Lincoln?"

"Yes?"

"Jim Polling. How you doin'?"

Rhyme realized that he hadn't seen much of the captain since early yesterday, except for the news conference last night, where he'd whispered prompts to the mayor and Chief Wilson.

"Okay. Any word on our unsub?" Rhyme asked.

"Nothing yet. But we'll get him." Another pause. "Hey, you alone?"

"Yep."

A longer pause.

"Okay if I stop by?"

"Sure."

"A half hour?"

"I'll be here," Rhyme said jovially.

He rested his head in the thick pillow and his eyes slipped to the knotted clothesline hanging beside the profile poster. Still no answer about the knot. It was—he laughed aloud at the joke—a loose end. He hated the idea of leaving the case without finding out what kind of knot it was. Then he remembered that Polling was a fisherman. Maybe he'd recognize—

Polling, Rhyme reflected.

James Polling . . .

Funny how the captain had insisted Rhyme handle the case. How he'd fought to keep him on it, rather than Peretti—who was the better choice, politically, for Polling. Remembering too how he'd lost his temper at Dellray when the feebie tried to strong-arm the investigation away from the NYPD.

Now that he thought about it, Polling's whole involvement in the case was a mystery. Eight twenty-three wasn't the kind of perp you took on voluntarily—even if you were looking for juicy cases to hang on your collar record. Too many chances to lose vics, too many opportunities for the press—and the brass—to snipe at you for fucking up.

Polling . . . Recalling how he'd breeze into Rhyme's bedroom, check out their progress and leave.

Sure, he was reporting to the mayor and the chief. But—the thought slipped unexpectedly into Rhyme's mind—was there someone *else* Polling was reporting back to?

Someone who wanted to keep tabs on the investigation? The unsub himself?

But how on earth could Polling have any connection with 823? It seemed—

And then it struck him.

Could Polling *be* the unsub?

Of course not. It was ridiculous. Laughable. Even apart from motive and means, there was the question of opportunity. The captain had been here, in Rhyme's room, when some of the kidnappings had occurred. . . .

Or had he?

Rhyme looked up at the profile chart.

Dark clothing and wrinkled cotton slacks. Polling'd been

wearing dark sports clothes over the past several days. But so what? So did a lot of—

Downstairs a door opened and closed.

"Thom?"

No answer. The aide wasn't due back for hours.

"Lincoln?"

Oh, no. Hell. He started to dial on the ECU.

9 - 1 -

With his chin he bumped the cursor to *2*.

Footsteps on the stairs.

He tried to redial but he knocked the joystick out of reach in his desperation.

And Jim Polling walked into the room. Rhyme had counted on the babysitter's calling upstairs first. But of course a beat cop would let a police captain inside without thinking twice.

Polling's dark jacket was unbuttoned and Rhyme got a look at the automatic on his hip. He couldn't see if it was his issue weapon. But he knew that .32 Colts were on the NYPD list of approved personal weapons.

"Lincoln," Polling said. He was clearly uneasy, cautious. His eyes fell to the bleached bit of spinal cord.

"How you doing, Jim?"

"Not bad."

Polling the outdoorsman. Had the scar on the fingerprint been left by years of casting a fishing line? Or an accident with a hunting knife? Rhyme tried to look but Polling kept his hands jammed into his pockets. Was he holding something in there? A knife?

Polling certainly knew forensics and crime scenes—he knew how *not* to leave evidence.

The ski mask? If Polling was the unsub he'd have to wear the mask of course—because one of the vics might see him later. And the aftershave . . . what if the unsub hadn't *worn* the scent at all but had just carried a bottle with him and sprayed some at the scenes to make them *believe* he wore Brut? So when Polling showed up here, not wearing any, no one would suspect him.

"You're alone?" Polling asked.

"My assistant—"

"The cop downstairs said he wouldn't be back for a while."

Rhyme hesitated. "That's right."

Polling was slight but strong, sandy-haired. Terry Dobyns's words came back: Someone helpful, upstanding. A social worker, counselor, politician. Somebody helping other people.

Like a cop.

Rhyme wondered now if he was about to die. And to his shock he realized that he didn't want to. Not this way, not on somebody else's terms.

Polling walked to the bed.

Yet there was nothing he could do. He was at this man's complete mercy.

"Lincoln," Polling repeated gravely.

Their eyes met and the feeling of electrical connection went through them. Dry sparks. The captain looked quickly out the window. "You've been wondering, haven't you?"

"Wondering?"

"Why I wanted you on the case."

"I figured it was my personality."

This drew no smile from the captain.

"Why *did* you want me, Jim?"

The captain's fingers knitted together. Thin but strong. The hands of a fisherman, a sport that, yes, may be genteel but whose purpose is nonetheless to wrench a poor beast from his home and slice through its smooth belly with a thin knife.

"Four years ago, the Shepherd case. We were on it together."

Rhyme nodded.

"The workers found the body of that cop in the subway stop."

A groan, Rhyme recalled, like the sound of the *Titanic* sinking in *A Night to Remember*. Then an explosion loud as a gunshot as the beam came down on his hapless neck, and dirt packed around his body.

"And you ran the scene. You yourself, like you always did."

"I did, yes."

"Did you know how we convicted Shepherd? We had a wit."

A witness? Rhyme hadn't heard that. After the accident he'd lost all track of the case, except for learning that Shepherd had been convicted and, three months later, stabbed to death on Riker's Island by an assailant who was never captured.

"An eyewitness," Polling continued. "He could place Shepherd at one of the victims' homes with the murder weapon." The captain stepped closer to the bed, crossed his arms. "We had the wit a day *before* we found the last body—the one in the subway. Before I put in the request that you run the scene."

"What're you saying, Jim?"

The captain's eyes rooted themselves to the floor. "We didn't need you. We didn't *need* your report."

Rhyme said nothing.

Polling nodded. "You understand what I'm saying? I wanted to nail that fuck Shepherd so bad. . . . I wanted an airtight case. And you know what a Lincoln Rhyme crime scene report does to defense lawyers. It scares the everlovin' shit out of them."

"But Shepherd would've been convicted even without my report from the subway scene."

"That's right, Lincoln. But it's worse than that. See, I got word from MTA Engineering that the site wasn't safe."

"The subway site. And you had me work the scene before they shored it up?"

"Shepherd was a cop-killer." Polling's face twisted up in disgust. "I wanted him so bad. I woulda done anything to nail him. But . . ." He lowered his head to his hands.

Rhyme said nothing. He heard the groan of the beam, the explosion of the breaking wood. Then the rustle of the dirt nestling around him. A curious, warm peace in his body while his heart stuttered with terror.

"Jim—"

"That's why I wanted you on this case, Lincoln. You see?" A miserable look crossed the captain's tough face; he stared at the disk of spinal column on the table. "I kept hearing these stories that your life was crap. You were wasting away here. Talking about killing yourself. I felt so fucking guilty. I wanted to try to give you some of your life back."

Rhyme said, "And you've been living with this for the last three and a half years."

"You know about me, Lincoln. *Everybody* knows about me. I collar somebody, he gives me any shit, he goes *down*. I get a hard-on for some perp, I don't stop till the prick's bagged and tagged. I can't control it. I know I've fucked over people sometimes. But they were perps—or suspects, at least. They weren't my own, they weren't cops. What happened to you . . . that was a sin. It was just fucking wrong."

"I wasn't a rookie," Rhyme said. "I didn't *have* to work a scene I thought wasn't safe."

"But—"

"Bad time?" another voice said from the doorway.

Rhyme glanced up, expecting to see Berger. But it was Peter Taylor who'd come up the stairs. Rhyme recalled that he was coming by today to check on his patient after the dysreflexia attack. He supposed too that the doctor was planning to give him hell about Berger and the Lethe Society. He wasn't in the mood for that; he wanted time alone—to digest Polling's confession. At the moment it just sat there, numb as Rhyme's thigh. But he said, "Come on in, Peter."

"You've got a very funny security system, Lincoln. The guard asked if I was a doctor and he let me up. What? Do lawyers and accountants get booted?"

Rhyme laughed. "I'll only be a second." Rhyme turned back to Polling. "Fate, Jim. That's what happened to me. I was in the wrong place at the wrong time. It happens."

"Thanks, Lincoln." Polling put his hand on Rhyme's right shoulder and squeezed it gently.

Rhyme nodded and, to deflect the uneasy gratitude, introduced the men. "Jim, this is Pete Taylor, one of my doctors. And this is Jim Polling, we used to work together."

"Nice to meet you," Taylor said, sticking out his right hand. It was a broad gesture and Rhyme's eyes followed it, noticing for some reason the deep crescent scar on Taylor's right index finger.

"No!" Rhyme shouted.

"So you're a cop too." Taylor gripped Polling's hand tightly as he slid the knife, held firmly in his left hand, in and out of the captain's chest three times, navigating around the ribs with the delicacy of a surgeon. Undoubtedly so he wouldn't nick the precious bone.

THIRTY-SIX

I n two long steps Taylor was beside the bed. He grabbed the ECU controller from beneath Rhyme's finger, flung it across the room.

Rhyme took a breath to shout. But the doctor said, "He's dead too. The constable." Nodding toward the door, meaning the bodyguard downstairs. Taylor stared with fascination as Polling thrashed like a spine-cracked animal, spraying his blood on the floor and walls.

"Jim!" Rhyme cried. "No, oh, no . . ."

The captain's hands curled over his ruined chest. A repugnant gurgling from his throat filled the room, accompanied by the mad thudding of his shoes on the floor as he died. Finally he quivered once violently and lay still. His glazed eyes, dotted with blood, stared at the ceiling.

Turning to the bed he kept his eyes on Lincoln Rhyme as he walked around it. Slowly circling, the knife in his hand. His breathing was hard.

"Who *are* you?" Rhyme gasped.

Silently Taylor stepped forward, put his fingers around Rhyme's arm, squeezed the bone several times, perhaps hard, perhaps not. His hand strayed to Rhyme's left ring finger. He lifted it off the

ECU and caressed it with the dripping blade of the knife. Slipped the sharp point up under the nail.

Rhyme felt faint pain, a queasy sensation. Then harder. He gasped.

Then Taylor noticed something and froze. He gasped. Leaned forward. Staring at the copy of *Crime in Old New York* on the turning frame.

"*That's* how . . . You actually found it. . . . Oh, the constables should be proud to have you in their ranks, Lincoln Rhyme. I thought it'd be days before you got to the house. I thought Maggie'd be stripped down by the dogs by then."

"Why're you doing this?" Rhyme asked.

But Taylor didn't answer; he was examining Rhyme carefully, muttering, half to himself, "You didn't used to be this good, you know. In the old days. You missed a lot back then, didn't you? In the old days."

The old days . . . What did he mean?

He shook his balding head, gray hair—not brown—and glanced at a copy of Rhyme's forensic textbook. There was recognition in his eyes and slowly Rhyme began to understand.

"You read my book," the criminalist said. "You studied it. At the library, right? The public library branch near you?"

Eight twenty-three was, after all, a reader.

So he knew Rhyme's CS procedures. That's why he'd swept up so carefully, why he'd worn gloves touching even surfaces most criminals wouldn't've thought would retain prints, why he'd sprayed the aftershave at the scene—he'd known exactly what Sachs would be looking for.

And of course the manual wasn't the only book he'd read.

Scenes of the Crime too. That's what had given him the idea for the planted clues—Old New York clues. Clues that only Lincoln Rhyme would be able to figure out.

Taylor picked up the disk of spinal column he'd given to Rhyme eight months ago. He kneaded it absently between his fingers. And Rhyme saw the gift, so touching back then, for the horrific preface that it was.

His eyes were unfocused, distant. Rhyme recalled he'd seen this before—when Taylor'd examined him over the past months. He'd put it down to a doctor's concentration but now knew it was madness. The control he'd been struggling to maintain was disappearing.

"Tell me," Rhyme asked. "Why?"

"Why?" Taylor whispered, moving his hand along Rhyme's leg, probing once more, knee, shin, ankle. "Because you were something remarkable, Rhyme. Unique. You were invulnerable."

"What do you mean?"

"How can you punish a man who wants to die? If you kill him you've done what he wants. So I had to make you want to live."

And the answer came to Rhyme finally.

The old days . . .

"It was fake, wasn't it?" he whispered. "That obituary from the Albany coroner. You wrote it yourself."

Colin Stanton. Dr. Taylor was Colin Stanton.

The man whose family had been butchered in front of him on the streets of Chinatown. The man who stood paralyzed in front of the bodies of his wife and two children as they bled to death, and could not make the obscene choice about which of them to save.

You missed things. In the old days.

Now, too late, the final pieces fell into place.

His watching the victims: T.J. Colfax and Monelle and Carole Ganz. He'd risked capture to stand and stare at them—just as Stanton had stood over his family, watching as they died. He wanted revenge but he was a doctor, sworn never to take a life, and so in order to kill he had to become his spiritual ancestor—the bone collector, James Schneider, a nineteenth-century madman whose family had been destroyed by the police.

"After I got out of the mental hospital I came back to Manhattan. I read the inquest report about how you missed the killer at the crime scene, how he got out of the apartment. I knew I had to kill you. But I couldn't. I don't know why. . . . I kept waiting and waiting for something to happen. And then I found the book.

James Schneider . . . He'd been through exactly what I had. He'd done it; I could too."

I took them down to the bone.

"The obituary," Rhyme said.

"Right. I wrote it myself on my computer. Faxed it to NYPD so they wouldn't suspect me. Then I became someone else. Dr. Peter Taylor. I didn't realize until later why I picked that name. Can you figure it out?" Stanton's eyes strayed to the chart. "The answer's there."

Rhyme scanned the profile.

- Knows basic German

"*Schneider*," Rhyme said, sighing. "It's German for 'tailor.'"

Stanton nodded. "I spent weeks at the library reading up on spinal cord trauma and then called you, claimed I'd been referred by Columbia SCI. I planned to kill you during the first appointment, cut your flesh off a strip at a time, let you bleed to death. It might've taken hours. Even days. But what happened?" His eyes grew wide. "I found out you wanted to kill *yourself*."

He leaned close to Rhyme. "Jesus, I still remember the first time I saw you. You son of a bitch. You *were* dead. And I knew what I had to do—I had to make you *want* to live. I had to give you purpose once more."

So it didn't matter whom he kidnapped. Anyone would do. "You didn't even care whether the victims lived or died."

"Of course not. All I wanted was to force *you* to try to save them."

"The knot," Rhyme asked, noticing the loop of clothesline hanging beside the poster. "It was a surgical suture?"

He nodded.

"Of course. And the scar on your finger?"

"My finger?" He frowned. "How did you . . . Her *neck!* You printed her neck, Hanna's. I *knew* that was possible. I didn't think about it." Angry with himself. "I broke a glass in the mental hospital library," Stanton continued. "To cut my wrist. I squeezed it till it broke." He madly traced the scar with his left index finger.

"The deaths," Rhyme said evenly, "your wife and children. It was an accident. A terrible accident, horrible. But it didn't happen on purpose. It was a mistake. I'm so sorry for you and for them."

In a sing-songy voice, Stanton chided, "Remember what you wrote? . . . in the preface of your textbook?" He recited perfectly, " 'The criminalist knows that for every action there's a consequence. The presence of a perpetrator alters every crime scene, however subtly. It is because of this that we can identify and locate criminals and achieve justice.' " Stanton grabbed Rhyme's hair and tugged his head forward. They were inches apart. Rhyme could smell the madman's breath, see the lenses of sweat on the gray skin. "Well, I'm the consequence of *your* actions."

"What'll you accomplish? You kill me and I'm no worse off than I would've been."

"Oh, but I'm not going to kill you. Not yet."

Stanton released Rhyme's hair, backed away.

"You want to know what I'm going to do?" he whispered. "I'm going to kill your doctor, Berger. But not the way he's used to killing. Oh, no sleeping pills for him, no booze. We'll see how he likes death the old-fashioned way. Then your friend Sellitto. And Officer Sachs? Her too. She was lucky once. But I'll get her the next time. Another burial for her. And Thom too of course. He'll die right here in front of you. Work him down to the bone . . . Nice and slow." Stanton's breathing was fast. "Maybe we'll take care of him today. When's he due back?"

"*I* made the mistakes. It's my—" Rhyme suddenly coughed deeply. He cleared his throat, caught his breath. "It's *my* fault. Do whatever you want with me."

"No, it's all of you. It's—"

"Please. You can't—" Rhyme began to cough again. It turned into a violent racking. He managed to control it.

Stanton glanced at him.

"You *can't* hurt them. I'll do whatever—" Rhyme's voice seized. His head flew back, his eyes bulged.

And Lincoln Rhyme's breath stopped completely. His head

thrashed, his shoulders shivered violently. The tendons in his neck tightened like steel cords.

"Rhyme!" Stanton cried.

Sputtering, saliva shooting from his lips, Rhyme trembled once, twice, an earthquake seemed to ripple through his entire limp body. His head fell back, blood trickled from the corner of his mouth.

"No!" Stanton shouted. Slamming his hands into Rhyme's chest. "You can't die!"

The doctor lifted Rhyme's lids, revealing only whites.

Stanton tore open Thom's medicine box and prepared a blood-pressure hypodermic, injected the drug. He yanked the pillow off the bed and pulled Rhyme flat. He tilted back Rhyme's lolling head, wiped the lips and placed his mouth on Rhyme's, breathing hard into the unresponsive lungs.

"No!" Stanton raged. "I won't let you die! You *can't!*"

No response.

Again. He checked the unmoving eyes.

"Come on! Come *on!*"

Another breath. Pounding on the still chest.

Then he backed up, frozen with panic and shock, staring, staring, watching the man die in front of him.

Finally he bent forward and one last time exhaled deeply into Rhyme's mouth.

And it was when Stanton turned his head and lowered his ear to listen for the faint sound of breath, any faint exhalation, that Rhyme's head shot forward like a striking snake. He closed his teeth on Stanton's neck, tearing through the carotid artery and gripping a portion of the man's own spine.

Down to . . .

Stanton screamed and scrabbled backwards, sliding Rhyme off the bed on top of him. Together they fell in a pile on the floor. The hot coppery blood gushed and gushed, filling Rhyme's mouth.

. . . the bone.

His lungs, his *killer* lungs, had already gone for a minute without air but he refused to loosen his grip now to gasp for breath, ignoring the searing pain from inside his cheek where he'd bit into the tender skin, bloodying it to give credence to his sham attack of dysreflexia. He growled in rage—seeing Amelia Sachs buried in dirt, seeing the steam spew over T.J. Colfax's body—and he shook his head, feeling the snap of bone and cartilage.

Pummeling Rhyme's chest, Stanton screamed again, kicking to get away from the monster that had socketed itself to him.

But Rhyme's grip was unbreakable. It was as if the spirits of all the dead muscles throughout his body had risen into his jaw.

Stanton clawed his way to the bedside table and managed to grab his knife. He jabbed it into Rhyme. Once, twice. But the only places he could reach were the criminalist's legs and arms. It's pain that incapacitates and pain was one thing to which Lincoln Rhyme was immune.

The vise of his jaws closed harder and Stanton's scream was cut off as his windpipe went. He plunged the knife deep into Rhyme's arm. It stopped when it hit bone. He started to draw it out to strike again but the madman's body froze then spasmed violently once, then again, and suddenly went completely limp.

Stanton collapsed to the floor, pulling Rhyme after him. The criminalist's head slammed onto the oak with a loud crack. Yet Rhyme wouldn't let go. He held tight and continued to crush the man's neck, shaking, tearing the flesh like a hungry lion crazed by blood and by the immeasurable satisfaction of a lust fulfilled.

V
WHEN YOU MOVE THEY CAN'T GETCHA

"A physician's duty is not just to extend life,
it is to end suffering."

—DR. JACK KEVORKIAN

THIRTY-SEVEN

It was nearly sunset when Amelia Sachs walked through his doorway.

She was no longer in sweats. Or uniform. She wore jeans and a forest-green blouse. Her beautiful face sported several scratches Rhyme didn't recognize, though given the events of the past three days he guessed the wounds weren't self-inflicted.

"Yuck," she said, walking around the portion of the floor where Stanton and Polling had died. It had been mopped with bleach—with the perp body-bagged, forensics became moot—but the pink island of stain was huge.

Rhyme watched Sachs pause and nod a cold greeting to Dr. William Berger, who stood by the falcon window with his infamous briefcase at his side.

"So you got him, did you?" she asked, nodding at the bloodstain.

"Yeah," Rhyme said. "He's got."

"All by yourself?"

"It was hardly a fair fight," he offered. "I forced myself to hold back."

Outside, the liquid, ruddy light of the low sun ignited treetops and the marching line of elegant buildings along Fifth Avenue across the park.

Sachs glanced at Berger, who said, "Lincoln and I were just having a little talk."

"Were you?"

There was a long pause.

"Amelia," he began. "I'm going to go through with it. I've decided."

"I see." Her gorgeous lips, marred by the black lines of tiny stitches, tightened slightly. It was her only visible reaction. "You know, I hate it when you use my first name. I goddamn *hate* it."

How could he explain to her that *she* was largely the reason he was going ahead with his death? Waking that morning, with her beside him, he realized with a piquant sorrow that she would soon climb from the bed and dress and walk out the door—to her own life, to a *normal* life. Why, they were as doomed as lovers could be—if he dared even to think of them as lovers. It was only a matter of time until she met another Nick and fell in love. The 823 case was over, and without that binding them together, their lives would have to drift apart. Inevitable.

Oh, Stanton was smarter than he could've guessed. Rhyme *had* been drawn to the brink of the real world once again and, yes, he'd moved far over it.

Sachs, I lied: Sometimes you can't give up the dead. Sometimes you just have to go with them. . . .

Hands clenched, she walked to the window. "I tried to come up with a ballbuster of an argument to talk you out of it. You know, something real slick. But I couldn't. All I can say is, I just don't want you to do it."

"A deal's a deal, Sachs."

She looked at Berger. "Shit, Rhyme." Walking over to the bed, crouching down. She put her hand on his shoulder, brushed his hair off his forehead. "But will you do one thing for me?"

"What?"

"Give me a few hours."

"I'm not changing my mind."

"I understand. Just two hours. There's something you have to do first."

Rhyme looked at Berger, who said, "I can't stay much longer, Lincoln. My plane . . . If you want to wait a week I can come back. . . ."

"That's okay, doctor," Sachs said. "I'll help him do it."

"You?" the doctor asked cautiously.

Reluctantly she nodded. "Yes."

This wasn't *her* nature. Rhyme could see that clearly. But he glanced into her blue eyes, which though tearful were remarkably clear.

She said, "When I was . . . when he was burying me, Rhyme, I couldn't move. Not an inch. For an instant I was desperate to die. Not to live, just to have it over with. I understood how you feel."

Rhyme nodded slowly then said to Berger, "It's all right, doctor. Could you just leave the—what's the euphemism of the day?"

"How's 'paraphernalia'?" Berger suggested.

"Could you just leave them there, on the table?"

"You're sure?" he asked Sachs.

She nodded again.

The doctor set the pills, brandy and plastic bag on the bedside table. Then he rummaged through his briefcase. "I don't have any rubber bands, I'm afraid. For the bag."

"That's all right," Sachs said, glancing down at her shoes. "I've got some."

Then Berger stepped close to the bed, put his arm on Rhyme's shoulder. "I wish you a peaceful self-deliverance," he said.

"Self-deliverance," Rhyme said wryly as Berger left. Then, to Sachs: "Now. What's this I have to do?"

She took the turn at fifty, skidded hard, and slipped smoothly up into fourth gear.

The wind blasted through the open windows and tossed their hair behind them. The gusts were brutal but Amelia Sachs wouldn't hear of driving with the windows up.

"That'd be un-Amurican," she announced, and broke the 100-mph mark.

When you move . . .

Rhyme had suggested it might be wiser to take their spin on the NYPD training course but he wasn't surprised when Sachs declared that that was a pussy run; she'd disposed of it the first week at the academy. So they were out on Long Island, their cover stories for the Nassau County police ready, rehearsed and marginally credible.

"The thing about five-speeds is, top gear isn't the fastest. That's a mileage gear. I don't give a shit about mileage." Then she took his left hand and placed it on the round black knob, encircled it with hers, downshifted.

The engine screamed and they shot up to 120, as trees and houses streaked past and the uneasy horses grazing in the fields stared at the black streak of Chevrolet.

"Isn't this the *best*, Rhyme?" she shouted. "Man, better than sex. Better than anything."

"I can feel the vibrations," he said. "I think I can. In my finger."

She smiled and he believed she squeezed his hand beneath hers. Finally, they ran out of deserted road, population loomed, and Sachs reluctantly slowed, turned around and pointed the nose of the car toward the hazy crescent of moon as it rose above the distant city, nearly invisible in the stew of hot August air.

"Let's try for one-fifty," she proposed. Lincoln Rhyme closed his eyes and lost himself in the sensation of wind and the perfume of freshly cut grass and the speed.

The night was the hottest of the month.

From Lincoln's Rhyme's new vantage point he could look down into the park and see the weirdos on the benches, the exhausted joggers, the families reclining around the smoke of dwindling barbecue fires like the survivors of a medieval battle. A few dog walkers unable to wait for the night's fever to break made their obligatory rounds, Baggies in hand.

Thom had put on a CD—Samuel Barber's elegiac Adagio for

Strings. But Rhyme had snorted a derisive laugh, declared it a sorry cliché and ordered him to replace it with Gershwin.

Amelia Sachs climbed the stairs and walked into his bedroom, noticed him looking outside. "What do you see?" she asked.

"Hot people."

"And the birds? The falcons?"

"Ah, yes, they're there."

"Hot too?"

He examined the male. "I don't think so. Somehow, they seem above that sort of thing."

She set the bag on the foot of the bed and lifted out the contents, a bottle of expensive brandy. He'd reminded her of the Scotch but Sachs said she'd contribute the liquor. She set it next to the pills and the plastic bag. Looking like a breezy professional wife, home from Balducci's with piles of vegetables and seafood and too little time to whip them into dinner.

She'd also bought some ice, at Rhyme's request. He'd remembered what Berger had explained about the heat in the bag. She lifted the cap off the Courvoisier and poured herself a glass and filled his tumbler, arranged the straw toward his mouth.

"Where's Thom?" she asked him.

"Out."

"Does he know?"

"Yes."

They sipped the brandy.

"Do you want me to say anything to your wife?"

Rhyme considered it for a long moment, thinking: We have years to converse with someone, to blurt and rant, to explain our desires and anger and regrets—and oh how we squander those moments. Here he'd known Amelia Sachs all of three days and they'd bared their hearts far more than he and Blaine had done in nearly a decade.

"No," he said. "I've e-mailed her." A chuckle. "That's a comment on our times, I'd say."

More brandy, the astringent bite on his palate was dissipating. Growing smoother, duller, lighter.

Sachs leaned over the bed and tapped her glass to his.

"I have some money," Rhyme began. "I'm giving a lot of it to Blaine and to Thom. I—"

But she shushed him with a kiss to the forehead and shook her head.

A soft clatter of pebbles as she spilled the tiny Seconals into her hand.

Rhyme instinctively thought: The Dillie-Koppanyi color test reagent. Add 1 percent cobalt acetate in methanol to the suspect material followed by 5 percent isopropylamine in methanol. If the substance is a barbiturate the reagent turns a beautiful violet-blue color.

"How should we do it?" she asked, gazing at the pills. "I really don't know."

"Mix them in the booze," he suggested.

She dropped them in his tumbler. They dissolved quickly.

How fragile they were. Like the dreams they induce.

She stirred the mixture with the straw. He glanced at her wounded nails but even that he couldn't be sorrowful for. This was *his* night and it was a night of joy.

Lincoln Rhyme had a sudden recollection of childhood in suburban Illinois. He never drank his milk and to get him to do so his mother bought straws coated on the inside with flavoring. Strawberry, chocolate. He hadn't thought about them until just this moment. It was a great invention, he remembered. He always looked forward to his afternoon milk.

Sachs pushed the straw close to his mouth. He took it between his lips. She put her hand on his arm.

Light or dark, music or silence, dreams or the meditation of dreamless sleep? What will I find?

He began to sip. The taste was really no different from straight liquor. A little more bitter maybe. It was like—

From downstairs came a huge pounding on the door. Hands and feet both, it seemed. Voices shouting too.

He lifted his lips away from the straw. Glanced into the dim stairwell.

She looked at him, frowning.

"Go see," he said to her.

She disappeared down the stairs and a moment later returned, looking unhappy. Lon Sellitto and Jerry Banks followed. Rhyme noticed that the young detective had done another butcher job on his face with a razor. He'd really have to get that under control.

Sellitto glanced at the bottle and the bag. His eyes swayed toward Sachs but she crossed her arms and held her own, silently ordering him to leave. This was not an issue of rank, the look told the detective, and what was happening here was none of his business. Sellitto's eyes acknowledged the message but he wasn't about to go anywhere just yet.

"Lincoln, I need to talk to you."

"Talk. But talk fast, Lon. We're busy."

The detective sat heavily in the noisy rattan chair. "An hour ago a bomb went off at the United Nations. Right next to the banquet hall. During the welcome dinner for the peace conference delegates."

"Six dead, fifty-four hurt," Banks added. "Twenty of them serious."

"My God," Sachs whispered.

"Tell him," Sellitto muttered.

Banks continued, "For the conference, the UN hired a bunch of temps. The perp was one of them—a receptionist. A half-dozen people saw her carrying a knapsack to work and putting it in a storeroom near the banquet hall. She left just before the bang. The bomb squad estimates we're looking at about two pounds of C4 or Semtex."

Sellitto said, "Linc, the bomb, it was a yellow knapsack, the wits said."

"Yellow?" Why was that familiar?

"UN human resources ID'd the receptionist as Carole Ganz."

"The mother," Rhyme and Sachs said simultaneously.

"Yeah. The woman you saved in the church. Only Ganz's an alias. Her real name's Charlotte Willoughby. She was married to a Ron Willoughby. Ring a bell?"

Rhyme said it didn't.

"It was in the news a couple years ago. He was an Army sergeant assigned to a UN peacekeeping force in Burma."

"Keep going," the criminalist said.

"Willoughby didn't want to go—thought an American soldier shouldn't be wearing a UN uniform and taking orders from anybody except the U.S. Army. It's a big right-wing issue nowadays. But he went anyway. Wasn't there a week before he's blown away by some little punk in Rangoon. Got shot in the back. Became a conservative martyr. Anti-Terror says his widow got recruited by an extremist group out in the Chicago burbs. Some U of C grads gone underground. Edward and Katherine Stone."

Banks took over the narrative. "The explosive was in a package of kid's modeling clay, along with some other toys. We think she was going to take the little girl with her so security at the banquet-hall entrance wouldn't think anything of the clay. But with Pammy in the hospital she didn't have her cover story so she gave up on the hall and just planted it in the storeroom. Did enough damage as it was."

"Rabitted?"

"Yep. Not a trace."

"What about the little girl," Sachs asked, "Pammy?"

"Gone. The woman checked her out of the hospital around the time of the bang. No sign of either of them."

Rhyme asked, "The cell?"

"The group in Chicago? They're gone too. Had a safe house in Wisconsin but it's been hosed. We don't know where they are."

"So *that* was the rumor Dellray's snitch heard." Rhyme laughed. "*Carole* was the one coming into the airport. Had nothing to do with Unsub 823."

He found Banks and Sellitto staring at him.

Oh, the old silent trick again.

"Forget it, Lon." Rhyme said, all too aware of the glass sitting inches from him, radiating a welcoming heat. "Impossible."

The older detective plucked his sweaty shirt away from his

body, cringing. "God*damn* cold in here, Lincoln. Jesus. Look, just think about it. What'sa harm?"

"I can't help you."

Sellitto said, "There was a note. Carole wrote it and sent it to the secretary-general by interoffice envelope. Harping on world government, taking away American liberties. Some shit like that. Claimed credit for the UNESCO bombing in London too and said there'd be more. We've gotta get 'em, Linc."

Feeling his oats, scarface Banks said, "The secretary-general and the mayor both've asked for you. SAC Perkins too. And there'll be a call from the White House, you need any more persuading. We sure hope you don't, detective."

Rhyme didn't comment on the error regarding his rank.

"They've got the Bureau's PERT team ready to go. Fred Dellray's running the case and he asked—*respectfully*, yeah, he used that very word—he asked respectfully if you'd do the forensic work. And it's a virgin scene, except for getting the bodies and the wounded out."

"Then it's *not* virgin," Rhyme snapped. "It's extremely contaminated."

"All the more reason we need you," Banks ventured, adding "sir" to defuse Rhyme's glare.

Rhyme sighed, looked at the glass and the straw. Peace was so close to him just now. And pain too. Infinite sums of both.

He closed his eyes. Not a sound in the room.

Sellitto added, "It was just the woman herself, hey, wouldn't be that big a deal. But she's got her daughter with her, Lincoln. Underground, with a little girl? You know what that kid's life's going to be like?"

I'll get you for that too, Lon.

Rhyme nestled his head into the opulent pillow. Finally his eyes sprang open. He said, "There'd be some conditions."

"Name it, Linc."

"First of all," he said, "I don't work alone."

Rhyme looked toward Amelia Sachs.

She hesitated for a moment then smiled and stood, lifted the glass of tainted brandy out from under the straw. She opened the window wide and flung the tawny liquid into the ripe, hot air above the alley next to the townhouse, while, just feet away, the falcon looked up, glaring angrily at the motion of her arm, cocked his gray head, then turned back to feed his hungry youngster.

APPENDIX

Excerpts from: Glossary of Terms, Lincoln Rhyme, Physical Evidence, *4th ed. (New York: Forensic Press, 1994). Reprinted with permission.*

Alternative light source (ALS): Any of several types of high-intensity lamps of varying wavelength and light color, used to visualize latent friction-ridge prints, and certain types of trace and biological evidence.

Automated Fingerprint Identification System (AFIS): One of several computerized systems for the scanning and storage of friction-ridge prints.

Birefringence: The difference between two measures of refraction displayed by certain crystalline substances. Useful in identifying sand, fibers, and dirt.

Chain of custody (COC): A record of every person who has had possession of a piece of evidence from the moment of its collection at a crime scene to its introduction at trial.

COD: Cause of death.

Control samples: Physical evidence collected at a crime scene from known sources, used for comparison with evidence from an unknown source. For example, the victim's own blood and hair constitutes a control sample.

DCDS: Deceased, confirmed dead at scene.

Density-gradient testing (D-G): A technique for comparing soil samples to determine if they come from the same location. The test involves suspending dirt samples in tubes filled with liquids that have different density values.

DNA typing: Analyzing and charting the genetic structure within the cells of certain types of biological evidence (for example, blood, semen, hair) for the purpose of comparison with control samples from a known suspect. The process involves the isolation and comparison of fragments of DNA—deoxyribonucleic acid—the basic building block of the chromosome. Some types of DNA typing produce a mere likelihood that the evidence came from a suspect; other types are virtually conclusive, with the odds in the hundreds of millions that the evidence was from a particular individual. Also called "genetic typing," or—erroneously—"DNA fingerprinting" or "genetic fingerprinting."

Forensic anthropologist: A skeletal-remains expert who aids crime scene investigators in evaluating and identifying remains and excavating grave sites.

Forensic odontologist: A dental expert who aids crime scene investigators in identifying victims through examination of dental remains and analyzing bite-mark evidence.

Friction ridges: The raised lines of skin on fingers, palms, and the soles of feet, whose patterns are unique to each individual. Prints of friction ridges at crime scenes can be classified as (1) plastic (left in an impressionable substance such as putty); (2) evident (left by skin coated with a foreign substance like dust or blood); (3) latent (left by skin contaminated with bodily secretions such as grease or sweat and largely invisible).

Gas chromatograph/mass spectrometer (GC-MS): Two instruments used in forensic analysis to identify unknown substances such as drugs and trace evidence. They are often linked together. The gas chromatograph separates components in a substance and transmits them to the mass spectrometer, which definitively identifies each of those components.

Grid: A common approach to searching for evidence whereby the searcher covers a crime scene back and forth in one direction (say, north–south), then covers the same scene in the perpendicular direction (east–west).

Gunshot residue (GSR): The material—particularly barium and antimony—deposited on the hands and clothing of a person shooting a firearm. GSR remains on human skin for up to six hours if not removed intentionally by washing or inadvertently by excessive contact when a suspect is arrested and handcuffed (a greater risk if the hands are cuffed behind the back).

Identification of physical evidence: Determining the category or class of material that an item of evidence falls into. This is distinguishable from "individuation," which is a determination of the single source the item came from. For example, a torn piece of paper found at a crime scene can be *identified* as coated 40-pound stock of the type often used in magazine printing. It can be *individuated* if the piece exactly fits the missing section of a torn page in a particular issue of a magazine found in a suspect's possession. Individuation, of course, has far more probative value than does identification.

Individuation of physical evidence: See "Identification of physical evidence."

Lividity: The purplish discoloring of portions of the skin of a deceased owing to the darkening and settling of the blood after death.

Locard's Exchange Principle: Formulated by Edmond Locard, a French criminalist, this theory holds that there is always an exchange of physical evidence between the perpetrator and the crime scene or the victim, however minute or difficult to detect that evidence might be.

Mass spectrometer: See "Gas chromatograph."

Ninhydrin: A chemical that visualizes latent friction-ridge prints on porous surfaces such as paper, cardboard, and wood.

Physical evidence (PE): In criminal law, PE refers to items or substances presented at trial to support the assertion by the defendant or the prosecution that a particular proposition is true. Physical evidence comprises inanimate objects, bodily materials, and impressions (such as fingerprints).

Presumptive blood test: Any of a number of chemical techniques for determining if blood residue is present at a crime scene, even if it is not evident to the eye. Most common are tests using luminol and orthotolidine.

Scanning electron microscope (SEM): An instrument that fires electrons onto a specimen of evidence to be examined and projects the resulting image on a computer monitor. Magnification of 100,000X is possible with SEMs, compared with about 500X in the case of most optical microscopes. The SEM is often combined with an energy-dispersive X-ray unit (EDX), which can identify the elements in a sample at the same time the technician is viewing it.

Staging: A perpetrator's efforts to rearrange, add, or remove evidence from a crime scene to make it appear that the crime he or she has committed did not occur or was committed by someone else.

Trace evidence: Bits of tiny, sometimes microscopic, substances such as dust, dirt, cellular material, and fibers.

Unsub: Unknown subject; that is, an unidentified suspect.

Vacuum-metal deposition (VMD): The most effective means for visualizing latent friction-ridge prints on smooth surfaces. Gold or zinc evaporated in a vacuum chamber coats the object to be examined with a thin layer of metal, thereby making a print visible.

Author's Note

I'm indebted to Peter A. Micheels, author of *The Detectives*, and E. W. Count, author of *Cop Talk*, whose books were not only wonderfully helpful in researching this one but great reads as well. Thanks to Pam Dorman, whose deft editorial touch is evident everywhere in this story. And of course thanks to my agent, Deborah Schneider . . . what would I do without ya? I'm grateful too to Nina Salter at Calmann-Lévy for her perceptive comments on an earlier draft of the book and to Karolyn Hutchinson at REP in Alexandria, Virginia, for invaluable help with wheelchairs and other equipment available for quadriplegics. And to Teddy Rosenbaum—a detective in her own right—for her fine copy-editing job. Students of law enforcement may wonder about the structure of the NYPD and FBI as presented here; tweaking the organizational charts was my doing exclusively. Oh, yes—anyone interested in reading a copy of *Crime in Old New York* may have a little trouble finding one. The official story is that the book is a fictional creation, though I've also heard the rumor that the one copy in existence was recently stolen from the New York Public Library—by a person or persons unknown.

—J.W.D.

About the Author

Jeffery Deaver is the author of nine suspense novels. He's twice been nominated for Edgar Awards and is the recipient of the Ellery Queen Readers' Award for best short story of 1995. His most recent thriller from Viking/Signet, *A Maiden's Grave*, was an HBO feature presentation. *The Bone Collector* is soon to be a film from Universal Pictures.